Also by Roberta Silman

Blood Relations

FOR CHILDREN:

Somebody Else's Child

BOUNDARIES

Roberta Silman's stories have appeared in
The Atlantic, The New Yorker, McCall's, and
Redbook, and were collected in *Blood Rela-
tions,* a runner-up for both the 1977 Hemingway
Foundation Award for fiction, and the 1977 Janet
Heidinger Kafka Award. Her children's book,
Somebody Else's Child, won the Child Study
Association Award for 1976. A 1956 graduate of
Cornell University, Silman received her MFA
from Sarah Lawrence College. She lives with
her husband and three children in Ardsley,
New York.

BOUNDARIES

a novel by
Roberta Silman

An Atlantic Monthly Press Book
Little, Brown and Company   Boston   Toronto

FIRST EDITION

LIBRARY OF CONGRESS CATALOGING IN PUBLICATION DATA

Silman, Roberta.
Boundaries.

"An Atlantic Monthly Press book."
I. Title.
PZ 4.S57234Bo[PS3569.I45] 813'.5'4   78-27089
ISBN 0-316-79109-1

ATLANTIC–LITTLE, BROWN BOOKS
ARE PUBLISHED BY
LITTLE, BROWN AND COMPANY
IN ASSOCIATION WITH
THE ATLANTIC MONTHLY PRESS

Designed by Susan Windheim

Published simultaneously in Canada
by Little, Brown & Company (Canada) Limited

PRINTED IN THE UNITED STATES OF AMERICA

For Bob

For Miriam — who will soon go off to find her own way

For Grace Paley and Jane Cooper — who helped me find mine

"Believe me — happiness is there only
Where we are loved, where we are believed."

— MIHAIL LERMONTOV

BOUNDARIES

CHAPTER 1

THE HUGE ARM of Hurricane Beulah scoured the easternmost tip of Long Island, lifting doors, windows, joists, beams, desks, paintings, and even refrigerators and freezers. Like dismembered carcasses the wreckage floated aimlessly over the drowned dunes and out to sea. July was too early for such a severe hurricane, yet here was proof that Beulah had come and gone. Even in the smallest, most protected town of all, Racer's Cove, the water climbed over the dunes dangerously close to the shops and houses.

Nestled in a knuckle of the Atlantic coastline, Racer's Cove was oddly hilly, as if some unknown glacier had stopped, then taken a hurried leap out to sea. Even its name was a puzzle. Some old-timers said it came from the whales. "This is where the fastest whales rested when they were fleeing the whalers — the men who did it for money and the crazy ones, like Captain Ahab." The thought of Ahab ever approaching a town as sleepy as Racer's Cove made the listeners smile as the storytellers continued, "Every once in a while an exhausted whale still comes ashore." Whale experts disagreed. They contended that whales were occasionally seen because the currents near the Cove behaved strangely. Other people insisted that the name came from the pirate ships that used to rove nearby waters. "This is where the pirates stopped to count their booty," they claimed. One very old man disputed both theories. He said the town had been called Dove's Cove and remembered being told by a great-aunt that some entrepreneur had cooked up the pirate story to get more business.

The entrepreneur would have been disappointed, for the Cove had never grown. Only a few hundred people lived there and the small business section of town was a series of charming culs-de-sac filled with small, mostly useless boutique items.

Luckily, the houses in Racer's Cove had been built by men who feared the sea. Beulah had torn away one patio and two porches and anything that had not been battened down was gone or cracked or broken, but the damage was nothing to what the newer towns had suffered. "Still, she didn't kill anyone, she gave plenty of warning," people comforted themselves as they stood next morning in knots along the dunes.

When she arrived in Racer's Cove later that day, Madeleine Glazer could hardly believe in the existence of Beulah. The day was so bright and sparkling and by now fast-moving cumulus clouds had brushed the sky to a clear luminous blue. Yet when she gazed at the ocean, the evidence of Beulah was there. It was a sea as wild as she had ever seen — far out the waves spun thunder, breaking quicker and quicker, faster than the eye or ear could count. Closer in toward shore they merged into enormous concavities of water as they sucked themselves up from the ocean floor, reminding Mady of the waves she had known as a child.

And even closer to her were traces of Beulah. With her forefinger she traced the scour marks on the damp sand. It looked as if an army had gotten down on its hands and knees and scrubbed this beach.

But what a beach! A long sheaf of sand before the ocean began, dotted only here and there with spots of color that meant people. Her friend Anne Levin had told her about this beach near Racer's Cove and when Madeleine looked to the left she could see the tiny unspoiled village. Next to her Foffy bent over her needlepoint. The child was still pale, for she had gotten sick from the car ride. Now as she moved, her blonde head glistened like a coin in the sun.

If she squinted Mady could see her two older children, Peter and Nina, at the water's edge. One kneeled and the other went back and forth with a bucket as they dripped sand into towers and turrets.

"Don't you want to help them?" Mady said.

Foffy shook her head and pursed her lips. The needlepoint was too hard for her but she had wanted it when Madeleine bought hers. Foffy's wispy hair fell into her eyes as she concentrated.

"Here, puss, let me help you." Mady gathered the flosslike hair into a loose ponytail. Still such fine baby hair, though Foffy was almost six years old. So different from the rest of them, who had thick dark hair.

"That looks like a great castle," Mady said and now Foffy looked up.

July was half-gone but it was the first time this summer or last that Mady had ventured to the beach. It had been easier to stay close to home, to swim in the artificial chlorinated safety of Westchester County, surrounded by familiar faces, only minutes from home. Now, alone with her children, listening to the pulsing of the waves, Mady knew why she hadn't come before. David had always wanted the sea — the smell, the salt, and that steady heartbeat of the waves which had been the sound he loved most in the world. If he were here he would be in it up to his neck, letting the waves sweep him upward, rock him, cradle him, carry him toward shore.

"A rough ocean is better than a roller coaster," he used to say, as he dried his thick curly hair while the water ran down his chest and legs.

Even when they had had no money, David had insisted on a

room within hearing distance of the waves. "Why be here and not be able to hear it?" he had reasoned. She and the kids had looked at three efficiency apartments; in each she stood by the bedroom window listening. The one they picked was closest to the sound of the sea.

"Now can we go in?" The older children's shadows enveloped her. Madeleine frowned as she looked up. "The lifeguards say it's better now, lots more people are going in," Peter reassured her.

"Okay." She stood up and helped Nina with her cap, then pulled on her own. At fifteen Peter was almost as tall as she was. And Nina, who was almost thirteen, had stretched, too. Friends exclaimed in amazement when they saw them, as if astonished that children could grow so well after their father had died.

"I'll look for shells, Mommy," Foffy said, then let go of her hand. She was afraid of the ocean even on lazy still days. "I'll collect enough shells so Grandma can make me a necklace."

"Don't go beyond the last lifeguard chair," Mady cautioned. Foffy nodded and waved.

The water sliced Mady's skin. A lifeguard saw her flinch. "It's because of the storm, everything's all mixed up because of Beulah," he told her. His eyes roved through the people as he spoke. The angry ocean frightened her, but she couldn't keep saying no to Peter and Nina. Children younger than they were battling the waves; besides, they were both good swimmers. She couldn't stay afraid forever. She straightened, then ducked beneath the surface. Nina took her hand and together they went up and down with the waves. Up, down, up, down. Each time they went up Nina drew in her breath; as they came down she let it out. Peter was farther out. Mady could see his black head bobbing up and down and for a few minutes she was fine. Then, without warning, panic filled her throat. The pull of the undertow, the endless clamor, that relentless surging of the waves against her body pushed her back to those first weeks after David's death — when the air itself pummeled her, when there wasn't any space or light or breath.

"I've got to get out, it's too cold," she shouted to Nina. "Are you okay?" Nina nodded. Madeleine swam in until she could stand, then she pushed her way through the surf and stood shivering at the water's edge. Her toes curled into the sand. After a few moments she walked backward, stumbled on her towel, and picked it up. Quickly she rubbed herself dry, yet her legs still trembled. She wanted to go back for her robe but she was afraid she would lose sight of Peter and Nina — as if their survival depended upon her watching them. Would she ever get over this? She fixed her eyes on the two bobbing heads; she wished she could turn away casually, yet she knew she couldn't.

Finally they had had enough. She watched their slow ramble toward shore and smiled and turned. Foffy was back at the blanket, crouching as she sorted her precious shells. Madeleine pulled off her cap and shook her hair and ears free of water, strangely aware that someone's eyes were on her. She turned again toward shore. A man about ten feet away was frowning at her. A middle-aged man with a graying beard and a stocky body. Most noticeable about his squarish frame were his muscular upper arms.

He stepped toward her. "You're shaking and your lips are purple," he said.

"I'm okay."

He shook his head. "You're still shivering and you've been out of the water for at least fifteen minutes." Mady shrugged. She couldn't tell him that her trembling legs had nothing to do with the cold ocean, that her legs had shaken uncontrollably for days after David died.

"It's very cold in there, Beulah has upset everything," she said as offhandedly as she could manage. He didn't answer and kept staring at her, as a doctor might. Was he a doctor? she wanted to ask, but he nodded briskly and turned away. Beneath his brusque manner was real concern. Why, she had no idea, but it was touching and she wanted to say something to him, thank him, perhaps, but before she could think of anything he had taken off his glasses and put them down. He jogged into the waves without a moment's hesitation. As she turned to walk back with Peter and Nina, she saw he was a strong swimmer.

All evening the tiny apartment hummed with the children's laughter. Here, away from the pitying troubled eyes that watched them constantly for signs of grief, the three children were freer, happier, than they had been since David's death. She was right to have come here alone with them. She had refused several invitations, she had wanted to go somewhere new — where no one knew her or her children. She closed her book and took a deep breath. She was reading *One Hundred Years of Solitude*. Someone had suggested it because he thought it was about living alone. Mady laughed out loud. It was a wonderful book and she wished David had read it, he would have liked its energy. She looked at the copyright date; they could have made it.

How comforting to live at such close quarters for a little while. She sank deeper into the pillows and turned off her light. As she dropped off to sleep, a cocoon of sounds surrounded her — Foffy's even breathing in the bed next to her, Peter and Nina whispering in the next room, occasional voices, coughs, laughter in the courtyard below — all against the endless soughing of the waves.

Next morning the sea was quieter, the sun scorching. Peter and Nina played catch with some kids they had met. Several yards from her Foffy dug a hole. Mady started the woman in her needlepoint. Doing something with her hands had saved her life this last year.

Into the rhythm of the needlework came a strange, somewhat throaty voice. "Are you all right?" She shielded her eyes and looked up. The man who had watched her yesterday stood over her. Now she could discern his accent — a blend of Germany and England.

"Fine, perfectly fine. The water was icy!" she insisted. He wasn't convinced and frowned a little, shrugged, started to back away. Suddenly she didn't want him to leave, she wanted to talk to him. She had prided herself on being able to fool almost everyone else, yet here was this total stranger who knew immediately that she was fibbing.

"Don't go," she said softly. He stopped, surprised.

"Please sit down." Mady gestured toward the blanket. He hesitated, then sat on the sand.

"The blanket won't bite."

He laughed, an unexpectedly deep laugh. "I like the sand, it's really amazing sand, you know, so fine. Not like the sand I knew as a child."

"Where was that?"

"Africa. Kenya. My family used to go swimming near Mombasa on our holidays. There the sand is pebbly, grayer." He took off his sunglasses and abruptly his face was younger. He was closer to her own age than she had thought, probably in his early forties. His eyes were a light hazel, with gold flecks in them; they seemed to be listening when he looked at her.

"I grew up in Africa on a coffee farm. My father's brother and my father owned the farm for a while together. We all lived in one big house." He stared into the distance and his glance rested on Foffy. "That beautiful child digging over there reminds me of my younger sister."

"That's Foffy, my youngest child."

"But I thought — yesterday I saw you with two older children."

"Peter and Nina. Foffy's the baby."

"She's so fair." He looked puzzled. Mady smiled, used to his confusion. People often thought Foffy was from a second marriage.

"Yes, no one knows quite where she came from. The other children have such dark hair and eyes. Her father's hair was almost black." She paused, waiting for the usual question in his eyes, but he wasn't even looking at her. Slowly he filtered the sand through his fingers. Madeleine took out more wool to thread her needle.

"Where is your sister now?" she asked as she moistened the tip of the wool with her tongue.

"She's back in Germany, in Stuttgart, where I was born. She's married to a writer, they have three sons."

Mady frowned. "I don't understand," she began to say. When he mentioned Kenya, she had expected him to tell her about one English parent.

"We were German, or at least born in Germany. But in the late twenties my father made some bad investments and he and my mother took me and my twin brother to Kenya when we were babies. His older brother, my Uncle Hans-Karl, owned a big coffee farm near Nairobi. We lived there through the thirties, but my father believed in Hitler and was very proud of his membership in the Nazi Party. As soon as·the war started he went back to Germany. In 1942 he came back to Kenya and took my brother Karl and me and my mother back to Germany. My sister was still little so she stayed in Kenya, and then after the war she and I went to school in England." His voice was flat, his expression distant, as if he had known as he spoke that she had stiffened, almost recoiled at what he was telling her. He had couched it as carefully as he could, but the fact remained, his father was a Nazi. That should have been enough to keep her silent, but she still didn't understand.

"How could you leave Africa in the middle of the war?" she asked, and stared at him with the curiosity of a child.

He didn't seem to mind. He smiled, shrugged. "Good question. I'm still not sure to this day, but from what I have pieced together, my father knew the right people and my grandparents had recouped some of the lost money. They bribed several people to get us out. I remember that we flew in army transports. My father was a very determined man, he believed absolutely in what he called 'the new Germany' and wanted us to be there when Hitler won." He looked away toward the sea. As he spoke his eyes had become more and more distant, and although she guessed the answer to her question, she knew she had to ask it.

"And your twin?" she said gently.

"He was killed in a training accident a few months after we joined the Hitler Youth. In the spring of 1943." His eyes still refused to meet hers.

"Oh, I'm sorry," she said quickly. The words came out like a reflex. In the past months she had learned to hate them, yet here she was, mouthing them herself.

"So am I. I still miss him." He looked at her now and shrugged again. She fought an impulse to touch his arm.

"Were you identical?"

"Yes." A shadow passed over his face. Seeing it, Mady knew he wasn't married. But she felt as if she had crossed some invisible barrier, so she turned and gazed at the ocean.

Suddenly the unlikely sound of "Gelati! Gelati!" came drifting toward them. The man smiled. "It's the only bit of phony chic on this beach," he told her. "The town elders didn't want the usual ice-cream stand and someone knew about an Italian family who make their own gelati. It's really very good." He stood up. "Would you like some?" Before she could nod he was gone.

How odd, she thought a few minutes later, to be sitting here, savoring the ice cream, holding it too long in her mouth exactly as the children did, with this man whose name she didn't even know but about whom she knew so much.

"What happened to your parents?" she asked.

"My mother had a nervous breakdown after the war and she and my father separated and subsequently divorced. I go back to see her every few years, but it isn't very comforting for either of us. Now she has a heart condition. My father died in 1960. My sister and I are fond of each other, but our lives are so different . . ." His voice dwindled.

Mady didn't know what to say. People's lives condensed into a few sentences left no room for words. Finally she said, "Why did you come here?"

"Well, it was here, or Australia, or someplace like that. I couldn't stay in Europe. I used to think I wasn't a political person, but I am. Everyone is, whether they know it or not. I thought about settling in England, which isn't really Europe, but I hated the climate so. I also considered going back to Africa, but then I decided to see America. I was on my way to Brazil when I stopped to see some cousins in Philadelphia and they took me to Montauk to visit a friend of theirs. Somehow this eastern end of Long Island reminded me of Africa. I think it's the sky, I don't know. Anyway, I decided to come here to live." He made it sound so simple, yet she knew it couldn't have been so easy.

Now she was afraid he would look at her with a question in his eyes; then it would be her turn. Quickly she asked, "What do you do?"

"These days, or when I first came?" He raised his eyebrows. They were still blond, though his hair and beard were quite gray.

"Both."

"I was trained as an engineer in England, so I worked as a designer for a construction company for the first few years. In my spare time I began to do ceramics and sculpture and after a while that took more and more time and I sold some pieces and bought a kiln and gave up my job. Now you might say I'm the resident potter."

"And sculptor?"

"Some. I teach art in the local high school and do the pottery in the summer." He smiled. "A very quiet life to someone with three children." He glanced at Foffy again, and they sat silently for a few minutes. Suddenly Foffy began to cry. She had rubbed her eyes with a sandy hand. Mady grabbed a Kleenex and hurried toward her.

"There, darling, you'll be all right." She wiped the child's face. The man followed her and watched them.

"This is Foffy. Sophia Anne Glazer," Mady said when Foffy stopped crying.

"Sophia was my great-grandmother," the child volunteered.

The man bowed. "I'm happy to meet you, Sophia." He shook her hand. "I'm Hans. Hans Panneman."

"You have a nice beard," Foffy said, "and you can call me Foffy."

"I'm honored," he called as she ran back to her digging.

The days melted into one another — white sand, pale cloudless sky, the steady foam of the surf. Peter and Nina browned, their faces grew calmer, Mady felt younger. The house that still echoed with their father's footsteps, laugh, voice seemed far away. Mady's needlepoint grew, the outline of the figure began to appear. Foffy needed a hat.

"I look like a cherry," she announced. On the beach she wore a long-sleeved shirt and pants except when she went into the water. Even her scalp was red.

Madeleine drove the green Volvo into Racer's Cove. They browsed through the quaint shops. Foffy tried on straw, denim, calico, and finally settled on the quilted cotton plaid with a very wide brim.

"You can't even see her face," Nina complained.

"It will protect her better than the others," Peter said with authority. Mady smiled as she paid. Then they meandered down the narrow streets, taking pleasure in each new window. She felt better than she had in months, and the children sensed it. After David's death she thought she would never be able to do this again. For so long she went scarcely anywhere — eyes followed her in the supermarket, the library, at school meetings, the local stores. Unrelenting, pitying, sad eyes — of her parents, her sister, David's family, her nieces, friends, the children's teachers, David's colleagues, everyone. She learned to welcome any impersonal transaction. The cruel appearance of the bills after David died (how could Con Edison, New York Telephone, the banks, the department stores not know of his death, her agony?) became, slowly, a comfort. No pity and proof of time passing. Now Foffy grinned from behind that silly enormous brim.

"Shall we have lunch out?" Mady asked her because she still loved a treat so much. But there wasn't time for Foffy to answer.

A familiar deep voice floated from somewhere. "Is that Sophia Anne Glazer behind that hat?" Hans was waving from a doorway a few yards beyond them. Above him was a hand-lettered sign with a sprightly bird painted on it — The Goldfinch Studio.

"What a pretty hat!" he said to Foffy, but his eyes were on Madeleine's face, hair, throat. She felt herself redden — how dare he look at her like that when he never came back to the beach, when she had watched for him for three days? She had looked him up in the local phone book just this morning, but no Panneman was listed.

"Foffy, you run ahead and tell Peter and Nina to wait," Mady said, then let herself look at him.

"I had to start teaching Monday — from ten to three, and by the time I got to the beach you were gone," he said simply. Then Mady could see him decide to go even further. "I drove around to a couple of places and asked for you. Where in God's name are you staying?"

"At the Sunset Efficiency Apartments. Behind the Dolphin Motel. They're new. I like to do my own cooking," she said. "And we usually leave the beach around two-thirty. The older kids play tennis." She was glad to see him. No use denying it. She wished she had put on better clothes.

But the whole thing is impossible, she thought, as she and the children ate a few doors from Hans's gallery. He was still giving a class. Since everyone ate a picnic lunch right there, he couldn't get away, but he suggested they come back at three. "How I happened to look out the door as you were passing by is nothing short of a miracle," he told her, then added, instead of good-bye, "You must come one night for a meal."

An hour ago she had wanted to stay on this strip of coast forever; now she was relieved they had only three more days here. The whole thing was impossible. They might as well be from opposite ends of the earth. In fact, they *were* from opposite ends of the earth. He didn't even look like anyone she could be interested in. In clothes he looked taller and thinner than he looked in a bathing suit. And she was faintly repelled by his stained European teeth, his graying beard and hair in sharp juxtaposition with his blond eyebrows and youngish face, his worn immaculate clothes. She remembered people like him in college — in the fine arts building or in the halls of the philosophy department. You could have a cup of coffee with them, but that was all. And that will be all, she resolved, as she lingered over her coffee.

She must be crazy, she suddenly thought as she watched her children eat huge desserts, to be thinking about his looks, his clothes. She was evading the real issue. He was a German, his father had been a Nazi, she was a Jew. Not much of a Jew, but after Hitler that no longer mattered. A Jew was a Jew. The evidence of what was now so carefully referred to as The Holocaust had stalked her throughout her childhood: her mother pressing her elbow and nodding at the blue numbers on someone's arm, her own thin small face framed by almost black hair. "Has anyone ever told you Mady looks like Anne Frank?" people asked while her parents nodded and hugged her tighter to them. She was always puzzled by the question because she had blue eyes and once mentioned it to her mother. "It's the shape of your face," her mother answered. And then all those movies, which never touched her so much as they seemed to touch everyone else, making her feel guilty for weeks afterward.

None of her family would have talked to a man who admitted that his father was a Nazi; her sister, Shelley, would simply have gotten up and moved away, and soon he would have had to leave, too. But she listened and finally learned that his "Germanness" had nothing to do with what he really was. Or did it? She had to admit she didn't know, yet what purpose did all this musing serve? Hans Panneman meant nothing to her; he was simply a man she had met on the beach, and if she chose to talk to a man who had been born in Germany, even if his father had been a Nazi, that was her prerogative.

When they returned to his studio, he was waiting for them. The room inside was cool, whitewashed, and instead of the dull earth colors that were so popular among potters now, his pieces were brightly colored and highly glazed: clocks, castles, mosques, villages, abstracts in spectacular shapes and colors, as well as the more ordinary flower holders, earrings, trivets, cheese plates, cachepots. Mady's eyes were greedy for more as she walked around. On the beach she had felt sorry for him, and in the restaurant she had almost scorned him. She hated to admit it, but she had. And now she was filled with admiration for him. What a careful craftsman he was! Each piece was further evidence of his talent. She wanted to touch everything she passed. She heard her children exclaiming, "Look at this one, show Mom, oh, Peter, did you see this one?" The class smiled at their reactions. One woman murmured, "I love to watch people's faces when they come here for the first time."

"It's such a surprise!" Mady said, then stopped, embarrassed. But Hans merely looked up from helping a student, an older woman with bright greenish-blue eyes. "I forgot to tell you I lived in Italy for a while, that's where I learned to do these glazes," he said.

"They're beautiful, I didn't expect—" Mady hesitated.

"Hans is an artist!" the older woman announced.

On the way back to the efficiency Peter asked, "How do you know him, Mom?" He clearly thought she had known Hans a long time ago. Whenever they went on vacation, she and David used to meet someone from their past.

"We talked a little at the beach on Sunday. When he said he was a potter, I pictured rows and rows of tan or brown pitchers."

"He doesn't look like rows of brown pitchers," Foffy interrupted. Peter laughed.

"Don't laugh, Peter," Nina said. "What does he look like?"

"He looks like Daddy."

A sigh rippled through the car. They had all heard that before. It began a few months after David died. An unfamiliar face smiling at her in a store, in a restaurant, in line for a movie, and Foffy announced, "He looks like Daddy."

"Oh, Foffy, I can't think of anyone who looks less like Daddy!"

"Now wait a minute, Peter." Nina's voice was thoughtful. "Foffy's not all wrong, there's something about his eyes. I can see what she means."

Madeleine's hands grew clammy as she drove. She could still feel his eyes on her, his pleasure when he saw her. After he had told her he was a potter she had been relieved. In addition to being a German, he was a potter, for God's sake! How could she ever get involved with a potter? Yet she had looked for him the next day, and the next, and the next. When they had met again, he had said, "Nothing short of a miracle," from a man who plainly didn't believe in miracles. And then his work — such beautiful, meticulous work. You'd have to be a stone not to respond to it; that woman was right. Hans was an artist. One look and you knew he toiled endlessly, patiently at his craft, and for a moment there in the studio she had envied him. To have something so important to you, to be able to work that hard. That was the kind of commitment she had always admired. But envy? She was surprised at herself. She was not an envious person, yet she knew envy when she felt it. As she drove she knew she would see him again, if only to sort out what she felt.

The main room of Hans's house took Mady back to those innocent years when she and her sister and parents used to visit endless restorations and museums. As you looked over the ropes into the mysterious silent rooms, you could sense the lives that had been lived there, but they were gone, evanescent, could only be guessed — and all that remained was a curious, well-earned peace.

Here was the same peace, yet the man was alive, handing her a glass of ginger ale. Did the surface of the room hide something? Or was it merely evidence of a life of solitude? The white walls were pure, unmarked — clearly this was a house without children. A few pieces from his studio were displayed; hanging above a small piano was a sun-filled painting of a picnic, below the chair rail were yards and yards of books, and mixed in with the low modern furniture were a few delicate antiques.

"How old is it?" she asked. The children were picking blueberries that grew near the south side of the house.

"The deed says 1803, but that's only the original room. The house was added on to three times after the Civil War, about twenty-five years apart. Some people say the deed is misdated and the original structure is the oldest in Racer's Cove. Hard to know." Hans shrugged, sipped his scotch. "The house hadn't been lived in for at least twenty years when I bought it, the owners had left it to their grandchildren, but they had settled in Arizona."

"How long did you work on it?" Mady looked up. The ceiling beams were very old.

"About a year. I lived in a tent for the summer, out there." Hans gestured to the flat piece of land on the east side of the house. "It was the only flat place, the rest of the land near the notch in the cove is so hilly. It's purely local, 'a geologist's delight' is what they call Racer's Cove. Anyway, I bought the house in May and by Thanksgiving I was able to sleep inside. I had to strip the walls and ceilings and redo them. At first I used the guest room for storage, then the next year, after I began teaching, I built the garage in my spare time and used the guest room for my classes. When they got too big, I rented the studio and now the house is really mine." His voice held a note of triumph. Their eyes met and they smiled.

"I'll be right back, I have to check the rice," he said.

When he had come to the beach, he had asked them to dinner. In front of Foffy and Nina, so of course the answer was yes before she had a chance to open her mouth. Now Mady wondered why she might even have been tempted to refuse. Seeing his life here and in his studio, she knew that what she had felt when they met again this morning was simply the fright that comes to a widow when a man, any man, looks at her with interest. For someone married as long as she had been married, being alone was so disconcerting, so dangerous. But here, certainly, was no danger. A man was settled into a life of work and solitude and art and books. As for the envy — well, that had more to do with her own restlessness than with him. When David had been alive, she had shared his life and some of his work. He had talked endlessly to her about his cases, and although she had never deluded herself that she actually influenced him, he had brought the world home to her. After his death she had been so busy with the endless red tape and financial arrangements that seem to be the American substitute for mourning that she had found her new isolation from the world a relief. Yet she couldn't retreat forever. Foffy would go to first grade in the fall and she had promised herself that she would begin to think about a job. When she saw Hans's studio, she felt that stab of envy. He knew so well what he had to do each day. He had made his work his life and once you saw the work you couldn't — if you were in your right mind — feel sorry for him. But what about her? What was she going to do? she had wondered as she walked around his studio. She sighed and sipped her drink and let her eyes scan the bookshelves. The key to the arrangement was nationality. Tasso, Ariosto, Dante, Boccaccio, Silone, Moravia, Morante, Montale. Then Romain Rolland, Rabelais, Montaigne, Flaubert, Valery, Colette, Camus, Proust. Across the room were the English and Americans, in front of her the Russians, but not in translation. Slowly at first she read the Russian letters: Pushkin, Lermontov, Chekhov, Tolstoy, Dostoevski, Paustovsky, Nabokov, Pasternak. Nabokov would be annoyed; he had only contempt for Pasternak, called *Doctor Zhivago* a fraud. She reached for the Mandelstam poems. Then she opened the page that was marked with a scrap of paper. Slowly she translated:

> *Can't sleep. Homer. Stretched sails.*
> *I've read to the middle of the list of ships:*
> *the lengthening flock, the stream of cranes*
> *that once flew above Hellas.*
>
> *Cranes in flight crossing strange borders,*
> *their leaders soaked with the spray of the gods.*

Where do you sail? What would Troy be to you,
O men of Achaea, without Helen?

The words came more easily than she would have dreamed. She was amazed.

"How do you know Russian?" Hans asked. She didn't know how long he had been standing in the doorway watching her.

"It was my major. I helped my Russian professor translate some Paustovsky stories and the early Akhmatova poems when I was a senior. But I got married right after college and never really used it except for my own pleasure. I haven't read any Russian for a while, though it comes back quicker than . . ." She shrugged. When she was in college, she had believed with all her heart that reading Russian was something that would help in grief. After David died all she read for months and months were picture books aloud to Foffy. She looked down at the book in her hands and leafed through the pages. Again she felt that inevitable shiver of delight at the sight of the curves and odd arches and curlicues that were the Russian language. A few passages were underlined, and occasionally a word meaning jotted in the margin. She looked at Hans.

"And you? How do you know it?"

"Our teacher in Kenya was a Russian, an emigre who thought the Revolution was going to solve everything and was disappointed, so he came to Kenya. When we finished our work he taught us Russian as a reward. We learned how to read and were beginning to learn conversation when we had to go back to Germany. He was the closest friend of my Aunt Johanna and my Uncle Hans-Karl. His name was Sergei Vladimirovitch. He and Johanna and Hans-Karl begged my father to let us stay in Africa . . ." Hans's eyes clouded for a split second, then he shrugged. "Perhaps someday I'll go to Russia and learn to speak it."

"What happened to him?"

"He died in 1962. I had gone back to see him for Christmas because by then Johanna and Hans-Karl were dead, too. When I arrived they told me he had died in his sleep in the night." He looked out the window for a moment. "I've been thinking of going to Russia the next time I visit —" But here was Foffy, bursting into the room with blue hands and mouth, streaks of purple across her forehead. "Look, Mommy, look at the fat blueberries!" she cried and held out the basket. Mady took one. It was tart, but juicier than she expected. She laughed.

"Good, aren't they?" Hans said. She nodded.

"Even better than the gelati."

Hans smiled and led Foffy to the kitchen. Mady put the Mandelstam poems back on the shelf and stood at the entrance to the kitchen. Like the rest of the house it was neat, sparse, but cheerful. Instead of a curtain, plants hung at the window. Now Hans was rubbing Foffy's hands with a piece of lemon. "That's how you get the blue off," he told the child. He filled the sink with water. "There, now hold your hands in this lemony water and you'll see most of it come off. Like magic." The water began to turn a purplish-blue; after a few minutes Foffy shook her hands and Hans released the stopper.

"Look, Mommy, come here," Foffy called as if Mady were miles away. "Come see the blue whirlpool." Madeleine stepped closer and watched the water swirl down the drain. Foffy held out her hands so Hans could wipe them. Watching the man and the child, each intent on that intimate act, Mady had to look away. Her ears pounded. She heard Hans's reasonable voice.

". . . has a funny name. It's named after a Frenchman, a man called Coriolis. I've forgotten his first name. The whirling is called the Coriolis effect. It goes from the right to the left north of the equator, which is here" — he stopped while Foffy looked up, nodded — "and in the part of Africa where I grew up, which is below the equator, it goes from the left to the right."

CHAPTER 2

A N INDIAN SUMMER EVENING. Soft unexpected warmth at October's end. Foffy and her friend Sally were blowing bubbles on the patio. David had come from Buffalo late last night and was going to Boston tomorrow, but now there was a peaceful space in between. Silently they sat and sipped the black espresso, watching the iridescences flying around their heads. David caught one.

"Don't, Daddy, it'll break," Foffy cried. But he held it on the tip of his finger and it swayed dangerously until Foffy finally popped it. She and Sally ran off to the tire swing that hung from the red oak whose leaves glowed in the tarnished light.

Around them was the garden David had planned and planted, adding a few perennials each year so that even now, late in October, there were masses of chrysanthemums and late-blooming roses and bushy impatiens and begonias and the last of the sweet alyssum, which had draped itself over a rock in a frenzy of growth like a lush waterfall. Mady sometimes tried to imagine how she and David would be once the children were grown. Would they be sitting here, still on this patio they had laid by themselves, stone by stone, the summer that Peter was born? She could feel David's eyes on her. Her glance met his.

"We'll be drinking Sanka," he said.

"Or else in some crazy, out-of-the-way place where someone needs a brilliant, aged lawyer," she replied. He chuckled. Only last week he had refused a job in Liberia.

How proud she was of his work! He had been on the commission to investigate the Attica uprising, tomorrow he was going to give a lecture at Harvard Law School where he and his old friend, Dan French, taught a course in a unique kind of partnership. She looked at him as he watched Foffy and Sally. Deeper lines, more firmly set features, but he was still very lean and his hair was still black and curly and his eyes had the same fierceness they had had when he was in law school and she was a sophomore in college.

He was the most interesting man she had ever known. She had married him years ago because she wanted to know everything about him. She couldn't believe her good luck, especially when she listened to other women, but she had the sense not to think too much about it. She only wished they could spend more peaceful time together. She felt cheated by his work, which was so important to him, and by his incredible energy, which kept him moving all the time. Most of all she felt cheated by time; all those years couldn't have passed, yet the proof surrounded them.

Now the two older children walked toward them. Nina had a book open in her hand, Peter carried his clarinet. He needed a lift to a rehearsal. The evening had just begun.

"I'll help Nina with her math and put Foffy to bed," David said as he gulped the last of his coffee. "You drive Peter."

The next morning dawned clear, bright. A gift to a wife who was uncomfortable when her husband had to fly, and he had had to fly so much these last two years. On nasty days he would make an exasperated call to the airport. Of course they were flying, he would reassure her (when didn't they fly? Mady sometimes wondered), and then he would give her the usual statistics, and, unless a storm were raging outside their window, he would fly. She always saved a lot of chores for those days so she could gradually work her way through them until she heard his voice say, "I'm at La Guardia."

Through a crack in the curtains she could see the sky, a brilliant blue. He was humming to himself as he shaved; he was always so lighthearted in the morning. She strained to listen. The theme from the *Trout*; they had heard it last night. She smiled and reached for her robe at the bottom of the bed. It had fallen on the floor. She sprawled across the bed and groped for it. When she looked up he was standing in the doorway, a towel around his waist. "You know, if I didn't have to make a plane . . ." he mused.

"Or a train, or a bus. You're all talk in the morning."

"Someday we're going to stay in bed for a week straight," he said so seriously that she laughed.

"Who's sick?" It was Foffy, rubbing sleep from her eyes, her favorite blanket twisted around her legs.

"No one, honey," Mady heard David say as she went into the bathroom.

He spent too much time playing with Foffy, so breakfast was rushed and Mady barely had time to say good-bye as he dashed out the door blowing kisses.

"Plane's in at six. I'll call," he said over his shoulder and crossed paths with the milkman.

"Mr. Glazer off to Buffalo again?" the man said. Everyone knew David was involved in the Attica investigation.

"No, Boston. He's teaching at Harvard every other week."

"Beautiful day to fly, everything's clear as a bell."

The day defeated her. Every time she looked up at the sky she dismissed the fear that had unexpectedly begun to mount in her blood, making her fingers and toes tingle. But how ridiculous, all you had to do was look at the deep blue sky. She was a little tired today, she must control herself. Everything was dangerous and certainly she had never wanted to be married to the postmaster. When David went to visit the prisoners at Attica, their friends had been worried, their relatives in a panic. Only she had remained calm. She was convinced nothing would happen to David in the prison. It was the damned flying that unnerved her so.

"If you flew more you wouldn't be so frightened," David said. "On a nice day it's lovely, exhilarating."

Foffy came home from nursery school with a temperature. "Will I have to stay in bed for a week straight?" she asked.

Mady laughed. "No, darling, it's probably a virus. You'll be fine after a day or so."

Her mother called at two. "Cousin Natalie had a boy!"

"Wonderful!" Mady said. "Everything okay?"

"Fine. Seven, three. The *bris* is next Thursday. I know David won't be able to make it but I hope you can," her mother said. The closest she could come to an order.

"You know how I hate *brises*," she began.

"Natalie is an orphan," her mother said brusquely. "Now, how's everything?"

"Fine, everything's fine, Mom. David went to Boston to teach today, he'll be home for dinner."

"He was just in Buffalo."

"I know, but he teaches every other Wednesday." Her mother was the only person Mady knew who wasn't impressed that David was teaching at Harvard.

"He does too much, much too much," her mother said. "But at least it's clear. I was just out and it's a perfect day. Where's Foffy? Let me speak to my darling."

"Don't tell her you're sick," Mady whispered as she handed Foffy the phone. The little girl winked.

The afternoon went quickly. Peter baby-sat for Foffy while Mady took Nina to her piano lesson. She shopped while Nina was there. Even though the prices were outrageous she liked shopping for her family. She didn't have to worry about what she was spending and she felt contented when she had filled the pantry and refrigerator. She also got depressed when she didn't

have enough food in the house. Once she had mentioned it to
their friend Fred Howland, who was a psychiatrist, and he had
said the usual things about security and feeling adequate and
being a woman. She thought that was too simplistic but she
hadn't sorted it out. These days it took longer to shop; like everyone else she was reading labels. She put a box of raw sugar in
the basket. David liked a spoonful in his tea in the morning.
Then some Grape-Nuts. She read the label on the cream cheese.
According to the date it would spoil in three months. Were they
all killing themselves with everlasting foods?

On the checkout line she met Gail Howland. She looked so
pale. They talked for a few minutes — nothings, details. Ap-
parently so civilized, but Mady knew that Gail's life was shat-
tering around her; she and Fred were separating, no one knew
why, Mady wasn't sure they knew why.

"Give David my love," Gail said.

"I will, and . . . " Her voice trailed off. She felt foolish. Should
she have sent her love to Fred? Then she glanced at her watch.
Four-thirty. Another hour and a half.

She watched Nina walk toward the car. Suddenly, as if in the
minute Mady was watching her, Nina became more graceful, no
longer the thin boyish girl. "The Mozart went well and we
worked on the fingering for the Debussy. And she gave me a
Chopin nocturne. The one you play," Nina said. Mady raised
her eyebrows. Nina sang a few notes. "The one Daddy likes so
much; he always says, 'Play that one again, Mady,' when you've
finished." Mady smiled in surprise.

Foffy's temperature was the same when she got home. She
called Anne Levin.

"Give it another day, Mady. There's something called 'echo
virus' around."

She had made the stew that morning. Now — salad, rice. She
got out the pot, put the water up to boil. Then she sectioned the
grapefruit. Over the sweet serene voice of Mister Rogers on the
TV she could hear Peter's clarinet, Nina on the phone. Both kids

were beginning to talk more on the phone. Should they get another? David was against it, yet — well, she wouldn't worry about it now. She picked up the extension. "Nina?"

"Yes, Mom?" Nina's voice had a slight edge. That was new.

"Honey, please don't be too long. Dad's supposed to call."

"Okay." Nina's voice softened. So calm, so reasonable. So different from when they were young. This used to be the witching hour when the two older ones were little, then again for a year or so after Foffy was born. Now it was such a luxury to be able to think.

Madeleine wondered how David's class had gone. She cut up the cucumbers and peppers for the salad, then shredded the lettuce and put the bowl into the refrigerator. She added the rice and some seasoning to the boiling water, turned the heat down, and used the next fifteen minutes to water some of the plants in the greenhouse. When David finished it a few months ago, the plants had been spaced widely apart. Now it looked as crowded as everyone else's greenhouse. She moved the fittonia, watched the prayer plants begin to close up, snipped some brown fronds from the asparagus ferns.

Later on, for weeks and months, probably for years, she sometimes thought, the details of that last hour would visit her in the strangest places, and once she thought of one detail her mind would be compelled to go through the entire sequence, searching perhaps for the moment when she had known something was wrong. But at the time she felt only that amorphous fear she had felt all day, fear she had known before. While she did the little chores that many wives do at the dinner hour, she was thinking nothing extraordinary — only how pleasant it was to have older children so that all this could be done so peacefully.

Then the telephone — late, yet not late enough that she was worried. But in place of his steady, "I'm at La Guardia," a cold official voice. Someone from the airline. An accident, he said. Could she come to the airport immediately, please?

"Is he . . . ?" her voice faltered.

"We don't know." Then an ominous click. And minutes later when she was still sitting numb, entirely alone with the burden of the news, before the truth or the trembling had begun to take hold of her body, another call. This time a long horrible wail. Only when a voice cried, "Mady!" did she realize it was Sarah, David's mother.

CHAPTER 3

"H IS MOTHER LIVES near the airport. She always asks details when anyone flies so she knew his flight number. There was a freak local storm that afternoon, they got caught in a powerful downdraft. You must have read about it. The plane crashed at the beginning of the runway, everyone was killed."

How flat her voice sounded. When she had begun to talk after dinner, Hans had given her a drink, the first drink she had had since David's death. She had never been much of a drinker — sherry, or an occasional vodka and tonic in summer, sometimes a few sips of brandy before they went to bed on a snowy night. With all the chaos, the trembling, the feeling of her mind just holding on, she had been afraid to have even one drink. Countless people had urged her to. "Just one, it will make you relax," they kept saying. But she was afraid. Her senses had worked double-time after David died; she had been so exposed, so vulnerable. She took offense at the slightest remark, she had fought at least once with everyone she loved. If she had a drink she might become even crazier than she alone knew she was, she had reasoned. Yet now, sitting in this interesting old house, with this bearded man she had met only a few days ago, she had begun to talk and when he handed her the scotch, she had welcomed its bitterness tearing at her throat.

"David's parents were older. His father died three years ago, his mother has a heart condition. I can still feel her voice in my head, her wail comes to me in my dreams." She looked up at him and went on. "One of the worst things that happened actually happened almost a year later. I'm not much of a television watcher, David and I never seemed to have time. We used to watch the news regularly, but during Vietnam it was hard to go to bed after watching." She stared across the room, unable to meet Hans's eyes.

"Even after he died I didn't watch much television. For the first few months I went to bed practically with the kids, and when I began to feel better, it was easier to read or listen to music. The voices on television made me lonelier; I think I was listening unconsciously for the sound of someone who would remind me of David. But one night I was waiting for Peter to come home from a dance and I was getting sleepy so I put on the news. Another airplane had crashed that day — and this time everyone got out before the plane began to burn. This plane crashed about five hundred yards from where David's plane had gone down and a bright young newscaster decided it would be interesting to show what these lucky people had escaped. So they ran clips from the crash David was in — no people, but a lot of fire and wreckage. They showed pictures of the temporary coffins as they loaded them from the scene of the crash. Blood was seeping through the raw pine coffins."

Now Madeleine looked at Hans. He was listening intently, absolutely still while she spoke. "I guess other people had seen them before, but somehow, for me, all those blood-stained coffins were the worst detail of all. I think right then, in my own living room, almost a year after he died, I finally *knew* it had happened." Mady put down her glass and turned her wedding ring on her finger. Then she added, "I've never told anyone else about that newscast. I don't know why I'm telling you, I barely know you." Hans was silent and looked into his glass. She was grateful for both his silence and his refusal to pity her even with a glance.

After that long silence they didn't have time to talk anymore. The children came in from their walk along the dunes; it was way past Foffy's bedtime. When they said good-bye, Mady noticed that Peter seemed a little cool toward Hans. Back in the apartment, with Foffy in bed and Nina in the shower, Peter turned to her.

"You didn't tell us he was a German," he said.

"I didn't tell you anything about him." Peter didn't answer. "Is it so important?" she added.

"Of course it's important! He said his father was a Nazi and he fought at the end of the war for Germany!"

"He also told you his twin brother was killed in a training accident and that he couldn't stay in Germany or even in Europe after the war. Doesn't that mean anything?" She looked at her son. His eyes were confused. Mady tried to think how David would handle this. How many times had she wished for his help when dealing with the children in this last year and a half! She sat down.

"Yeah," Peter said, and sat down next to her.

"He was terribly hurt by his brother's death. He made it clear that he didn't agree with his father or the Nazi Party and he certainly wasn't close to his father after the war."

"But he could have refused to leave Africa, he could have refused to fight if he didn't believe the way his father did."

"Peter, he was fourteen years old. Almost your age. If your father told you you had to go back to a country and fight for it and he really believed it, wouldn't you fight?"

"I don't know." Suddenly Peter looked like a little boy. She moved toward him. He blurted, "Sometimes I can't even remember what it was like to have a father!" And he was crying and she had her arms around him and his tears were in her hair. He was all bones.

"I don't know what to think — about anything. I can't believe

Dad is dead. Night after night, sometimes every night in a row for a week, he's standing over my bed, talking to me before I turn off my light the way he used to, and then I realize it's a dream and I wake up sweating and crying . . ."

"Why didn't you tell me, why didn't you say so?"

"I don't know. It didn't start to happen till a few months ago and by then everyone else was much better. You were smiling more, not sleeping so much, I didn't want to make it worse . . ." Peter shrugged and wiped his eyes with the back of his hand, smearing his face.

Quickly Mady reconstructed the weeks after David's death. They had all gone for crisis therapy. At the time Peter seemed the sturdiest of them all. "He's amazing," the psychiatrist said. "A very unusual boy, he takes after his father," said the man, who was a friend of Fred Howland. "Peter's fine," everyone had reassured her. Yet he was the boy, the oldest, the most sensitive child she had. The loss of his father — it was so complicated. He'd bounce back quickly, they said, and she wanted — perhaps too much — to believe that. Worse, she had become the child, and had let Peter take care of her. But now he was exhausted, and frightened. She knew the feelings well. Guilt overwhelmed her as she groped for a tissue and wiped his face.

So here, in this tiny kitchen that smelled slightly of mildew, miles from home, Mady and Peter, and later Nina, finally talked about David's death. How painful it was! Mady's shoulder blades fluttered with tiredness as she again discovered what David had reminded her so often but what she had forgotten (or ignored, perhaps, because it was easier) — that children know everything and feel everything and there is no use trying to protect them. How much better to share the pain with them. As they talked Mady realized how sturdy, how intelligent, they both were. The sun was beginning to break through the dawn mist when they finally kissed good-night and crawled into bed.

The next day Hans postponed his class until after lunch and headed for the beach. He might meet one of his students and be

called upon to make some excuse for the class, but he would figure that one out when he needed to. Now all he wanted was to
see her — not even speak to her, just reassure himself that she
was real, that he had not dreamed her, or last night. Perhaps he'd
be smarter to walk endlessly on the beach and never find her.
Then he could go back to his quiet life, his uneventful middle
age. But of course that wasn't going to happen. It was a glori-
ous day and she would be here with her children and her
needlepoint.

He parked in the town lot and pulled on his beach jacket. The
radio was predicting temperatures in the nineties, and he had to
be careful not to burn. Lotions, jackets, hats, glasses, and *voilà*,
you didn't burn. So easy to protect yourself against a powerful
sun. He wished it were so easy to protect yourself against other
things.

Since she had left, somewhat hurriedly, with her children last
night, he had been unable to sleep, or even to sit down for long.
He kept going over their conversation, hearing her somewhat
high vibrant voice, her laugh; he kept seeing the way she ate her
food, slowly, with not much appetite, the way she watched her
children, never missing a motion or a facial expression, the way
her body sometimes seemed a poignant extension of theirs
(especially Foffy's) when she leaned toward them, talked to
them, admonished them. She had covered herself with her children in the same way, he supposed, that he had covered himself
with his work and his furniture and his books and house. Even
her appearance gave her away — the way she tied back her thick
dark hair and wore her somber darkish clothes and her old one-
piece bathing suit. Don't touch me, she was saying, there's nothing here for you. And that was exactly what had attracted him. In
the midst of all the exposed flesh on the beach he found himself
wondering why such a long and lean body wasn't in a bikini, or,
at the very least, a two-piece bathing suit.

He scanned the beach for her. There she was, bending over
that infernal needlepoint. It was a copy of a reclining woman by
Matisse. He had seen the original once — he couldn't remember

where, maybe in Zurich, and it was a lovely thing — sensuous curves, Matisse's vision of woman, filled with a kind of suppressed sexual electricity. She concentrated on it so hard, as if endowing it with all the energy and passion her clothes denied.

Someday — maybe — he would point out the irony to her. But for now . . . For a second Hans closed his eyes and wished she weren't there. Then he wouldn't have to deal with this absurd anxiety. He had thought he was finished with this by now. He had known only a few women well, and he had thought he loved the last one — a childless divorcée whom he had met a few years ago while on a vacation in Maine. But he couldn't remember ever feeling quite like this. God knows he had never canceled a class for the divorcée — even after they were lovers — or gone running along the beach trying to find her. "You're so goddamned controlled," she had told him when they parted. "A typical German." He wished she could see him now, a knot in his throat, stepping tentatively toward the clump of color that he knew was Madeleine Glazer and her possessions.

From her profile, from the way her shoulders sloped, he could see that she was tired, and when she looked up he saw dark circles beneath her eyes. For a second he had a glimpse of what she must have looked like for months after her husband's death.

"Where are the kids?"

She pointed a few yards away where Foffy was playing. "Peter and Nina are still sleeping, we stayed up very late talking, and they're exhausted. But Foffy wanted to come." She bent her head over her work as if she realized how tired she must look and didn't want him to see. He was filled with a desire to lift her chin with the tip of his forefinger and tell her she didn't have to hide from him. But he merely stood there, waiting, hoping she would ask him to sit down.

"We were up very late talking," she repeated. "Peter and Nina and I . . . " She shrugged. "It's hard to explain." When her eyes met his he could see they were a little confused. Or was he imagining it? She bent to her work again.

"They're teenaged now, it must be hard to bring them up

alone," he said. Instantly her head snapped up, now her eyes were distant, and she answered curtly, "It's too complicated to explain to someone who's never had a family."

"You don't have to explain," he said. He groped for something to break the tension; when he found it, his words were stiff, matter-of-fact. "Get to bed early tonight," he said.

She laughed. "You sound just like you did that first day, when you said, 'You're shaking and your lips are purple.' I thought you were a doctor."

He tried to smile but he couldn't and he could see a wariness creeping into her eyes that mirrored his own, he knew. Both needed to retreat a little. Still, he couldn't bear the thought of not seeing her again. As his brain searched for a solution his glance fell on Foffy, who looked up and waved.

He tried to make his voice businesslike, kind. Dale Carnegie, you would be proud of me, he thought. "Will you stop by tomorrow at the studio? I have some things for the children."

"Oh, Hans, you shouldn't. After dinner and the evening, you've done more than enough," she protested.

For a second he thought her eyes glistened, but why on earth would she be crying in the middle of the morning in front of him? He wished the gelati man would come by and they could sit for a few moments and get their bearings. For once he didn't feel like respecting someone else's privacy, but in the end his manners, his control, his Germanness, whatever it was, won out. He stood there and said, "They're just small things, please don't deprive me of that pleasure." Then he backed away from her, put down his jacket and towel, and let his legs lead him into the rocking waves where he took a long exhausting swim. When he got out, she and Foffy were gone, though their things were still there. He looked along the shore and saw Madeleine patiently holding the bucket while Foffy gathered her second thousand shells.

In the morning Peter found a tennis game and Mady drove into town with the girls.

"Peter says Hans is a Nazi," Foffy said.

"Oh, Foffy, Peter didn't say Hans was a Nazi, he said he was a German," Nina objected.

"Then after you left, Nina, he said a German in World War Two was a Nazi and everyone should hate Nazis."

"Have you and Peter talked about this a lot?" Mady asked.

"No, just yesterday afternoon at the beach. I wanted to look for Hans and I asked Peter to come with me and he said, 'I don't want to talk to a Nazi and neither should you.'"

"I think Peter's getting a little uptight about this, Mom," Nina said.

"So do I, we'll have to talk about it later," Mady promised.

"He doesn't mean it anyway," Foffy told her. "He really likes Hans. I heard him tell Roger and his family to go to Hans's studio."

They stopped for a light. Mady looked at Foffy. "Sometimes it's hard to put people's lives together, Foffy. That's what's giving Peter trouble now. Hans is not responsible for his father's beliefs. He could even have fought for the Germans when he was a boy and be a perfectly nice person at forty."

"He's forty-six."

"How do you know?" Nina demanded.

"He told me."

"You mean you asked."

"So what if I did? Men don't care. Besides, Mommy, I don't think Hans was a Nazi, he wouldn't hurt anyone. Ever."

"If you say so, Foffy," Mady murmured.

"When do you leave?" Hans asked.

"Tomorrow. We have to be out by eleven so they can clean for the next people." She felt such a fool. She had come to his studio exactly as he had asked and now she was uncomfortable. She should ask him to dinner, he was so kind and she had been rude to him yesterday on the beach. But he confused her so, and with Peter feeling the way he did, how could she ask Hans to dinner? Oh, why had they ever gone to his house? She would have to be as detached as she could, but when she turned to him again, he was smiling at her with gold lights in his eyes. Really extraordinary eyes.

"That's wonderful! Then you can come folk dancing. The kids will enjoy it. A very good man from Brooklyn comes once a week and calls. Eight o'clock at the Community Center."

"I don't know," she hesitated. Peter would probably say no.

"I hope you make it," he said and gave the girls their presents. "Now don't open them until you get home," he said and handed Mady a present for Peter. That could have been good-bye.

But Peter had heard about the folk dancing. Everyone was going, so here she was with Foffy at her side, facing Hans and an attractive woman of about fifty-five. Hans had introduced her as the "musician-in-residence." She wore an intricately embroidered blouse and skirt and was very small and slender and she had a gray topknot. Her name was Rosa. When the dances began, it was obvious that Rosa had done a lot of dancing. So had Hans.

In the beginning Mady's legs were tangled rope, but after a bit the steps came easier, the rhythms took hold, the swish-swish of soles brushing against the floor in the *pas de bas* comforted her. In the fuzzy blur of color that surrounded her, Hans's face occasionally smiled or bowed, but most of the time they were part of the swirling movements of the dancing circle. When the caller announced the Salty Dog Rag, she asked Nina to look after Foffy and sat down on the edge to watch. Hans joined her.

She rubbed her hands along her thighs. "Am I going to ache tomorrow!" She pushed her hair away from her face; her hairline was wet.

"You'll be fine," Hans said and together they watched the dancers. The teenagers were beautiful. Their shirts were stained with sweat, their hair was rumpled, but their young bodies moved gracefully through the steps, each one more complicated than the last, and their faces glowed as they danced faster and faster. What a good way for Peter and Nina to spend an evening. When she got home she would ask around; perhaps they had folk dancing nearby.

The next dance was a Macedonian folk dance. "This one is slow, meditative, almost. It is done during the haying — when everyone is involved in the one task together. Let's all join hands," the caller announced.

As Hans took her hand in his Mady realized they had never touched. When they greeted each other they always stood stiffly apart; it had been like an unspoken agreement between them. Now the physical longing she had been denying since she first saw him surfaced. She felt that sensation of her blood thickening throughout her body. Ribbons of blood raveling from a knot of desire. She had thought she would never have that sensation again, and it came as such a shock that she felt dizzy and went through the motions of the dance as if in a dream. She felt her body reach toward him, reach away from her caution, her plans, her very self. Whether he knew what was happening to her she didn't know, couldn't even care. But when she looked at him, she saw that he knew. Once more, as in those few moments near his studio, his eyes caressed her, could not get enough of her, but now she was glad. How good it felt to know she had a body again! She let herself bend and sway to the languor of the music and when the dance was over she kept her hand in his. She wondered if Hans and Rosa were lovers. Now she could imagine him making love to someone, his touch warm, tender.

They stood with hands linked for a few minutes, then he pulled her toward him as the next dance was announced. "I must go now," he said quietly. "I'm leaving for Germany very early in the morning. I got a cable this afternoon. My mother's ill. I'll call you when I return."

"But our address?" Mady said, then felt stupid. She was so bewildered, so disappointed, so — yes, she might as well admit it — angry.

"Foffy gave it to me. Don't worry. I don't know how long I'll be — it may even be months — I'll write. I'm sorry, really I am," he added. Just then he sounded like a boy, and in that second all her anger dropped away and she wanted to put her arms around him, but of course she didn't. The circle formed around her and he slipped away and waved and as the next dance, a polka, began, she got a glimpse of him near the door shaking Peter's hand. On the way home Nina and Foffy told her he had kissed them both good-bye.

CHAPTER 4

THE HOUSE WELCOMED THEM and that moment of fear as she entered, almost that David's ghost awaited them, disappeared as they put down their suitcases and shopping bags and opened the doors and windows and collected the mail from next door. The only strangeness, and finally it jarred Madeleine, was the empty greenhouse.

After the funeral the plants had wilted, some were near death, and still Mady had not gone near the greenhouse. One day Mady's mother arrived with several large cartons and Peter and Nina helped her load the plants into her car. Her parents' living room looked like a jungle and Mady felt guilty every time she saw it, but she could not ask for them back.

Until now. "I think it's time for the plants to come home," Mady told her mother on the phone that evening.

"Oh, darling, that's wonderful. I can't tell you how pleased I am when I hear you say that. I have nothing planned tomorrow. Dad can help me load them into the car tonight and I'll bring them in the morning. You don't think anything will happen to them overnight in the car, do you?"

"It can wait until the weekend, Mom. They've waited this

long, they can wait another few days. The children and I can come get them Saturday."

"No, darling, tomorrow will be fine. Besides, it will give me a chance to see you all, hear about your time at the beach."

Madeleine's mother arrived from the north shore of Long Island by nine-thirty the following morning. Her skin glowed with a golden tan and people still referred to her as a pretty woman, but to Mady she was a shadow of herself.

Libby Hayman had always been carefree, even a trifle flighty. She was the only child of high school teachers and they had sent her to Hunter, where she studied French, and at twenty she had met Max Hayman at a friend's and although he was "in business" she had fallen in love with him. To her astonishment. Sometimes Mady thought her mother had never completely forgiven her husband for being a businessman instead of a professional, yet even Libby had admitted the appeal of falling in love against all one's well-founded expectations.

More than forty years later, Mady's parents shared a contented marriage, as long marriages go. Max and Libby respected each other and enjoyed many of the same things, and when her life didn't go as smoothly as she might have wished, Libby's wry sense of humor saw her through. To her daughters she saw life as a series of steps — a huge straight staircase, in fact. First she had had her babies with their French names — Michele and Madeleine — which made them immediately different. Then she had brought them up to love books and music and museums and the theater and the ballet and she had even spoken French to them at home. They had gone to college; Shelley had majored in French, Mady in Russian, and they had both married professional men. Shelley's husband, Mel, was a physician, David was an attorney. No such simple words as doctor and lawyer for Libby. Mady was always amused as her mother waited until all the women she met talked about their families and then, casually, she pulled her happiness out of her hat. A physician and an attorney and five grandchildren and no one maimed or deformed or divorced or even in therapy. Libby had the Midas touch.

Why, just look at her! people exclaimed. Still tall and thin and so lively. She played tennis with her grandson, she compared modern dance movements with her granddaughters, and she collected rocks and shells and pinecones for the one who was still little. The night David's plane crashed she did a little dance up the steps to Mady's house, never suspecting why Shelley had asked her to meet them there after dinner. Max was away and Libby never listened to the radio before eleven o'clock when she was doing her exercises. She made some funny clown movements while Foffy watched at the front window, then she frowned because this youngest grandchild (her secret favorite) wouldn't laugh.

"What's wrong with Foffy?" she had said, but then she saw all their faces and the blood seeped out of hers.

Madeleine waited month after month for the blood to come back into her mother's face. Libby developed a tic in one eye for a while but that disappeared. Still, Libby's skin had that pale, waxy hue. Mady found it hard to be with her mother for a long time; guilt overcame her when they did the most innocent things together, for it was she who had brought such tragedy into Libby's unblemished life.

"Libby will never get over it," people said. She had sat next to David's mother, Sarah, when they sat *shiva,* and it was Sarah, the older woman with a severe heart condition, who had comforted Libby. As the months passed Libby's hardy laugh became a narrow smile, her energy seemed sapped, she was often "very tired." Her stubborn silence, her refusal to speak openly about David's death, became a judgment on Madeleine, who suspected that if she had spoken Libby would have blamed David for his own death. For doing too much, for traveling too much, for being almost famous, for caring about Attica and his students, for wanting to fight injustice. A woman like Libby could turn virtues in life into flaws in death. David had wrecked her beautiful staircase, and now she was building again.

"Well, that's the first step. They'll perk up after a few days, but you must give me credit for keeping them alive. Every last one!"

Would she leave now? Mady hoped so, for seeing the plants in their places had given her a jolt; as she walked around the greenhouse she heard David's voice, talking, lifting leaves here, plucking stray stalks there, whispering, murmuring, making love to his plants.

Fortunately, Libby left before lunch. "I'm supposed to meet Helen at her club," she explained. Mady couldn't tell if it were true. Her mother had trouble staying in the house too long; she preferred to see Mady and the children at Shelley's or in her own apartment overlooking Long Island Sound.

After her mother left Mady sat on the patio. A heavy airless day had settled on Westchester County. How different from the beach where the seawind blew almost constantly, calming down only during the long, dreamlike twilight. Mady looked out onto the garden. Gnats and mosquitoes whirred, forming a sultry mist around certain plants. The garden looked so forlorn — wild where she hadn't weeded and pruned, or neglected where they used to put in the annuals. Only the roses were oblivious to all that happened and bloomed luxuriously, almost defiantly, although she had not fed them or sprayed for two summers. The first year she hadn't even been able to look at the garden; last spring she had thought about doing some planting, but she kept making excuses, and now it was almost the end of the summer again. But at least she could sit here and gaze at it; at least she didn't want to run.

After lunch she and Foffy went to the swim club. Nina and Peter were in a trips program and at the Metropolitan Museum today.

They found a cool spot under a large maple near the fence. Anne wasn't here yet, but Gail Howland was talking to someone Mady didn't know. Gail waved. Mady sighed. Only a few more days of sitting here among these large-hatted women; next week Foffy went to day camp. Each woman was a good person, she supposed, as she watched them stand, sit, scold their children, sip their iced tea, smile, laugh, talk, crochet, knit, rearrange their breasts as they entered or left the pool. Still, it was hard for her to spend too much time here. Their conversation was filled with clues that they were working their way through the leisure of a summer's day until their husbands arrived home. These were not working women, by and large. They still had young children at home, and those who did work were teachers or somehow tied to the schools — with the summer off. Listening to them Mady felt like an adolescent, eavesdropping while Shelley and her friends talked about their dates. Occasionally, one of them would sense Mady's plight and the talk would shift abruptly, become deliberately impersonal, though filled with their nameless guilt that they had husbands and she didn't. She sometimes wondered if she wouldn't be better off in Manhattan, but the only person who encouraged her was her old friend Dore, who was divorced, whose children were grown, and who had become a painter and lived in a feminist co-op in Chelsea.

So she stayed in the small town and learned to smile a lot in public. The anger she had felt and sometimes showed soon after David's death was so much more honest, but it got her into trouble. Family and close friends tolerated it in the beginning, but only for so long. Acquaintances never wanted her pain. She was constantly praised for her cheerfulness. Even today, as her mother was leaving, she had said, "You've been a brave girl, Mady, I'm proud of you." As if the necessity for bravery were over. If Libby only knew. "Still, it's better than being known as 'the town weakling,' or 'a drag,'" Anne once said. Now Mady was glad to hide under her hat and read Jane Austen's *Emma* after Foffy went off with her friends.

First she looked at the other book she had brought with her — a study of women in the arts. She stared at the author's photograph. The woman was wearing a coverall over a bathing suit and was holding tightly onto her husband's hand. He had been standing behind her, Mady guessed, and a second before the photographer clicked the shutter he had reached over her shoulder and grabbed his wife's hand. You couldn't see much of him, only his arm and hand and torso, but the connection between them was so obvious that Mady started to cry.

To hide her tears she opened the newspaper. The editorials were a blur. She turned to the obituaries; since David's death she had felt compelled to read them every day. Today no names she knew. Then she glanced at the facing page; usually it had some interesting small items. Now she could see and her eye caught the headline: CRASH CAUSED BY CONFUSION BETWEEN PILOT AND FLIGHT CONTROLLER. In a plane wreck near Cincinnati two men had been hurt but the rest were able to get out. The pilot had disobeyed the orders of the flight controller and crashed; he claimed that if he hadn't everyone would have been killed because of strange air currents caused by a sudden thunderstorm. The circumstances were uncannily close to those of the accident in which David died. She read the article again. What had happened to David's plane? Had he known? Had he been reading or talking, or dozing? Had the stewardess had time to demonstrate that oxygen contraption, or had it happened too fast? Had he awakened, blinking his eyes very fast? Or tried to comfort the person next to him? Had he screamed? Were his eyes wide open with surprise when he died?

Why did she want to know all this? Why did she let it haunt her? Too many questions that could never be answered. Her eyes searched for Foffy and found the blonde head bending over a deck of cards. Her hands sought her needlepoint. In and out, in and out, the rhythm of the work calmed her and she lay back in the chaise and dozed. When she woke, Gail was next to her, reading.

"Good sleep?"

Mady rubbed her eyes. "God, it was such a deep sleep! I scarcely knew where I was. That hasn't happened to me in a long time. I'm sorry."

"Nothing to be sorry about. I enjoyed watching you so relaxed. Things are better, aren't they?" When Mady heard the wistfulness in Gail's voice, she knew that Gail and Fred had decided, at last, to separate. She waited.

"Well, it's finally happened," Gail said slowly and looked down, smoothing her beach robe over her knees. She let her eyes meet Madeleine's.

"Is there someone else?"

"No, he says not, he says he's tired of being married, he wants to live by himself and do all the things he's always wanted to do. He says he's not interested in women or sex. But I'm not sure I believe him. Fred likes women, always has. You remember how he was in college. 'The Jewish Casanova,' they called him, didn't they?"

"Yes, but we were all so young then, and after he met you and went to medical school, he changed," Mady reminded her.

"That's what I thought. But now he sees himself as a savior of sorts and I have the feeling that what he really wants is to show some lonely repressed woman the light." Gail shook her head. "It's happened before, but I thought, well, let him have a fling. Then when he came back both times he was more settled, really more loving. But now he wants out. He wants to be free! That male cry for freedom — they all sound like fugitives on the Underground Railroad, for Christ's sake."

Mady had never heard Gail talk like this and now she looked as if she had been slapped across the face. The skin stretched over her cheekbones was ashen. "Has he told the kids?" she asked.

"No, he's supposed to — tomorrow night, but I'm not holding my breath. He's such a coward. Sometimes I think that's the worst thing, to discover you've been living with and loving — because we did love each other for a long time though he denies it now — a coward. For almost eighteen years. He says nothing will change, he'll see the girls. He doesn't understand we aren't a family anymore."

Mady didn't know what to say. "Let me get you a cup of coffee, I bet you haven't had a thing to eat all day." Quickly she made her way through several hellos and smiles and questions about how her summer was going. Gingerly she stepped around the jacks games, the sandbox, the swings, and the arts and crafts project. By the time she stood in line she was furious. How could they throw out a marriage? They were both alive, healthy, they had two beautiful daughters. Didn't they see what they were doing? She blamed Gail as well as Fred. Why didn't Gail fight harder? Yes, Fred was a successful psychiatrist who saw lots of women, but she was an intelligent attractive woman, how could she be so helpless?

Gail's eyes were brighter now; she was actually smiling.

"You're angry, Mady, I can see it in your walk. Sparks are ready to fly. You think I'm throwing away what you would give everything to have back," she said quietly. Mady didn't answer and started to arrange the food on the table next to them.

"Listen, Mady, we've been living in the same house like strangers. We get into bed and he goes to his side and I go to mine and it feels as if there's an ocean between us and if one of us were to venture into it we would drown. Occasionally I get very brave and he says, 'Not now, Gail,' as if I'm a child. A few months ago I started sleeping on a cot and that was better. It's even better when he doesn't come home at all. It's lonely when someone is gone, like David is, but it's even lonelier when someone is less than a foot away and doesn't want any part of you. I know it looks crazy to you, Mady, and it seems crazy to me, too. I didn't want this and I would take him back if he wanted to come back. But he doesn't." Gail swallowed hard.

Mady regretted her anger. "What about Dr. Oshinsky?" she asked gently. "Have you seen her?" Dr. Oshinsky was old now. She was Fred's teacher and the Howlands' close friend.

"She says things change, marriages change, people change, nothing is permanent, everything is in flux, especially these days."

Still, Mady didn't give up easily. "A mule," her mother used to call her. "Do you want me to talk to Fred?" she said.

"No. There's nothing you can do, nothing anyone can do.

You can't will this to change any more than you can will David back. No one can talk to Fred these days." Gail sighed. "I have to get used to the idea of divorce. It's so nutty, I'm the squarest lady in the county and now I guess I'll have to learn how to swing."

Mady shook her head. While both pretended to read, she decided to call Fred. She had been wanting to ask him about Peter anyway, she had a perfectly good reason to call him. And maybe she could talk to him about his marriage, make him see what he was doing. She would remind him how madly he had fallen in love with Gail.

"Well, if it isn't my foul-weather friends!" Dore's voice penetrated the thick silence surrounding Mady and Gail. They looked up.

"My God, Dore, you've lost so much weight!" Gail gasped as they both rose to greet their old friend.

"Yes, I'm writing a book called 'How I Lost Seventy-Five Pounds and Found My Collarbone.'" Dore laughed and hugged them both.

"How are you, and who are you visiting and why haven't we heard from you? I thought you were in New Hampshire," Gail said, as they sat down.

"Wait a minute, one question at a time. I'm here with Nan and we didn't tell you I was coming because I wanted to surprise you. At the last minute I rented the house and decided to stay in New York because I'm working on a new cycle of paintings. I'm also going to behavior modification class. That's how I lost the weight."

Mady was shaking her head. "I can't believe it, Dore, you look like a different person."

"Almost as thin as you, Mady. That's what I told them: I have a friend back in the suburbs who is never really hungry, she just pushes the food around on her plate, that's what I want to learn to do."

Mady laughed. "That's not true. I'm just not a very big eater.

I've never cared much about food, and you know that David used to do a lot of the cooking on the weekends."

"I sure do," Dore said, "but what you don't understand is that it was another way to make you more dependent on him."

Mady groaned. "Okay, Dore, let's not beat that one to death anymore. What are you working on?"

"*Green Spring.* A cycle of five paintings in shades of green, blue, and yellow. You must come in and see them." Dore's husband, Jake, and David had worked together years ago and they were the reason Mady and David had come to live in this small town. Then, one day, after their younger child went to college, Dore had announced that she and Jake were separating and before anyone knew it she had moved into a loft in Chelsea. Everyone was stunned. She had been the perfect suburban matron — president of the League of Women Voters, the moving force in the peace movement for the county in the sixties, an activist in civil rights, the only woman member of the school board. The only person who didn't seem surprised was Jake, and as soon as the separation agreement went through he moved to Chicago with a much younger woman and now they had a child.

"Foul-weather friends, that's what you are, both of you," Dore said again.

"That's because every time we came in it was raining," Gail reminded Mady. But Mady remembered. They had thought she was in a trance the first few months after David died and when she had to go in to transact business with the lawyers or the banks or the federal agencies that suddenly descend on a woman when she becomes a widow, Gail had often come with her. After the business was finished they used to take a cab down to Dore's place.

"And what are you up to?" Dore narrowed her eyes. They laughed.

"You might as well lie to the Sphinx as to Dore," Mady murmured.

"Fred and I are separating," Gail said in a low voice.

"That's the best thing that could have happened to you," Dore said. "I know you think I'm cruel and crass, but you'll see that marriage isn't the answer to everything. Today women have to learn to make it on their own, and independence is the most important ingredient in a woman's life."

"Leave her alone, Dore, it's all so new, she needs time to get used to it," Mady said in an irritated tone. "She doesn't need a lecture on the women's movement."

"You're right, absolutely right. I am crass and cruel, but everyone knows that," Dore said. She put her hand on Gail's. "Forgive me, ducks."

Dore turned to Mady. "Well, what about you? Has the bereaved widow found a job yet?"

"Oh, Dore, you are incorrigible. No, the bereaved widow hasn't found a job. She told you very clearly that she was going to think about that when Foffy went to first grade, which gives her six weeks."

"Good," Dore said firmly. "I saw Foffy. She's absolutely gorgeous. Before you know it, all those *Kinder* are going to be out of the house, Mady." She stood up and looked at Mady's long body stretched out on the chaise. "You really are thin."

"So are you now," Gail said.

"Now, the question is, can I keep it off? Aye, ducks, there's the rub." She glanced around at the other women.

"Everyone's wearing a two-piece bathing suit this year, Mady. For God's sake, why don't you go out and buy a new suit? With that figure it's the least you can do." Mady looked up at her, but didn't answer.

"Listen, Mady, all the people behind the desks interviewing for jobs aren't sadists and there are no rapists waiting for widows in the dressing rooms at Bonwit's. Get yourself out of the house, and come see me soon, both of you," she said and kissed them and left.

"She's wonderful," Mady sighed. An evening of Dore used to be enough to make even David sleep late.

"Wonderfully nuts. I only hope she can keep the weight off,

she's not getting any younger and there's heart disease in her family," Gail said and they both leaned back and dozed.

That evening, after the children had gone to bed, Mady sat for a while in the dark living room. Spidery threads of darkness enveloped her as a cool breeze finally floated in from outside. She put her head back into the pillows. It was almost ten. Fred Howland was probably in his office, yet something stopped her. Her fear that he would be with someone? Two figures undressing while a gray sooty curtain billowed toward them? No, it wasn't the image that put her off. She was too lonely to make the call; she knew his voice would make her lonelier. She had once read a story about a man who was so lonely he used to get dressed in the middle of the night and walk around the streets near his apartment and talk to the cops for an hour or so before he could go home and get to sleep. But for her the sound of voices deepened her own isolation. Tonight should have been easy. She had had a full day. She was upset about the Howlands but she had expected it. No, that wasn't why her body felt weighted down.

When she stood up, she couldn't remember a thing she had thought for the last hour. She dragged herself through the house, checking the children, and then she went into the greenhouse. Softly she stroked some of the larger plants and as she ran her fingers along the leaves she imagined she could feel the imprint of David's fingers. During the day the air had thickened with humidity and now it held that moist heady smell. Why had she avoided the greenhouse? Now her lungs welcomed the heavy sour air; she could, literally, feel her pores open, her whole body open. Before she knew what she was doing she had unbuttoned her blouse and loosened her bra. Slowly she let her breasts graze the leaves of the larger plants, waiting for her body to feel something. But after a while all she felt was foolish, ashamed. She almost ran to her room and undressed in the dark. Her sleep was fitful. Helplessly she kept moving to David's side of the bed, groping for his elbows, reaching with her toes for his heels. She woke several times in the night, startled that no one was there.

CHAPTER 5

THE NEXT MORNING Shelley called. "Listen, Mady, can you come to dinner Saturday night? We met a smashing man when we were away."

"Oh, Shelley, not again. We went through all that last spring." Then for some reason the whole ghastly spring struck her funny. She began to laugh.

"Are you really laughing?"

"Yes, I'm really laughing."

"Okay, laugh. But come. He's a terrific man, his name is Larry and he's tall —"

"— and dark and handsome and he's a doctor."

"No, he's sandy-haired, getting a little gray, very distinguished looking, only at the temples, silver-rimmed glasses, and he's an oral surgeon."

"Oh, Shelley, you can't be serious."

"He's also a cellist. A beautiful cellist. He led a chamber-music group at our hotel, he's sensitive, bright, well-read — honestly, Mady, you'll like him, I promise."

Mady sighed. Shelley had already asked him to dinner. "Okay," she said, "but no fancy food. Just a chef's salad or something like that. I can't bear the thought of you being cooped up in the kitchen on a hot day."

"We'll see," Shelley said. Mady waited, hoping she would say something more, that he was widowed, perhaps. But nothing. She wished she could stop feeling this way, but she couldn't help it. Each divorced man she met was like someone else's leftovers.

For as long as she lived Mady knew she would remember the spring of 1974 as the spring of the dinner party. The respectable year had passed since her husband's death, then winter closed in. She and the kids had seen her family, close friends, David's mother. But with the appearance of the first snowdrops the conspiracy began. Everyone had found a prospective husband for her — as if they had agreed among themselves, "The divorcées will manage, it's Mady we have to concentrate on."

At the first dinner she felt foolish, like a teenager on a date. She had known other men besides David — when she was in college, but that was such a long time ago. And now she was almost middle-aged: thirty-eight years old, with graying hair and crow's feet.

"But such a smashing figure." "And a lovely sculptured face." "Wonderful bones." "Doesn't Mady look stunning tonight?" Her friends said to one another as if she weren't there. She was tall and lean — painfully skinny when she was a girl. Then as styles changed and thinness became more fashionable and she gained a few pounds as she got older, she had an outstanding, elegant figure.

"I don't work on it," she told the first man guiltily. "All my family tend toward thin."

"You're so lucky. All I do is diet. Since I've been divorced, all I think about is food. I feel like a pregnant woman."

His name was Jerry. Sweating profusely, he made pleasant conversation with her through the gazpacho, Chinese pork, wild rice, endive and mushroom salad, homemade French bread, and chocolate mousse.

The second one was Ira, an analyst. He had left his wife because he wanted to read mythology and go to the movies. He had intended to go back to his family again, but his wife had found someone else and they were now getting a divorce. He was miserable. "I love those kids, I have three girls, they're gorgeous. I never intended to stay away forever, she knew that, but how can you read *The Golden Bough* with three little kids under your feet? So I took Frazer and Heinrich Zimmer and Joseph Campbell and all the myths (Edith Hamilton is better than Bulfinch) and spent the weekends in the office." He seemed so genuinely puzzled. As he spoke everyone nodded. During the lobster bisque he put his hand on her mohair skirt. She picked it up and put it back on his knee. After that he was more relaxed and when he talked about the presence of mythology in all aspects of our lives he was interesting — straight through the veal stew, sourdough biscuits, rugola and lettuce salad, and, again, chocolate mousse. By the time the espresso came Mady had a headache. She excused herself and when she came back he was gone.

"His wife called. She was hysterical. His youngest daughter was having an asthma attack," the hostess told her.

Then Myron. This one had been a mistake all around. "I'm looking for a good sexual relationship," he told her over the fruit cup. "Sex is a necessity, like exercise, or food. It's good for your heart, your lungs, your muscles, especially the stomach muscles." By now he was announcing his credo to the entire table. The hostess looked pained. Myron was her husband's find. He was an engineer who was devising new ways to recycle garbage. He was almost as interested in garbage as he was in sex.

"You make sex sound like one of the distribution requirements we used to have in college," one woman said.

"They don't even have those anymore," a man muttered.

But Myron was delighted with the analogy. "That's exactly what sex is, a distribution requirement for life," he said triumphantly.

Mady stifled a smile. Soon after David and she were married, they had lived in Richmond, Virginia. David was in the army. Every day they passed a huge sign for Climax soda. "Had your Climax today?" it said. She could hear David's laugh and suddenly she was furious with herself. Why was she sitting here next to this idiot, wasting this evening? After the shish kebab she pleaded sick and left.

The next time she left the children was to go to a concert with some close friends. Afterward, in the lobby of Philharmonic Hall, a Nathaniel appeared. Strictly a coincidence, they insisted. Nathaniel, it turned out, was intelligent and pleasant. A sociologist, he was interested in prison reform and knew about David's work at Attica. He showed up at a party a few weeks later and they had an animated conversation about Moog synthesizers — he was for, she was against — over the cheesecake, but when he wanted to stop in after he had driven her home, she refused. From the way his hands had lingered along her back when he helped her with her coat, Mady sensed he was an advocate of casual sex and she wasn't ready for that yet.

Then two Martys, a Harvey, the very last a Jacques. An extremely thin man with huge expressive hands and attenuated fingers, he spoke thoughtfully and placed his fingertips (joined to a point) just below his chin. "Jesus was probably fatter than we have been led to believe. When I was fatter I was a rabbi and I think spirituality and fatness are inevitable corollaries. I am doing a paper on this and I have found evidence that Saint Augustine, Thomas Aquinas, Luther, Spinoza, and several others were closet eaters." Mady couldn't wait to get away from him. His fingernails were dirty, his hair greasy. All through the guacamole, paella, and, strangely, carrot cake, she never discovered why he and his wife had parted or if there were children. Before she excused herself he told her, behind one of his hands, that a small inheritance had set him free from his fatness and the rabbinate. He now called himself a philosopher.

After Jacques her friends gave up and Shelley took over. The middle of May to the middle of June were evenings at Shelley's house, two towns away. They fused in her mind: cold soups, crisp salads, stroganoffs or veal cordon bleu or shrimp creole, discreet help, the inevitable chocolate souffle or lemon mousse for dessert.

After the fourth evening at Shelley's she was filled with hatred for all the people at these dinner parties, she hated even the older sister she knew she loved. She admitted it to no one, for how could you be so ungrateful when people were spending hours in the kitchen on your behalf? Still, she hated them — all of them. She had the feeling that she was becoming "poor Mady," whom other couples discussed as they undressed slowly, filled with the sweet anticipation of the sex to come after such a long lovely dinner, or, if they were too tired now, that would be there whenever they were in the mood again.

Could she ever explain it? Could anyone understand? Could she have understood when she was married and mostly content, that someone like her didn't have a body left, barely cared what she looked like, didn't want any of these men, even to talk to? That she came to these dinners because she had been brought up not to be rude, that philosophically she thought she ought to be open to new experiences and that — the real reason — she was lonely. Lonely for adult company, lonely for little stories to tell the children, lonely to know what other people besides Anthony Lewis and Tom Wicker and James Reston and her father and her brother-in-law Mel and her good friends the Levins thought about Nixon, Watergate, Kissinger.

By now people were tired. "It's too depressing," some said and refused to discuss it.

"He'll have to resign."

"He'll never resign." A verbal tug of war, but no longer interesting enough to give up evening after evening for.

No more dinner parties. The week after school was over Mady had announced to her children, "We're going to the beach in July." They had gone and come back and now it was almost August and she was going to another dinner party.

By Saturday afternoon she had still not told her children she was going out. She had left the pool early and made a chicken salad with nuts and grapes and she had a banana bread baking in the oven. Anne Levin was bringing the kids home a little later. Peter's friend Ricky was planning to stay for the night, Nina was reading *Gone with the Wind* and would be happy to spend the evening on the porch, Foffy would watch her television program. She was certainly not neglecting her children if she went to her sister's for dinner.

After her shower she turned back the bedspread and lay down. She threw her robe over her. It was really David's robe; she had begun to wear it after he died and she loved the feel of the worn Viyella against her skin. She felt like a Victorian. Her own, or anyone else's, nakedness had never bothered her; in fact, she liked it, especially in the heat. A cool unexpected swath of breeze grazing her body was a pleasant sensation. As a child she had loved to go skinny-dipping and once, when Peter and Nina were very little and they were vacationing in Wellfleet, she and David had left them sleeping and gone swimming nude in Gull Pond at dawn. If she hadn't been so anxious about the kids they would have stayed and made love, sheltered by the small pitch pines. Of course, the children were fast asleep. She had tried, a long time afterward, to tell David how much she regretted that dawn, but he had answered cheerfully, "Just one more reason to go back."

He had thought he would live forever — but isn't that what we all think? she wondered as she lay there, absolutely alone, yet needing his old robe over her. He wouldn't even know her. How many times had he cautioned her to close the curtains? Now she forced herself to recall how, when David was away, she sometimes stepped out of the shower late at night filled with such a strong desire for him that she had masturbated. She never told him. A pity, really; it might have pleased him. Was she afraid of that now? she wondered and looked out the large window opposite the bed and the lilies nodded at her as the sun began its long descent in the west.

She dozed a while, then pulled on her robe and laid out her two long dresses on the bed. Tonight was too hot for the black, perhaps a scarf around the plain neck of the gray. She was picking out a pink and raspberry scarf when she heard the door open. The children tumbled into the house.

"Mom, Mom, where are you?"

"In my room," she called.

They dropped their towels and zories and dripped water along the hall.

"She sure is a card," Ricky was saying.

"Anne was telling us this crazy story —" Nina began, then looked at the bed. "Where are you going?"

"To Aunt Shelley's for dinner." No one answered. Foffy shifted from foot to foot. Then she and Ricky mumbled something about changing and Mady was left facing Nina and Peter. Peter's eyes were angry.

"I thought you said 'no more dinner parties' in June," he accused her. Nina bit her lip and looked down.

"I did."

"So why are you going to Aunt Shelley's?"

"Because she invited me."

"But you said 'no more parties'! "

"And now I've changed my mind. I don't see why you're making such a fuss," Mady said.

"You were so miserable after all those dinner parties last spring. Sundays were awful, we hated them! " Nina said. Her voice was not as hard as Peter's but it reminded Mady of someone's. Who? She frowned, then realized it was the same voice that David had when he was trying to bully her into doing something she didn't want to do. How many Sunday nights when the kids were little had she wished they could stay home and watch television like everyone else? Those freezing snowy drives they had taken to hear Boccherini, or Dvořák, or the Rasumovsky Quartets, when all she wanted was to get into her nightgown and robe and go to sleep early. Once she had said so. "But how could you be tired?" he had reasoned with her. What he left unsaid was that he had done most of the cooking over the weekend; that night he had done chicken with vegetables in a wok, she remembered.

Now Nina even looked like David, especially around the

lower lip and chin. But David was dead. She wasn't going to be bullied by him and certainly not by his child.

"I can handle it now. We've had a vacation and I'm getting my bearings better and I said yes to Shelley," she said quietly.

"I think you're a masochist," Peter shouted. She didn't answer. "And all those men you keep meeting are just divorced suburban jerks!"

"Peter!"

"Well, they are."

"You said you wanted to start Doris Lessing's new book," Nina reminded her. "And we're supposed to practice a duet for my next lesson."

Then Foffy was back, smiling like a marionette.

Madeleine straightened and said firmly, "Now look, kids, stop bossing me around." Their heads shot up, their eyes flooded with relief.

"Peter, please take the bread out of the oven, and Nina, get a towel and wipe up the rug, and Foffy, the table needs setting." The girls left willingly; Peter was not so easily put off.

"Listen, Mom," he began.

"I'm going, Peter," she interrupted, surprised at how stubborn she, too, could sound.

"I know you're going. That's really your business, you're right about that." His tone was different now. He had stopped wanting to fight with her and was trying to talk to her.

"Listen, Mom," he hesitated, then spoke quickly. "Don't think you have to find a father for us." Madeleine stepped toward her son. She wanted to gather him into her arms, but as she approached he ducked as if he were on the basketball court and backed deftly into the hall. She felt as if he were drifting away from her, and she was helpless.

The scene with the kids upset her. Those small unexpected eruptions of truth were as unsettling as the shouting matches she and David had had during the early years of their marriage, when she couldn't understand his incredible energy and his need for excellence not only in himself, but in her and the children as well. After those arguments she had felt devastated for days. Each time she had adjusted to what she thought was the inevitable ebb and flow of married love, and more and more her marriage had seemed to be the solid ground of her life. Then his death and she was left — drowning at first, then floundering, groping, doubting her senses, her reason, everything. But was it so simple as she had thought? She wondered. She had done what David expected, what she herself expected, but wasn't that phrase "the ebb and flow of married love" deceptive? Naive? A euphemism? Who knew? The past was so complex, so layered, a palimpsest of emotions and incidents that could never be separated. "Don't look back," everyone advised. Yet didn't she have to look back before she could look ahead?

There was no time to think about it now. Shelley's large house loomed as she turned the corner. She parked the car and caught a glimpse of herself in the mirror. She had forgotten eye makeup. Too bad, they would have to take her as she was. She reached into the back seat for her shawl; if they sat outside later it might be cool. Her stomach began to churn as she walked up the manicured flagstone path.

Still, she had to confess, Larry was a gentle considerate man, with intelligent brown eyes. Tall, slightly hunched with the burden of his divorced life and a weltschmerz that was a hangover from his rabbi father and uncles. "He and his wife were married for almost ten years, she had lots of miscarriages, but they never had any children. They parted amicably," Shelley whispered in the kitchen. How do couples part amicably? She would have to ask Shelley one of these days. Not now, though; tonight Shelley was trying to please her and although there were fourteen for dinner, the meal was simple and there was no help. By dessert it was clear that Larry wanted to take care of someone, preferably several someones. Now Mady knew why Shelley had been so insistent that she come.

And he knew music. He had wanted to be a professional cellist, but after college he decided he wasn't good enough so he took some extra science courses and got into dental school and was now a successful oral surgeon.

"It's a strange way to spend one's life — inside people's bloody mouths — but it's not as bad as I thought it would be," he admitted. He was about to say something else when Mady's younger niece, Bonnie, came into the room. Cynthia, the older, was in Europe for her junior year in college.

"You're the one who plays the harp," he said as Bonnie kissed Mady, then shook his hand.

"Yes," Bonnie said with a sigh. Soon someone asked her to play. How could she refuse? Harpists were so rare. Obediently she sat down and played a Bach prelude and fugue, then a piece by Saint-Saëns. Bonnie's light brown hair blended with the harp's strings so that a gossamer of gold shimmered against the dark walnut of the open piano behind. Out the window, beyond the child and her harp and the piano, was Shelley's garden, tastefully lighted.

It's all too perfect, Madeleine was thinking. Still, this was what they had dreamed of as girls. This was what their parents had wanted. Yet wasn't there something forced about it? Or was that her own bitterness?

Larry touched her elbow. "Mady, Bonnie's asking you something."

She looked up. Bonnie's eyes held hers. "Play with me, Aunt Mady, please," she said.

"Oh, I couldn't, I haven't played for months, more than months . . ." Mady stopped, confused. She hadn't touched the piano since the day David's plane crashed except to play duets with Nina and folk songs for Foffy; once in a while she accompanied Peter on his clarinet. Shelley and Bonnie knew that. Mady looked around the room. The encouraging faces seemed part of a plot. Mady could almost hear her mother say, "If you could just get Mady to play the piano again." Well, she would surprise them. She went to the piano and sat down and glanced for a brief moment at Shelley. Then she and Bonnie looked at

the music and began. Mady's fingers seemed to play without
her, apart from her. They went through "The Girl with the
Flaxen Hair" without a stumble. She was embarrassed by the
applause, she felt that she had had nothing to do with the playing. But no one would believe her, and when she looked up she
saw that everyone's eyes were misty.

She had to get away from them. As soon as she could, Mady
slipped outside. She sat on the rock wall and breathed deeply.
The smell of the tobacco plants blended with the dying smoke of
the barbecue coals. She used to love that thick, pendulous smell;
now she had to move a little to free her nostrils of it.

A heavy tread upon the flagstone path. Larry was coming to
look for her. Even his walk sounded worried. She smiled. He
was such a good man, she knew he wanted to see her again. He
was exactly the sort of man she should be interested in. She let
her mind wander as she listened vaguely to his tentative walk.
She could imagine their wedding — probably right here in this
lovely garden — her parents' relieved happy faces, her children's shy wariness, Shelley's triumph. Larry would be a devoted husband, a good father. She could imagine them sitting
across the table at countless pleasant meals. They would go to
concerts, museums, and even the smaller galleries; she could
picture them talking for a long time in front of a painting like
Cezanne's *The Great Bathers;* she could even see them walking at
Mianus Gorge or Ward Pound Ridge on a sparkling golden day.
Yet she felt no connection with him, so it was all delusion, like
those dream games Nina and her friends played when they announced so gravely over milk and cookies that they were going
to be doctors or teachers or nurses or lawyers and have two boys
and a girl each two years apart when they grew up.

Larry sat down next to her, her shawl draped over his arm.
"Do you want this?" His voice was attentive, concerned. From its
timbre Mady knew he could become the shadow of someone he
loved. She shook her head. Then he seemed to relax and they sat
for several minutes in silence. She liked that in him — to know

that silences were as much a part of speech as words. Not many people knew that; perhaps she had been too hasty.

Then Larry put his hand over hers and took a deep breath. His voice was low, husky. "Feel like talking?"

Her first impulse was to say no, but when she saw the look on his face — plaintive, concerned — she shrugged and laughed a little. "Yes, I guess I do. But how did you know?"

"Because you're lonely, too," he said softly. She stiffened and tried to disengage her hand, but he held it tighter. "No one can hide all that pain. Some give in to it and others fight it."

"How do you read me?" she said, fascinated yet also irritated by his cool analytic way of speaking.

"Oh, you're a survivor." He grinned a little lopsidedly and let go of her hand and looked directly at her. "Do you think you'd want to go out with me?" He had a hard time getting the question out.

"Of course, you're an attractive, interesting man," she heard herself say.

"And you're an attractive, interesting woman," he said. "But if we go out I'll fall in love with you; I think I'm half in love with you already. And I wonder if you're going to settle for someone like me, Mady — an honest Abe, reliable as they come. I couldn't bear being rejected. I'm getting too old for that." His voice had an unmistakable finality. His eyes were hurt. Yet what could she say? She let him arrange her shawl around her shoulders, let him kiss her tenderly on her forehead, and when they rose together she took his arm and they walked in silence back to the rustling, lighted house.

CHAPTER 6

THE NEXT MORNING Madeleine walked up to Anne Levin's house. She hadn't seen Anne since she had returned from the beach because Anne knew her better than anyone in the world now that David was dead, and she wasn't sure what she would say to Anne if Hans's name came up. It had been easier to stay away and talk casually over the telephone. But this morning she needed to talk to Anne.

Anne was in the kitchen stirring borscht. She taught French in a private school and spent the summer cooking and refinishing furniture. She handed Mady a cup of coffee. "I read in an article that beets prevent aging so I thought I'd give it a try," she said. Mady smiled and sat down. Everything in the Levin kitchen was old and creaking and noisy — the plumbing sang as loudly as the electric coffee pot and the refrigerator had a repertoire of bass arias. One wall was a huge pegboard filled with hanging pots, colanders, shining copper molds, woks, and every hand utensil Mady had heard of. Mady could not think of a room she loved more.

"Well, how was the beach?" Anne asked as she settled herself with a pile of mending. Anne called herself dumpy, but stocky was more accurate, and she had a beautiful face — milky skin, green eyes, and wavy reddish hair.

"Wonderful. The kids ate like horses and we swam every day and found friends. Spectacular weather, so clear and fresh after the hurricane. The best time we've had together since before David died."

Anne nodded, then peered over her sewing glasses. "Foffy told me about a man named Hans."

"Oh, that big mouth. Hans is a potter we met at the beach."

"So I heard. I also heard about his studio and his house and the blueberries and his books and his beard and the Coriolis effect, which I had never heard of till I went to college and took physics."

"He's an interesting man. We saw him at the beach a few times, then went to his house for dinner. He had to leave suddenly because his mother was sick in Germany. The last night we went folk dancing and I felt myself attracted to him. I haven't felt that with anyone since David — but I'm sure it was just loneliness. He took our address. I'll probably never hear from him again. He's very independent, self-contained."

Anne didn't answer and Mady picked an imaginary thread off her skirt. Finally, to cover the silence, she said, "Shelley had a dinner party last night and I went."

Anne nodded. "I knew she was planning it. She called while you were away and told me about a Harvey or a Larry, or was it Gary? The oral surgeon who plays the cello." Anne's voice was amused. "Shelley said he was smashing. Have you set the date?"

"Hardly. He's a lovely man and knows a lot about music and is obviously anxious to remarry. He also wants a family, the more children the better. I was the one who was ugly," Mady replied.

Anne raised her eyebrows.

"I played the piano with Bonnie and was practically in shock because my fingers seemed to play without me. It's amazing how much the brain stores, and I never would have believed I could play through that piece so easily after not practicing for so long." Mady shook her head, then her eyes met Anne's. "Anyway, when we finished I couldn't stand the pity in everyone's face, so

I went out to the garden. Before I knew it I was thinking that this Larry was someone I should be interested in, that I should go out with him because he was gentle and wouldn't make too many demands, and that if I did he could provide me with a way into the world again. Then I realized that he would probably want to marry me, since he is absolutely frantic to remarry. I was actually manipulating him in my mind, even to the point of imagining our wedding. When he came outside and sat down next to me, he virtually read my mind. He was tactful, but he practically said he didn't have the strength to be used."

Anne put down her sewing and stared. "You don't use people, Mady."

"I know I don't, but I did last night. I was sitting there thinking only of myself, never considering any of the risks for him and he sensed it and closed the door. It's horrible to be so calculating and, at the same time, so thoughtless. To think in such a premeditated way must be close to losing your mind, and then to be caught at it! It was terrible. I've never acted like this before."

"You've never been in this spot before. And you didn't act, you were just thinking," Anne replied.

"But that's just the point. He knew it, even though it *was* only thinking."

"Did you tell Shelley?"

"No. She called this morning. She's totally confused. Before he left, Larry told her it would never work. She thinks he's strange. It never occurred to her that it was my fault. And if I tried to explain, she wouldn't understand. She's too practical. It was so mental, so cerebral, like something out of Henry James. You know, Anne, at one point I felt as if I had no control over my mind, as if my mind had divided and one half of it was saying here was the kind of man I should be interested in and the other half kept saying no."

"Then he was right. You can't see him, there's no point in it, for either of you," Anne said sensibly.

She should have known. In all the years Mady had known her,

Anne had never lied to her, or embroidered or softened the truth. Yet now, as she looked at her old friend, Madeleine filled with anger. Today she wanted something more than the truth. But what? She couldn't even say it because she didn't know what it was.

Now Anne's voice was gentler. "What do you want me to say, Mady?" she asked. Mady bit her lower lip, looked away.

"Listen, Mady, I can't help you, no one can help you, even the ones who think they're helping you — like Shelley and your mother and the rest of them who think that by getting you out of the house or making you play the piano they can bring you back to life. Mady, you've got to help yourself, you can't want to live the rest of your life as you have this last year and a half — doing what everyone tells you to, trotting off to those dinner parties like a trained dog, looking over all those men with such a cold eye, holding yourself aloof, apart from everything. To live you have to take risks, that's what you did when you married and had kids, that's what we all did . . ." Anne hesitated, then she looked down.

"And look what happened," Mady retorted bitterly. "Listen to me, Anne, there's no future in people, they can always die."

Anne's head lifted slowly, her face darkened with pain. Mady hated to see it, but now, at last, she could talk.

"It's easier to stay aloof, apart, whatever you want to call it. I think of it as living each day as simply as possible, letting time pass to do its work. You know, Anne, that's what that man at the beach was doing — that potter, Hans. That's why the kids and I were so interested in him, we wanted to learn his secret. He had no one, no family, probably only a few friends. All his emotional connections were to inanimate things — his house and his books and those pieces of pottery he created. And you know something, Anne, I envied him."

Now Anne was frowning. "No, Mady, you can't do that. Sure, it may look easier and it's a lot safer, but that's not living. To live you must take risks, sometimes they work out and sometimes they don't. But not to take them?" Anne stared at her. "No, Mady, you can't want to do that, you're too alive. You can't do that to yourself and you can't do it to your children. It isn't fair to deprive them of you, the woman you are, the woman you can be." Anne stood up, paced a little, rubbed her palms together. "I don't know how to say it . . ."

"Just say it."

"They want a mother, a woman they can respect, not this stick-like . . . not this stick figure you've been since David died." The words echoed coldly even in this friendly room.

How dare Anne? She looked around and for a second her vision shifted and the pots and pans and colanders and molds threatened to fall in on her and she could hear a voice she didn't recognize but knew was her own. "How can you?" it demanded. "How can you talk that way to me? Haven't I held my family together, haven't I made all the financial arrangements that drive some widows crazy? Haven't I shopped and cooked and fixed everything, and gone to all the school events and helped the kids with their homework and driven thousands of miles? Didn't I take them on vacation to a place that I had never seen before? How dare you?" the voice shouted, and then she saw a face and heard a voice she hadn't heard for decades:

— Start with a stick figure and fill in the neck, the shoulders, then the arms, the torso, the legs. The idea is to give it life, to put some flesh on those bones, to breathe life into it. Be bold, Madeleine, you mustn't be afraid, draw in those curves and then fill it in, give it the substance it needs —

But what about the brain, the nerves, the heart?

She could feel her body fill, and all the heaviness she had felt for so long — the yearning, the anxiety, the fear — seemed to pour out of her and she was no longer back in the splattered art room of her childhood but floating with the wind, as fast as a suddenly stringless kite in the cool metallic blue. The air she breathed was not going out but staying inside her until she filled and billowed and nothing could hold her, so it was such a surprise when she heard the scrape of a chair and felt the smooth touch of Anne's arms and heard Anne's voice: "Cry, Mady, it's time you cried."

As a girl she thought healing took place in spare darkened hospital rooms filled with shadowy starched figures and the comforting hum of subdued competent voices. Another dream game from childhood, she thought as she stood up to leave, her throat scratchy with all the shouting and crying she had done.

Anne walked her to the door. "Try not to try so hard, Mady, don't worry so much about the kids, start thinking about what you want to do." But that meant she would have to dig deeper into her heart, into her mind, and for so long it had been easier to avoid doing that.

"There are no answers, that's why I get so angry at Shelley, or Dore," Anne continued. "They see life only one way. For Shelley you must be married, for Dore you must not. But you're you, Mady, and you have to find out what's right for you."

Mady decided to go home through the woods. Although it was midsummer they were cool, green, fragrant as spring. Mostly pine and hemlock, some gray birch and hickory and ash. Fifteen acres of woods ran along the edge of the neighborhood and were part of an old estate. The owner had finally died and a developer was trying to buy the land. This fall there were to be hearings. Anne and her husband, Woody, and several others wanted the woods to be designated as a park, what the county called a "greenbelt." Mady had given money for the park, but she should get more involved, she thought. What a pity it would be to lose these old trees.

Her sandaled feet padded softly on the pine needles. Voices floated from the tree house that Woody and his sons had built years ago.

"Now, Nadia, you're the father and I'm the mother," Foffy's voice drifted toward Mady.

"No, I want to be the mother."

"Next time. First I'll be the mother. We're going to a party."

She could hear the tops of the storage seats bang to as the children took the clothes out of them. Mady didn't stop, though she usually enjoyed watching the little girls romp in her old nightgowns. She needed more time by herself. As she walked she realized Hans's name had not come up after she cried. Yet she might have slept with him if he hadn't had to leave. So what? Was it so terrible to admit to herself that she had been attracted to him? He wasn't the last man in the world, and neither was Larry, and now she had other things to think about. Anne was right, she had to start getting out of the house. She had to think about a job, and she wanted to call Fred Howland about Peter. Lately she had been having dreams about her Russian teacher. One night last week she had dreamed she was in class and had come unprepared and he was shaking his head in disappointment.

Now she glanced at her house. A brief but hard rain early this morning had stained its cedar exterior so that it had a mournful look.

She pushed open the side door. She could hear Peter. His voice was low, harsh. "So she played the piano last night. What's so fucking great about that?"

"I guess Aunt Shelley thinks it's important if she mentioned it on the phone."

Mady went into the kitchen expecting them to look embarrassed; instead Peter glanced at her and said curtly, "You might as well hear this." He shrugged and then said, as if he had rehearsed it, "Aunt Shelley gives me a pain. I don't know why she's so anxious for you to remarry." He looked at his mother. "There are plenty of women whose husbands die who don't get married. Mrs. Wheeler's husband died when Michael was two and she was left with five kids and she hasn't remarried."

Nina narrowed her eyes apprehensively and took a step toward her mother. But Peter ignored that. "Aunt Shelley and Grandma Hayman and some of those creepy ladies you call your friends are all wrong, Mom. You feel a lot better now, I know you do, and you don't need them to find someone for you to marry. It made me sick to see you getting dressed up every Saturday night last spring. Like a — " he stopped, then whispered, "like a whore, or something."

"Peter!" Nina cried.

"I didn't mean exactly that, Mom, I'm sorry. I don't know . . ." He stared at her and ran his hand through his thick hair. But he did mean it. She knew that now as she watched him. He had been wanting to say it for a long time. And somehow she was relieved. It was better to have it out in the open.

"It's okay, Peter," she said. "It's a free country." At the sound of that old childhood expression they relaxed and looked at her shyly. In their eyes was a new respect; she was not as passive as they had thought. Children need to know who's the mother and who's the child.

CHAPTER 7

O N TUESDAY ANNE CAME BY. Mady had spent the last two days almost entirely alone. The older children were in an all-day sports program and Foffy had started camp.

"I've been reading and playing the piano, and I took down some of my Russian books," she said and pointed to a large gap in the shelves. "And I haven't worked on my needlepoint for almost three days," she told Anne, amazed.

Anne laughed. "You and that needlepoint. Woody was beginning to call you Madame Defarge." She looked at Mady cautiously, but Mady laughed, too.

"I saw Gail yesterday," Anne said. "Fred has moved to New York. He keeps saying it will be the same as always, for heaven's sake."

Mady's vision clouded with anger, sorrow, frustration; she didn't know which. If she were Catholic she would probably be praying for compassion. She pressed her lips together.

Anne continued, "Gail thinks they stayed together this long partly because of David's death. But the last month has been unbearable, he barely speaks to her, she's lonelier than she's ever been. She said she told you about it."

Mady looked down at her hands; they were planted tensely on

her knees. Who was she to judge, to condemn? Everyone's life was different. Why should she expect couples to stay happily married? And why couldn't she keep her feelings to herself? Gail had enough problems without her disapproval.

"I feel as if they're throwing away their lives," she finally said to Anne.

"They're throwing away what you think they might have had. What you had. But, obviously, they didn't have it. No one knows what goes on in other people's houses."

"That's true," Mady agreed. "But you have to fight to keep something good. It wasn't always smooth around here, it's not always smooth around your house. But you want to keep it. I wanted to keep it. Sure, I bent a lot to David, when I was doing it I didn't think much about it, you don't know when you love someone. Now I see that sometimes he was wrong and I didn't speak up. Maybe now I would be less passive, more honest, maybe even more demanding. But if I compromised then it was to keep what we had. Fred and Gail aren't fighting hard enough to keep the marriage. Gail's too passive."

"I don't agree with you, Mady. She's handling it her way." Anne's voice was tight, and Mady knew they wouldn't discuss Gail again. Anne wanted her to promise to call Gail. She couldn't do that yet, but she would call Fred this afternoon. Maybe she could persuade him not to throw away eighteen years.

She dialed Fred Howland's number at ten minutes to three. She knew from past experience he would be between patients.

"I've been wondering how you were," he said.

"We're fine, Fred, we even got away for a week to the beach."

"How are the kids?"

"Fine, well, not absolutely fine. Peter's having some problems. That's why I'm calling, I'd like to talk to you about it."

"Of course. I'm always happy to talk to you about the kids, Mady. You know that. I'll be up to see the girls Saturday. I'm taking them out for dinner. Can I stop by about nine?" His voice was so casual, as if he had been coming up to see his daughters on designated days for years. Her heart sank. She had expected more emotion.

"That's fine. Peter has a party and Nina has a sleepover. I'll see you then."

Saturday afternoon was hot and sultry. Between conversations at the swim club, Mady tried to rehearse what she was going to say to Fred. She finally concluded she would talk about Peter and see what happened after that. Still, she was nervous. Calling Fred was the first thing she had initiated in so long; what if he refused to discuss his marriage?

She was out on the porch when he rang the bell. Foffy answered the door and he scooped the child up in his arms, startling her, for she hadn't seen him for months. Besides, Fred was such a tall man, and now it looked as if he had put on weight. He used to be a jogging nut, but he certainly hadn't been getting much exercise lately.

"I made a cheesecake yesterday," she told him. "Tea or coffee?"

"Gin and ice and a little lemon. And skip the cheesecake for me, though you should have a piece. Don't you ever put on any weight?" he said, grinning. The whites of his eyes were red.

"How much have you had to drink tonight?" she asked.

"None of your goddamn business, Mady," he growled. "I'm drinking more and I love it." If they had been children he would have stuck out his tongue, she was sure.

But still, it was pleasant to sit on the porch on a summer's night with an old friend. She had known Fred as long as she had known David; she remembered him parading all his gorgeous tall gentile girlfriends on Saturday nights; she remembered how excited he was when he met Gail, how relieved Fred's Zionist family had been that Gail was Jewish.

"Now, tell me about Peter," he said kindly after a few minutes.

"He seems to be having a delayed reaction, he says he dreams that David is back and talking to him at night. And then the

other day he said he hated the way I went out, he said I reminded him of a whore, and then he mentioned Cathy Wheeler,
his math teacher, who was widowed with five children years ago
and never married again."

Fred nodded. "It's all very normal, and very understandable.
He's transferring the anger he feels toward David for dying to
you. The first impulse is to huddle close to the surviving parent,
then the child tends to step back, see things more objectively,
and that's when the anger appears. Actually, I'm glad to hear it, I
was beginning to wonder when it would happen."

"But if what he feels is so normal, why is Nina so calm?"
Mady asked. Fred had worried her.

"Nina is more like you, Mady, Peter is more like David, at
least outwardly. She's able to accept more, she compromises
more easily, and besides, she's a girl and she identifies more
closely with you. Peter is your first child, a son, he had to work
out his Oedipal impulses with his father, and now he fears having to work them out with some stranger. He's not a child, he
feels threatened by men who may want to sleep with you."

"He called them 'divorced suburban jerks.' "

Fred gave a harsh laugh. "He's probably right."

She looked at him and raised her eyebrows.

"That's what you think I am, don't you?" he said.

"No," she replied, but her voice was tentative. She didn't want
to talk about him yet. Selfishly she wanted to talk more about
her children, she wanted to know what to do.

"Listen, Fred, should Peter be in therapy? I don't want not to
do something that should be done, even if this is 'normal,' as you
put it. Should he be talking to someone?"

Again Fred laughed his harsh laugh. Was it the drink or was it
him? He was so different from the man she had known when
they were young. But how naive she was! They were all
different.

"Honestly, Mady, you sound like all those other mothers. You
think you can solve a child's pain by paying fifty bucks a few
times a week and letting him talk to someone? Someday I'm

going to write a book called 'Talking to Someone.' Listen, Peter is in pain, just like you are in pain, and he has to live through it. Maybe it would help if he saw someone. I doubt it. It might even help if he went to a group with other kids whose fathers have died, but he probably won't agree to it, and you can't force something like that. Someday Peter will want to talk to someone, but then he'll be older, more able to know what's happened to him. Now he has to live through it and if he doesn't like it when you go to dinner parties, then the two of you will have to struggle that one out."

"But should I be seeing someone — so I understand better?"

"What for? You understand what's happening, you're really a very intelligent girl, far brighter than you think you are."

Mady gestured his words away. The last thing she wanted was a lecture on her own lost possibilities. "You don't seem to have much faith in your profession these days," she murmured.

For a second there was a glimmer of the old Fred. "When I was in medical school I thought psychiatry was going to save the world. We were our generation's Jesus freaks or Moonies. Freud was God, Jung was Joseph, Karen Horney was Mary, and somewhere, floating around among us, was our generation's genius, our Jesus. Well, it wasn't that simple. Working with patients for fifteen years — really sick patients — makes you realize that it's like anything else; sometimes it works and sometimes it doesn't, and God knows, psychiatry cannot alter the underlying sadness and pain and loneliness of the human condition."

"Oh, Fred, it can't be that bad, you make it sound so hopeless."

Fred slumped a little and averted his eyes. "Well, that's how I feel. Don't worry about the kids, Mady, they'll be all right. They had you and David when they were young and they have you now and they don't live in poverty and aren't abused and have plenty of male role models around and they'll be as fine as everyone else's children. The kids of divorced parents are probably worse off, and that immediately puts yours ahead of the game."

Mady frowned. If he was so sure of that, then why was he doing what he was doing? She looked down. When her glance met his, Fred's eyes were laughing at her, as if she had just told him a funny joke.

"Do you remember how you felt about Gail when you first met her?" he said sardonically. "Isn't that what you were going to ask me?" He chuckled.

Helplessly, she nodded.

"Oh, Mady, of course I remember. I was drunk with happiness — the thought of her body when I was twenty-one could give me an orgasm. All I wanted was to marry her and the first year we were married we barely got out of bed — only to eat and go to the movies. I practically flunked out of medical school that year, and I never even tried to study at home, it would have been impossible. But it was all physical and after we had been married for about twelve years I realized we didn't have a thing in common. She had become so dull."

"Fred, that's not true. Gail is one of the brightest people we know. She was always reading when the girls were little; I remember her reading Montaigne when she was nursing Suzy."

"So do I," Fred said grimly. "Gail was born a hundred years too late; she would have been a wonderful founder of some woman's college, like Emma Willard or Mary Lyon. Absolutely solid, the rock of Gibraltar, but she's not open to new things."

Mady stared at him; she knew the answer, but she also knew she had to ask the question. "What kind of new things, Fred?"

This time Fred's laugh sounded more like a hoarse snort. "Okay, Mady, you've got me. I should have known I couldn't lie to you. There's nothing wrong with Gail's mind, we all know that. But she's very conservative, she won't ..." His voice dwindled.

"She won't act out all your sexual fantasies, isn't that it?"

"Partly."

"And she also doesn't like it when you act them out with other women?" Mady said bitterly.

Fred stood up. "You can't understand it, Mady, but there are thousands of people in cities all over the world who are exploring their senses and trying new things and opening their minds and bodies to what this century has to offer."

She stared at Fred. Did he really believe that crap, that propaganda, from *New York Magazine*?

"But what about the children?"

"Ah, yes, that is the question, isn't it, Mady?"

"It sure is."

"Well, the children will have to manage. I love them and I want to see them and I'll support them, but I've given them a lot of years and now it's time to take care of me. I feel as if I'm choking when I'm in the house with Gail. I can't help it, Mady, but I do, and if I stay there I'm going to suffocate."

"Fred, you sound like something from a soap opera."

"I feel like something from a soap opera, but if this is how I feel the best thing is to get out so we can start new lives. Gail will meet someone, one of those 'divorced suburban jerks' who likes the missionary position and an intelligent, good-looking wife. It's really me you should be worrying about — thick-in-the-middle, drinks-too-much Fred who is disillusioned with life and love." He put his arm around her and they walked together through the living room to the front hall.

He looked at her thoughtfully. "Don't frown so much, Mady, you'll get wrinkles," he said and added, "Then you'll never be able to swing, and someday you may want to." He winked at her, then ducked out the door. "See ya around the quad," he called softly and was gone.

What an exasperating man he was. Had he always been like that? She tried to remember, but realized that after he had married Gail she had had very few conversations alone with him. He hadn't been in this shape when she had talked with him after David died, but a year and a half, almost two, had elapsed since then.

Well, she had tried. At least allow yourself something for effort, she thought as she helped Foffy into bed and turned off the child's light. And she had known Fred long enough to know that he was miserable; he knew damn well that the kids wouldn't manage. He was absolutely right. It was he who was in trouble, not Gail. And she had thought she could help them. What a fool she was! She had probably made the situation worse. She now knew more about their marriage than she needed or wanted to know. She felt as if she had gotten a glimpse of Fred's soul, and no one needed that. She had enough trouble with her own. Worst of all, she felt sorry for him now, and pity was harder to deal with than anger.

CHAPTER 8

FINALLY NIXON RESIGNED. Glued to their television set like everyone else, they waited for the announcement. When it came, Mady felt a surprising surge of pity for him. Not for what he had done, but because he didn't know it.

"Well, it's over," Mady's father said, his eyes brimming with excitement as he kissed her.

Momentous political events intoxicated Max Hayman. He could never hope to sleep tonight, so he had talked Libby into going to see Mady. When they arrived, the neighborhood throbbed — car doors slamming, people chatting in high daytime tones, teenagers laughing and singing as they trudged by: "We have overc-o-me, we have overco-o-ome." Even her neighbors who had Nixon stickers on their cars seemed jubilant. "Idiots!" David would have shouted.

"Now, what do you think of Ford?" Max asked Peter. He put his arm around the boy's shoulders and they walked onto the porch where the television was on with the sound turned down. The voiceless people flitted across the porch furniture and foliage outside.

"Ghosts," Libby murmured.

Now Peter shrugged. "I don't know, Grandpa, what do you think?"

Nina broke in. "Lyndon Johnson said he couldn't walk down the stairs and chew gum at the same time."

Max smiled. "Lyndon Johnson was no Einstein either."

"A lot better than Nixon," Peter said. Libby and Mady exchanged glances, remembering the fights Max and David had had. David wanted Johnson out, had hated his position during Vietnam. Max defended Johnson. "What we get after him will be worse," he said. "Nothing could be worse!" David retorted. Later David reneged. As unbelievable as it was, Max had been right.

Now Mady went to get some food while Libby put Foffy to bed. "Did George Washington resign?" Mady heard Foffy ask as they went down the hall.

"That child is precious," Libby announced as they carried the trays out to the porch. Everyone was starved; it seemed days since they had eaten dinner.

"It reminds me of 1948," Mady murmured as she poured the coffee.

Libby and Max smiled at each other. The old English Tudor house on Long Island overflowing with volunteers working for a haberdasher named Harry Truman. Mady was twelve, she had looked up haberdasher in the dictionary and was amazed to discover how harmless it was. That night all the leaves were in the dining room table, index cards were strewn over the maroon table pads, the phone was clicking on and off, Max was urging, "Just get them out to vote," as she and Shelley brought platter after platter of food out and then washed the endless stream of dishes. Cora, their maid, was campaigning in the black part of town. The only paper Cora had read since coming north was *PM*.

When Mady and Shelley woke the next morning, the volunteers were back — sorting cards, emptying ashtrays, making last-minute calls, comforting each other. Their villain that day was a man with a shoe-polish black mustache and hair to match, whose voice irked them, whose mustache was too reminiscent of Hitler's, and whose policies would bring disaster. "Dewey!" They spat his name like a curse.

Max looked at Mady as she handed him his coffee. "Dewey was a saint compared to Nixon," he admitted, though she had not uttered a word. She laughed, delighted at his ability to read her mind.

Then Max described to his grandchildren the issues surrounding Truman's election in 1948. The rejoicing a few nights later. Again the house full, but now an enormous ivory linen cloth on the table, champagne bottles popping, petits fours from the best bakery in town set on large silver trays lined with paper doilies. So many doilies to peel and place, like confetti at a victory parade. And so many faces — all bathed in triumph! No one gave a second's thought for the losers. Let them drink their bitterness in silence. The little man had won again. Wasn't America truly the land of the free?

Not once, in all those years when she was growing up on the living legend of Roosevelt and the surprising victory and energy of Truman, did Mady think of those who were frustrated by the policies her family endorsed. Until she was on the losing side. On the day when she woke up to find that Eisenhower had defeated Stevenson, she had felt the rage of the helpless loser. And later when the country had been absurd enough to elect Nixon. But there had been so much lunacy in the sixties that Nixon's victory seemed more logical, more acceptable, than the rejections of Stevenson in 1952 and 1956. Mady said so now.

"You were also younger then. You wanted to save the world. You and David and Adlai and that running mate of his who didn't have too many brains in his head, who was it?" Max stared at her in an uncomfortable lapse of memory.

"Sparkman."

"Sparkman," he repeated. "No sparks from Sparkman, let me tell you," he said and the kids joined him in laughter. Max continued to give them a capsule history of the late forties and fifties. How happy he was to tell it. Politics and history were nourishment for him. When she and Shelley were kids, they thought everyone knew the names of Arthur Vandenberg, Styles Bridges, Walter George, Lister Hill, Kenneth Wherry, Warren Magnuson. They were as familiar to her as neighbors down the street, and it had taken her some time to realize that her father had never been in the same room with Robert Taft or Owen Brewster or George Aiken or Alexander Wiley. Once she dreamed that Max had a fight with Pat McCarran. She and Shelley had learned those names the way other children learn butterflies, or wild flowers, or tools.

But Max wasn't telling it all. He omitted Truman's attorney general's list, which led to McCarthy's savage accusations, and he oversimplified. Did he do that then, too? she wondered. Still, Mady didn't have the heart to correct him. Was he any different from the books that distorted history? "Men like Max can be dangerous," David once said. "They see the world too clearly." But when he was finished, Nina and Peter believed that Nixon's resignation was the end to corruption and a chance for a new start. Maybe that was what you had to believe when you were young. Or old.

"I hope you're right," Libby said sensibly.

"Of course I'm right," Max retorted. "It will be better. It has to be. Even if Ford can't do two things at once he will have the sense to surround himself with decent advisers," Max assured them. "We must give him a chance, he's not Taft, after all."

But Libby insisted on having the last word. "We'll see," she said as they left. "We'll see."

When Mady opened her eyes the next morning, it was five minutes past five. No use trying to stay in bed; she was awake for the day. She pulled open the curtains. Outlines of plants and shrubs were emerging in the trickle of dawn light. Showers in the night had made the plants stand at attention, protected by an iridescent dewy armor. From the window seat she could see almost the whole garden, and in the half-light the places where

David used to put in the annuals were not so large or gaping. A beautiful garden, it had a grace that not even almost two years of neglect could spoil.

On the flattest part, at the south end, were the roses. Now in bloom were the Chrysler Imperials — four bushes planted on a gray day late in November 1963. Their color a deep winy red, the true color of arterial blood before it hits the air. In her mind she could see David digging furiously into ground already edged with rime, beginning early in the morning, before breakfast, angrily digging into the frozen earth so that it came up in clumps that looked like rocks. He moved so quickly that the memory was a speeded-up movie — David digging, then feeding and pulling the roses out of their neat boxes and roughing up the roots the way she had read later you were supposed to, the way David knew instinctively because (he once told Peter) no living thing should go into the ground in a cardboard box. Shaking the roots, then spreading them tenderly, each in the right-sized hole, then covering and watering and feeding them again, and still in a fury after hours of work, coming into the house and drinking cup after cup of black coffee and making a huge fire, which they didn't really want, because he needed to expend the physical energy required to split the wood and bring it in and get the blaze going steadily.

That afternoon friends called. Would they like to come over? David shook his head. He couldn't face the sitting around, the helplessness, the attempts at comfort. Later, after Nina woke from her nap, he packed some sandwiches and two thermoses into a rucksack and, wordlessly, they dressed the children in warm clothes and put Nina into the Hike-a-Poose and walked for miles along the aqueduct until dusk. Peter's eyes were glazed from the chill wind and exhaustion, but he never complained, not once, that awful day. And then that night, after they had put the children to bed and pushed some food around on their plates and were drawn into the magnetic field of the television set, she had lain in bed trying to read, waiting for him as he locked up and checked the children, wondering how long it would take him to relax enough for her to take him into her arms (for she didn't yet know that you don't wait for someone you love to be able to come into your arms), when he appeared with two brandy glasses and a bottle and they drank a little Napoleon and their eyes winced as it ripped through their throats and they talked disconnectedly about nothing and just as she was about to drowse into a half-sleep he began to make love to her with an intensity and a ferocity they had never known before or since. The next morning, after he watered the roses, he said to her in a cracked rasp of a voice, "Only in this damn country do they name roses after cars!"

The Chrysler Imperials thrived without him. So did the heather at the other end of the garden. "It's hard to grow," the man in the nursery had said when they went to buy it. "It wants damp and cool, like England, but it's beautiful if you can get it going. I'm from Scotland myself." They had been speechless at his ability to make small talk while they were still numb from the news of Martin Luther King's assassination. "He doesn't understand, he's not from here," she had whispered, but David shook his head. No excuses today, his piercing eyes said. He had walked with King in Selma, had heard the man's mellifluous voice, had watched his gentleness from not more than a few feet away. No excuses, and the same grayness in his face that she had seen almost five years before, and the next morning the planting, but now more resigned than furious. Again the television set pulled her to it; the day was sunny and unseasonably warm for April; the children's laughter as they played outside, happy for a holiday from school, made the muted blackness on the screen surreal. Black people in black (be careful when you drive at night, you can't see them, they had told her when she was a girl), hovering over the blackness that had once been their hope. A baby was beginning to grow in her womb (she knew for sure now), yet she felt the joy tainted by a sickening ambivalence. Religiously, for there was no other meaningful ritual, she watered the heather every few hours. And that Sunday they walked — this time in a long line of darkly dressed people — for several miles to remember the best marcher of them all. The children were quiet, too subdued, and when they got home, Peter finally said, "That reminded me of something, but I can't remember what."

"When Kennedy was killed," David replied, then explained, his voice flattening with each word.

Such flatness, such weariness. It frightened her more than the fury. Later he undressed slowly, taking his clothes off as gingerly as if he had been burned. She watched him from behind her book and their eyes met. "I think this one is going to be a girl," he said softly.

Of course the heather bloomed. Everything David put his hand to bloomed. He had placed it well, its rough prickly texture a relief among the smooth pachysandra and myrtle and a lovely complement to the more delicate daphne and columbine he had planted in the shadier section of the garden.

Behind and to the right of the roses were the azaleas, their shiny leaves glittering in the pale dawn. In front of them was the potentilla, and in front of that one of his favorites — the mountain cranberry. It never grew as large as he expected it to, but he liked its sturdiness, especially when its leaves changed from a startling glistening green to a deep lasting purple in the fall.

"We've gone nuts," he muttered to himself as he dug the holes for this small perennial and she stood over him in a red maternity dress with little yellow flowers on it. "You look like an English garden," someone had told her the day before. Now the baby was a weight within her, as if it, too, felt the inertia that hung in the air around them. "Sirhan Sirhan is just a symptom, Mady, this country is going crazy," he said quietly as he smoothed the soil around the roots. "*Vaccinium vitisidaea minus*," he read the label aloud. This time he didn't frighten her. His movements were deliberate; he was thinking, weighing each pro and con and coming to a decision. The summer and fall after Robert Kennedy's death he made a stubborn and finally suc-

cessful effort to extricate himself from the big corporate ac-
counts and by October he had announced his intention to leave
the large law firm he was working in. He wanted a different kind
of practice; he didn't want to spend the rest of his life figuring
tax loopholes, arranging mergers.

"Mountain cranberry, a relative to cowberry," David explained when people pointed to the small plants. The most experienced gardeners shook their heads in wonderment. Now
Madeleine could distinguish the different leaves — the skimmia,
the leucothoe (for Malcolm X), the fluted ruffles of the germander (George Jackson) nestled in among the andromeda,
something David called partridgeberry, with the wild flowers
and that tenacious creeping blue Wilton juniper. He had put in
the wild flowers when Nina was born — the trillium, Dutch-
man's-breeches, Johnny-jump-ups, herb Robert, Solomon's seal,
galax, bleeding heart, hepatica. Then, in October, two months
before the baby was due, he had come home early on a Friday
with a plastic bag tied to his briefcase. "It's wild ginger. A client
heard I liked wild flowers and brought it with him from
Chautauqua."

He put the ginger in before supper and they lingered over
coffee. Her legs were swollen and her back ached, but she didn't
tell him how weary she was when he began to stroke her shoulders later. They made love, yet her mind was elsewhere, even
her body was elsewhere. Later she remembered wondering why
she had been so distracted, then dismissed it and went to sleep.

At exactly 3:56 in the morning she was awakened by a warm
uncomfortable sensation along the inside of her thighs and legs
and when she stood up she realized she was bleeding.

"Sometimes happens after sex," the doctor's busy voice said
impatiently at eight in the morning. "It looks like more than it
is — don't worry, the baby isn't due for a long time. Forget about
it." She nodded and put the phone down. She could feel the
baby moving inside her. He was probably right. The other two
children had quieted down just before they were born.

"Not to worry," she said cheerfully to David as he entered the kitchen. "Here" — she took his hand and put it on her abdomen — "the baby's still kicking, he wasn't concerned at all."

"Was it because . . ." he started to ask, then turned away.

"It has nothing to do with that," she lied.

But his frown deepened and he kept watching her as she sipped her coffee, as she moved slowly toward the kitchen and back to the table again. The children's questions washed over them and Nina began to cry because no one was answering her. Madeleine was grateful when David turned to talk to the child; what a relief not to feel his eyes so intently upon her. She was so tired. Unbelievably tired. In the hour since she had spoken to the doctor she felt as if a stone were pulling down the muscles of her back — nothing like pain, just that extraordinary pulling.

Finally he said, "I'm calling the doctor again."

"No, I'll be all right," she protested. "I have to go with Nina and get a present for Laurie's birthday party. She's supposed to be there by twelve-thirty."

David shook his head. "I'll buy the present later, now I'm calling him. I want you looked at."

When they were about to leave he brought her an old sweater that was beginning to ravel in a seam and she thought about asking him to take it back for a less shabby one, but when she saw his face she didn't. Quickly he called the Levins and they dropped Peter and Nina there on their way. Anne came to the car. "It's nothing, don't worry," Mady said, but she could see fear in Anne's eyes.

"I must look terrible," she said as they drove.

"You've never looked terrible in your life," he replied.

The leaves were turning. As she lay on the examining table she could see a huge red maple outside the window of the small room — it must have been dying, for its colors screeched — too sharp and strident, as if screaming it didn't want to die, she thought as she put her feet into the stirrups and felt the doctor probing inside her.

"She's going to have this baby in a few hours," the doctor said quietly to David, who was standing by her head. He spoke as if she weren't there. 10:16. They helped her into a wheelchair and the doctor pushed it down the hall himself, barking orders as he went. "Lucky I was here in the hospital," he muttered, then called to David. "I'll see you in the labor room."

". . . to call Anne," David was saying to her. She barely nodded. She was counting the weeks between the middle of October and the beginning of December. Almost eight weeks to go. The baby was thirty-two, maybe thirty-three weeks old. Her body stiffened with fear. Images of Peter and Nina as infants floated in her brain, but her fear rendered them motionless, still — dead? Newsclips of Martin Luther King and Robert Kennedy pushed themselves before her eyes. She wet her lips.

"Doctor," she said as he approached. He was smiling over his blue operating gown and his mask was slack across his chin.

"I've just ordered an incubator for the baby," he said cheerfully. He seemed charged with excitement at this unexpected turn of events. "That's what makes medicine interesting," she had once heard a doctor say. "All those surprises."

She wished David were here. Where was he, anyway? "Listen, Doctor," she said, but now he was talking to a nurse at the door.

Finally he turned. "Yes?"

"It's very early, isn't it?"

"You must have miscalculated, happens all the time, women can't count, never could." At that moment she hated him.

"If the baby's not . . ." She wet her lips again, her throat and mouth felt baked dry. "If the baby's not . . ."

The doctor looked at her sternly. Would she have to begin again? Her eyes were on the door. If only David would come! "If the baby's not . . . right — " She stopped.

The doctor's face went hard. "We'll cross that bridge when we come to it. *If* we come to it." His words fell like ice cubes into a glass. She lay back wearily. The pulling that she remembered from the other births had begun. It felt as if some enormous invisible hand were tugging at the baby within her, yet she knew it was the baby itself that was pulling.

She concentrated on the pain. Off in the distance she could hear David's voice. She couldn't speak, her throat was sand-paper. But she could hear. "I've given her a caudal," the doctor was telling David. "She won't feel much from the waist down."

"But she's always had very easy, natural births," David said.

"I know, but this is different. That fetus is only thirty-two weeks old, we have to be cautious." Madeleine couldn't believe how gentle his tone was with David.

The caudal distorted her vision. As they put them into the stirrups her legs were mammoth — thick trunks of blue legs. The anesthetist had no face, only a great shock of white hair and gargantuan fingers as he stroked her own hair away from her forehead. One part of her brain wanted to ask him if he didn't have anything better to do, the other half was comforted by the stroking motion.

"Where's David?" she whispered. The man bent his feature-less face toward her. "David?" Her voice rasped in her head. From his frown she gathered that no sound was coming from her but he understood anyway. "Outside," he said and nodded to his left. A second later she heard, "It's a girl!" and the baby's cry.

Then, silence. She became afraid.

"Where is she?" Her voice cracked. The anesthetist bent his white head. "Is she dead?"

"No, no, of course she's not dead, you silly girl. They've gone to clean her up and show her to her father. She's a fine baby, very much alive," he said loudly.

The clock said 12:19 as she closed her eyes.

David sat in the easy chair near the bed with a pad and pencil. "How about Ginger?"

Mady shook her head. "Too cute."

He frowned.

"What time is it?"

"Almost two."

She leaned back into the pillows. The time she slept had meant nothing, probably too short a time to make a dent in her consciousness. She was still back in the labor room and all the anger she had felt swelled through her, up into her throat. For a second she thought she was going to be sick, then it passed and she sat up a little.

"He was horrible," she whispered.

"Who?" He was doodling on the pad.

"Dr. Wynfield. He told me I couldn't count, he told me women didn't know how to count the weeks of a pregnancy, then when you came in he was all sugar. Why did he treat me like a child, or, worse, as if I wasn't there? I was having this baby, for God's sake." Her voice rose, quivered. Why was she so shaky? Why couldn't she get her voice to come out properly?

David sighed and got up and closed the door to the room.

"You're tired, Mady, we'll talk about the baby's name when you get up from a nap," he said.

Ragged lines of rage darted before her closed eyelids. "Don't tell me I'm tired, and stop treating me like an invalid. I want to talk about Dr. Wynfield."

"Okay," David said. "What do you want to talk about?"

"I told you, how horrible he was."

"Oh, Mady, he was tense, too. He knew how old the fetus was and he was scared, he wanted you to have a nice baby." David's voice was so reasonable, the words flowed so easily; she could feel the anger rising in her again.

"But he was so condescending to me, so patronizing. He was disgusting. Then when you came in he was so respectful, he talked to you like an equal, and I was simply a stupid woman. When I tried to talk to him about the baby, what he would do if she wasn't right, he was hostile." She looked up. David was staring at her.

"What's wrong?"

"What's wrong? You're asking me what's wrong? That's what I'd like to know. I think you've gone crazy."

She put her head down, pressed her lips together.

He came over to her and sat on the edge of the bed, took her hand. "Listen, Mady, he got you a healthy baby, didn't he?"

She nodded. Now he was treating her like a child, he was no better than the doctor, he didn't understand, how could she make him see?

"But, David, it's not what you say, it's how you say it. I saw what a terrible man Wynfield was in that labor room."

David practically flung her hand away from his and stood up. His eyes were blazing. "Jesus, Mady, you *have* gone crazy. What you saw was a scared doctor who wanted you to deliver a normal baby. What you saw was a man who is human, and not a God like your mother thinks. He was in a bind so he treated you badly, but he got you the baby, didn't he?" His voice was rough and when he sat down on the chair his shoulders slumped from tiredness, but she knew from the way his mouth was set that he had said what he had to and wasn't sorry. He would never humor her because he knew that telling the truth was part of loving someone. Even now — less than two hours after their baby was born. Her eyes brimmed with tears as she turned her head so he wouldn't see, and she was filled with an overwhelming love for him that she knew she could never express.

When she woke, he was doodling again. "You're sure about Ginger?" he asked and smiled.

"What if she doesn't turn out to be a redhead?" Now the baby had a wild halo of red curls. "Besides, when she's fifty she'll want a real name."

"Like what?"

"Like Sophia," Madeleine said quietly and settled back into the pillows. Sophia was her father's mother's name. She could barely remember Grandma Sophie, she had died when Mady was eight and she spoke only Yiddish, but she could still smell Grandma Sophie's immaculate white kitchen. If she stretched her brain she could even recall the warm smoothness of Grandma Sophie's palm on her face.

"It's old-fashioned," David warned, but she knew from his eyes that he liked it.

"Peter and Nina will find a nickname," she assured him. "And we can give her Anne for a middle name, in case she hates So-phia. Spelled with an e, like Anne Levin." She watched David write the name on his pad, pictured the letters in her head, then remembered Nina's party. "Did Nina go to Laurie's?" she said.

"Yes, Anne got her dressed and Woody got the present. He said the toy store was obscene." Their eyes met and finally they laughed.

On the day Foffy came home from the hospital David an-nounced, "The wild ginger took." Now its wide, heart-shaped leaves lay almost on the ground and its curious pipelike blos-soms were a dried brown in the brightening dawn light. Mady's eyes swept the entire width of the garden from the wild flowers to the more cultivated part — the roses, the verbena, the daisies (Viola Liuzzo), the phlox and the lilies (Medgar Evers) to the far right.

How beautifully David had tamed the large mound of grass and bracken and rock they had found when they moved here! The only plants he kept were the wild dogwoods, the water grass that had been brought years ago by a former owner from Cape Cod, and the yucca whose thick white roots tunneled stubbornly through the soil no matter what they did to stop them from spreading. A magnificent garden that burgeoned endlessly with life, but also with death and anguish, she thought as she gazed out the window. David's memorial to the sixties. Now it struck her as strangely significant that there was nothing out there to remember the men who had died at Attica. Nor was there any-thing to remember him. "Ironic, isn't it?" his voice said in her head.

A month after David's accident a young black woman rang the doorbell.

"Yes?" Mady's voice was wary, the children were in school, she wasn't dressed yet. At first Mady took her for a Jehovah's Witness, but this woman had none of that sect's passive serenity. Her small figure was defiant, her breasts thrust upward, her eyes scorched the air in front of them. She didn't even have time for a hello, but her voice was surprisingly gentle.

"My brother Frank was killed at Attica. I knew your husband. He was the only one who understood what happened there. Then he was killed. But that's always the way, isn't it?" she said as if Mady were a stranger who didn't yet know all the facts. "I'm Cassandra Layton. My mother didn't know Cassandra had to do with doom, she just liked its sound," the girl added with a shrug. She was twenty-three years old, she told Mady. She had been at Howard University when her brother Frank was killed. "When he was eighteen he was caught looting a grocery store after a fire there. It was two weeks before Christmas. Nothing like this had ever happened in our family before. Frank was supposed to start at Bronx Community College in January. Instead he went to jail." Madeleine nodded. David had told her about Frank Layton, about his proud, strict, hard-working parents, and this sister who, after her brother's death, had been obsessed by a need to vindicate him and the men who had died with him.

Cassandra had come under the guise of giving her comfort, but what she really wanted was Madeleine's help. She wanted Mady to work with her and other relatives of the Attica dead to discover what had happened there. Fierce, articulate, angry, she only frightened Mady.

I still find it hard to get up in the morning, get dressed, get the car out of the driveway, walk into the supermarket. Buying food is one of the biggest ordeals of the week. At first it was so hard I think I wanted to starve us so we could die, too, Mady wanted to say to her. But how could Cassandra understand that kind of inertia? She would have thrown a disgusted look at Mady and gone on her way.

Today Mady wasn't ready for Cassandra, she didn't know if she would ever be ready for the Cassandras of this world. Yet she admired the girl's straight back, her body that seemed charged with electricity, her devotion to her cause. At least her brother had died for something she could grasp, hold in her mind. There was an enemy, and there were allies.

Mady had none of that. To die in a plane crash in 1972 was a completely anonymous death, something Aldous Huxley might have invented.

Now Cassandra was looking out the back window. "You have a beautiful garden," she said quietly, when, at last, she understood that her visit had been fruitless, when she saw Mady in almost full retreat behind her glazed blue eyes.

"It was David's garden, he loved working in it, there are several unusual plants out there, many that are hard to grow this far north." Mady's voice was eager, alive. She took Cassandra's elbow and propelled her toward the window. "There's the Connemara heather he put in to remember King, and the leucothoe for Malcolm X and the pink lilies for Evers and the rare white magnolia for Schwerner and Goodman and Chaney . . ." She wanted to lead the girl outside. *Come, come close to them,* she wanted to say, as if their touch and smell could compensate for what she couldn't do. But Cassandra had drawn away from her, her face tight, her eyes remote. "I hear what you're saying," she murmured, "but you'd be wasting your time. I don't know one plant from another."

Mady hadn't thought of Cassandra in all these months. A lot of events soon after David's death had simply fallen out of her memory.

She stood up. She could see the outline of her body under her white nightgown in the mirror. What was left of her after almost two years alone. As she looked her body seemed to curl into itself. That was ridiculous. She was still young. And he was never coming back. The garden was a mess, but alive. Like his plants, she would have to discover how to live without him. She thought she had learned it when she spoke to Hans, but she now realized the healing process was a long, slow unwinding of events that would help her learn to survive. Maybe she would be learning for the rest of her life. Again Mady forced herself to stare at her reflection. This time her eyes didn't look away and they weren't as frightened.

By the time the children awoke she was out in the garden and had filled a huge plastic bag with weeds. After breakfast she found the bulb catalog and later in the day Peter helped her dig out a piece of ground near the back door. Foffy found the trowel and began to edge the bed. Nina was weeding nearby.

"It's for a kitchen garden, herbs, mostly. Daddy and I talked about it a hundred times but we never got to it. He was more interested in the flowers," she told her children. Working together like this made them all feel better. Tonight they had plans to see *Harold and Maude.* Yesterday she had refused two dinner invitations. School would soon begin.

Suddenly Foffy's head popped up. "Hans had a nice herb garden."

Mady's throat thickened, she had to sit down. It was seven weeks since they had said good-bye to Hans. She had been positive he would try to get in touch with her. But nothing. The humiliation she felt practically took her breath away and she was an adolescent again; her children's eyes upon her were her mother's eyes when she played the piano badly or when she forgot some lines in a well-rehearsed play.

Nina's voice saved her. "Yes, he did. Remember the basil, Foffy? It was so tall." Mady nodded and rubbed her hands along the front of her jeans.

CHAPTER 9

"**Y**OU'RE ALL WRONG," Max Hayman snapped irritably. He and Libby and Shelley and Mel were trying to linger over dessert at the Russian Tea Room, but the restaurant had changed; you no longer lingered here. The place was as noisy and frenetic as a low-budget fun house. The smartest thing would be to leave as quickly as possible. Still, he couldn't let them lie to themselves this way. They had actually convinced themselves that Mady's options were theirs.

Shelley stared at him. Her eyes were troubled and she wore too much makeup; sometimes her face looked pasted together with it. She was unwilling to be a day older than thirty-five and all her efforts to stay time only accentuated its passage. Max wished he could tell her so.

A waiter in a red fez bumped into the table. "More coffee?" he asked brusquely and poured.

"This place is getting worse than Moskowitz and Lupowitz," Libby murmured.

"At least there they used to call the girls *sheine meidela*," Mel said. When the girls were first married, they would meet Max and Libby at Moskowitz and Lupowitz before going to the Phoenix Theatre. Eating there was always a personal triumph for Max over his early life in America when he had been too poor to eat anywhere but home and had stood outside Moskowitz's window, pretending to be studying the menu. David had brought them first to the Russian Tea Room; in the fifties it was filled with people from the musical and art worlds. How David had loved it! When would he stop influencing their lives? Max wondered.

"Dad, are you listening?" Max looked blankly at Shelley. "Why are we wrong, I've been asking for five minutes why we're wrong," she said earnestly.

"You're wrong to think you're going to find a husband for Mady. If she wants another husband, she'll find him, she doesn't need you."

"What do you mean, if she wants one? Of course she wants one," Libby interrupted. Her mouth was a thin grayish line across her face. She behaved as if David's death were Max's fault and now he had to make everything good again.

"You said that cellist, whatever he is, the oral surgeon–cellist, was perfect. What happened?" Libby accused Shelley. Max knew Libby didn't mean to be so difficult; she couldn't help herself.

"I don't know. It didn't work out. I was wrong. Let's get out of here." Shelley sighed and reached for her handbag.

Then Max remembered why he had said they were wrong. Now they were standing, annoying the people around them and the busboy who wanted to clear, but he had better say it while he thought of it. Libby was convinced that only she had suffered since David's death. How mistaken she was. Max's memory, which used to be legendary, now resembled a reliable knife that has inexplicably gone dull.

"You're wrong to think Mady will marry someone who is divorced," he said. "I don't think she would be comfortable with that." To Max's surprise Libby was nodding, her eyes agreeing with him.

"A widower, that's what we need, a widower," Libby repeated.

"What about a bachelor?" Mel asked.

"No. Anyone who's never married by the time he's in his forties has something wrong with him," Libby muttered as they left.

For Max Hayman the last year and a half had been the most terrible in his life. Nothing that he had experienced as a young man making his way in America, not even the long anguishing deaths of his parents, had prepared him for the unexpected finality of David's death. Max was not a practicing Jew and he didn't believe in rituals or synagogues or funerals or any of the protective, caring devices that religions all over the world had evolved for themselves. But Max did believe in time. Yet time was failing him. In the morning he awoke as desolate as he had been the month before, or six months before. His insurance business went along, if anything, better than ever, getting more and more prosperous, but he didn't really care. He and Libby had gone to the English Lakes and stayed in that delightful place in Keswick, but they had returned as washed out as they had been before they left. Watergate and the excitement surrounding it had been a relief, and a trace of the old interest in government and politics had surged within him. The night Nixon resigned he had felt for a few hours like his old self, but that had been short-lived and Ford's pardon of Nixon had been unforgivable. The unchanging state of the country had pushed Max back into his personal malaise.

Depression was something a man like Max had only read about, never understood. You get up in the morning, you take a shower as hot as you can stand, you get dressed and have orange juice and a piece of whole-wheat toast and a steaming cup of coffee and you go out to face the day. You walk briskly under a bower of maples in your pretty suburban town, you greet people on the train, at the newsstand, at work. The habits of fifty years do not fail you because of one event in a life of seventy-odd years, he had always believed. Yet this was harder than he had ever thought possible. He still dreamed conversations with David, sometimes so vivid he would be startled out of sleep and filled with a yearning to see him so deep that it resembled physical pain. His ears would strain to hear certain slightly nasal inflections that reminded him of David's, he would find himself telling people who had never known David "David stories." He would read the paper, then reach for the phone to talk to David and be numb with helplessness for hours afterward. He dreaded going home and watching Libby's listless movements through dinner and into the long evening. The weekends were endless, and Libby found it hard even to be with Mady and the children.

"Scrawny! She's positively scrawny!" Libby would rail at him through tears as they drove home from Mady's house. As if he could make Mady eat more, so that her cheekbones didn't look covered with rice paper, so that her back didn't become permanently curved from discouragement.

For a while the weight loss and the tiredness and the sleeping (which he inferred from hints the children dropped) and the fright appeared to be building in a geometric progression and he had feared for his child, had begun to call her every morning to reassure himself that she was up and about. But then the progression stopped. And when they saw Mady last month, the night Nixon resigned, she had looked beautiful — her prettiness in youth had become real beauty in middle age. She had picked up some weight, her body was less awkward when she moved, her voice sounded more musical, more lilting, her eyes had a glimmer of that expectant attentive quality that had made them so compelling when she was a young girl.

She had met David when she was nineteen, beginning her junior year in college, and from then on she had filled her life with David. She had finished her Russian studies (Max was still in awe when he saw the original Chekhov and Babel and Akhmatova and Pushkin and Bely on her bookshelves), and she had taken a minor in music in case she ever wanted to teach piano, but the focus of her life had been her husband. There had been no thoughts of her own career — strange, now that Max thought about it, because 1958, the year they married, wasn't so very long ago. Undoubtedly, it had been her choice; with a husband as brilliant and energetic as David she had had enough to do, at least while the children were still little.

"Only the good die young, surely you know that, Max," a cousin had comforted him at David's funeral. But to die so senselessly, so unexpectedly! He and David had only begun to talk. It had taken Max a few years not to be intimidated by David's intelligence, his intensity. At first Max had been a little jealous of David: handsome, Harvard, tall, with such black hair and those incredible dark penetrating eyes. And the quickness of mind. It awed everyone who met him. But the jealousy was soon replaced by enormous pride. In David's work, in his refusal to compromise, in his absolute belief in justice and the law, in his physical courage. For most men unshakable beliefs lead to fanaticism, a hunger for power, even a slight yet unmistakable craziness, and often disappointment. Not for David. When David began to be quoted in *The New York Times*, Max could scarcely believe that one of his children (for David and Mel had become the sons he had wanted) could be so respected, so admired, so correct. Whenever Libby complained that he was away too much, Max said, "He has important things to do. He'll stay home when he's old." How many times that remark had come back to haunt him. If only Libby could begin to forgive him, forgive David, even forgive Mady for marrying him. Then maybe time could begin to do its work.

And now they were on the lookout for a widower. Well, he would look. God knows there weren't as many widowers as widows, but he would do his best. United effort. One family. He didn't understand the urgency, though. Mady looked fine to him now. And she was financially secure. Most of David's insurance had been doubled because of his accidental death.

"But what about her physical life?" Libby asked him a few nights later. They were sitting over dessert and coffee. Libby was trying, she had signed up for a drama course at the library, she had consented to be chairman of a music committee for the Cultural Arts Association in town. Tonight she was wearing a new apricot-colored sweater with a cowl collar, but her throat and neck were so lined with tension that she looked like a rabbit peering out of its hole.

"What about her physical life?" Max stared. He had never thought of either of his daughters as having a sex life, or a physical life, as Libby persisted in calling it. He had watched their faces age, their minds develop, he knew they had borne children, but in his head their bodies were the smooth, hairless, beautifully curved entities they had been at about eight years old, just before they became too shy to run around the house naked.

"She's still very young, Max." He must seem an idiot to Libby. Of course she was right; Mady was thirty-eight. When Libby was that age, she had had an early hysterectomy and they had begun to enjoy sex. He conjured an image of Mady's head on Libby's body — an angular, yet appealing, fragile body, the left breast larger than the right, the stretch marks near the navel still visible from pregnancies so long ago, the startlingly dark pubic hair. Then his mind drifted back to Mady in a black bathing suit that was covered up in front and very low in back. He could see David rubbing suntan oil on her back and legs as she lay on her stomach, reading, then David whispering something to her that made her laugh. Max had had to turn away that day.

Now he looked at Libby. Her eyes were patient, smiling. He hadn't seen that look for a long time. They hadn't made love since David's death, as if by silent agreement. He had thought that part of their life was over. When Max looked at his wife again, she seemed bemused, a little puzzled. Embarrassed, he mumbled, "Yes, she's very young." Libby folded her napkin and they cleared the dishes slowly, and that night they made love.

CHAPTER 10

Now THAT THEY HAD the neighborhood to themselves, the birds made a terrible clatter. Three robins and a blue jay were teasing each other, harmlessly at first, then, without warning, fighting in earnest.

It hadn't been an easy morning. The children were nervous. New teachers, questions, forms to fill out. Last year Peter's homeroom teacher had handed back his emergency slip and said, "You forgot to put down your father's office number." This morning Nina had tried on three outfits; her room was strewn with discarded clothes and when she came home she would say she wore the wrong thing.

From the corner of her eye Mady could see the clutter on the kitchen counter. She should clear it away, the food would spoil; it was the usual hot first day of school. But she didn't want to leave the greenhouse yet. Slowly she washed the sponge she had been using and looked at the chart for watering: David's invention. The plants were watered in succession so that someone would be near each one for a few minutes every day. "They're like babies in cribs," David had explained to the children when he hung up the chart.

"Anyone home?" Anne walked toward her, carrying a plant.

"It's a sick African violet, maybe you can revive it." She sat down in the corner of the greenhouse. "I have some lemon mousse for you in my freezer. I made a double recipe — one last orgy before I go back to work." Anne's school started in a few days. Before Mady could thank her she said, "Shelley called this morning."

"Already?"

"Yes, she said to be on the lookout for a widower."

Mady smiled. "Why a widower?"

"Your dad said you would never marry someone who had been divorced."

"Very perceptive of him."

"And your mother says bachelors are out."

"Oh?"

Suddenly Anne's tone went from slightly mocking to serious. "How can you stand it, Mady? All their manipulating, conniving, call it what you like, on your behalf. They act as if you're a child."

"They don't mean any harm. That's the way they love people — Mom and Shelley. They want to make everyone's life good and whole again."

"Whole?"

"Whole by their definition. In my case, whole would be remarried. In a man's case, whole would be having work he cared about. Like David and Woody."

Anne nodded. "But don't you resent it? Don't you hate Shelley calling me and talking about you like you're an invalid?"

"I suppose I should, but I don't. I guess I'm used to it. They can't help themselves. I resent other things, but not that."

"I would hate it."

"They're well-intentioned . . ."

"Still, I would find it oppressive," Anne interrupted. "They treat you like a sensitive plant and you're not, you've done so well."

Now Mady felt herself getting annoyed — at Anne and at

Shelley for calling Anne. "Shelley shouldn't have called, I'll tell her to stop," she said.

"It's not Shelley I'm concerned about. I've already told her I wasn't on the lookout for anyone, I told her you don't need me or anyone else to find you a husband."

"I'm sure she loved that."

"As a matter of fact, she did. She doesn't think I'm serious." That was true, Mady knew. Well-intentioned people like Shelley assumed everyone else agreed with them.

"I care about you," Anne said and looked around. "One of these days you're going to want to move out of the greenhouse and . . ."

"But for the time being it serves," Mady said, "and the plants thrive."

"The more interesting ones live out in the air," Anne said, and they went into the kitchen.

Mady tried to listen while Anne drifted from topic to topic. Once Anne's job began their conversations would be the shorthand that sustained the friendship of busy women. She wished she could relax and enjoy Anne now. She had given herself a week to do all the chores that needed to be done, and then she was going to look for a job. She had one interview already scheduled, but no one knew about it.

Now Anne was talking about the park. "There's a meeting early next month. Woody says we need as many people as we can get to attend. Could you plan to come?" The Levins cared so much about this park and they wanted her to care, too. She did, in an abstract way, and she promised to go, but she knew she had disappointed Anne with her lack of enthusiasm. This was such a logical project for her to be interested in, and it would get her out of the house with a legitimate reason — instead of those trumped-up dinner parties — but somehow she wasn't very enthusiastic. Perhaps it was because she had more to do inside her house, inside herself. It had come to her as she was watering the plants, before Anne arrived. And now she wanted to get down to it. She didn't want to have to wait. Anne sensed her impatience.

"Well, I've got to go and attack the clutter. Three days to do what I should have done all summer." She paused, but Mady said nothing. Quickly the two women kissed good-bye.

When David had first died she had been in a tunnel, suffocated by dark threatening air that had actually pushed at her, pressed against her so that she had felt continually bruised. She remembered examining her body for black and blue marks, amazed that there were none. Then, one day, she had been flung from the darkness into a glittering brightness. Surrounded by strands of flaring light, she had felt that everything she put in her hands was dangerous. Words flew out of her mouth like unexpected licks of flame, singeing whatever they touched. She became afraid of herself and tried to go through each day very slowly, deliberately, often keeping the curtains in the house drawn so that the sunlight wouldn't add to her mental delusion. At one point she was sure she was going insane and was about to call the doctor when, abruptly, the light disappeared. She was left with an endless weariness and that was when she had begun to do the needlepoint, when she had begun to move slowly, more deliberately, and though she could see her behavior exasperated those close to her, she had been afraid to go faster, she had been afraid that what came next might be worse.

Since that day in Anne's kitchen when she had cried, she had felt more adventurous. She had noticed, if no one else had, that she could walk faster and talk a little faster. In the greenhouse this morning she could actually feel herself divided — one self watering the plants and the other self observing her. And for the first time there was a conflict; the watching self wanted to pull away from the self it observed, wanted her to move. But where, how? She had thought survival depended upon doing each task in a given day as thoroughly as possible. Just go from one task to another and the days will pass and time will slide by and you will feel better. But that was nonsense — at least for her. If you keep doing that you can become a piece of wood, a stick figure, as Anne had said, and you end up living a half-life. To begin to live again you had to look back. In these last weeks, actually since that night in Hans's house, she had begun, and this morning, as she breathed in the thick smell of the newly watered earth, as she walked through the palpable greenness, she finally felt brave enough to handle David's clothes.

They had waited for her in his closet like obedient, fairy-tale children while she did all the other things that had to be done — the funeral arrangements, the financial details, the government forms, the taxes, the meetings required with his partners. And when all that was finished she had still been afraid to go near his closet. Actually, physically afraid. Once Clair asked if she could help her with it and Mady had stared dumbly at the kind black woman and their eyes filled and they hurried away from each other.

Wouldn't Clair be surprised? she thought as she opened the door. Everything David wore was here — built-in shelves held his underwear and shirts and sweaters and socks and handkerchiefs and small things. On the other side of the closet were two poles for his suits and jackets and slacks. They had had the two closets built the summer before he was killed, when they finally got rid of the maple chests that were hand-me-downs from her childhood. With all their clothes in the roomy closets, their bedroom had become larger, more like a sitting room. A retreat, they had called it, delighted with their foresight, now that the children were getting older.

The closet smelled musty. The summer clothes were in the front, the winter things still in camphor-filled bags. Mechanically she carried them over to the bed, a few suits at a time: the tan worsted, the brown and blue plaids, the checked summer blazer, David's favorite that was falling apart. He had been wearing a gray glen plaid suit when he left that day — with a yellow shirt and a yellow and blue tie. She had bought the shirt and tie for Father's Day the June before. Over the months she had tried to envision David hurt, with blood spreading over that gray suit, but all she could see was blood spilling over Jackie Kennedy's pink suit in Dallas.

Even after so much time on the hangers the jackets bore signs of his body — the puckered places near the shoulders that could never be perfectly altered, the drooping of the left side because he always carried more than he should in the inside pocket, the right sleeve a little longer than the left. Slowly Madeleine took the suits off the hangers and went through the pockets. Ticket stubs, Kleenexes, a few crumpled handkerchiefs, paper clips, mint Lifesavers, a package of unopened peanuts. Why wasn't she feeling anything? She had expected, as she anticipated doing this, to experience something, but nothing like that was happening.

Now she saw a sequence of images — tilting images, but clear and quickly moving: David running toward her down the runway, his black and red polka-dotted tie picked up by the wind he created in his need to reach her as fast as possible, David in a blue checked L. L. Bean shirt giving Foffy a piggyback ride through the garden, David loosening his tie and rolling up his sleeves as he talked to a client on the phone when she surprised him at his office, David in a dark blue wool suit at his father's funeral, refusing to wear an overcoat though it was only fourteen degrees, as he helped to carry the coffin into the hearse, and, finally, David in a tuxedo and white ruffled dress shirt, holding her arm so tightly that she was almost lifted off the floor as he guided her down the aisle, the Mendelssohn blaring into their ears. Tilting, swirling images that threatened to throw her off balance if she let them continue. She groped for the window seat and sat down, trying to reason with herself. She was doing the same job she had done for years and years each spring and fall, only this time she wouldn't take the suits to the cleaners but to the Goodwill store in the next town. One winter blazer he had never worn. They had bought it on sale at Saks at the end of the season; tickets still dangled from it. She held the jacket up. Navy blue, single-breasted, brass buttons, a red lining. "Smart," the saleslady had kept calling it. David had winked at her. For them "smart" had to do with brains, not clothes. It might fit Peter; maybe she should ask him to try it on. No! She must be crazy!

Why should a kid wear his dead father's clothes? Out, all of it out!

She was sweating, her underwear was clammy, once she stopped to wipe her face and the back of her hand was wet, her lips salty. She straightened for a second and heard a low whimpering sound, then realized, startled, that it was coming from her throat.

Yet still she pushed and pulled and slammed and piled till the mountain of clothes toppled and made two hills. Her mind was stretched into two masses. Stretching and stretching into two pieces held together by a thread. Then a cold click. Her brain came together, she was spent.

The empty closet loomed in front of her like a naked thief. Slowly she closed its silent louvered doors. It was one o'clock. She climbed over the pile of clothes to get onto the bed, dragging with her a few sweaters and jackets which she then pulled over her. Quivering with cold and sweat, she fell into an intense dreamless sleep.

The telephone must have been ringing forever. She rubbed her eyes, sat up. Why was she waking at two-twenty-five in the middle of the afternoon?

Anne's voice was urgent. "Are you okay?"

"Fine, fine," she said thickly.

"Oh, I woke you, you were napping."

"No, it's okay. I have to get up, Foffy will be home soon."

"Do you feel all right?"

At first she was tempted to say yes, and let it go at that. Then she decided to be truthful. If she was going crazy she might as well know it. She told Anne what she had done. "Do you think I'm going nuts?"

"No, I don't," Anne said quietly. "As a matter of fact, I think you're going sane. I'll be down to help you pack it up."

Mady stared at the pile. How could she throw out all those good sweaters? Peter and his friends could divide them up, even Nina could wear some of the things now that she was getting so big. *No.* She sat up, put her feet on the floor. Her brain was floating, she was light-headed. She hadn't eaten since breakfast, but it was more than that. A job like this required energy you got from way inside; no wonder she had put it off for so long.

Her feet sought her espadrilles. Slowly she folded the clothes she had thrown over her when she went to sleep. Sometimes she imagined she could smell David, sometimes she dreamed of how he smelled when he slipped into bed beside her, then later, after they had made love. How the loneliness deepened the longing. She held the beige cardigan up to her face. It gave off an odor of dust, neglect. When she was a child, she believed that houses mourned the people who had moved out of them. Did clothes know when their owners had died? Tenderly she smoothed and folded the sweater, then took the other garments and placed them into neat symmetrical piles. A car door slammed. Anne was at the door with large cartons under each arm.

"Do you think I'm going crazy?" Mady repeated.

Anne pulled her close, wiped her face with a tissue.

"No. People like us don't go crazy. That's for flashier folk. The only thing that happens to people like us is that we get mugged when we're old. But you shouldn't have done it alone."

"That's just the point, I had to do it alone."

"Okay, maybe you did, but you've been there and back and we have only a few minutes to load this stuff into my car before Foffy comes home," Anne replied. Then she added, "Cathy Wheeler told me that for weeks after her husband died, she got a baby-sitter and drove to the station for his train and waited until everyone got off. Only then could she turn her car around and come home for dinner."

CHAPTER 11

AROUND HER IN THE WAITING ROOM were books that had never been opened, their jackets glazed with a newness that gave them the look of wax. Suddenly Mady knew why she preferred libraries to bookstores; books were never meant to be new.

"Mrs. Glazer?" A young woman crept up behind her on the thickly carpeted floor. Mady jumped. The girl smiled; it must happen all the time. "Mr. Solomon will see you now." Mady followed her down a tiled hall, comforted by the sound of footsteps, then paused for a moment. Her fingers tingled with fear.

A tall, well-dressed man looked up expectantly, then stood and moved toward her. He seemed to be coming through the desk, which, she now realized, was entirely Lucite and which, when the sun touched it, appeared to be on fire. Here was this man rising out of quivering prisms of fire. The effect was startling, and in spite of all her intentions, Mady stepped away from him instead of toward him.

"Maximilian Solomon," he said warmly as he shook her hand. "Everyone calls me Mack."

She nodded and sat down. She was like a tongue-tied schoolgirl and to give herself more time she pretended she was warm and took off her sweater.

Quickly she reviewed how she had gotten here. Eli Houseman, one of David's partners, had always been impressed that she knew Russian and when David died said he knew someone who would give her a job. She had called him when she got back from the beach to say she was interested, and when he called back last week he had told her that Mack Solomon was one of the smartest men in publishing. The appointment had been for ten-thirty; at exactly ten-thirty-four Mr. Solomon began to speak.

"As Eli may have told you, we have set up a translating division, and we are planning to do retranslations of many of the classics. You, of course, would fit into the Russian department. Coincidentally, that's the first area we would like to tackle. Eli told me you were a Russian major at Radcliffe, translated some Akhmatova, he said. He also told me about your husband, whom I think I met once, and whom I had read about. Terrible loss, terrible . . ." Mr. Solomon shook his head and stood up and looked out the window for a moment. Because of the way the sun hit the desk now, the seat of his pants seemed to be on fire. Mady blinked. Then he walked around the desk and sat on its edge, which, of course, made him appear to be sitting on air. Mady sighed and tried to concentrate.

"Although you might have expected us to start with Tolstoy, we are beginning with Chekhov. We plan to do all the stories." Mady straightened. That interested her and while Solomon started to explain her mind pulled her back to Foyles bookstore in London in 1955. She had just completed a year of college, and for some reason — still unknown — she had wandered into the Russian-language section. When she picked up a paperback volume of stories, when she saw the mysterious lines and loops and curves that made up the Russian words, she had known, in a remarkable flash, that this was what she wanted to do with the rest of her time at school. Untangle that strangely forlorn configuration of lines which seemed to beg for her understanding into words and the words into sentences and paragraphs and stories and plays and even novels. She had bought a Russian dictionary and grammar from an elderly Englishman wearing a wig that looked as if it were on backward and when everyone else went to the theater those last nights in London, she had been drawn to the Russian books (the paperback turned out to be Chekhov's short stories), and by the time they landed in New York she had a few pages of one story — "The Beggar" — written out. She had picked that one from the table of contents because it was the shortest title. Reluctantly she forced her brain to leave the dusty, homey English boardinghouse and listen to this exquisitely dressed man in his bizarre office.

He was reading a list of the stories they were planning to do. She would ask for "The House with the Porch" and "Gooseberries" and "The Name-Day Party." "You want me to do a few stories, then," she said, but Mack Solomon was smiling at her and shaking his head.

"No, nothing like that old-fashioned method. We're planning to use a team approach. Each phrase will be done by several people, all together, sitting around a conference table. It will be an excellent way to use our new conference rooms, which are the most elaborate in the publishing world, but more important, we feel that the interaction of various intelligences will give us truly superior translations. None of this Constance Garnett business, sitting alone in a room with a dictionary and five thesauruses, thesaurusi?" He raised his eyebrows and chuckled.

Mady wasn't amused. Her head shot up. "There's nothing wrong with the Constance Garnett translations, they stand up wonderfully, in fact. Garnett was a pioneer, a —" But he didn't let her finish.

"Constance Garnett had a pedestrian mind," he said, "and her translations are dated."

Mady shook her head. "No, they're not. Garnett was a remarkable, intelligent woman. Her translations have a rhythm and tone that are true to the Russian. Her translation of 'The Lady with the Dog' is still the best I've seen." Mady was surprised at how belligerent she sounded and she knew she wasn't endearing herself to him but she didn't care. Now she stared directly at him, challenging him.

"But all my experts say they're dated . . ." His voice dwindled.

"What's wrong with being a little dated? Spenser and Milton and Shakespeare are dated, too."

"Well, you certainly have a point." He smiled weakly. "And you do have strong opinions. Eli didn't tell me that."

Mady shrugged. "Russian happens to be something I care about."

"Yes, I see." Now he was sitting at his desk again and looked at the *curriculum vitae* attached to her letter. "You do seem to care about it, but why didn't you do anything with it all these years?" He waved the sheets in the air.

"I did," Mady answered.

He frowned and looked at her letter again.

"For whom? Who did you work for?"

"No one, Mr. Solomon. I read Russian for pleasure when I was home with my three children."

"Oh. Well, that's quite unusual. Most people don't read things like Russian for pleasure, they usually need the discipline of classes or work to make them do that, unless of course, we're talking about Edmund Wilson. Remarkable man. I knew him, you know." Now he had turned and was digging into a cabinet. He pulled out a small tape recorder on which someone had taped a card with her name. "But of course now that you're alone a job is more important to you." She knew there was no point in disagreeing with him. He had made up his mind that she now needed the money, and once he made up his mind — oh, forget it, she said to herself, and listened.

"Now, Mady, what I want you to do is read something and translate it at sight. Since you did some of Akhmatova's poems, we thought you might have a look at this one by Mandelstam." He looked up quickly to be sure she knew who Mandelstam was. Later she knew it was at that moment that she decided she would never work for Maximilian Solomon, but she also knew that she would go through the charade, if only to show him she knew Russian. He handed her the same edition of Mandelstam's poems that Hans had had.

"Here." He shoved the book at her with a marker in it. "Try this one."

She opened the page to the poem she had read in Hans's living room. It was uncanny, eerie, and for a second she considered telling him to pick another, then she heard David's chuckle in her ears. "Let him have it, Mady, and when he offers you a job, hold him up for more money."

She read the poem first in Russian, then in English.

"Well, well, well!" He grinned. "You certainly are fluent. Very fluent, indeed. My wife reads French for pleasure, actually this whole translation project is her idea, but she isn't nearly as fluent in French as you are in Russian. Well, Eli was right. A trustworthy man, that Eli, I should have known he wouldn't send me a housewife who *thinks* she remembers Russian. But of course I should have known. Radcliffe, after all."

"No, Mr. Solomon. Smith." Now she knew why she hadn't corrected him the first time.

"Oh, well, Radcliffe, Smith, makes no difference. Ivy League. And so good-looking, too. I always knew Eli was a man who had taste." He flashed his best Ultra Brite smile. She looked away, and she knew he thought she was politely embarrassed, but at this point it didn't matter. Sleazy, that's what he was, despite his excellent diction and well-cut clothes and gobs of money. Sleazy and horrible, and all she wanted was to leave and never come back. He could offer her a fantastic salary and she would never work here. Ten people sitting at a table picking over Chekhov and Tolstoy and her beloved writers! It was enough to make her skin crawl. She pulled her sweater around her shoulders and started to back toward the door.

"Protocol dictates that this tape be heard by our team of Russian poetry experts — people like Karlinsky and Yarmolinsky and Magarshack have been retained by us — but I can assure you personally that we will offer you a job. At least twelve thousand, five hundred."

"You have my address, Mr. Solomon," she said wearily.

"Oh, no, Mady, Mack. Just call me Mack. Everyone does,

even the mail boys. And I hope I may call you Mady. I'll phone you. We want to have a volume of Chekhov stories in the bookstores by summer. And it will be a pleasure to work together."

She should have known better, she thought, as she sat back into her seat on the train. She had been back onto the street by eleven-thirty and all her plans to go to the Gotham Book Mart and Bloomingdale's had vanished. Her knees were weak, her head spinning. She had trudged back to the station and had a cup of coffee and a Danish and she was on the twelve-thirty train home. Her big day in New York. Her first job interview in twenty years. She was going out into the world! she had told herself proudly. How ridiculous she was. How tired she felt.

Why couldn't she hoard a little triumph; after all, she had put him in his place. Maximilian Solomon. What an absurd name, his mother must have been insane. She could hear David, even Woody and Anne and Shelley and Mel advising her. "Roll with the punches, use Solomon a little, it's a way into the world, you can leave after six months and go somewhere else." But then she thought of Chekhov, fighting to write each word, refusing to leave Russia, afraid he would lose his gift, and dying for his stubbornness. No, she would never see Solomon again, and what's more, she would never tell anyone about today. She had tried to get out of the house — and had failed miserably because she couldn't compromise. As the train ribboned its way through the abandoned houses of the south Bronx, she thought, what will I do? She felt as tired as those stalwart buildings that had long ago outlived their usefulness. She dozed a little, grateful to be able to hide her disappointment, and when the train reached her stop, she waited a few minutes in the small garden that had been planted around the station to be sure she wouldn't meet anyone she knew.

She was reading the paper over a second cup of coffee when Foffy came up the front steps, crying.

"What's the matter, what's wrong?" Mady hurried to the child; she expected to hear about a fight. Last week Foffy's lunch had gotten stepped on, and yesterday a child had asked her if her parents were divorced because she never talked about her father.

"He didn't write me." Foffy threw the mail on the table.

"Who?" About a year ago someone had told Foffy dead people could write from heaven. Were they going to go through that again?

"Hans. He wrote to Peter and Nina and you, but not me."

Mady riffled through the mail. Two bills, one circular, *The Harvard Magazine*, two cards from Germany, and an envelope for her addressed in a chicken-scratchy hand with many of the letters left open.

"Yours will come, I'm sure of it. Tomorrow, and it will be the prettiest of them all." Foffy still looked skeptical.

Mady held out her arms and Foffy climbed into her lap. School all day was tiring for the child, but after her milk and cookies she perked up and began to give her mother every detail of her day. The small voice went on and on and Mady's mind wandered. So he had finally written. After she had given him up. She might have expected to feel relief, but now her body was tight with caution. Maybe he was never coming back to the States. Anything seemed possible, especially after the surreal interview today.

"You're not listening, Mommy," Foffy complained. Mady smiled at being caught and they talked for a while and finally Foffy went to play. She sat there fingering the blue envelope, oddly touched that he hadn't sent a card. His handwriting was almost illegible. She reached for her glasses and read,

My dear Madeleine,

I am writing this as I stand in the airport on my way to Zurich. So much has happened I scarcely know where to begin. When I arrived my mother was in hospital. She saw me and pressed my hand, but I don't know if she knew who I was. Then she fell into a coma for three weeks. During that time it was like living in limbo. I felt like a child again, as if I had never left Germany. I was surrounded by old aunts and uncles who behaved as if the war, my brother's accident, my parents' divorce, my father's death, my self-imposed exile had never happened. They treated me like a teenaged boy and watched me constantly. Their ministrations exhausted me, the food they kept preparing — as if I were some gargantuan monster — only depressed me more. When I couldn't bear another day of it, my mother died. On August 16. After the funeral I had to sell my mother's house and divide her possessions. My nephew got pneumonia so my sister couldn't help, and that is a partial explanation of why I have not written till now. But not all. I will tell you more about it when I see you.

In Zurich I must attend to some financial affairs and will be taking a plane home on September 20th. I would very much like to see you after I return and will call you then.

> Yours,
> HANS

She traced the words with her forefinger. Yours, Hans. Well, she would wait and see. As she stood up she suddenly thought, he would have understood why I couldn't work for Solomon, and that comforted her.

Peter and Nina admired the scenes of Heidelberg on the cards Hans sent. That night, at supper, Mady described the city to them. She had been there in the mid-fifties. "The most interesting part is the old section, where the university is. And the castle has a wonderful long view over the Black Forest. Most of the city was intact, and such a relief after Cologne and Frankfurt where there was still so much rubble left from the war. People were living in buildings with cardboard and tin windows."

Peter's eyebrows flew up.

"Yes, we bombed them, too," Mady murmured. He didn't answer. Foffy held the cards up to her nose. "The air smells so good," she said. Mady smiled.

"It was terrific air, not too hot or too cold and dry and it smelled of pine and balsam, like the souvenirs."

Nina looked up. "I'd like to see Mozart's birthplace in Salzburg," she said shyly.

Peter nodded. "But first Rome. The fountains and the Sistine Chapel." Peter played his records of Respighi almost every night, and Rachmaninoff's Piano Concerto, and *Victory at Sea*. But the Sistine Chapel was news.

"And Michelangelo's *David*," Nina said.

Mady stared. How grown-up they sounded.

"It's that new art teacher, Mom. Mr. Donahue. He's fabulous," Peter explained.

"He must be, to have done so much in a couple of weeks."

Nina nodded. "You'd love him, Mom. He's straight out of college, and I think he looks like Daddy did when he was in law school."

Peter's face went pale; in seconds it was papery. His voice was low. "It's the eyes, goddamn it! I knew he reminded me of someone. He has Daddy's eyes!" He mumbled an excuse to leave the table.

Watching him leave, Mady thought, they were all moons to David's planet. How could they free themselves? When?

Later Peter told her, "Sometimes I think I'm mad at Daddy for dying. As if he had a choice. It's crazy. I hate myself. How can you hate someone for dying in a plane crash?"

"I do it, too," she admitted. Peter looked up, startled. "It's that we were left so suddenly, I think. Abandoned, in a way."

"Do you think if someone dies slowly, of cancer, say, we would feel the same?" he asked.

"I don't know. People are relieved then. You watch someone suffer and the end is more logical. With us there was never any beginning, or middle, just the end."

"That's true." Peter sounded wary. Then he asked, too casually, "When is Hans due back?"

"He mentioned a plane from Zurich next week. I thought you didn't like him."

"I never said that. I said I didn't like his past." Peter sounded so old, she thought as they kissed good-night.

Slowly she moved through the house, shutting lights, closing windows, locking doors. A filmy breeze filtered through the rooms. Her bare feet glided along the oak floors, her body savored the dark. That first winter after David died she had scurried through the shrouded rooms, afraid of every sound and shadow. Sleep was fitful, she woke up angry. Slowly she realized that the anger came partly from not allowing herself time without the children. By going to bed with them she had become one of them. So she devised a plan to stay up a little later each night — the first week, a half hour, the second week, an hour, and so on. She read Agatha Christie, Simenon, Dick Francis, Ngaio Marsh, and by the following fall she was able to stay up hours after the children had gone to bed. For the last few months she had even been playing the piano at times. The notes resounded through the quiet house, comforting the children. How much easier it had been, as a child, to go to sleep when there was company. Voices, laughter, dishes tinkling, cards slapping had given her a sense of being in the world, not entirely alone beneath the goosedown quilt where she had carved out a bit of warmth for herself. Now their company was Mozart, Schubert, Debussy, Fauré, Scott Joplin. And she had Shelley to thank for it; if she hadn't played with Bonnie that night she might not be back at the piano yet.

She stopped at the mail basket and held Hans's letter in her hand. Peter's words echoed in her head. "I didn't like his past." Only when you're young can you blame someone for his past. She remembered doing it herself. But the past is so complicated, you can barely understand your own, how can you hope to understand someone else's? Especially someone from such a different past.

For her the war meant her mother standing in a long line in the butcher's, her father wearing a white helmet that said "Air Raid Warden," her aunts learning to drink tea without sugar, her and Shelley sitting in the dark halls of their school singing songs during air raid drills. Or that gray March day when her mother said in shocked quavering tones that the Stangs had lost a son. Mady had an image of a boy in a forest trying to find his path back, but then her mother said, "He died instantly." It was better to die instantly, but why, she didn't know. The next time they visited the Stangs Mady had stared at the picture of Arthur

Stang on the piano. Once Mrs. Stang clutched it to her breast and said, "He was such a good boy."

What did living through a war mean? When David phoned from Attica the first time, he said, "It looks like a war."

How young and arrogant of Peter to judge Hans's past! Yet how understandable. She thought of Hans, surrounded by that ineffable weariness, yet his back straight, his eyes filled with that golden light. He was a contradiction, perhaps that was what interested her. Who knew? She hoped he would keep his promise and call.

CHAPTER 12

Finally Hans was flying home. His mother's body lay exactly parallel to his brother's, the cemetery authorities in Munich informed him. In a drenching rain he had watched as rivulets of muddy water kept disturbing the diggers' careful work. After they had smoothed the earth as best they could, Hans knelt a few feet away near the stone that marked his brother's grave.

"Hans, come along, you'll catch a death, Hans, you're getting soaked!" his aunts and uncles admonished him, but he stayed, kneeling over Karl's grave, welcoming the water that streamed down his face and beard in place of the tears he could not weep.

The plane climbed higher and higher, then it dipped a little. They were in a patch of bad weather, the pilot announced. Hans wondered if he would ever go back to Germany. What baffled him was their lives. They behaved as if the war had never happened. From their faces, from the scraps of conversation, Karl might have died of some childhood disease, or in an auto accident, instead of in the war. Once Hans referred to Karl's death and they had stared at him with widened wary eyes. They were like the characters in Sergei Vladimirovitch's favorite tale, "The Snow Queen." Splinters in their hearts and eyes prevented them from seeing the real world. When the carton of photographs had been unearthed in his mother's cluttered attic, they had pressed them on Hans.

"Are you sure you want these on the plane?" customs men had asked, first in Munich, then in Zurich.

"Absolutely sure," Hans replied.

"A lot cheaper to send them by boat," the man in Zurich persisted.

"I know," Hans assured him. "But I prefer it this way." He couldn't have described to this sensible stranger why he needed to drag along these boxes of photographs that were costing him more than a hundred dollars in overweight. Yet he couldn't part with them; in some mysterious way, they defined his past, contained it, made it manageable. If he lost the photographs he might have to keep going back and back to Germany. When he had tied the last piece of twine on the cartons, he suspected that if he and the boxes arrived safely in Racer's Cove he would never see Germany again.

In the Zurich airport they had insisted on examining his hand luggage. "Now what do we have here?" The man turned the piece of walnut over and over in his hands.

"A block of wood."

"I can see that, my friend. Are you a sculptor?" The man narrowed his eyes. Hardly the typical taciturn Swiss of public places.

"Yes, I'm going to use it for a head. Or try to."

The man nodded. "It's good and hard, the best for sculpting. I used to do some myself, a long time ago," he offered. Then he put out his hand. "Good luck, my friend."

Now Hans's fingers sought the wood. He had found it in a souvenir shop where the owner carved wooden candlesticks and miniature Christmas figures, but wasn't enough of a craftsman to hoard this splendid piece of walnut. Greedily he held out his hand for Hans's money, his eyes flickering disdain. But when he rose to get change, his body was lopsided, his walk a painful limp. The man had believed in Hitler, just as Hans's father had, and he had lived the last thirty years in shock at Hitler's defeat. Men like the woodcarver were scattered in the dank poorer sections of every city in Germany. The young had no patience with them and their own generation didn't trust them, so they sat doing small jobs and waited for death to deliver them. "Melancholic," their families called them. But at least they had not forgotten the unforgettable. Their eyes showed signs of a struggle with the past; they were more human than the amnesiacs.

Hans held the wood in his hands. Warm, smooth. He wasn't sure if he would be able to do what he wanted with it. So much depended on the circumstances. A vague vision of what the wood might become hovered around the edges of his brain as he dozed through the last hours of the flight home.

As the patchwork quilt of land emerged through the clouds, Hans felt an unfamiliar tension rising in him. Was he afraid? He who for years had flown without a thought? Hard to believe, yet his palms were wet, he was nauseated, the walls of the plane were closing in on him. He hadn't felt fear for years and years. Yet here it was, crawling through his limbs. To his astonishment his mind welcomed it, and he was a little sorry when the plane touched ground.

"Fear!" His Aunt Johanna spat it out. "All your mother knows is fear! It rules her life!" She had risen at five so she could finish the jackets before they left that afternoon. Karl stood in the doorway with his over his arm. Both boys were embarrassed; jackets like these were for smaller boys, English schoolboys.

"They don't need jackets, they will be given uniforms of the Nazi Youth," their father explained to Johanna when she dragged the bolt of flannel into the sewing room.

"They'll need something to go to church in, or the theater, or whatever. I want them to have these jackets," she retorted through clenched teeth to Friedrich's retreating back.

"There!" Now she was triumphant as she opened the large gold watch that always hung around her neck. Hours to go and she had only to sew the lapels and collar on each jacket. Now it was Karl's turn to stand on the small platform in the middle of the sewing room. As Hans sat down in the easy chair he could hear his mother's worried step. Gingerly, she crossed the threshold.

"Johanna, Friedrich says we may have to go earlier than we thought. Whether or not the jackets are finished."

"They'll be finished," Johanna said grimly through the pins.

His mother moved closer and smoothed the jacket over Karl's back. If she kept that up Hans knew that Johanna would explode. It came sooner than he expected. "Berthe, stop touching him, I'll never get it right, and here you've come to tell me you're going earlier. How can I work with you fussing over him? Leave him alone!" Johanna said. His mother backed away and held her hands in front of her mouth. Suddenly Hans rose and put his arm around his mother. Her bones felt as small and frail as Margot's. She trembled at his touch.

"So, you don't want me to be mad at your mama?" Johanna looked up and smiled for the first time all day. "You are a good son, Hans, better than she deserves."

Johanna motioned to Karl to take the jacket off. Then she put her arm around Karl. It had been that way before. Berthe Panneman could never have handled twins by herself in this strange, seething land so different from the Bavaria she had known. Between them Berthe and Johanna had brought the boys up and it was Johanna who had become the authority in their lives.

For years Johanna had refused to believe in Hitler, she had laughed continuously at Friedrich's fervor. Here, close to her beloved mountains — Kenya and Kilimanjaro — surrounded by the natives she had grown to love, pounded at by the vicissitudes of life on the large and productive farm, Johanna had felt protected from the increasing madness in Europe. "That Hitler is demented, daft, a true lunatic," she would mutter to Berthe and Hans-Karl as she read the papers. Even after Friedrich had gone back to Germany she felt no danger. "Let him go, good riddance," she said as she looked around the capacious oval table. But finally the war encroached on her life.

In the last year letters. More letters. Back and forth. Trying to reason with Friedrich. "We are Germans," he wrote. "This is where we belong."

"We are Germans by birth," Hans-Karl wrote back, "and Africans by adoption. Our home is this farm. We have been here so long that we are accepted by the English, we are not aliens, and this is where we shall stay." Besides, Johanna had a Jewish grandmother, but that was left unsaid.

Settled, or so Johanna thought. The silence stretched from weeks to months; she breathed easier. Then, suddenly, a cable. Friedrich was returning to Kenya to take his wife and children back to Germany.

"They are babies," Johanna protested, wishing irrationally that she had never let Hans-Karl teach them how to shoot.

"They are German youth," Friedrich insisted. "When the war is over, they will be proud to have fought for a new Germany."

"Germany will not win. Hitler is a maniac, maniacs don't win," Hans-Karl replied.

Arguments lasting deep into the night. Night after night. On the fourth morning of Friedrich's return, Hans and Karl were again shunted into the study. Raised voices grew louder and louder. Then, abruptly, a frightening stillness. From what they could piece together later, Berthe had finally asserted herself. In quivering tones she announced that since Friedrich was the boys' father he knew best, and he had survived part of the war and soon it would be over and Germany would be victorious and Hans and Karl and she would go to Germany and Margot would stay here till then. After the war they would all be together again.

Sergei Vladimirovitch gathered the largest copybooks he had; in them he made long meticulous lists. History, Biography, Fiction, Science, Art, Music, Philosophy. "Books for a lifetime," he said, blinking his glistening eyes too often. Uncle Hans-Karl kept touching their shoulders; Johanna shouted a lot as she concentrated on the jackets; Friedrich pressed his lips together and spent a lot of time with Margot, who was seven years old and totally confused. Berthe dabbed her eyes as she followed Johanna around, hoping for the forgiveness she knew was to be denied. The servants tiptoed through their chores and looked frightened.

Hans began to wish they could stay. He saw that the natives were very afraid for him and Karl. Then, as Johanna pulled the last stitches through the blue flannel and said, for the last time, "There!" Sergei Vladimirovitch appeared in the doorway. Johanna's face went gray, she dropped the jacket and put the back of her hand to her lips and began to sob.

"Johanna," he whispered. "Johanna, my darling," he said and held out his spindly arms. She went to him and they stumbled to the couch and he rocked her back and forth while she cried and cried. Hans and Karl watched, their feet frozen to the floor. "There, there, my poor Johanna, my darling Johanna," he murmured into her thick hair. But he never said, "Don't cry."

When they left for the airfield, Johanna's eyes were steady, her voice as cool as daylong rain. "Germany will be defeated and being a German will be a curse for the next hundred years." Then she looked down at the boys. "Kiss the walls, and then you will come back."

"Oh, Johanna, surely you don't believe that native nonsense." Berthe smiled as she watched her sons obey their aunt.

"Of course I believe it, and so do they. Some people in this house have learned to respect what should be respected." Now Johanna's voice was soft, warm, as it was when she had been teaching them some difficult task, or when she said, "Sleep well," in her most lilting tone. Then Johanna hugged them each to her and for years and years afterward Hans remembered the feeling of her ample body as she held him close.

Only Hans returned. In 1950, when he was twenty-two years old. When he saw Johanna he drew in his breath; her body had lost a third of its bulk and she peered from behind watered-down, weary eyes.

"There are so many shadows here, Hans," she said to him one morning while they strolled through her kitchen garden. She picked basil, sage, rosemary, mint, lavender and laid them haphazardly in the old basket. She, who had been such a tyrant when a servant mixed up the herbs! Hans could hardly believe it. Then she said, "Germany is a grave, but there are too many shadows, they follow one everywhere, it is so hard to live among them . . ."

She died in 1957. A few years later Hans-Karl died of stomach cancer. The natives continued to run the farm, but it was no longer profitable. Sergei Vladimirovitch moved into the big house, which he converted into a school for the grandchildren of the first Kikuyus who had worked for the Pannemans.

While Hans was on his way to see him in 1962, Sergei Vladimirovitch died in his sleep. The natives greeted Hans with red eyes overflowing with relief. They didn't handle their dead and had been terrified by the old man's corpse. Now Hans could prepare his old teacher for his coffin.

The next day dawned clear. A cool sharpness whistled through one's nostrils, but the high vault of cloudless sky meant a hot midday. Such cruel heat. It singed Hans's back as he kneeled with the rest. Then the ground jumped up, playing tricks with his vision in the tremulous air. Perhaps it was the sun, perhaps the small lonely cemetery. Hans didn't know, but suddenly his body crumpled beneath him, he felt like a spark ignited by the dazzling sun, and there, in the hot dry landscape of his memories, he finally wept. In his brain was the image of Karl's clenched mouth and blazing eyes as he refused to follow yet another stupid training command. Then the warning and Karl's stubborn silent refusal and finally the wrenching of his brother's body into the air and the thunderous crack of the rifle, which always came last in his mind.

After he woke in his old room Hans knew that the natives would watch over him until he was well. And when he recovered he did what he knew he must. There was no choice. He went to Nairobi and sold the farm for a pitifully small fraction of its worth. He gave some of the money to the natives, as Johanna and Hans-Karl had stipulated in their wills; what was left he sent to his mother.

He packed the books, Johanna's baskets, one antique chest, two rockers, several quilts, and the Danish silver and sent them back to Racer's Cove. The rest he divided among the servants. On the last day he visited each of the native homes that formed a circle around Johanna's gardens. At the stonemason's house he instructed the old man to carve a stone in memory of Karl and place it next to Johanna's grave.

The night he returned from Europe Hans dreamed reels of dreams filled with strange images of animals and natives and finally of baskets of wool, thread, the large spool-board that was Hans-Karl's invention, the hemmer, the forms, tapes, pincushions, scissors (his favorite, the pinking shears, looming larger than the rest), and the printed flower couch, the rocker, the old treadle Singer. And superimposed on all these — stones. Gravestones in a cluttered sewing room filled with yellow morning light. Flat stones and standing stones, even stones flying like bodies that have been hopelessly wounded. Spinning stones.

In the morning Hans pushed away the covers and stood up, glad for the firm hard feel of the floor. He looked around his room. His bed was hardly rumpled; he could still see the outline of his body. Then the bare floors, white sheets, cleared trestle desk. Everything neat, austere. The only spots of color were the quilt Johanna had made, the drapery of his clothes, and the *Newsweek* he had read on the bus home. He walked into the bathroom and saw himself in the mirror. Even his pajamas were a dull ivory. How lifeless it all looked! How disappointed Johanna would be!

Hans rubbed his hands over his face, his beard. The hair in his beard was wiry, grayer than the hair on his head or in his eyebrows. He had grown it almost twenty years ago, soon after he moved into this house. By then he had stopped moving listlessly, by then it was almost ten years after Karl's death and he had accustomed himself to living. No more, no less. He had learned, simply, how to live. Not to be a great person, or even "somebody," as Johanna had promised so often when he and Karl were children, but merely to live. He had found solace in this house, he had heeded the lists of Sergei Vladimirovitch, he had his books, his work, his students, a few friends. He had known a few women, he had thought he was in love once, yet nothing had come of it. More than that he had never dared to desire.

Yet for these last eight weeks, he had been haunted by the image of a woman he had seen only a few times — a woman whose beauty flickered in and out of sight even when she was sitting across the table from you, whose face was alternately bewitching and plain, and who, to some, might be too worn and too intense and thin ever to be called beautiful, but whose eyes held a grace and wisdom he had thought were gone from this world. He had written her on an impulse from the Munich airport. Did she think he was brazen? Perhaps he was. He was so far from what she knew in men, what she had been prepared to know. Wouldn't it be wiser to leave things alone? Live his peaceful life that he had so carefully constructed? He was middle-aged. Maybe that was the clue, maybe this was merely a last gasp before he faced growing older. Yes, I am still interested in sex, in women, no, my quiet life has not emasculated me. If that were the case there were a half-dozen women he could have sought out. Why her? A Jewish widow with three children. He must have lost his mind. How could he dare to see her again? The very question threatened to smother him, and an unfamiliar confusion flooded through him. Yet in his letter he had promised to call when he got home.

One more time. Then he would be able to know what was happening to him, then he could be more rational. He looked at his reflection thoughtfully, and when he finally moved his gestures were deliberate, sure. He filled the sink with water and took out his razor and slowly, methodically, Hans shaved off his beard.

CHAPTER 13

THE MAIN ROOM of the village hall was so crowded that when Joe Carpenter, a neighbor of the Levins who was a structural engineer, came in, he said to Woody, "Jesus, I hope the damn place doesn't cave in." Large portraits of the village elders stared down severely, silently exhorting the noisy crowd to be quiet, well-behaved, staunch. Staunch they certainly were. Each side was utterly convinced it was right. A grim seriousness pervaded the room as thick as the smoke that swirled above their heads.

"Or burn up," Woody said. He stood next to Mady and kept blinking his eyes. Anne was on the other side of her, and though she was taller than either of them, she felt like their child. A few people had looked approvingly in her direction, smiled, nodded, cocked their heads. Their approval had nothing to do with the side she was on, but rather with the fact that she was out at all. Village Widow Attends Meeting, she could see the headline in her mind. One husky, outspoken woman in an outlandish straw hat mouthed a stage whisper, "Glad to see you back in the world again." She was a big meeting-goer.

If this is the world you can have it, Mady thought and smiled back. She believed in the park Woody had worked so hard for, but was this sort of thing really necessary? All this humanity crammed into a room, talking excitedly, passionately. And on top of that, the smoking. She could feel her eyes beginning to tear.

"They'll make them stop," Anne assured her. "As soon as they call the meeting to order."

"By that time we'll all be dead," Woody muttered. He was such a solitary man. Besides, he was dressed too warmly — in a heavy chamois shirt. He and David used to order those shirts from L. L. Bean together. Anne and she called them their Teddy Bears. Mady had given away two nearly new ones, but Woody was slighter than David. And you didn't ask a man to wear his dead friend's clothes, she reminded herself.

"Order. Meeting called to order." The gavel pounded on the lectern. An announcement about smoking. Proctors passed ashtrays, then the talk began. First one side, then the other. Consultations with the village attorney. More talk, as if their lives were at stake. How far removed from it she felt!

Currents of passion eddied through the room, exposing nerves there, wounds here. Faces distorted by zeal attacked minute points of law as though they were alive and could wiggle away. It was easy to spot the ecologists: they were leaner and had more gray hair than their opponents. Most of them had marched against Vietnam, gave to Common Cause, and wouldn't dream of having a Twinkie in their refrigerators. But tonight their intelligence was exhausting itself upon clauses, phrases, details. On and on they droned. Mady wished she had been lucky enough to get a seat, then she could be doing her needlepoint. She looked at her idle hands, then her feet. She straightened, tried to listen. She caught Gail Howland's eye and they smiled. Next to Gail Fred was grinning — whether at her or at the scene she didn't know. He had come home last week, they were going to have another go at the marriage. Fred had stopped by a few weeks ago for a drink and then called her to tell her he thought Peter was doing fine. She had thanked him and hung up. Later in the week he had called and asked if he could come see her that night. He was working late, he could stop by at ten, he said. But Nina was playing in a concert, she told him, with some relief. Something about his voice was different, and he hadn't called again. The next thing she had heard was from Anne — that he was home again.

As she watched them, Mady wondered about the marriage. Fred kept fidgeting, and even at a distance Gail's face was so tense that her skin appeared to be pulled too tightly over her high cheekbones.

Suddenly she heard a rustle beside her. Woody had taken a few creased papers from his pocket and was being recognized. He straightened. Sweat trickled down her breasts, along the insides of her arms.

Woody's flat Boston speech sounded too dry in the high-ceilinged room. He coughed, began again. Mady loved to listen to him. Despite a slight hesitation that sometimes occurred in his speech, he was one of the most articulate men she had ever known and had one of the clearest minds. He taught literature at a nearby college and all that he had read in his forty-nine years had filtered quietly through his mind so that his speech had the weight and balance of the written, rather than the spoken, word. Tonight he spoke of the environment and documented his statements with figures on run-off, bird life, plant growth, pollution. His conclusion dealt with our responsibility to the next generation, the need to reject the easy profits. Finally someone had addressed himself to the real issues.

Clapping, cheering. Then the recapitulation of the other side. Taxes, expenses to the village, the necessity to bear in mind the profit motive, America's rugged individualism, the benefits of capitalism, rising costs. Then a final coda. Exposition, development, recapitulation. A desecration of the musical terms, Mady thought, wondering why the scene didn't move her more. After all, here was democracy at work — a small village having a town meeting. Opposing opinions expressed. Wasn't this part of the

American dream? Why John Adams said he must study politics and war? Wasn't this why she had encouraged Peter and Nina to come tonight, even though, in the end, they both had too much homework and stayed home? Why couldn't she be more enthusiastic?

Mady didn't know. But she felt isolated, an estranged on-looker. "IT ISN'T LIFE AND DEATH!" she wanted to scream to them as they listened, then clapped a final time.

Of course she said nothing and breathed with relief when the doors were opened and the cool evening air flowed in. People converged on Woody, so Mady stepped back and found herself face to face with Fred Howland. His eyes were bloodshot, bleary, his liquory breath brushed along her face. He bent to kiss her hello, but she turned deftly so he caught her on the ear. His tone was caustic.

"Amazing how some people get their kicks, isn't it, Mady?" She shrugged as they floated slowly with the crowd toward the entrance. She would wait for Anne and Woody in the parking lot. It was such a pleasure to be able to move again. She looked for Gail. Surely she would be along.

The night was warm as summer. She breathed deeply as Fred held the huge front door. The village hall was a reconverted barn, the door one of the village prides. "Amazing, isn't it?" Fred persisted.

"I don't know what you mean," she said.

"Oh, come on, Mady, you were as bored as I was."

"Bored isn't exactly right. Depressed is more like it." He didn't answer and they walked silently along the wooded rim of the parking lot.

"Woody's car is over there," she said. He nodded. "So is mine." By now most of the cars were leaving, people were ex-changing last words of instruction, comfort, encouragement to their friends as they pulled out. Mady's clothes were clammy, she longed for a hot shower. "It feels so good to be out of there, it was so oppressive," she confided. Fred looked down at her and

smiled — his usual crooked, somewhat indulgent, smile, but
then a different smile, one she had never seen before. He rested
an arm against a tree and took her hand with his free hand. "You
know, Mady, now that Gail has decided sex is a reward, I have to
be a good boy to get mine, and these days I'm not a very goo'
boy." He stopped, as startled as she was at the slur in his speech.
"Good boy," he corrected himself. "And we, Mady, you and I,
we could make such beautiful music together." With that Fred
planted his fist in the small of her back and pulled her toward
him. She could feel him hard against her. Her voice formed a
lump in her throat, she couldn't make a sound. She tried to lift
her free hand to push him away, but he anticipated her and
clamped his hands on her wrists. His mouth was open, he was
lunging toward her. How strong he was! She knew she couldn't
stop him by fighting him, so she turned her head away to avoid
his open mouth and appeared to relax. He chuckled, a triumphant little snort, and let go of one wrist. She wedged her
pocketbook between them and kicked him in the groin.

"You bitch!" he growled in pain. "You cold bitch! One lousy
kiss, for old times' sake. It's been two years since you've had
any, I thought you'd be dying for it!" Rage muffled his voice, he
looked as if he wanted to spit at her, then turned on his heel and
left.

Mady's knees were weak. She leaned for a few moments
against the tree. The deep striations of the bark pressed into her
upper arms but she was grateful for the pain. It gave her time to
put her mind in order. She couldn't believe it. Fred was a good
man, their friend, David's friend from college, a devoted father,
a good husband for almost twenty years. She wondered now,
was Fred a psychiatrist because he had a prurient streak? Did he
need to listen to other people's sex lives? As she slumped against
the back of the Levins' station wagon, Mady reviewed what she
remembered of Fred. He had always been scrupulously polite.
Very sympathetic and helpful after David died. One Sunday
morning he had fixed a broken toilet for her. The last time she

could recall his putting his arm around her was that evening a few weeks ago, before that it was when she was pregnant with Foffy and David had teased him that pregnant women turned him on.

Jesus Christ! She felt as she had in college after wrestling with some absolutely determined nineteen-year-old in the dark room of a fraternity house. But then she was stronger, or the college boy wasn't as tall and large-boned as Fred. Yet the sameness of it astonished her — the sour breath, the panting, the lunging movements. She had thought she was through with that forever, but here they were, in a suburban parking lot, and she was thirty-eight years old. "Youngish widow up for grabs." She had read about such things but had not believed them. Her naiveté was absurd. Suddenly she began to laugh. The sound of her laughter only made her laugh harder, till she cried. She knew she couldn't tell a soul what had happened, but she had coped with it. In a bookstore she had recently noticed — among the Fiction, Biography, History, Gardening, and so on — a section called Coping. Well, she had coped.

As Anne and Woody approached the car Mady was waiting for them near it, as if she had just arrived. Woody looked uncomfortable.

"Woody's speech swayed several key people," Anne told Mady. "Everyone thinks we have a better chance now."

"When will the decision be announced?"

"In a month."

"Do you think we'll win?" Anne turned to Woody. "I do."

"Now don't get your hopes up, Anne, anything can happen," he said.

"Oh, Woody, don't be so cautious. You influenced a lot of people there tonight."

"Yes, but it was only a hearing. The real decision will come from behind closed doors."

Mady listened to them wistfully. Two heads were better than one. This was what she missed so much — that give and take in conversation with someone who knew you well, maybe even better than himself. As they neared her house the Levins urged her to come back to their place for a cup of tea, but she refused.

The next morning the phone rang at eight-forty-five. Fred was on the other end. Sober, sorry, actually mortified. "I don't know what got into me, I've been drinking a little too much these last few months, but that's no excuse. I seemed to have lost my mind there for a few minutes. I'm sorry, I hope you'll . . ." his voice dwindled. He wasn't used to apologizing.

In the old days, when David was alive and even soon after his death, Mady would probably have said, "It's all right, don't feel so bad, it's okay, no harm done . . ." until she would end up comforting Fred, practically asking *his* forgiveness. Now she didn't feel like doing any of that. She was outraged by his behavior, she was furious on behalf of Gail, his wife, her friend. She had also had a nightmare and lost some sleep. Her voice was hard and she spoke slowly and firmly so he couldn't mistake what she said. "You really are a bastard, Fred. The person I feel sorry for is Gail. She didn't deserve you."

Silence. Then the psychiatrist's voice. "I'm sorry you feel that way, Mady." Smooth, professional, distant, the voice went on, "Someday, when you can control your own anger, someday when you work your own problems out, perhaps we can talk about this." Click.

The nerve of him! She placed the phone back on the receiver and shook her head. Well, at least David would have been proud of her. "You don't have to be so nice to everyone," he used to say when she felt pulled to pieces by her children, her parents, her friends. "You can say no, you can even be nasty, occasionally." But niceness had been her code; what she had been brought up to respect. If you can't be good, at least have good manners, appear nice, something like that. Well, the truth was, she was sick of it. She hadn't felt nice after David died, but those who loved her excused her irritability and called it grief. She hadn't felt nice during all those weird dinner parties, but she hadn't had enough confidence then to do anything but pretend. She hadn't felt nice last night, being used, and she had finally been able to say so this morning.

Mady stretched her arms over her head. She could have danced. Quickly she rummaged through her closet and found her oldest pants and a stained sweatshirt she had inherited from Nina. The house was filthy — Clair was sick — but she didn't care. She was going out to clean the garden: David's garden, now hers. Instead of creeping around the greenhouse watering the plants, then tidying up the house, she was going out. This morning there had been a tartness in the air. The bulbs had to go in, the place needed a good raking, the azaleas and roses and germander needed to be mulched. She would do the house later, maybe even after the kids came home from school. She didn't have to have everything spick and span when they walked in the door. They knew that she was not going to die of grief. She had kept this household going for almost two years without David, she could allow herself a day to do what she wanted. Besides, a dirty house signified nothing more than a dirty house. How wonderful that she could say it! She pulled on her sneakers and admitted one last thing to herself — she didn't want to spend another day wandering through the rooms waiting for Hans to call.

When Nina came home from school (she had gotten an unexpected ride so she was the first home) and saw the house, she became frightened. Some emergency must have pulled her mother away. A bottle of milk standing in the sun had soured. The butter was puddled in its dish, the chairs were still pushed away from the table. What had happened?

She ran through the house calling, "Mom! Mom? Mommy, Mommy?" The beds were unmade, the pile of laundry Peter had dumped on his bed was still there. Where could her mother be? Something terrible had happened, she was sure of it. To Foffy? Maybe they were in a hospital somewhere. Having a dead father wasn't the only thing that could happen to you. "Mommy, Mommy?" she called, panicky, then ran outside. She stopped dead still.

In a frayed lawn chair, covered with an old blanket, lay her mother, asleep. Her face was so peaceful, so young. The frown lines that reminded Nina of a quotation mark between her eyebrows had almost disappeared, her forehead was smudged with mud, the hand that curled under her chin was grass-stained. A trowel and claw and big shovel were near the chair, the grass was dusted with bone meal. Underneath a leg of the chair were an empty bulb bag and a chart of where the bulbs were planted, which meant that her mother had put in two hundred bulbs all by herself. No wonder she was tired! Nina stood still, not wanting to break the strange spell that had fallen over them both. She felt as if she were seeing her mother for the first time. Suddenly, in a rush, she understood what she had not understood before, what Peter didn't understand either, what maybe only Foffy could know because she was little: that their mother was still so very young. She was a widow and she had three children to take care of, but "widow" and "mother" didn't mean old. Nina couldn't have thought about that before; if you thought about that you had to admit to yourself that your father was dead. Stone-cold dead. Gone. Never going to return. For two years they had pretended that Daddy was gone for a while and they were waiting for him to come back. Each evening, for a few seconds, she thought, maybe tonight he will push open the front door with "Anybody home?" But he was never going to push open that front door again, and here was this pretty thin woman asleep in a chair after working all day in the garden. Here was this woman who happened to be her mother, but she was also a woman, not yet forty, and it was utterly foolish to think that she would spend the rest of her life simply taking care of them.

As Nina stood there a breeze blew over them, lifting a few strands of her mother's hair. Gently Nina pulled the blanket up around her mother's shoulders, and that small tender movement did it. Mady opened her eyes; for a second she didn't know where she was. Then she saw her child's brown eyes staring down at her.

"Darling! Are you sick?"

"No, Mom, it's almost three. I got a ride home." Nina laughed.

Mady looked at her watch and shook her head. "I feel like I think you kids used to feel after your afternoon naps." She sat up and rubbed her legs. Her thighs hurt and then she remembered. She looked at the garden. The beds were a testament to her work — scarred with all the raking. Her stomach growled.

"You haven't had lunch, have you?" Nina asked. Mady shook her head like a guilty child. She felt dizzy and when the phone rang, she let Nina get it. All she wanted was a cup of coffee and something to eat. It was the first time she had felt hungry in months, maybe even in years!

"There's a man on the phone, Mom." Nina frowned, shrugged. "He has an accent."

Puzzled, Mady looked up. Then her eyes flashed. "That's Hans, that's Hans on the phone." Relief flooded her blood. "He doesn't recognize your voice, say hello to him while I get some coffee," Mady instructed Nina. She wasn't sure why she was doing this, but she needed to savor these few moments of anticipation. She poured herself some coffee and made a cheese sandwich and watched Nina smile while she talked to Hans. She even took time to greet Foffy and tell her who was on the phone. The little girl said hello, but then became tongue-tied. She handed her mother the phone. Slowly Mady put it to her ear. Wasn't this called delayed gratification? She didn't know, but she had to admit to herself as she heard his voice, which was more accented than she remembered (was it the telephone or the trip?), that she felt as if she were being given a reward. For what, she couldn't have said.

CHAPTER 14

F ROM THE KITCHEN WINDOW Mady saw the red Fiat pull up to the curb. Her palms were sweating, her fingers tingled. Fear that he would or wouldn't be as she remembered him? She watched him get out of the car, heard its door slam, saw his raincoat slung over his shoulder and his arms full of packages, and she could feel the fear replaced by something else. Her blood thickened, as though it were clogging her veins and arteries and vital organs. Desire is such a physical thing, so much easier for the body to take when it is young. In her twenties it had made her feel light, euphoric; now there was a heaviness about it that approached pain.

He came up the stairs two at a time and when he reached the top she knew something was wrong. He didn't look like the man she had met, the man she had recalled these last months. For a second she was confused; then she saw what it was. His beard was gone and where it had been his skin was luminescent, as if reflecting a bright sun. Why hadn't he told her about the beard? But why should he?

Foffy opened the door. "I'm looking for a distinguished personage named Sophia Anne Glazer," he said. But the child was also confused; her eyes filled as Mady hurried to her.

"His beard is gone," she whispered. Foffy blushed until her scalp glowed pink. "And his clothes are different."

Then the child laughed and said, "I'm Sophia Anne Glazer." Hans grinned and handed her the largest package. He put the other presents down and clasped Mady's hands. She couldn't believe how well he looked. How could a beard matter so much?

"You look so different," she fumbled. He laughed his deep hearty laugh.

"It's so good to see you," he said and handed Peter and Nina their gifts. How pleased they were. Even Peter lingered with the string. Of course Foffy was first.

"Oh, Mommy!" Two beautifully dressed dolls lay side by side in the box. The child's voice was choked with pleasure as she ran her thin hands over their fine hair, their porcelain faces, their handmade clothes.

"They're Kate and Jancsi from *The Good Master*. My mother collected dolls," Hans explained. Foffy nodded as she hugged the dolls to her and hurried to her room. When Mady turned, Hans was helping Nina fasten the silver filigree bracelet. She twisted her arm to let the silver catch the light. "I love it," Nina told Hans.

Peter's present was the game, Go. Mady gasped when she saw it. She and David had been talking about buying it the night before the plane crash. Mady had forgotten that conversation until this very second. She stared at the box.

"What's the matter, Mom, it's supposed to be a great game. Why are you staring?"

"Nothing. It is a great game. Daddy used to play it in college," she lied, grateful that Peter and Nina were showing Hans around.

From the shape of the package left on the table Mady knew it was a plant. Suddenly she was filled with anger. Why did he have to bring them these extravagant presents? And especially Go? And a plant that would go into David's greenhouse? They had been so peaceful, the four of them, and now she felt so confused. What was it? Was this the way she would be with any

strange man in the house? Or was it Hans? And why had he cut
off his beard? More to the point, why should his not having a
beard matter so much to her?

"Why are you mad?" Foffy was looking up at her.

"Who said I was mad?"

"No one, but you're wearing your mad face. And your mad
eyes."

Mady laughed. "I think I need a drink. Why don't you ask
Hans what he wants and I'll put this in the greenhouse?"

After dinner Foffy begged for a fire and Hans showed the
children how to make paper logs. When they brought him a pile
of old newspapers, he asked, "Have you got any *Posts?* It burns
better than the *Times.*" They shook their heads, no one wanting
to volunteer the information that they hadn't seen *The Post* since
the day before David was killed. He was addicted to it.

But after that it was calm. Foffy concentrated on her needlepoint while Mady worked on hers. The woman's body was almost done and soon she would begin the blue background. As
Hans helped Nina and Peter play Go, the soft firelight glistened
on their hair and faces. Now and then the wood crackled and
hissed.

He was thinner than he had been on the beach. How, she
didn't know. From what he had told them, all his relatives
wanted to do was feed him. Yet he looked thinner and his body
seemed more graceful than it had before. Or was she imagining
it? Or was it the fire, that coverer of all blemishes?

"They've got the basic rules now," he said and sat down next
to her.

"Who taught you?"

"Sergei Vladimirovitch and Aunt Johanna used to play with
us. Karl was a whiz at it." Then he glanced at Foffy. "You know,
the resemblance between Foffy and my sister is amazing. I told
Margot about her but she didn't believe me. Nothing in America
is real to Margot, it's so strange."

"Your visit sounded awful."

"It was. You can't go home again — Wolfe was right — especially to Germany. You know, Madeleine, they've had to rewrite the Second World War in order to survive, and as a result they live in a curious vacuum. Events in the rest of the world don't really affect them. They were so detached about Watergate, they felt sorry for Nixon. *Der Spiegel* ran that photo of him and Julie hugging and everyone kept saying, 'All politicians do things like that, the Americans take things too seriously.' " Hans stopped, fiddled with the thread that lay between them on the couch.

"The only person I felt anything for was my cousin who is an engineer. He married a Greek girl and they live in Innsbruck, which is better than Hamburg or Berlin, but he's thinking of leaving. He says there's no intellectual life left. That's because they've had to deny so much of their own history. They can't analyze the past, or the present, either. All they want is what's new — like Russia after the Revolution. Historical process has no meaning there; he says he doesn't want to bring up his children in Germany."

"Where will he go?"

"He'd like to go to England, but it's so hard to make a living there. It's really the most civilized place on earth with the worst economic situation. Honestly, Madeleine, the world is topsy-turvy."

Mady smiled at the incongruous informality in his speech. "What are the young people like?" she asked.

"I don't know. My nephews are quite young, Foffy's age, and my cousins in their twenties scattered after the funeral — one is a pediatrician, two are lawyers, another works in the government as an economist. But the young people I observed looked familiar — lots of motorcycles, leather jackets, sports cars. They have plenty of money and like to enjoy themselves. Rock concerts advertised all over the place. Margot and I went to the opera one night but it was filled with middle-aged people — like us."

Now Mady raised her eyebrows. He laughed. "Like me. You know, you look marvelous. So much younger than you did at the beach. You must have had a restful summer."

She stared at him. Was he teasing her?

"No, I mean it. You're so tanned, and, well, relaxed. Not as tense as you were then," he added. He was talking to her like an old friend, like Dan French or one of David's colleagues. He had been invited for dinner and he had settled himself in her house and he was treating her as if he had known her for years. How dare he tell her she looked tense at the beach? He had liked her well enough then! Her hands trembled as she went back to her needlepoint, but he was oblivious. He was sitting on the floor again, showing Peter a fine point of the game.

Abruptly she put down the needlepoint and stood up. She had to walk, move a little. "I'm going to get another log," she told Foffy, then hurried out to the back door. She pulled on an old gardening jacket and stood in the crisp moonlight. She took a few deep breaths. The air held a scent of autumn. When she was a child, she had always loved winter, and now, for the first time in two years, she didn't dread it. Hans was right. She was more relaxed. So why was she so angry? Because he could see the truth? Or because the seeing implied intimacy? But what did she want? She had waited to hear from him and when she hadn't she had been disappointed. Then he had finally written and called. She couldn't deny the pleasure she had felt at hearing his voice on the phone. Yet now she wanted him to keep his distance. Oh, damn it, why was she so bewildered, she was behaving like a child!

She walked toward the woodshed and pulled the hook from its ring. The door creaked open. On one side was the neatly stacked woodpile, exactly as David had left it. Next to the woodpile were the flowerpots that had been tossed in carelessly. In the moonlight their open empty tops were gaping mouths. Strands of soil dripped like blood from their lips. She shuddered. Death lurks everywhere. She put down the log and spent a few minutes to set the pots into neat harmless stacks.

She would ask Hans to go. Now. She wanted to put Foffy to bed alone, she didn't want him lingering with her in front of the fire. She had fed him dinner, she had heard about his trip, she had reciprocated for the meal at the beach, now she wanted him to go.

She was being absurd. This meal had nothing to do with the meal at the beach; she had invited him tonight because she wanted to see him again, to talk to him, to sort out her feelings, which had frightened her when they were folk dancing. And he had come to see her as a friend. Maybe more than a friend. He was an intelligent man, and what did she expect? They weren't children, after all. Yet, in an uncanny way she had the feeling that David was watching her every moment of this endless evening, and that if she allowed Hans to step further into her life she would be betraying her dead husband.

Her voice was cold when she entered the living room. "Come along, Foffy, time for bed." The child jumped a little. The older children looked up, they knew that tone of voice. Where had it come from? Nina's eyes asked. She was blaming everyone but herself for what was clearly her problem. An old friend of Libby's once said that people get married so they have someone to complain to. Another more forthright woman had disagreed: "No, it's so they can have someone to blame for whatever goes wrong." That last remark sounded like her friend Dore, but Mady had heard that conversation when she was around Nina's age. Was she looking for someone to blame? she wondered as she and Foffy walked down the hall.

She sat on Foffy's bed while Foffy brushed her teeth. She had crowded herself, she had painted herself into this corner. But then, she told herself, try to be reasonable. This is the first time a strange man has stepped into the house, there were bound to be problems. It couldn't be easy for him, either. To walk into her home, David's home, surrounded by his children, his garden, his presence in the furniture, the rugs, the pictures, the books. On the coffee table was David's report to the Attica Commission, published after he had died.

"I pity the exile's lot. / Like a felon, a man half-dead / Dark is your path, wanderer . . ." Akhmatova's lines surfaced in her head. But Hans had chosen his exile's state, she wasn't responsible for him or his predicament.

She took a long time tucking Foffy in. "Tell me a story," the child teased, knowing it was too late.

"I'll tell you a story about Jack-a-Nory and now my story's begun, I'll tell you another about Jack and his brother and now my story's done." She gave Foffy one last hug and walked determinedly into the living room.

Hans sat with the atlas on his knees. Peter and Nina were on either side of him. "This belonged to the Kikuyu and that to the Masai. It was fascinating to live so close to both, they're so different," he was saying.

"Is there really a frozen tiger at the top of Kilimanjaro?"

"They say there's one on Kibo peak, that's the one with the glacier. Mawenzi, the other peak, doesn't have a glacier." Now Hans looked at Mady. "It's a good story, isn't it?" he said. She softened, smiled.

"A wonderful story, maybe the best thing he ever wrote." She had had a professor in college who said everyone should read "The Snows of Kilimanjaro" every five years. "It's about lost possibilities," he had said. He was a thin, almost bald man in his thirties with silver-rimmed glasses. "And laziness and temptation and unused talent and facing oneself." How hard it was to do that! She hadn't had an inkling of what that meant when she had sat in that young professor's office.

Peter got up and rubbed his back against the warm chimney. "Didn't you want to go back?" he asked Hans.

"I thought I might, but I couldn't. I felt that my brother's shadow was following me. My Aunt Johanna felt that way, too, and although she and my uncle wanted me to come back to the farm, they knew it was better for me to make a fresh start in a new country."

"But you had no one here, it must have been scary," Peter said.

"Some cousins in Philadelphia, an uncle on the coast. But I was in my twenties, hardly a child."

Still, Peter shook his head. He was trying to fathom the alone-ness of it. She couldn't have understood it at Peter's age, or even while she was still married. Being alone had always been half a life then, you must cling to your family. What were they for? she had thought. She had even thought that after she was widowed, and now — well, she was changing her mind, but she certainly didn't want to discuss it.

"Come on, Peter, time for bed," she said. She was exhausted and relieved when Nina and Peter finally left.

"They are wonderful children," he said and closed the atlas. Was he going to give her a lecture on her children? She concen-trated on her needlepoint. In Foffy's room she had been sure she would find the right words to tell him to go; now the air between them filled with a stubborn silence.

Finally she whispered, "I think you'd better go." She couldn't look up.

"What?"

"I think you'd better go," she repeated, then looked at him.

"Is that what I traveled two hours each way to hear — 'I think you'd better go'?" His tone was incredulous, his eyes amazed.

"What did you travel two hours each way to hear?" she asked in a defiant voice. If he thought he could bully her he was wrong.

"Well, certainly not to be told to go as soon as we have a min-ute alone," he said. For him the discussion was merely begin-ning. She bent her head to her work.

Silence hung between them. When she looked up she saw she had made a horrible mistake in asking him here. He had taken it as a sign she cared for him; he was gazing at her now with be-nign amusement, waiting for her to relax, maybe even fall into his arms. Her body stiffened, she avoided his eyes.

"Why did you ask me here?" he said gently and stood up and leaned against the mantel.

I wanted to tell you about that crazy interview I had with Maximilian Solomon, I wanted to hear about your trip, maybe I even wanted to desire you, but I wanted the man I remembered from the beach — that more for-mal, distant, shyer man who looked older, less attractive, who wanted companionship, she would have liked to say. But she was lying to herself. This man standing here was the same Hans she had danced with. Maybe he looked different, but he was the same man. Yet now the sight of him frightened her.

"I don't know. Maybe I did know when you called. I was glad you called, I wanted to see you again, but when you came into the house something happened. You're the first man who's been here since David died, and the minute you walked in there were ghosts of him all over the place. I'm sorry, terribly sorry." She bit her lip and shook her head. She sought his glance, expecting sympathy.

Instead, fury raged in his eyes, contorted his mouth. When he spoke, his voice was cold. "So am I." Then he turned, a variation on some military turn he must have learned when he was in the army, and stopped and stared at her again.

"Do you think people are puppets that you can manipulate? Did you think I was some sort of sideshow for your children? What did you think when you invited me here?"

"I told you. I wanted to see you again, I felt drawn to you, but when you came you brought David with you."

"I brought David with me? That's absurd, Madeleine, and you know it."

"What are you saying?"

"I'm saying that it's difficult to extricate yourself from the past, no one knows that better than I. It took me years and years to accept Karl's death and all that it meant to me and my family. But at least I did it alone, I didn't involve other people. I certainly didn't invite people to dinner, then kick them out."

"I'm not kicking you out."

"What would you call it?" His voice was harsher now than ever. She could feel her eyes begin to fill, she was starting to hate him. What did he want from her, why had she ever gotten involved with this intense strange man who wouldn't even leave when she wanted him to?

"You sit there and work on that needlepoint that you drag with you wherever you go like a cripple drags his crutch and it's as if all your feelings are being sewn into that damned thing just so you won't have to deal with them."

"What do you mean?" She put down the needlework and stood up and faced him. They were almost the same height. "How dare you talk to me like that, you barely know me."

"I know you well enough to know you're running for your life and blaming David for it. Ghosts. I brought David with me! That's crazy, Madeleine. David's dead and you have to face it. And grow up. We're not teenagers, after all!" He practically flung the last sentence at her as he turned and walked to the hall. For a second she couldn't move, she felt as if he had slapped her. Then she hurried after him. His raincoat was thrown over his shoulder and his hand was on the doorknob. Now he was the tight controlled man she had seen on the beach, but that control was more frightening to her than his outburst.

"You didn't think I had a temper, did you?" he asked. Before she could answer he was gone.

She watched the Fiat pull away. Not a look backward, not a wave, nothing. A proud angry man. More than she could cope with. "A man half-dead / Dark is your path, wanderer . . ." But he wasn't half-dead. At times, when he hid beneath that controlled exterior he appeared half-dead, but now she knew why she had been interested in him. Beneath that controlled exterior was a man with feelings, and passion, and a temper. Nor was he a wanderer. He was better rooted in his life in Racer's Cove than most of the people she knew who had had easier, less eventful lives. What was he? That was what she had wanted to know, that was part of what had pulled her toward him, but now she would never know. Slowly she walked to her room. She would do the pots in the morning. Then she remembered the garbage. Let the ants come, let them devour every bit of it, she didn't care.

As she undressed, her body felt sore, as it had soon after David died. She had hated that soreness then, but now it was a relief from that bleached dryness she had been feeling for so long. How she had looked forward to seeing Hans. She had made a fantasy of him these months. She was good at that. For almost two years she had created a fantasy out of David and he had stayed close by her, as all obedient fantasies do. But even she had known she couldn't live like that forever. So when she met Hans she had fantasized about him. But he was too compelling, too fierce for her, and it was just as well that this evening had happened now, that they hadn't gotten more involved and then had to part. For the future he would be a man she had met at the beach, with whom she had spent a few evenings. She lay there rigid in bed, her neck muscles taut. She had made a terrible mistake, and that was that. In the morning she would write him a note, and one of these days, when she least expected it, she would meet someone else.

Then she remembered that she hadn't told him about Maximilian Solomon, and for some reason that made her feel worse than ever.

CHAPTER 15

THE NEXT MORNING she awoke feeling lethargic, still depressed. When the doorbell rang during breakfast, she opened the front door eagerly. Woody Levin stood there with a long white paper in his hand. He looked sheepish, uncomfortable. A visit from Woody was rare. Like her parents he couldn't stay in the house long, and although he was quick to help her if she needed him, he never just dropped in.

"Coffee?"

"Okay." He sat down.

"What's that?" Nina pointed to the paper.

"A petition to the county for the creation of David Glazer Park," he said quickly and looked toward the doorway as if he expected David to be standing there, laughing a small mocking laugh. "A lot of people on the hill want the name. And he did do the preliminary legal work for it."

How strange to see Woody behaving so awkwardly, Mady thought. He would probably be surprised to learn that what touched her even more than the petition was his discomfort. Woody was probably the most private man she knew and his wish to have something tangible in David's memory and his journey through the neighborhood with this petition in hand moved her more than he could know. But Peter was frowning.

"What's the matter?" she asked.

Peter shrugged. "I don't know. Except that I don't think Dad would have liked it too much."

Woody nodded. "I know how you feel, Peter, I felt that way at first. But then I began to think — what can a man leave behind? His children, his work, which will certainly be remembered, and then something of his spirit, which is harder to point to than you kids or the work on Attica. A small park tells something of David's spirit, what he cared about, what we all care about. We all felt so helpless . . ." His voice trailed off. ". . . At least we can preserve a little of his spirit." He looked totally defeated. He had once admitted to Mady that there were days when he woke and started for the phone to tell David something. Maybe Woody needed an actual piece of land, formally named, to have the realization complete and final. Mady prepared herself to convince Peter, but her son had seen it for himself; he was nodding.

"I get you," he said and held out his hand for the petition. "I'll sign for all of us," he said and wrote The Glazer Family.

Now suddenly, everyone was starving although they hadn't been much interested in eating before Woody arrived. While she made the eggs Mady heard the children tell Woody about Hans. They were so enthusiastic, what was it that attracted them to him? It couldn't be just the gifts. Was it that he had never known their father? That he didn't remind them of David? His foreignness? She didn't know, but whatever it was, they would have to get over it, because they weren't going to see Hans anymore. After the kids left the table she was surprised by Woody's stony expression. She frowned at him.

"He's a German, you know how I feel about Germans," Woody said.

"Oh, Woody, you're jumping the gun, that's not like you." She hesitated, but he didn't answer. "You're wrong, dead wrong. He's not for me, he's too intense, too serious." Woody stared at her now, relieved, yet not quite sure she was telling the truth.

She sighed. This was ridiculous, but on principle she felt compelled to come to Hans's defense. "Really, Woody, I'm not going to get involved with him, but not because he's a German. And he's not your typical German, if there is such a thing — which I doubt. He left Germany because he couldn't live there after the war. He was brought up in Africa. If anything, he's more English than German because of the tie to Kenya. His twin brother was killed in the war and he hates Germany. Even this last visit when his mother died was painful for him."

Woody shook his head, virtually interrupting her with the gesture. He murmured, "A German is a German is a German," then looked at her hard and added more firmly, "is a German."

"Honestly, Woody, you're more stubborn than even David knew," she muttered and began to clear the table.

"I'm sorry, Mady, I have a blind spot on that subject."

"Obviously." Her voice was harsher than she intended. She sat down in an attempt to make peace.

Let's change the subject, his eyes said. *I'm only your dead husband's old friend, I'm not your keeper.* But Mady didn't need a keeper. Damn it, why was everyone so eager to tell her they couldn't help her, what was she, an invalid? Well, maybe that's what she had looked like these last two years, but that was over. She tried to make her voice as casual as she could. "Do you think there's a chance the village will vote for the park the first time?"

Now Woody relaxed. "It looks good. I think the national situation will help, too. Now that Nixon is out and Ford is in people are more interested in honesty, grass roots, ecology. It's the right time to push something like this through. And if it does go through, why shouldn't it be named for David?" he added, unsure of himself again.

"It should, Woody. He would be pleased," she said.

Woody nodded gratefully. When he rose his voice was subdued, bewildered. "Gail called last night. Fred's gone again. He's very depressed. He told her there was someone he had loved for a long time, but she doesn't want him and now he has to sort out his life. He has to be by himself, he said. Gail says she's relieved but she sounds as if she'd like to scream at the top of her lungs."

Mady could feel the color leave her face; even her hands

blanched as she looked down. How could she have been so stupid? She was the woman Fred referred to. She was the lonely repressed woman he had been planning to save. As she reviewed the phone calls, his visit, she realized she had only been encouraging his self-deception. She was to be next in Fred's line of women that probably extended from the Hudson River to Long Island Sound along the lush, spiraling streets of Westchester. And she had encouraged Gail to stay married, and had thought she could convince him to be sensible. What a fool she was! How naive! Shame for what she had done overwhelmed her and for a moment she wanted to tell Woody the whole thing. But that would be useless, no one would understand. They might even think she had intervened because unconsciously she saw Fred as a man on the loose. Maybe in some primitive way she had. Who knew? In the last day her assumptions and emotions seemed so unreliable. She was grateful when Woody walked to the door.

"One month he's home, the next month he's gone," Woody said. "It must be like living on a seesaw for her. Fred's gone crazy, Mady, the whole world's gone crazy," he said, then kissed her briefly and left. Watching him go down the steps, Mady felt more vulnerable right now than she had ever felt in her life.

So it was a comfort to drive a few hours later into an area untouched by the craziness of the world. Where Sarah Glazer lived had the sepia tranquillity of old photographs, and as Mady drove through the orderly grid of streets with their symmetrical attached houses and impeccable stoops and postage stamps of grass, she marveled at how little of the present had intruded here. Visiting Sarah was walking into the past, into David's childhood, into safety.

Today only Foffy came along. She liked to sit in Sarah's living room and watch the sailboats tacking in the nearby boat basin. She had brought along her Kate and Jancsi dolls, she wanted her grandmother to make a quilt for them.

Sarah was waiting for them on the front steps. Creases of pleasure outlined her eyes as she embraced them, but when Mady circled Sarah's body with her arms she was taken aback by its fragility. They hadn't seen each other since the fourth of July weekend — first Sarah had visited her son Gil and his family in Boston and Cape Cod, then in August she had gone to Lakewood and spent six weeks with her cousins. In a few short months she had aged; her small bundle of a body stopped more frequently on the dim-lit stairs, and even though she wore heavy support stockings her ankles were swollen. At the top of the stairs Sarah hugged Foffy to her again, but Mady knew it was a stalling mechanism to give her time to catch her breath. Mady's fingers throbbed with fear.

Mady and Sarah had always loved each other, and now that Mady was older she knew it wasn't luck, as she had thought, but because Sarah had welcomed her from the beginning, from the day David first brought her home to meet his parents. Such devotion between a woman and her daughter-in-law was unusual, but then Sarah was unusual. She fascinated Mady. An intensely religious woman who believed unequivocally in God, Sarah accepted whatever happened with an incredible sense of calm and dignity. Whatever happened was fated, *beshaert*, ordained in the Book of Life. One must find the strength to live. And to love. His mother's orthodoxy had exasperated David. "It strangles her mind," he had said, but as Mady matured she had disagreed. The more she watched Sarah go about her daily life, the more she saw how Sarah's religion was the foundation of her existence. It regulated her days, it gave her a sense of knowing who she was, why she was here. By *Shabbos* one finished one's work and could rest and pray; if joy came one laughed, if sorrow came one survived. God's will be done. Don't torture yourself with questions, there are no answers even if the questions themselves are magnificently phrased.

Grief was not a personal punishment, it was part of the cycle of life, the endless flow of events. When questioned about catastrophes — an earthquake or Hitler or Vietnam or Kent

State — Sarah would answer, imperturbably, "There is a reason, it may not be clear to us, but there is a reason."

Yet her passive response to the big issues was balanced by a remarkably active life. Never was she still as she made a home, cooked and cleaned and sewed and shopped and comforted her family and the community around her. Sarah was a *neshuma*, a gift. For her the true sin was cruelty and as long as she had to live she would be kind. She also believed in happiness and music and could not go to bed without reading *The Jewish Daily Forward*.

When David died, those close to Sarah feared for her. She was seventy-nine years old, her husband had died the year before after a long struggle with stomach cancer, David was her youngest child. Yet Sarah survived better than anyone. After the funeral she came to stay with Mady and the children; everyone thought Sarah would move in with them. But one morning Mady woke to find Sarah's suitcases in the front hall. "I'm going home," she said serenely as she set out breakfast. Mady's limbs had gone numb with apprehension. She tried to persuade Sarah to stay.

"No," the old woman had said, her gray eyes as piercing then as David's black eyes had been so often. "You've got to learn to live alone with your children, you must find the courage to go on and the longer I stay, the harder it will be for you to begin."

Of course she was right. And they had both known it then.

Now, as they entered the apartment, Sarah pulled a hankie from her cuff and wiped her perspiring face. Her flowered housedress was crisp, her black shoes reflected the light, she sat erect, but she wasn't well.

"I'm so tired," she said after she had sent Foffy for her sewing basket. "After that wonderful summer I'm still so tired. Maybe people like me shouldn't go on vacation."

"Now, Ma, don't say that. It was so good for you. This just isn't a good day, you should have said so when I called, we could have come next week. Do you want to lie down?"

Sarah refused and she and Foffy began to sift through scraps of fabric for a quilt. Mady looked around the apartment. A dust ball, formerly unheard of in Sarah's home, was making its way along the periphery of the room. And the pillows, usually straight as soldiers, were limp, crushed. The silver behind the glass doors of the china closet was tinged with the glint of tarnish, pictures on the walls were crooked.

Suddenly, Mady knew that Sarah was going to die very soon and that Sarah knew it, too. Death had settled into the room, weighing down the air, and even if you tried to chase it, as you might the skittering dust ball, it would only seem to disappear. Panic rose into Mady's throat, filled her eyes. She tried to reason with herself: Sarah would be eighty-one in April, she had had a heart condition for years, she had had edema during the last several months, her skin had lost the shine that used to annoy Libby so much. Sarah was an old woman; if you saw her on the street you might admit, practically, it was time. Yet watching her white head bent so close to Foffy's blonde one, Mady wanted to shout, "It's not fair!" although Sarah would be the first to say, "No one promised it would be fair, but I have had my chance, so let me go in peace, please don't make such a fuss."

At lunch Sarah picked at her food. "I didn't have much of an appetite even when someone else was cooking," she confessed ruefully. The hot coffee was the only thing she welcomed; she hugged the cup in her small time-roughened hands as she watched Foffy pin the scraps of material together.

"Do red and orange go, Grandma?"

"Of course they go, everything goes, nothing clashes anymore. So you remember when people wouldn't wear green and blue, Mady?" Sarah said, her voice trembling with forced gaiety.

The end was near, but who knew what near meant? When Foffy lay down for a rest, Mady poured Sarah a second cup of coffee, then said, "Ma, have you thought about coming to us for a while?" The thought of Sarah dying alone was more than she could bear.

Sarah looked at her with approval. She liked direct questions.

"Yes, I have, and I've decided against it. But Mrs. Wadler's niece is staying with her until she can save enough to get her own place, and their apartment is small so I've asked her to sleep here with me. Some of her things are in the guest room already."

How matter-of-fact Sarah sounded. Resignation emanated from her, yet she was still in charge of her life. Mady wished David could see his mother now. And after Mady's question, which she had clearly been expecting, Sarah seemed less tired. She wanted to know about Nina and Peter, and then Max and Libby. "How's Mother?"

"Fine, I guess. I don't know, maybe a little better, she has more color lately. I'm not sure," Mady admitted.

"Be patient with her, Mady, it's hard for people like Libby to accept the accidents of life."

Why should it be harder for her than for you, you were his mother, Mady wanted to ask, but it was useless. In Sarah's code, the more privileged your life was, the more privileges you deserved, because you had never learned how to cope with adversity. She could take sorrow better than Libby for the simple reason that she had known more sorrow.

Then Sarah said, "And what about you? What have you been doing now that Foffy is gone all day?"

"I'm going to look for a job, something part-time to start, and close to home. I don't think I'm ready to go into the city yet."

Sarah nodded. "With your music?" she asked. She had always been convinced Mady should teach piano; whenever she came to visit them when the children were little, Mady had had to play. Were it not for Sarah she wouldn't have kept up with the piano, she often said.

"Maybe, I don't know. I'm very rusty. I heard about a publishing house that was doing some translation of the Russians, but it didn't work out." She wanted to go on, but now Sarah's eyes were distant, distracted. When you were going to die, did you know it every second, or did that knowledge visit you at odd unexpected moments?

"Are you sure you don't want to lie down?" Mady asked.

But Sarah straightened and her eyes brightened. "Now, who is this Hans who brought Foffy the dolls?" she said.

Mady chuckled. Leave it to Sarah to know what to ask. "Oh, we met him at the beach and then he had to go back to Germany because his mother was ill and she died and when he came home he called and then came up for dinner last night." She smiled at her run-on explanation; she sounded like Foffy. When her eyes met Sarah's, she hoped for the remoteness she had seen before; instead, they were filled with curiosity.

"Foffy's crazy about him. She also said she thought you liked him, especially at the beach."

Mady laughed with relief. "That little gossip. Well, she's right. I did like him, and we spent a few evenings together, but when he came last night it was terrible, all wrong. I'll never see him again, though God knows how I'm going to tell that to Foffy."

"Oh?" Sarah's eyebrows were raised and now she didn't look so old. "What happened?"

"Everything. The minute he walked in I felt as if we were both trespassing in David's house. David was watching us, disapproving. You know, I had forgotten this until now, but a few nights after we met Hans at the beach I dreamt that he and David were walking toward me on the shore. They were talking at first, then arguing. By the time they reached me David was angry. I had the feeling David was angry last night."

"But David is dead, Mady."

"I wish I could convince myself of that."

"You must convince yourself. You're too young to be living with a dead husband. Believe me, I know what that's like, I still live with Daniel, but I'm an old woman. You are still so young!"

Mady felt her eyes fill. She shrugged. "I can't help it. David was still in the house last night. When I asked Hans to go, he got angry, he said it was hard to extricate yourself from the past but that I had to do it, he also said I had to grow up . . ." The words cascaded out of her in such a rush that even she was surprised.

"Well." Sarah smiled. "He sounds like a man who speaks his mind."

Mady nodded. "He didn't seem to, until last night. He's very controlled most of the time, too controlled. Seeing that he has a temper came as a bit of a relief, but it doesn't matter, I'm not going to see him anymore. He's too intense, complicated . . ."

"All interesting people are intense and complicated," Sarah observed quietly, then took off her glasses and wiped them. "It sounds as if this Hans cares for you, Mady."

Mady shook her head. "He's so different." Her shoulders slumped for a moment, then something stirred in her, and she wanted to explain it to Sarah. If she could tell it to Sarah, maybe she would understand it herself.

"He seems to have made his peace with the world in such a passive way. His brother was killed in the war in a training accident while they were fighting in the Hitler Youth, he had to leave Europe, he couldn't go back to Africa where he had been brought up, and he has this house in Racer's Cove and he works in the school — he teaches art — and does his ceramics. It seems like such an ordinary life. Yet I have the feeling that he's not at all passive, I have the feeling that if you could get through to what he really is, you would find — oh, I don't know, Ma. After last night, I think it's useless. I have the children to worry about, and myself. I've got to get out in the world, I have to find a job, and I don't think I have the energy to deal with such a difficult man. He needs someone younger, with more strength . . ."

"But you are young, you have practically another lifetime ahead of you," Sarah interrupted.

"Maybe for someone else, but not Hans. And besides, he isn't Jewish," she said, then blushed at her stupidity when Sarah burst out laughing. How good to see Sarah laugh! Well, at least this discussion about Hans had served some purpose.

"Of course he's not Jewish. How could he be Jewish, you silly child?" Sarah said as she wiped the tears from her eyes and continued to chuckle. With anyone else Mady would have felt like a fool, with Sarah she leaned back and smiled and tried not to think of the future when Sarah would be gone.

Sarah looked out the window; when their eyes met her expression had changed. "Do you think you're the only Jewish woman who has been attracted to a gentile man?" she asked, and her voice flowed as if through lazy still water, and she smoothed her dress over her knees. "Let me tell you a story, Mady," she said, then tucked her hankie into her cuff and began. "You remember that my family had money before the First World War, that my father was a lawyer and his mother and father had been close to people in the Austrian palace. My father went to the University of Linz and we lived in a small town not far from Vienna. I was the youngest of eight children — three daughters and four sons and then me. My parents didn't like to leave me alone when they went on holiday, and by the time I was a teenager my brothers were at college or working and my sisters were married. Two had had children before I was born." Mady nodded. She and her children were always fascinated that Sarah had nephews and nieces who were older than she was.

"In the summer of 1912 I wanted to visit my brother Robert, who was in Paris, but my mother thought I was too young, so she and my father took me with them to Mont Blanc. My father was a great hiker, and so was my mother after she got finished having children.

"The first night after we arrived I remember looking out over those Alps in utter amazement, for they were much higher than the Austrian Alps I knew in the Öztal or Kitzbühel. These were real mountains, just as my father had promised. I couldn't wait to go out with him the next morning. But that very night I became ill, with a fever and stomach cramps, and wouldn't you know it? I had appendicitis. The regular doctor in town was away, so they sent a young man only a few years out of medical school. But he was well-trained and with the help of the local midwife and my mother, who was an incredibly brave woman, he took my appendix out. It was very exciting, really the most excitement that little town had had for a very long time, and to make it even more wonderful, the hotel keeper started a rumor that we were wealthy Austrians from an excellent family, related distantly to the nobility. That my father was a Jew who had reached the top of his profession and made lots of money never seemed to occur to them. And it didn't matter to anyone but me, in the end.

"The young doctor came to see me every day. I had been his first operation, and it went so well. I was also young and pretty and he was uncommonly handsome — very fair and tall, almost Scandinavian-looking. He might have had some Danish blood. Magnificent gray eyes and a wonderfully easy manner. We would spend hours talking while my parents were out hiking. The waitresses would bring an enormous tea and he used to lick his fingers after he ate the sachertorte. The hotel had a Viennese cook. 'Never was there such sachertorte!' he would exclaim.

"Now, remember that I had been very sheltered. I didn't even go to school, tutors came to the house, and here was this beautiful young man. Of course I fell madly in love with him. He had a new theory — that mental health affected the recovery in tuberculosis and if he could treat people in an entirely different way he was sure he could cure them faster. His plans sounded marvelous to me. He talked to me as an equal, and I had never been happier. As I got better we would stroll around the gardens. In the background were the snowy glittering peaks — you would have had to be made of stone not to have fallen in love.

"After we got back to Austria he came to visit us and a few months later my sister's family went skiing and they took me along and he met us. My sister's marriage wasn't very good and she was an incurable romantic — really a child in many ways — and she encouraged me in what had now become a love affair. Not that I blame her, Mady, I was so happy, and it never occurred to either of us that he would not marry me. I was going to be nineteen in April. And he was earning a living. Besides, we were not orthodox Jews. My sister and I were sure we could convince my parents to let me marry him, and all during that long winter we kept rehearsing what we would say. But soon after my birthday I received a letter from him. He had met a very rich woman who was several years older than he. He didn't love her, but she had offered to give him the money he needed for the sanatorium. He would always love me, but I was young and would have lots of chances for happiness. He was older than I — already in his late twenties — and such an opportunity might never come again. Besides, I was a Jew and he was not, that would cause complications when children came, and so on. He had a dozen reasons. None of them meant a thing to me. I wrote back and told him how much I loved him, certain he would come and get me. He never answered my letter but sent my sister a clipping from the newspaper that announced his marriage.

"I thought I was going to die. My mother, who knew the whole story by now, kept me busy from morning till night. It was during that time that I became so religious. My mother had the idea that religion could help a person get through all kinds of difficulty so she had a tutor come and teach me Hebrew and the Talmud, as if I were a young boy about to be bar mitzvah, and even though the war had begun.

"Then after the war so much changed. Austria was no longer a separate entity, and my father had always hated the German influence. Anti-Semitism, which had been suppressed for years, surfaced again with a vengeance. We had to leave a great deal of money behind for my sisters and brothers who felt they had to remain, but in 1919 we came to America — my parents and I and my brother Robert, whom you know, and my brother George, who stayed here for a while and then settled in England and died just before you and David met. We had cousins in New York and we stayed with them and one of them was a close friend of a young doctor named Daniel Glazer. The minute my mother saw Daniel she said he would be my husband, but I didn't even want to speak to him. I thought all doctors were the same."

Now Sarah's eyes were filled with laughter. "You know, Mady, I never told Daniel the whole story although one of the first things he wanted to know about after we were married was my appendectomy. He admired the scar — it was the thinnest line you can imagine. Now I can't even find it. At first I felt badly about not telling Daniel. He was such a good husband and I loved him more than I had loved that young Swiss because love grows if you're lucky like Daniel and I were. But before my mother died she said, 'Better not tell him, there are things no one needs to know.' After she died and my sister was killed in the camps no one knew but me. For years and years I would forget it, then some item in the news or some casual remark would bring it all back. Now, after sixty years, it seems impossible that it happened, but it did."

Sarah wiped her hairline with her hankie and took off her glasses and rubbed them. Her upper lip was beaded with perspiration. Mady didn't know what to say, but the silence between them was comfortable, pleasant.

After Foffy woke up, Mady said, "Why don't we leave the quilt and Grandma can finish it when she has time?"

Sarah and Foffy shook their heads. So she sat there and leafed through the paper while they sewed and chatted. Had Sarah been afraid after that first drastic plunge? Or had that first experience been enough to satisfy her for a lifetime, and was that the answer to her outward acceptance?

Finally the quilt was finished. How uneven the stitches were! For a second Mady considered calling the children and saying she and Foffy would stay here overnight, but that was the last thing Sarah wanted.

"Isn't it beautiful, Mommy? Grandma Sarah is the best sewer in the world."

Sarah smiled wanly. "Used to be a good sewer, Foffy darling. Now Grandma is tired."

When Foffy went to put the basket away Sarah said quickly, in a whisper, "Don't be afraid of love, Mady, it's all that matters in the world. You had it with David, but that's gone, you can't live on memories, you're still so young." Her voice was a thread.

And again, when they kissed good-bye, she said, "Don't be afraid." Foffy asked, "Afraid of what?" But no one answered.

The house blared with Bob Dylan when she opened the back door. Peter and his friends were sprawled in the living room and she could hear voices from Nina's room. She liked the feeling of the house being full, but now, as she thought of Sarah, the noise was too much. She resented the bodies of Peter's friends all over the furniture.

"Anyone call?" she shouted.

"Aunt Shelley and Grandma Libby," Peter answered and for a moment total silence. What a relief! But they were only turning the record over. Mady practically ran to her room.

How big Peter's friends had gotten! And in such a short time. She felt overwhelmed by their physical presences, their awkward deference when they greeted her. They were almost men. She slipped out of her shoes and lay down on her bed.

How hard it was to see someone you loved get so old, so frail. When she was a young girl she had imagined that one would be more accepting as one got older, but to her Sarah was no older than the woman she had first met when she had come home with David from college. And soon Sarah would die. Knowing that, perhaps she should heed Sarah's words. Maybe the dying see more clearly than we do. Perhaps she should call Hans; it was 1974, after all, and she could make a move. Especially if she was sorry about what had happened last night. And the more she thought about it, the sorrier she was.

From where she was lying she could see the note she had written to Hans early this morning. A cold distant note calculated to push him away, into safer territory. After listening to Sarah she wasn't sure that was what she wanted. She was utterly confused, but the one thing she knew was that she didn't want to do anything precipitous. She got up and went to her desk. The tiny pieces of ragged paper fluttered quickly to the bottom of the wastebasket and she went into the kitchen to make dinner.

CHAPTER 16

"WELL, DO YOU LOVE HER?"

Hans stared. He and his friend Rosa Whitman were sitting on the deck of his house. A fiery sun spread a film of ochre over everything in sight — the waves glistened with a coppery tinge as they curled toward shore, and the trees and scrub pine and old slate roofs were bathed in a fine amber translucence. In a few minutes the light would become pinker, with mauve tones. It was now, these few minutes of an autumn sunset, that Hans loved best. The brief eerie light had the tawny luster of his childhood. He had seen it in some of Georgia O'Keeffe's paintings and he had even taken a trip to Arizona in the late fifties, but it wasn't there. Then, the following fall, when he returned to Racer's Cove he had found it one cool clear evening, and now, as he sat here with Rosa, he savored the light the way other men might savor fresh bread or a favorite perfume.

Only five days had passed since he had been to Madeleine's home. It might have been weeks, months. Each day he went to work and vowed to stop thinking about her, but he had failed, miserably. He had tried to work on the wooden head; the few strokes he carved were dull, lifeless, so he had put it aside, afraid of ruining the fine wood. By this morning the tension in him was so unbearable that he needed to talk to someone about Madeleine, so he had asked Rosa, his oldest friend in Racer's Cove, to come to dinner. She sat across from him in her elegant black peasant blouse and off-white pants and an unusual paisley shawl thrown over her narrow shoulders. Hanging from a chain around her neck was a Victorian baby's rattle that she wore very often. It was the first thing they had talked about when they met years ago; Hans had thought it was a shepherd's whistle from Europe and when she told him it was American he had been delighted. Now she fingered it and the tiny bells made a small sound as she repeated her question.

"Do you love her?"

Hans walked to the railing and looked down at Rosa. "I don't know. I don't know if I know what love is. I don't think I've ever been in love. Certainly I have never felt like this." He felt like a fool and sounded like an idiot. Rosa's eyes were amused, she had lifted her eyebrows, and her mouth was getting ready to laugh. That expression of hers usually gave him pleasure, but now he was annoyed at her and at himself. Still, he had gone this far, he couldn't turn back.

"It's true. I was fifteen when Karl was killed and for the next ten years I can't remember anything in detail — only the blurry veil of grief. Later, I must have been in my twenties by then, I read an article about sexuality in males, and when it talked about the strong sex drives in males in their late teens, I felt that I was reading about some ancient or faraway tribe. I had experienced none of it. Or if I had I couldn't remember it. But then I couldn't remember smelling or tasting or hearing either. I do remember visiting Johanna and Hans-Karl at the farm in 1950 and how happy I was to be back there in that tremendous space. But then I had to face my own isolation in a new way and I saw that as much as I may have wanted to, I couldn't stay. I had to go somewhere else, not burdened by memories. My next real recollection is of Montauk Point — how I responded to the sweetness of the morning sky, how homesick it made me for Africa until I realized that this was where I could live. Beyond those two incidents there isn't much from those years. My memory begins again when I started to rebuild this house, and by that time I was twenty-eight, I had been in America for two years, I had worked in Riverhead for a construction company and had had my own apartment. You know, Rosa, I can't even remember that apartment and it's only an hour away. Details begin to come back from the summer that I worked on the house. But the time in between — beginning with Karl's body twisting up into the air, suspended for a second, then exploding into fragments — those years are a blank."

Rosa began to try to form a sentence, then words failed her and she bent her head. He had never tried to describe Karl's death before.

"Tell me what happened! Try to tell me what happened!" His father said over and over, at first softly, then in a stifled scream. They were in the small office of the training camp. He sat there, staring straight ahead, seeing the contortions of his father's face, hearing his pain, but he couldn't open his mouth to speak. How could he ever hope to describe the impatient command that Karl refused to obey, then the threatening repetition of the command, then his own terror that the person giving the command had every intention of carrying it out, and then that air-splitting crack of rifle shot that ripped open his brother's body. As he sat there unable to obey his father, he could feel the images embedding themselves into his mind, and they stayed there for years and years, more years than he would have thought possible, even then.

"Leave him alone, please try to leave him alone," the commanding officer had pleaded with Friedrich. The man blamed himself for this tragic accident; he had not been there for that part of the training and his fanatic underling had killed Karl. "Maybe he can't remember, maybe it's nature's way of protecting him," the officer said to Friedrich in a tight voice. By then they were walking across a large field, perhaps the same field where the accident had occurred. Then Hans vaguely remembered riding with a long raw wood box that must have held Karl's shattered body, but where they were going he didn't know and had never figured out.

Hans shrugged under Rosa's steady glance. "I should have gone for therapy, but I didn't. I wasn't smart enough, I was ashamed of having to admit to someone that my father had dragged us back to Germany. I couldn't tell a stranger how much my father had adored Hitler. He talked about him the way another man might talk about a mistress. And then I was ashamed that I hadn't realized how much Karl hated the army, Europe, that training camp. If I had, maybe I could have prevented his death."

Still Rosa said nothing.

"You think I'm a fool, don't you?" He was surprised to hear himself sound so belligerent. "I guess I was. But all I wanted was to be able to get out of bed in the morning and support myself and then, after a while, to have this house. Sleeping within the sound of the waves was the first comfort I felt — the first night I slept here I felt as if I was being born again. It was like a heightened daydreaming all night and I could feel my body reaching for the sound of the waves, and after that I began to be able to see what was around me. Little things — the flowers, the swallows, the gulls strutting and the pipers struggling to keep up with them, the copper beech tree over there, the sky, the weather. Something had pulled me here and when I found the house — well, it was as if I had come to a home I didn't even know I had." Finally Hans smiled and Rosa found her voice.

"But after you settled in, wasn't there anyone you were attracted to? When I met you, you must have been about thirty-five, but I recall hearing you had gone out with someone at school, and wasn't there a woman who ran a gallery here in the summers? I remember some innuendoes about her."

Hans laughed. "The gossips are so imaginative — really failed writers, you know. There was a woman who ran a gallery, we used to have dinner sometimes. She was a wonderful woman, very lively and sharp, and something might easily have come of it, but she was mad about a married man. He used to come for part of the summer."

"Then what about the teacher?" From Rosa's expression Hans knew she was going to pursue this discussion as far as she could. But he had only himself to blame; he had started it.

"We were close for a time, I guess it was a bona fide affair. She wanted to marry. She was interested in art and a very bright woman — she was a French teacher. At first we seemed to have a lot in common. But we didn't, really. She wasn't much of a reader and she kept interrupting me when I was reading or if I wanted to listen to music, and by the time we met I wasn't ready to give either of those things up. We tried to talk about our differences and she finally admitted that she wasn't sure she really loved me, but she wanted to have a child more than anything else in the world. That was about" — Hans scratched his head — "I could have sworn it was about five years ago, but it seems to have been more like twelve." He shook his head in disbelief.

Rosa nodded. "It would be about that, because I've been here about eleven years."

"It doesn't seem possible," Hans murmured. There had been someone else, the woman he had met on vacation in Maine not long after Rosa moved to Racer's Cove. Hans had thought he loved her, they had considered marriage, then, abruptly, she had decided she wanted out. She was the one who had called him "goddamned controlled" and "a typical German" when they parted, and he had never told Rosa about her and he wasn't going to break his long silence now.

"So many years. I can't believe I'm forty-six." Now Hans looked at Rosa and said, "You know, I hadn't thought of my age in a real way for years and years, and then Madeleine's little girl, the very fair one, asked, 'How old are you?' and I had to think twice. I know she thought I was out of my mind."

Rosa laughed. "I know. I also know why my mother was always so angry on her birthday. She couldn't believe it was happening."

Rosa Whitman was fifty-five years old. She had grown daughters and had been divorced for almost fifteen years. She taught music in the local high school, she and Hans saw each other every day. She was also writing a biography of Clara Schumann. Her eyes had retreated with helplessness as he had talked about Mady. He should never have called her and burdened her with his problems.

"I've got to check the meat," Hans said now. He needed to be by himself for a minute. How had he been so foolish as to think that talking to Rosa would have helped? Her directness had only confused him more. How could a normal forty-six-year-old man not know whether he was in love? Was this feeling of panic that he felt each morning what people call love? When he opened his eyes all he wanted was to see Madeleine, to hear her voice. Once or twice he had been stricken with the irrational certainty that she was dead. By evening he had a ball of pain in his chest. Was pain what those songs and movies and books were all about? Or was this the form love took when you weren't young?

Rosa was standing at the railing looking out over the small village. Soon it would be black, for there were few lights in Racer's Cove to relieve the darkness; misty clouds obscured the moon and the pinprick lights of the autumn sky. From the back Rosa's body looked like a girl's. All those years of dancing had kept her straight and lithe, even her almost totally gray hair looked youthful as it fell in a thick mass down her back. Suddenly Hans realized what he had done. Here they were — close friends. Out of habit they spent at least one, often two or three evenings a week. When she finished chunks of her biography, he would read them, talk to her about them, suggest changes. It was a comfortable relationship, and the most meaningful one he had had since he moved to Racer's Cove. He and Rosa had never been intimate, but still — Rosa was a woman and he was a man and their friendship had the tension that is always there when friends are not of the same sex. He was close to his friend Hugh, he saw several couples in town, he loved his cousins Alfred and

Ernst and their wives and children, but his tie to Rosa had always been in a special category and they both knew it. And now he had asked her to come here so he could tell her he had met a woman who haunted him so steadily he could scarcely live with it, and he had expected Rosa to be sympathetic, to advise him. How crass he was, how thoughtless! Is this what love does to one's reason?

He took her arm and stood beside her. He looked down at her familiar fine features, her slight figure. "I'm sorry, Rosa, I have been an idiot, expecting you to help me work this out. Utterly stupid," he said. Dinner was pleasant but Rosa looked relieved when Hans suggested after coffee that they drive to Montauk and see *Lies My Father Told Me*.

The next morning Hans was up at dawn. While shaving he decided he would call Mady. Perhaps she could meet him at the Museum of Modern Art tomorrow. He had to go and pick up some slides. The radio was announcing a frost — was she digging around in the closet for heavier jackets for the children? He pictured her making breakfast, the children's lunches. Was she wearing a robe or did she get dressed before she went into the kitchen? Now that he had seen where she lived he was hungry for the details of her life. Which were, of course, none of his damned business. Perhaps it was that last fact that made him lose his nerve, for he didn't call her at lunch or when he got home after school. She knew where he was, she could get in touch with him if she wanted him.

For the first time in years the weekend loomed ahead of him and he was depressed by the thought of filling the next two days. How had he lived all these years alone? But he was being ridiculous. He was invited to Hugh's Saturday night, he planned to be in New York most of the day, and on Sunday there was a chamber-music concert that he and Rosa had tickets for. He would barely have enough time to prepare his classes and get the storm doors and windows on and finish reading *Doctor Zhivago*, which he had never read till now. Plenty to do, but none of it was very important, somehow. He wanted to see Madeleine, he wanted to go to the telephone and pick up the receiver and dial her number and speak in a reasonable, somewhat businesslike way about seeing her this weekend. But he knew he would frighten her if he called, so for the rest of the weekend he did everything he was supposed to do and spent whatever dead time there was between his obligations on the most tiring chores. By Sunday night the storm windows were on, the wood pile was twice as high as it had been on Friday, and the spare room had been painted a smooth alabaster.

By the end of the following week Hans was in a state of resignation. If he called her, what would he say? That he was sorry? For what? Losing his temper or falling in love with her? Obviously she wasn't going to call, or write. With her busy life she had undoubtedly put the evening into the back of her brain where it would slowly recede into a blur. He was certainly not going to come upon her in a library, as Zhivago had discovered Lara. New York in 1974 was far more complicated than Pasternak's vision of Russia during the Revolution, and, comforting as it was to read about lives so dependent on coincidence, one could not hope for that in real life. Hans put down the book and went to the kitchen to make a cup of warm milk. He had been sleeping badly all week, now it was Thursday night again. Another weekend to be gotten through. His whole body ached with this incessant waiting, and for what? Nothing. He would have to forget her, and he had lived through enough to know that he could. The brain can adjust to anything in time. That much he knew, even if he didn't seem to know much else. More time would have to pass before he could wrest the images of her and her children and her car and her house from the whirling that continued so rebelliously in his mind.

CHAPTER 17

MADY HUNG UP THE PHONE. Well, that was done; she had called Gil and Martin, David's brothers, and told them about Sarah. They would make arrangements to come over the weekend. Now she dialed Sarah's number and sighed, relieved, when she heard the equable voice of Mrs. Johnson, the nurse who had been hired only three days ago to stay with Sarah.

"I don't want to die in a hospital. Since Daniel's illness I've hated hospitals," Sarah had said simply. She even knew the name of a nurse who could come and stay. Mrs. Johnson was a large, kind black woman and well-known in the neighborhood. A specialist in dying. Whenever they spoke, her velvety, still southern voice comforted Mady.

"She's sleeping quietly. She doesn't have much strength, but she's holding her own. Her pulse is good, and the doctor called a little while ago. He said he'll stop by tomorrow."

"I know," Mady replied. The doctor had called her and told her it was time to get in touch with Gil and Martin. "I'll see you tomorrow afternoon, Mrs. Johnson, have a good night."

How long would Sarah last? No one knew. How wearing this was! When David died, she had thought it would be easier if death gave a warning, if they had had a little time. But this anxious limbo was terrible, more terrible in some ways than a sudden death.

She picked up the small address book near the phone, then leafed through it. She had called everyone she should about Sarah. She could call her mother again; Libby had been coming over each afternoon to meet Foffy's bus so Mady could visit Sarah. But nothing had changed, and they would talk in the morning. She glanced at the clock. Nine-fifteen. She could hear a record from Peter's room mingling with the strains of Chopin that Nina was practicing. Foffy was already asleep. She could read the paper or look at *Speak, Memory*, which she was reading to Sarah each afternoon, or she could give in and shower and go to bed. Waiting for death was exhausting, her body was weighted down, she could feel her shoulders slump as she stood there. She could call Anne, but she knew Anne was correcting papers, and they had talked before supper. She could try Gail, but she didn't know what to say, how she would begin, for she knew that someday they would have to talk about Fred and Mady's oblique involvement in his leaving. Not now, though, she couldn't go through that now. Then, without thinking, she found the number she wanted and dialed it. Later she tried to figure out what had possessed her, but while it was happening she felt as if someone else was moving her fingers.

"It's Mady, Madeleine Glazer," she said slowly, for it was a bad connection.

"I know," he replied.

"Hans, I hope it's not too late."

"No, no, I was reading, how are you?" His voice was padded with caution, but she had come this far, she might as well make a complete fool of herself.

"I'm fine, but Sarah, David's mother, has been very sick," she said. "I've been going to see her every day since I saw you." She paused, then waited, but she should have known better. He wasn't going to offer her any false comfort and it was his silence that made her long to see him again. He would let her talk about Sarah's coming death; he wouldn't make her feel guilty if she wanted to talk about it.

"Hans, I've thought a lot about what you said, and I'm sorry. I don't know what happened to me." Still he didn't answer. Why couldn't he make it a little easier for her? She stopped, trying to find the words to say she would like to see him again, when he offered, as a sign of truce: "My mother used to say I had a vile temper."

"Then she never saw a really vile temper," Mady said with a laugh. "How are you?"

"Fine, just fine. Getting the house ready for winter." Now his voice was more open. She breathed more normally. But what else could she say? She hesitated, almost defeated, then Sarah's words pounded in her ears. *Don't be afraid, don't be afraid.*

"I'd like to see you again," she heard herself say.

"I'm so glad," he said. And then, of course, it was easier.

"I've got to go back to the Museum of Modern Art on Saturday to return some slides. Could we have lunch?"

She thought for a moment. By Saturday Martin would surely be here and Gil said Saturday afternoon. She could let Max and Libby take the kids to Sarah's and she would meet them there. But wasn't this bizarre — to be planning a lunch date when Sarah was so plainly dying? Or maybe not. Maybe it was possible only then. "Don't be afraid." "You've been a brave girl, Mady." "You have a lot of courage, Mady." Little did they know, she thought, then acquiesced.

"Yes, I can. I'll take the train and then I can take a subway to Sarah's. My parents will drive the children out."

"I'll drive you to Sarah's," he said firmly.

"But why should you leave the city because I have to?" She found it comforting to try to work out the details; it made her forget what was really happening.

But Hans wasn't interested in them. "We'll talk about it Saturday. I'll see you in the main lobby at twelve noon," he said as casually as if they had been meeting every few weeks for months and months.

The large gray entrance crawled with people. Mady scanned the bench near the coat checkout. He wasn't there, but at the end was the woman who was always there. Dressed in a shabby green hat and coat and those ugly plastic galoshes (it had rained earlier), she sat, waiting. The last time Mady had come to the museum she had been with Gail — about six months ago — and Gail had told her the story of the old woman. She and her daughter were supposed to have fought and the daughter never called, but the old woman waited for her here almost every day because the daughter had majored in art history in college and this was as good a place as any to try to catch her. The woman stayed about an hour each day, then got up and left. Between the woman's veined legs was the same frayed Bloomingdale's bag she had had months ago. Today she looked more like a disappointed Harpo Marx than Mady remembered. Her white hair flew wildly around her hat, two deep lines extended from her large nose to the edges of her weary mouth. Her eyes darted endlessly as people kept pushing through the revolving doors.

"Ah, here you are!" He touched her lightly on the shoulder. She turned. She had been expecting him to whirl through the doors.

"I was in the library, they let me in before the museum opened. I have a special pass," he explained and took her arm and maneuvered her through the line, flashing his pass at the dour old ticket taker who had been here for as long as she could remember.

She liked being on his arm, she liked standing on the main floor of the Museum of Modern Art with Hans Panneman. Here she was no one's mother or widow or child or daughter-in-law. Here she was simply a woman in her late thirties standing next to a man she liked, going to look at these illustrious paintings or going to eat a simple lunch. She had so enjoyed walking, even in the rain, along Fifth Avenue from the station, and now she was enjoying the anonymity that freed her from her children and house and town.

But the anonymity was short-lived.

"Why, Mady Glazer, it is Mady Hayman Glazer, isn't it?" A well-dressed woman with determinedly red hair touched her arm as they stepped off the elevator. Mady stared for a second, then remembered. It was Roz Abrams, they had gone to grade school and high school together, and she and David used to meet her and her husband at the theater when they were first married.

"Hello, Roz," Mady said.

"How are you, Mady? How are you and the children doing?" Solicitude oozed from Roz's voice. Mady recalled that she had gotten a particularly beautiful note from Roz after David died. Then she had been touched, now she knew Roz hadn't meant a word of it; Roz merely wrote excellent notes.

"We're fine, really fine. How's your family?"

"Terrific. Couldn't be better. We just got back from Japan." Then Roz let her very observant eyes rest on Hans. He had slipped away and was talking to the hostess and gesturing toward the window.

Roz turned to Mady. Approval was in her eyes. She wanted to be introduced, but all Mady wanted was to get away from her.

"You're looking marvelous, Roz, you haven't changed a bit," she said hurriedly, and hoped the elevator would come soon, as the red light promised.

Roz looked thoughtfully at her. "I exercise an hour and a half a day. And it's my hair," she whispered proudly. "You ought to do something about that gray hair, Mady, especially now . . ." Roz suddenly looked trapped, then recouped. "You should go for a consultation at Kenneth's, they have a spectacular woman there. She's *fabuloso*. Say I sent you," she said, and thank God, the elevator came.

Instinctively Mady touched her hair. As if to reassure it, she thought with a wry smile, then made her way toward Hans. He was standing next to the table, gazing out onto the street below.

"Hi," she said softly.

He turned, smiled. "An old friend?"

"Old acquaintance. She told me to do something about my hair."

He frowned. "Oh, Mady, you don't want to look like that, do you?"

"I don't know. She's attractive."

"Until you get up close," he said, then looked at the menu. She sensed he was afraid of overstepping that invisible boundary that often hung in the air between them. That was why he had left her with Roz. To her relief. But now she realized that her relief came not only from Roz's unabashed curiosity or her hard stunning looks. It stretched farther into the past — when Roz's older brother was killed at Normandy. A hot June day, they were in the third grade, Roz wore a plaid dress with a big bertha collar, and someone dressed in black had come to school to take her home early.

"These things happen," Mady's mother had explained. "People die in wars and death is a fact of life." Facts of life. Sex. Death. And caring for someone whose past might look suspect? But to whom? Why should she care about Roz Abrams? Or anyone else? But how much easier it was to say than do.

"Some sherry?" Hans asked gently. His face was puzzled; she knew she had been frowning, wearing her "mad face."

"Fine." Then she told him about Sarah. At first the details of her illness, but then a little bit of their discussion, then about her interview with Maximilian Solomon, and when he laughed so heartily over that, she wanted to tell him about Sarah's story.

"At the end she told me this astonishing story — of an early love affair she had with a Swiss doctor when she was still living in Europe. Years before she met Daniel, David's father. It was so hard to believe and she was so determined to tell it, as though she didn't want it to die with her."

"Were you shocked?" he said.

"No, just a little surprised. You would be too, if you saw Sarah. She's the last of the true ladies."

"But there's always a kind of suppressed passion in women like that, don't you think?"

"I didn't think about it before she told me the story, but you're probably right. I always thought she was so simple, so good, almost otherworldly. People who know her call Sarah a saint."

Hans nodded. "Most saints know a good deal about temptation."

Mady smiled. How comfortable she felt sitting here talking to him. She looked around the dining room, she liked its informality.

"Do you come here often?" she asked Hans.

"Usually if I'm in town for the day. It's pleasant."

They sat quietly while the waitress put their plates before them. Then Hans said, "You know, Sarah's story reminded me of my Aunt Johanna. You could never call Johanna 'the last of the true ladies,' she had an earthiness about her that denied that, but she always seemed to have some marvelous secret. And she did. My mother told it to me before Johanna died, almost as if Johanna had instructed her to tell it so that if I had any questions I could ask them. But I didn't; the story told me all I wanted to know."

His voice sounded so young, it flowed so easily. And his eyes had a lightness about them that she had seen only that first day when he spoke of his childhood.

"You remember our teacher, Sergei Vladimirovitch?" Hans asked. Mady nodded. "Well, I had never thought much about him when I was growing up — he was there, that was all. But when my mother started to tell the story, it fit together like pieces in a puzzle you didn't even know existed." He paused, enjoying the expectant curiosity on her face.

"When Hans-Karl came to Africa and bought the farm, he wasn't married, but after he had been there for several years he returned to Germany for a visit and fell in love with Johanna. He was thirty and she was nineteen. Everyone was delighted, but Hans-Karl didn't want to marry her and take her back to Kenya like a bonded servant. At least that's how he described it to my mother, so he arranged for Johanna to come for a visit, to see if she liked the life she would have to lead if she married him. When Johanna arrived in Nairobi, she stayed in the hotel there for a few days before coming to the farm. At the hotel was this Russian man whose family had lost everything in the Revolution and who was planning to teach school in a small village. When he saw Johanna he fell madly in love with her. He was in his early thirties and so thin and tired that everyone assumed he was a consumptive, yet his intelligence seemed to shine from his face. Johanna was attracted to him and they became lovers right there in Nairobi, under everyone's eyes. They were an unforgettable couple — he so frail and drawn and she the picture of health and youth. She was tall and striking, with her light skin and dark eyes and thick brown hair. A presence. When we were children, the Kikuyu women told us they thought Johanna was a queen when they first saw her.

"Well, you can imagine how shocked people were. Here was this beautiful girl who had come to visit her fiancé and instead had taken a lover. And a sick Russian, at that! It was a scandal. Everyone was dismayed. Except Hans-Karl. He was the only one who understood that Johanna could be temporarily in love with this interesting Russian. He said she was young and everyone young was entitled to a love affair; he predicted she would tire of Sergei Vladimirovitch and he would wait it out. Of course Hans-Karl was right. Johanna wanted children and Hans-Karl was strong and handsome. When she came to the farm, she loved it. A few months later she and Hans-Karl returned to Germany for an enormous wedding and then came back to Kenya to live.

"But Sergei Vladimirovitch couldn't bear to be parted from her. He said he could live quite happily for the rest of his life if only he could see her every day. He and Hans-Karl had liked each other on sight, and they had a lot in common. This probably couldn't have happened in a city in Europe, but the white community in Nairobi was still small in those days, so Hans-

Karl got Sergei Vladimirovitch the job at the English school and the three of them became good friends. Of course no one expected Sergei Vladimirovitch to live as long as he did, or Johanna and Hans-Karl to be childless. By the time we were growing up everyone had forgotten the scandal and regarded the friendship as touching. Which it was." Hans looked at Mady. He expected to see pleasure in her eyes. Instead she was frowning, pushing the food around on her plate. "What's the matter?"

"I don't find it so touching. I find it rather selfish of Johanna. She liked having two men tied to her. It sounds to me as if she was an egomaniac."

"I don't think so." Hans shook his head. "They say love is blind, and God knows I loved Johanna, maybe better than I loved my mother or my father, but I think it was a strain for her some of the time."

"She could have stopped it," Mady retorted.

"It wasn't that easy. She and Hans-Karl couldn't leave the farm and she couldn't send Sergei Vladimirovitch away."

"Yes, she could, if she had wanted to."

"No. His home was near the farm. He was an exile, he belonged there, it was the only home he had after he left Russia." His voice was firm, he wanted this discussion to be over.

"It sounds so pretty — this strong beautiful woman with the two men she loved and who loved her. But it was also sick," she insisted.

"But it isn't as if she played one off against the other. She never did that, it was why my mother admired her so."

"Oh, Hans, you're seeing what you want to see. Johanna had no children, she needed Sergei as well as her husband to feel complete. She should have tried to free Sergei, let him make a life for himself elsewhere. But she didn't, she let him stay and be a watcher of other people's lives."

"No, Madeleine, you don't understand." Hans hesitated. "You can't understand, I guess. He had no place to go, and if he was a watcher of other people's lives, as you put it, then that was what he wanted."

"She could have helped him find something else, someplace else to teach," she said stubbornly.

Hans sighed. "And then he might have been miserable, lonely. He was an exile . . ." He shrugged. "You can't understand, but I don't know why you came down so hard on Johanna. She was a remarkable woman, and she loved Sergei Vladimirovitch very much."

"She also used him."

"And he used her, too, I guess. But don't we all use people we love?" Hans asked her, then looked down. He didn't want to talk about it anymore. When the waitress came to clear they were silent, withdrawn. The quarrel floated in the air between them. Why was there so much between them? Hans wondered, as he watched her walk to the ladies' room. All he had wanted was to see her again, and then, magically, she had called, and when he had touched her shoulder an hour ago, he had been sure that everything would be fine. He had told her what he thought was a moving story — perhaps to balance Sarah's story — and she had gotten angry. The irony was that she was behaving exactly as Johanna had sometimes behaved when he was a boy. Now, finally, he understood his Uncle Hans-Karl's bewilderment.

As they walked down the street to the parking lot Hans saw people staring at Madeleine. She was wearing a gray skirt and a white turtleneck sweater and a softer gray cardigan that had some angora in it. Her eyes were brighter than usual — because she was still angry, but what did these onlookers know? — and she would have been surprised if he could have found a way to tell her that she commanded the stares of strangers. Of course he didn't; instead he enjoyed the buoyant feeling of walking beside a woman whom people noticed, whom he happened to love. For he did love her. Now he knew that what he had been feeling these last weeks was love. The joy of sitting across the table from her, watching her eat, listening to her story of the job interview, then seeing her decide to trust him and tell him about Sarah, and even later, witnessing her anger. In the space of two hours he had felt responses so deep, so pleasurable that he almost didn't want his mind to find them, for fear that if he knew his own joy it would disappear. "Yes," he would tell Rosa Whitman the next time he saw her. "Yes, I do love Madeleine."

As he heard their footsteps mingling with hundreds of others on the pavement below, Hans suddenly understood that wonderful scene in *Anna Karenina* when Sergei, Levin's half-brother, is walking with his old friend Varenka. He wants to propose and she expects his proposal, but, mysteriously, the right moment passes. Sergei doesn't propose and they both know they will never marry. Perhaps one has to be middle-aged to know that such moments can pass, irretrievably, Hans thought. Now, walking up Fifty-third Street while the sun struggled to grace a Saturday afternoon in the fall, Hans was filled with a fear that he would be like Sergei Levin — lonely, yearning, never declaring his love. No, he vowed. Now was not the time, and she might not return his love, but somehow, some other time, a moment would be right and he would have to seize it. If he had learned nothing else today, he had learned that. There was nothing passive about love — even in middle age, and he would have to act.

In the car she relaxed a little and while they talked about her children, he kept hoping for some clue that they would see each other again soon, but she said nothing and soon they were on Sarah's block.

"Thanks so much for driving me, Hans, it was more than kind of you," she said in a curiously formal way. He started to try to park the car so he could help her out but she said, "Don't bother to park, I'll hop out here." Helplessly he waited and watched her climb the steps to Sarah's house and then wave, casually. As if they were old friends. As if his heart were in its usual place and not pounding in his mouth. He tried to see what was in her face, but it was futile, she was too far away. Besides, it probably had nothing to do with him. As soon as they had turned into this neighborhood she became distracted, worried, and from the little she said he knew she was thinking about Sarah. But what did she feel about him? Anything? Would he ever know? He felt so separate from her, so inadequate, so gauche, so — goddamn it!

He had never felt this way before; he had thought if he could see her again his problems would be solved, and now he knew that though they had spent the last few hours together, his problems were merely beginning.

He pressed his foot down on the gas pedal and drove back to Racer's Cove too fast. The red Fiat became a garish streak of metal against the splashes of fall color that still flanked the highway. Filled with longing and the pain of physical desire he found himself pulling into the street where Rosa lived. For once in his life he didn't want the safety of his neat spare home.

When Rosa came to the door she was in her robe. From her scrubbed face and the tendrils of hair that curled near her cheeks he knew that she had just bathed. As he followed her into the living room he could see the outline of her slender body. They tried to talk over a drink. He had thought if he could talk a bit he would feel better, but it was no use and they both knew it. Dusk was beginning to spread its lovely amber glow over the sleepy village when, as in the half-light of other people's dreams, Hans and his old friend Rosa walked into her bedroom and made love.

CHAPTER 18

MUFFLED VOICES thickened the air. Hundreds of faces and bodies converged into a huge shroud, drew her and her children against silk, worsted, polyester bosoms; a few fingers grazed the fine wood of the casket.

"Such a shame, so soon after David," a distant cousin whispered.

"First Daniel, then David, now Sarah. Too much," another agreed. Peter pressed her arm in anger. When she was a child, she read a person died every minute. Does a person die every second now? Every five seconds? She shrugged, looked for her parents. Late, always late.

"Where are Grandma and Grandpa?" Nina said.

"They'll be here, they must have had traffic."

Then a flurry at the door and the shroud parted, like the Red Sea. Shelley and Mel and Bonnie rushed in. "Dad locked his keys in the car and Mom didn't have hers," Shelley said and pulled Mady's face toward her own.

Max looked bewildered, his features awry, out of control. *So much death, when will it end?* his eyes asked. Libby took Foffy's hand, smoothed the child's cornsilk hair. Her small face was wan; in her arms she clutched her doll Kate, who was wrapped in the quilt Sarah had made. As they walked into the chapel

Mady saw Libby press her lips together, straighten her shoulders, stare ahead. Her mother's face had more color today than it had had for months, years.

Libby had helped her prepare Sarah for the coffin. Slowly, silently, they had undressed Sarah, then washed her and put her into fresh clothes: fragrant almost new underthings, a white silk blouse, and a navy blue suit she wore last spring. They had had to tuck a few inches of the skirt behind her, but when they finished, she looked as if she had tottered and fainted just as she arrived at someone's house for dinner.

"Such a pretty woman," Libby murmured, and dabbed a hankie with cologne and put it in Sarah's hand. The fingers were getting stiff by then, but Libby wasn't frightened. The ritual of preparing Sarah for her coffin had helped them both. This was part of healing — handling the dead. This was what she had not had with David.

"You can't see him," they had said over and over again, so instead of the reality of his body she was left with her own nightmarish imaginings. "You mustn't see him, you will never get over it, cherish the memories of him alive," they had repeated. A fool in her grief, she had obeyed. But neither she nor they knew the power of the imagination.

Now they walked down the path to the cemetery. Crisp air and full sun a relief after the dim funeral home and dark limousine. The coffin awaited them — sleek, shiny. Suddenly Mady saw that the grave was in the wrong place. Sarah was to lie next to Daniel, but the freshly dug grave was beside David's. When she looked up, she saw Max approach the man in charge. No one else had noticed.

Max's eyes seethed, his voice was tight. "Idiots, they're idiots. They know they made a mistake, but the gravediggers leave at three-thirty, they will change it tomorrow."

The thought of lowering Sarah, then pulling her up and lowering her again was more than Mady could bear. "Let it be, leave her next to David," she said wearily. Perhaps there was some logic to the mistake. When a child died before his mother, perhaps he should lie protected forever by his parents.

At the end everyone threw a handful of dirt into the open grave. "Sleep well," Max whispered, then turned to Mady. But she wasn't ready to go. So he took Libby's arm and they trailed after the rest of the funeral party. Funeral party. What a ridiculous expression, Mady thought, as she watched the crowd hurry away.

Mady and her children stood over David's grave. The stone was still so white. DAVID GLAZER 1932-1972. Nothing more. Plague. Diphtheria. Drowning. Choking. Small blackened stones that mark the children's graves in New England sometimes gave reasons. DAVID GLAZER 1932-1972. Death: unreasonable. Death: random. Either would do but silence was more appropriate. What did that mean — appropriate? Another silly word invented by the same people who invented these rituals of religion. Rules, rituals, guidelines. Whatever you called them, they were created so that those giving birth, marrying, burying the dead would not have to think. Follow the rules, practice the rituals, survive. But to live that way can also grind life into meaninglessness. Mady looked around. How crazy to use stones to remember those who throbbed with life. Hundreds and thousands of stones in those endless Long Island cemeteries. Weathered battered stones that stretched as far as the eye could see. Dead stiff pieces of matter to commemorate people who had walked, run, danced, argued, laughed, cried. Why not trees and shrubs and flowers instead of these awful cold stones? As they left the cemetery, Mady saw it miraculously transformed into a huge orchard of graceful apple and pear and peach and cherry trees — some weeping, some sturdy and straight — and people walking as they pleased.

When she returned home, the house was filled with people. Clair and Shelley and her friends and neighbors had already set out the food. Funerals made people hungry. Was that to hide their silent guilt? Had each one admitted in some small secret place in his heart — better Sarah than me? Did each see death as a roaming wild animal — a lion or tiger, perhaps — searching the landscape for its next victim? Were they relieved that death had been satiated, and their small circle, according to the laws of statistics, was safe for a while? Or was she the only one to have such thoughts? She couldn't remember having them when David died. Was this bitterness or maturity? she wondered, as she walked slowly through the clusters of people urging them to eat, to help themselves.

Suddenly Nina grabbed her arm. Her face was pale.

"What's the matter?"

"Foffy. Foffy's sick. Grandma's with her in your bathroom."

Foffy hung over the toilet bowl while Libby held the child's forehead. Foffy gagged, her skin a yellowish green.

"Now it's just bile, there's nothing more left," Libby said. "She must have eaten something that disagreed with her. Or else it's a virus." Mady carried Foffy to her room. Libby was turning down Mady's bed. "What did she eat last night, can you remember what she ate?" Libby kept asking.

Mady didn't answer and sat on the bed, cradling Foffy in her arms. Foffy had vomited for no other reason than that her Grandma Sarah had died; she was gone into the ground and she would never tell her a story again, or read to her, or sew with her, or hug her, and it was more than the child could bear, more than the child's body could bear. But Mady knew that Libby would never believe that a person could be sick for any reason that wasn't physical.

Peter stood in the doorway and watched his mother and grandmother flutter around Foffy. "I want Kate," the child said. Peter remembered that the doll was in the den and went to get it, glad for something to do. He hated all these people in the house, he didn't know what to say to his uncles, Gil and Martin. Every time they looked at him they had to look away, sadness drooping from their faces. Did he look so much like his father? Peter wondered.

When he brought the doll back, Foffy's head was propped on some pillows and Libby and Mady were cleaning the bathroom. For a moment he envied Foffy. At least she could get sick and get it out. He was stuck with this awful lump in his throat that he knew would stay for days and days and no amount of water or crusts of bread would get rid of it.

"Is it true that worms can get through the coffin?" Foffy asked.

"Where did you get that idea?"

"That song, you know, 'The worms go in, the worms go out, they eat your guts and they spit them out . . .' Are they going to do that to Grandma Sarah, did they do that to Daddy? I thought Daddy went to heaven and became a star, that's what Mrs. Parks told me in kindergarten. I didn't know he was in the ground." She shuddered and grew very pale again.

"But you saw him lowered into the ground, you were there," he told her. "It was two years ago, you were four."

"No, I wasn't. I never saw any such thing, Peter, you're a liar!" Foffy buried her head in her pillow and began to cry.

How lucky she was, Peter thought. How lucky she was that she could forget or pretend and vomit and cry! He sat on the bed and stroked her hair until her shoulders stopped shaking and she finally fell asleep.

The next morning Foffy was better. Nina and Peter were helping Clair tidy the house. People had stayed till after ten last night and more would be arriving soon after lunch to pay their condolences. Gil and Martin and their wives Sally and Eve and their children had stayed at Shelley's. "Now I know why I have that big house," Shelley had said so cheerfully, and Mady was grateful. A lot of Sarah's relatives from Brooklyn were planning to come this afternoon. "Thank God she didn't wait till winter," one had just said on the phone. Mady couldn't even smile.

"Tell whoever calls that we'll be here today and tomorrow, we'll be sitting *shiva* till Thursday night," she told Clair. She was standing in the kitchen with a long list in her hand. Peter was waiting in the car. Foffy's face was hidden in a huge mug of tea.

"And you, miss, can get back into bed for the rest of the morning." She bent to kiss her. Foffy was cool but her eyes had deep circles under them.

When she and Peter returned, Clair said, "A Mr. Panneman called. Just a minute after you pulled the car out."

"Oh?"

"He asked how you were. He didn't seem to know Mrs. Glazer had died, but I said you would be home all afternoon. He seemed a little surprised. That was the only call, except for your mother. She'll be here soon, she said she was bringing lunch and some more fruit."

"Ye gods, we'll be drowning in fruit," Mady groaned. As soon as she had helped with the packages she hurried to her room. She needed to be by herself. Since she had gotten out of Hans's car on Saturday she had not been alone, except when she fell into an exhausted, numbed sleep.

Sarah had died, quietly, in Mrs. Johnson's arms late Saturday night. Sunday had been taken up with funeral arrangements, phone calls, details, and preparing Sarah for the coffin. The funeral was Monday, today was Tuesday, and she had not had time to sort out what had happened with Hans on Saturday. And now he might be coming to see her. She hardly knew what she felt. She sat down on the window seat and leaned back into the pillows.

Why had she and Hans quarreled? The afternoon they had spent together was only three days ago, yet she felt that she hadn't seen him for months. She had wanted to call him late Saturday night, she had even begun to dial his number, then stopped. No, she had decided, she would get through this crisis by herself. But now he had called and she had to face what had happened on Saturday.

She sat there mulling over their lunch, as if she had all the time in the world, as if her house wouldn't be bustling with people in an hour or so. And she realized she hadn't been reacting entirely to what he was saying but what it might mean for him.

Was he going to be another Sergei Vladimirovitch — forever watching people's lives, never having anything of his own? He had told the story so placidly. This is the way it was, he was saying with such acceptance. Now she knew it wasn't the story or even Johanna she had been angry at. She had been angry at him. Hans. As an adolescent he had been thrown against the borders of life. He had watched his twin brother die. Yet he had survived. For the last two years she, too, had lived near those same boundaries, and when they met in Racer's Cove, particularly when she saw his involvement with his work, she had thought he had the secret of survival. If she could learn his secret, she had thought, then she, too, could survive, then she would be able to function better.

But in the museum, sitting across from him over lunch, she had realized that she had been absolutely wrong. It wasn't that way at all. You can't hover on the edges, playing it safe forever in that no-man's-land. You have to make your way back to the center of life and to do that you must take risks, just as Anne had said. While she was telling Hans Sarah's story, everything had been turned around. Abruptly. Strangely. As she had spoken, she saw his face change, soften. In the space of a few minutes she experienced what was possible only when you're older, not so self-involved. She had seen a man fall in love with her at a specific moment. Suddenly she knew that if he could help her survive, she could also help him, she could show him the way back, if he would let her. She had almost stopped telling the story about Sarah and said, "If only we could stop time and have this moment together and stay forever suspended in it." But of course she hadn't; she had continued telling her story and he had responded by telling her about Johanna and Sergei Vladimirovitch. Instead of being moved as he had intended, she had been filled with anger and disappointment.

Perhaps he was incurable. Perhaps all the love in the world wouldn't change him, perhaps he was a man destined always to live on the fringe, never really engaged. Perhaps he would have been this way even if his brother hadn't been killed, or his father weren't a Nazi and he hadn't lived most of his adult life away from the countries of his birth and adoption. She didn't want to believe it, yet the only evidence she had — against those long years of isolation and acceptance — was that marvelous light that occasionally emanated from his eyes, spreading a radiance over his features, and that flash of temper she had seen that evening when he came for dinner. Not much to go on, was it? she thought, as she opened the door to her closet. Yet it was all she had and she knew now, as she had known when she stood on the steps to Sarah's house, that Hans had entered her life during that short time over lunch on Saturday. For better or worse, as they used to say.

She pushed the hangers slowly and remembered a line of Nadezhda Mandelstam's: "The only good life is one in which there is no need for miracles." But Mandelstam's widow was wrong; every life, even the most ordinary life, needs miracles. Sarah knew that best, Mady thought, as she found a print silk blouse and a black skirt.

The crowd was larger than she expected. She had to send Peter up to the Levins for more chairs and she was unfolding them near the back door when she heard Foffy call, "Mommy, Mommy, Hans is here!"

Immediately heads were raised. Who was this stranger who was kissing Foffy, whom the older children were so glad to see? The silence buzzed with curiosity as Mady greeted him. She had her back to her audience, but she knew what they looked like. When she was young, she had thought these relatives believed a person's well-being depended on three nourishing meals a day, clean sheets once a week, avoiding constipation; they would probably claim that the quality of a person's sex life was directly dependent on the quality of the bed. Now she knew better. They were all canny enough to spot something different, and though she couldn't see their faces Mady knew that not one of them was overlooking Hans.

How she wished Sarah were here! One look from Sarah and everyone behaved better.

Finally, someone coughed and they went back to their conversations. One deaf cousin kept asking, "Who is he?" until they shushed her. Despite herself, Mady was amused that no one mistook him for a long-lost relative. He was wearing the suburban uniform — a navy single-breasted blazer, gray slacks, a light blue shirt, and the same tie as David's brother Martin, yet no two men looked less alike, she thought as she watched Martin's wife, Eve, take Hans over to meet her husband.

Martin was a plastic surgeon well known for rebuilding the faces of children. He had gone to California to study with a man who had done many Japanese faces after Hiroshima and Nagasaki, and he had met Eve and settled there. Martin was passionate about his work and entirely devoted to the children who needed him; he refused to do noses or breasts or face-lifts. He had almost no time for his family, he hadn't read anything but a scientific journal for years and years (with the exception of David's report to the Attica Commission), his idea of recreation was a UJA fund-raiser, his only outside interest was Israel. Like Gil, who was a pediatrician in Boston, Martin lived for his work. Both men were enormously successful, their work was praised and quoted, and their wives and children seemed to adore them. If they were lonely or resentful, Sally and Eve and the six kids kept it to themselves. In the last two years, since the senseless death of their beloved kid brother, Gil and Martin had escaped further and further into their work. In the operating room or in the clinic it was easier to forget that David wasn't in his law office. But here, in his house, watching Mady and the children, especially Peter, who looked like a reincarnation of David, they were both miserable. Usually so decisive and responsible, they had both been listless — distracted and depressed by their mother's death, which forced them to relive David's death. They had been only too glad to leave the details to Mady, who seemed so much better than she had been last spring.

And now they were being asked to make conversation with a

man, who, he had just told them, was a potter and a sculptor, and who couldn't have been more different from everyone else here if he had marched into the house off a UFO.

When Hans told them what he did, Mady could see Martin almost wince. Either Hans didn't notice or chose not to see it. Politely he explained to Sally and Eve, who showed interest, the details of his work, but Gil and Martin were no longer listening, and Gil had begun to move away while Hans was talking. How bigoted those two men were! The sons of a doctor, they believed that the only life for a man was medicine or law or architecture or engineering or, if you came from a rich family, college teaching. She had believed it once, too, as had many of the women of her generation. A man's sex appeal in the fifties directly depended on his occupation, and in some cases even money didn't help. A struggling lawyer was infinitely more pleasing than a jeweler or concrete salesman who earned a decent living. Was this only Jewish? Mady now found herself wondering, amazed by the way Hans kept his dignity although he had been clearly written off by the two doctors, who had moved to a corner to talk to an old uncle.

Hans had lived through so much that he knew some things didn't matter, he refused to define his life by others. When he saw her the first time on the beach, he had been concerned and had expressed his concern, he hadn't cared what she thought. He had known Sarah's death would be hard for her, and he had come. Now he was answering questions and he didn't care how the answers were received. I am Hans Panneman, I teach art in a rural high school, I live in an out-of-the-way place, I am a potter and a sculptor. What freedom that was! Maybe that was why Peter was so interested in him.

As she said good-bye to some cousins of Daniel Glazer, Mady saw from the corner of her eye that Sally was introducing Hans to Max. Her father had come directly from his office, and she hadn't yet greeted him. Now it was impossible to walk over to them; a river of people wanted to reminisce with her. Quickly she clasped their knotted hands, gently she brushed against their papery faces. Then, rather than try to get through more people, she slipped through the kitchen (where Clair looked at her quizzically) through the greenhouse and garden and into the dining room.

"You're from Bavaria, near Munich, or Stuttgart?" Max was saying. He had an amazing ear for inflections of European speech.

Hans nodded. Her father's face had constricted into a stony coldness which softened only a little when she tapped his arm and kissed his ear. Max's mouth was a thin line. *I'll be damned if I'm going to make conversation with a Nazi*, his whole bearing shrieked, and he used the first opportunity he had to move away from them.

Mady could feel her throat fill as she watched him. Stay, stay, she wanted to say, I can explain. But now he was angry as well as depressed and lonely.

For a second Mady felt trapped; then her mother was approaching her and Hans. Mady knew Libby wanted to cover Max's rudeness, which she could not help but see, since she had been watching Max carefully ever since he arrived.

"You must be an old friend of David's," Libby said warmly.

"No, I met Madeleine and the children at the beach in July."

"Oh?"

"My own mother died this summer and I know how hard it is to deal with all this." Hans gestured toward the people, the laden table. "I wanted to see her and the children," he said.

"I see." Then, "What do you do?"

Mady stiffened, almost anticipating her mother. But Libby surprised her. As she heard Libby ask Hans more about his work, Mady was overwhelmed by a sudden rush of love for her mother. She found it hard to swallow and moved away from them to say some good-byes.

At one point Nina insisted on showing Hans all the things Sarah had made — pillows done in crewel, needlepoint, quilting. "She was wonderful with her hands," Nina was saying as they passed Mady. Then Hans followed her to Peter's room to see the quilt on his bed, Sarah's masterpiece. Later, when she passed Peter's room, Hans was still there, with a book in his hand, talking to Nina and Peter. Peter was laughing a little. What a relief to hear it! These last few days had been hardest for him. Last night he had announced he wasn't sure he would marry. Ever. "Families make me uncomfortable," he had said. Then, "Do I look that much like Daddy?"

Well, at least Hans wouldn't keep telling him how much he looked like David.

In the kitchen Shelley and Gail were emptying the dishwasher. Gail was such a loyal friend, and she, Mady, had been — oh, what had she been? Mady didn't even know, but whatever it was, Gail didn't hold it against her. Seeing Gail hard at work in her kitchen, Mady wanted to tell Gail the whole story. Now.

"Please, Gail, leave that. You, too, Shelley. Clair can finish it later. Sit with me a second."

Gail came into the little breakfast room, but Shelley continued with the unloading. From the way Shelley's back was set Mady knew she was angry, probably about Hans, but she had been expecting that since the moment Clair told her a Mr. Panneman had called. It would wait. Now she had to talk to Gail. She looked down and moved the plates into a pile, not yet able to meet Gail's glance.

"I've got to tell you something," she said quickly. "Even though you asked me not to, I called Fred and tried to make him see what he was doing, but it was all wrong, and I think I did just the opposite, I think . . ." Helplessly Mady looked up. Gail's eyes were kind.

"I know, Mady. I know all about it. When Fred kept talking about this woman he thought he loved, I assumed it was a colleague or a patient, because that's what it was before. But then, from the few things he said, I realized it was someone he had known since he was young, and one day, about a week before that village meeting, I realized it was you. Later, when he admitted it was you, he claimed he had been in love with you before

David; he had made a whole fantasy out of you. Then after you got angry at him, his lovely fantasy got smashed and he went back into therapy. He told me the other day it's going so well that he might come home one of these days. But what he doesn't know yet is that I don't want him. Ever again. I think I've finally faced what he is, and the girls and I can make it on our own. You know, Mady, I don't think I've ever told anyone this, but when I was a student in France I once overheard a conversation between a man and his wife that I have always regretted. I used to eavesdrop all the time when I was there, to test myself, and one day I saw this elegant couple sitting in the Tuileries. They looked so perfect — he had wonderful gray hair and she was a beautiful blonde, though she had faded a little. Anyway, as I inched closer and closer I could hear that they were talking about their marriage, and of course I should have moved away. But I was young and stupid then, and I listened, and she finally said, 'Too many deceits have occurred for me ever to be happy with you again.' I remember it because my translation of it was so literal. Then they rose and as I looked at her face I saw an unhappiness that I could never forget. I vowed that I would never look like that woman. If I stay with Fred I will. I must leave him, even if I never find anyone else." Gail reached across the table and grabbed Mady's hand.

"I hated you for about a week," she admitted. "Then I realized that all those clues he kept planting about this woman — how much she cared for him, how she respected his opinions about her kids — weren't true. He was making it all up. He finally told me the truth when he was too furious to lie anymore. When you kicked him in the parking lot near the village hall, I wanted to call you and say, 'Hurrah!' But of course I didn't."

Gail smiled and stood up. "I'm so glad it came out. I didn't think it would today, with all this." She looked around. "But sometimes good things do happen unexpectedly." The two women kissed and Gail left through the back door.

She sat there remembering Gail at her wedding, Gail after she had given birth to her first child, Gail reading Montaigne in the original with two little girls in diapers, Gail telling her she was going back to school, Gail at Fred's fortieth birthday party.

Then a voice interrupted. "I think she's crazy to kick him out. It's not easy to live alone in middle age," Shelley said as she wiped her hands on the dish towel. Mady looked up.

"She'll be all right. She's attractive and she has her work."

"Translating New Wave French novelists isn't exactly going to make her a millionaire," Shelley snapped.

"She'll get alimony and child support. And at least she likes what she's doing," Mady answered.

"Oh, Mady, you're so naive. Do you know that about two-thirds of the divorced men in this country stop paying alimony and child support within five years?"

"Fred will pay, but you're right, I didn't know that charming statistic."

"You think Fred will pay. Why can't you ever face the truth about money?" Shelley goaded her. "You act as if it's something dirty, you always have, even when we were little."

Mady stared at her sister. "But I don't need to worry about money now. David had more insurance and legal advice than anyone needed. He left me with an annual income of almost fifty thousand dollars."

"That's what I mean," Shelley said disgustedly. "Haven't you heard of inflation? The cost of living keeps going up and you have three kids to educate."

"Then I'll get a job, I've already begun to look for one." Finally, Shelley looked surprised and Mady thought she was safe. But then Shelley turned sharply and demanded, "Who is he?"

"Who?"

"Who do you think?"

"His name is Hans Panneman."

"I know his name, Mom introduced us. I want to know who he is."

"We met him when we were on vacation, he lives in Racer's Cove. He's a potter and he teaches art in the local high school and he has a beautiful —"

"—and he's in love with you."

"You certainly seem to know an awful lot about him in a few minutes."

"I know what I see and I saw how he looked at you. When I think of Larry, how perfect he would be, how successful he is, what a good father he would make, what an intelligent gentle man he is, I could cry!" Shelley rubbed her hands as if they were covered with poison.

"What makes you think Hans isn't an intelligent gentle man?"

Her sister stared. "He's a high school art teacher and a potter. He's also a Nazi. A Nazi hippie. That's terrific, Mady, what we've all always dreamed for you. David must be turning in his grave!"

"You leave David out of this!" Mady said, louder than she intended.

"I wish I could," Shelley whispered. "What about Dad, have you seen his face?"

"Of course. But Dad's wrong and you're wrong. He's not a Nazi and was never a Nazi. Why must you jump to conclusions when you don't know anything about him?"

"Whatever he is, he's in love with you and you're falling in love with him," Shelley said through clenched teeth.

But Mady didn't even hear that last. What had struck her during this bizarre angry whispering (for the only thing they agreed on was that they couldn't yell) was that an explanation wasn't necessary. Whereas the Nazism of Hans's father would matter very much to Max, it was beside the point to Shelley. His politics were not nearly as important as what he did and what he looked like. Mady looked at her older sister and felt something close to pity.

"You're falling in love with him, I know you, Mady," Shelley said.

"Shelley, stop being crazy, people our age don't fall in love like that. This isn't a movie."

"Don't tell me what it is and what it isn't. Some movies are made from real life — or they used to be anyway —" Shelley stopped, confused, and in any other circumstances the two sisters would have laughed and hugged each other and that would have been that. But Shelley wasn't laughing today. She pulled a few more plates off the counter and put them in the sink. "I know you, Mady, you're practically in love with him already. Don't think you can fool me, I know you better than anyone, I remember the day you were born, and you're going to make us all crazy!" Her words hung in the air. Crazy, crazy, crazy, crazy. The echo of Shelley's whisper drowned out the voices and clatter around her. Wearily Mady got up and wished she could retreat into her own room.

She's so tired, Hans thought when she came out into the living room. Her shoulders were round with tiredness, and her face was pale. He should go. He didn't belong here with her family, with people she had known all her life. He had intruded, yet when he heard Sarah had died he had to see her. And although it had not been pleasant, Hans was glad he had come. He had met David's brothers and their wives and he had met her parents and her sister, Shelley, and Shelley's husband, Mel. Of them all, only her mother had been civil. Clearly, the others had higher hopes for Mady than a man like him. Given that, perhaps he was doomed. He had never thought about it before, but now he had all sorts of questions about her. Did her well-dressed and affluent parents support her? Or was she financially independent? He had assumed she had enough money because she didn't have a job, yet when she had told him about that disastrous interview she seemed to want to have a job. There was still so much he didn't know about her. He looked around. Across the room was the Steinway grand and here and in the dining room were old Orientals, fine furniture, some of it antique and inlaid. The dishes and crystal and silver bespoke a certain standard of life; even her well-cut skirt and blouse were expensive and clearly different from the faded cottons she had worn in Racer's Cove. In her home she looked the most conventional of women, yet when she had talked at lunch last Saturday about that interview, when she had defended Constance Garnett and revealed her passion for the Russian language, even when she had disagreed with him about Johanna, she was a woman who could take charge of a life very different from the one she was now so comfortably living.

Oh, what we don't know about each other! In a sense that was what they had talked about that day — what they didn't know about Sarah and Johanna. If she could know what he had done after he left her, would she understand, or would she hate him? He didn't know, but the strangest thing of all was that Rosa didn't hate him and he didn't hate himself. He had thought he would, but he didn't. He regretted it, but he had not lain awake these last few nights filled with disgust and contempt for himself. Maybe one gets easier on oneself as one grows older, he thought, and held out his hand to someone new — a lovely-looking stocky woman who had a voice like wind.

"I'm happy to meet you," Anne Levin said and her eyes confirmed her voice. Here was someone who knew about him, and though Anne didn't have time to talk (someone came up behind her and hugged her and drew her away), the knowledge he had gotten from Anne's eyes gave Hans courage. He waited a few minutes, then followed Mady into the kitchen.

"You'll stay for dinner?" she said. "Nothing very elaborate, but there's plenty."

He shook his head. "No, it's a long ride. I must go now, but perhaps we can meet in New York on Saturday, for dinner." Then he looked around and felt his face fall. "Or is it too early, will you still have this?" He gestured to the dishes and platters spilling over the counters.

"No, this is over by Thursday. Jews don't mourn on the Sabbath. And Foffy is better now."

He was amused to hear her justify her answer, and he knew that unless he pressed her, she would stall and say she would let him know.

"Can you come?" he said again.

She was startled by the urgency in his voice, and once again his face appeared to have gathered all the light in the room and was reflecting it. She looked away from his penetrating eyes to get her bearings, but when their glances met again she knew that, despite her father and Shelley and the rest of them, despite the word "crazy," which was still echoing in her ears like a dying bell, she would be wherever he wanted her to be on Saturday.

CHAPTER 19

DAWN. Icy light seeping through the crack in the curtains. Too early, but she couldn't stay in bed. Quickly she threw off the covers and wrapped up in her robe. She opened the curtains. A hard frost last night had blackened and bent the marigolds and asters. The leaves of the water grass were no longer a rough elastic green but a listless, yellowish gray, their tops dry and strawlike. Cardinals and jays pecked at the tops, shaking loose the seeds. When had all that happened? She had been so busy all week she had not marked the changes and now felt cheated.

She pulled the taupe corduroy suit from her closet. She had never worn it, she had bought it the day before David was killed, and afterward had put it back into its box, ashamed to admit she had been doing something so frivolous as shop that week. Then she had forgotten about it. The other night she had found it, when she was wondering what to wear when she met Hans on Saturday.

As she brushed her teeth she listened to the weather report — cool and quite cold tonight. She had the white turtleneck sweater she could wear. She poured a few drops of bath oil into her bath. It was an old bottle and the scent had thinned. Antilope, by Weil — the only perfume she had ever used — and a few weeks ago Shelley told her she had read they were going to change the scent. As the fragrance rose in the hot steam, Mady wondered if she would ever talk to her sister of small things again. Of course she would, Shelley would get over her anger. What was so absurd was that Shelley had made assumptions that simply weren't true, not yet, anyway.

She must have dozed, for it was almost seven-thirty when she got out of the bath. Now she could easily have gone back to sleep, but Foffy would be up soon. Slowly the water whirled out of the tub. She watched the Coriolis effect, for once you knew about it you became mesmerized by it. It affects the tides, the sea, the weather and winds, she had read when she looked it up. It was never-ending and knew no boundaries, it could take place in a bath or in an ocean.

Slowly she rubbed her arms and legs with moisturizer. Her elbows were rough, her breasts and thighs had those odd random red spots she had observed on her parents' bodies, and there was a small burgundy-colored maze of veins on the back of her left leg about the size of a baby's fist. When had that appeared? As she rubbed it (it was smooth), she thought of the Hawthorne story she had read as a child. "The Birthmark." It was in a skinny volume of Hawthorne's stories her father had found in one of the endless antique shops her mother was always dragging them to. In the story a man and woman marry; the woman has a tiny birthmark on her cheek in the shape of a miniature hand. Some people think it enhances her beauty, others think it mars her otherwise flawless face. Her husband, who is a scientist, doesn't think much about it before they marry, but afterward he becomes obsessed by it. He wants it removed, for he feels it destroys her beauty. She senses his loathing and knows he will never be happy until it is gone. She submits to his experiments to remove it. As the mark gets lighter and lighter she becomes weaker and weaker. When it is gone she dies.

Now Mady rubbed the broken capillaries again. Thin women's bodies aged, too. She saw her sagging breasts; she touched the stretch marks on her belly that had been there since Nina, her biggest baby, was born; she traced the lines on her forehead, around her mouth, near her temples. What was it that Anna Magnani once said? "Don't you take those lines out of my face, I worked hard for every one of them!" There was pride in age, and whoever loved her would have to take the lines and marks. But how scary to contemplate. She and David had known each other for so long they didn't even see each other's bodies. She thought of Hans's body and again she felt that compelling connection with him. Could it be loneliness? Could she merely be starved for physical contact? Yet what about those men at the dinner parties? She had felt nothing for them, less than nothing. Even Larry. She would have avoided sex with him as long as she possibly could. Now she wished she had been curious and courageous enough to go to bed with one of them so she could be surer of herself now. Maybe the one who believed in sex as exercise? Why couldn't she have subscribed to his philosophy at least once and used him as men had been using women for hundreds, maybe thousands of years? She was an anachronism in today's world. She had slept with one man in her life — David. She was something out of Jane Austen.

The house was still quiet when she went into the kitchen. Mady went to Foffy's room. She was sitting up in bed reading *The Littles*. The curtains were still closed.

"Oh, Foffy, you'll ruin your eyes," Mady whispered as she turned on the light. "Isn't that better?"

Foffy barely nodded. How fast they grow up. "I have to finish this chapter," she murmured to her mother.

Mady went through yesterday's mail again while she had toast and coffee. When the phone rang, it was Anne.

"I hate to bother you so early, Mady."

"That's okay, I've been up for hours."

"Then maybe you can help us. We're trying to get people to help clean the woods. Now that the Republicans are out, the county wants to put through the park. We had thought they wouldn't move till spring, but they're planning to send a committee to the woods at the end of the week. Can you and the kids help today?"

Mady hesitated. She was to meet Hans at the Metropolitan Museum and after that they were to have dinner. Peter was going to a basketball game, Nina and her friend Ramona were baby-sitting for Foffy. Now it was nine. The chores she planned to do could wait. It was too beautiful to waste the day indoors.

When she and Foffy entered the woods, several men were clustered in a small clearing. Machetes, axes, pruning shears, rakes, and thick coils of rope lay scattered on the ground. As she approached, the men nodded respectfully and averted their eyes. She wished they could treat her like any other woman who had come to help, but of course they couldn't. This was to be David Glazer Park, she was his widow. She was relieved to see Anne coming, and soon Foffy's friend Nadia and her mother arrived.

"The kids are over by the playhouse, it's a mess around the trees there," Anne told them and the little girls ran off.

Anne handed her a pruning shears and some chalk. "Come on, Mady, you and I can mark what needs to be cut away at the entrance."

They worked in silence. A cool wind drifted through the trees and when she paused to rest, it felt raw. It was better to work steadily and pleasant not to talk. She had already told Anne about her fight with Shelley, but Anne had not mentioned Hans. She wasn't the sort of woman who made quick judgments. She didn't know that Mady planned to see him today. No one did, not even Nina and Peter.

Knocked off their limbs by a recent storm, some of the leaves on the ground were green; they had the resilience of still-living things and a sweet elusive odor. "That's fine. Woody doesn't want too clear a line, he wants you to feel as if you meandered into the park, discovered it yourself. He's also planning a wild flower garden near the brook," Anne said and pointed east.

Mady wiped her hands on her jeans and returned to the marking. Some of the saplings were stringy, bent; others were straight and already thickening. She mentioned it to Anne.

"Funny, isn't it, like people," Anne replied.

When Mady stopped to rest, she felt utterly relaxed. Now the wind was refreshing; even the clamminess it gave her clothes didn't bother her. She should be out here this morning, she should help make this park. She knew why Anne had called at the last minute; she might have refused if she had had time to think about it; she might have wanted to avoid what once seemed pity but what she now saw was merely acceptance. She pushed her hair behind her ears and got up, ready to work again.

Suddenly a sound shot through the trees. A high sharp cry, then a man's voice calling what sounded like "Foffy!" Anne's face grayed, she grabbed Mady's hand and turned her toward the playhouse. Mady heard voices, the swish of running feet on the damp leaves, then, "Run! Call the police!" Her heart was a stone when they reached the clearing.

Foffy was propped across Woody's lap with her head back while Joe Carpenter breathed into her mouth. Nadia and the other children stared down at Foffy. A blanched silence hung in the air; eyes were riveted on Foffy's red shirt. Anne took Mady's arm and led her slowly toward her child, then restrained her from stepping too close. Mady could feel her fingers digging into Anne's arm. Woody looked up; anguish filmed his eyes. No one moved as glances flickered from Foffy to her and back again. Even the arms of the trees were motionless, waiting, pleading. "Breathe! Breathe!" a voice in her shouted silently to her child. Joe grunted with the effort. Then, at last, the small red chest began to move. Up and down, up and down. A sigh rippled the air. Mady's legs trembled as she fell into a bed of leaves. She heard Woody murmur, "She'll be fine, it was only a few seconds, she'll be fine."

Then the exquisite purple hue of Foffy's eyes. "Hi, Mommy," she said and held out her arms. Only when Mady pulled Foffy to her did she notice the rope looped around the child's hips.

Joe took off his jacket and wrapped it around Foffy but shook his head when Mady looked at him.

"The kids were trying to pull out a fairly large sapling and they got this idea of tying ropes around their waists and pulling. They made slip knots by mistake and Foffy was at the end and the rope climbed up around her chest and —" Woody's voice broke.

Now Joe spoke. "We were damned lucky we came through here then." He shuddered and ran his fingers through his thick hair and shrugged.

"The rope got tighter and tighter, Mommy. I couldn't even yell. I had no voice left, no air. My mouth felt like pudding." Foffy's arms grew limp. "I'm so sleepy," she whispered.

"No, you can't let her go to sleep, she's got to stay awake!" Joe grabbed Foffy and walked back and forth, jostling her in his arms. "She can't go to sleep, she could go out again." Mady knew you couldn't let them go to sleep after they had fallen or banged their heads, but why now? Foffy was breathing, she was awake, she had spoken clearly, reasonably. Mady tried to form a question, but the words stuck in her throat. Then the noise of the ambulance and Nina and Peter running toward her, encircling her in their arms.

She had been here for stitches and burns so she wasn't afraid when she entered the small emergency room behind the stretcher, but when they hooked the child up to an oxygen tank and she saw Nate Tolliver's face, Mady knew she had come close to losing her child.

"The oxygen is a precaution," he said. "We're not sure how long she was out. We'll do some X rays and after a while we'll run a few tests."

Someone put a chair behind her and she sat down. Her legs shook, but her voice was steady. "Are you talking about hours or days?"

"We don't know. We'll do a cardiogram and some other things and if everything looks okay you may be able to take her home today. I have another emergency, a baby who can't breathe, but I'll be back as soon as I can."

While they were wheeling Foffy to the elevator, Mady spoke with Peter and Nina. Nina's face was streaked with mud, her lips salty. Peter's mouth was tense, his eyes dazed. "We found your note and were walking through to the playhouse when they found her."

Mady nodded. "I wish you could stay but they don't want us all in Intensive Care. That's where she's going after the X rays."

"Don't worry, I'll be with them," Anne said. She pressed Mady's arm and led the children away.

More than anything Mady wanted to get out of her mud-spattered clothes. With them still on her back she was in the woods, helpless, overcome. Here it was different, here Foffy could get well. She would sit here all day and all night and for days and nights after that if she had to.

At the entrance to the Intensive Care Unit a nurse handed her a green gown, mask, paper slippers. "Everything off, wash up and put these on," she said brusquely.

"How is she?"

"Fine, just fine." The nurse had no idea how Foffy was. Why did they lie?

In the cubicle Foffy was asleep, but the gown bunched above the sheet moved in a regular rhythm and the young nurse standing over her smiled. From the way she bent over the child Mady knew she could be trusted.

"Everything's normal." She pointed to the machines.

"Is it okay for her to sleep?" Mady asked. "Joe Carpenter said she shouldn't, he kept her awake till the ambulance came."

The nurse nodded. "He had the right instincts, but now that she's monitored it's okay. Poor thing, she's exhausted. And so beautiful, I've never seen such hair, like floss." The nurse pushed a strand away from Foffy's ear. "I wouldn't be surprised if you could take her home today," she said softly and moved on. But even she might be lying. Mady had once heard someone say that hospitals were a conspiracy to fool the dying.

She sank into the chair. The child across from her was Foffy, but now she existed in a vacuum, connected only to the machines that recorded her life signs. Once Mady would have thought she would be weak or nauseated, now all she felt was a deep loneliness. Whatever happened to her child was apart from her. She was alive, the markings that trailed from the machines, those mysterious bird-scratchings, said she was fine. Surely a cause for joy, but all Mady felt was utter loneliness. Each moment was simply to be endured. Her mind was a piece of the purest Carrara, and all her brain could encompass was Foffy in the past — Foffy naked in the incubator, Foffy crawling on the window seat with a wooden man in her mouth, Foffy finishing her first meal of spaghetti and meat balls looking like an Indian, Foffy crying the first day of nursery school while she fought the impulse to scoop her up into her arms. Then Foffy at David's funeral — a small paper-doll figure in a gray and yellow plaid coat squeezed in among the dark clothes, never flinching as the glossy black coffin was swallowed by the earth. Foffy gathering shells on the damp sand singing to herself, Foffy straightening Sarah's sewing basket, Foffy sick after Sarah's funeral, Foffy trying to breathe, the rope tightening . . . No! She forced herself to see the child before her and her eyes seized the motes of sunlight and miraculously she found a thread of them to connect her to her child. Mady didn't know how long she concentrated on that thread. When Nate Tolliver walked in, she started, overcome with guilt; she had been within a hair's breadth of falling asleep.

"Mady?" His voice was low.

She pushed herself upright. Behind Nate was a tall man; she could hear Anne's voice in the hall. Her watch said five past one.

"This is Mark Sauer, Mady. He's a surgeon with a specialty in chest problems, he's at Babies Hospital, and he's going to have a look at Foffy." The child's eyelids fluttered open; she shut them quickly.

"Come Foffy, time to get up, someone's here to see you." Nate bent over her, took her hand. "Come on now, honey, open your eyes." The eyelids quivered, then opened wide. "Hi, Mommy.

Hello, Dr. Tolliver," she said in a clear cool voice. She had no idea how she had gotten here or why she had tubes and needles connected to her.

"Hello, darling." Mady's voice was a whisper, her blood ice water.

"Now, Foffy, while Mommy has something to eat Dr. Sauer's going to examine you," Nate said. Foffy looked around, her eyes bewildered. Mady said, "You had a little accident, you became unconscious. That's why you're here." Foffy got the message and for a second Mady felt faint, but the feeling passed. She wasn't quite steady on her feet. The young nurse gave her her arm, Nate smiled, the other doctor avoided her eyes.

Why couldn't Foffy remember? Was this the beginning of a lot of forgetting? Foffy often didn't remember waking in the night. Don't torture yourself with what hasn't happened, David's voice said in her ears.

Anne handed her a thermos cup of coffee that was so heavily sugared she wanted to gag. "Drink it slowly, you need the sugar," Anne said. She sipped the sticky liquid as the kids pulled chairs around her.

"Nate says Sauer is the best in the country," Anne said and offered her half a sandwich. Mady shook her head; she would be sick if she ate. She couldn't even form the words to tell Anne that Foffy hadn't remembered.

Peter and Nina told her who called, what the mail was. They had convinced themselves Foffy was all right. Her hands were folded in her lap, the reflex made her smile. She glanced at her watch. Almost ten to two. What was taking so long? Fear pricked her throat, her stomach, her chest. Anne was pacing the hall. Two. Two-ten, two-thirteen.

Finally Nate's voice — cheerful, buoyant. "I think Foffy needs an ice-cream soda." His face creased into a grin. "Nurse is removing the intravenous, you can take her home. Mark says we were very lucky."

Mady looked at Dr. Sauer, expecting a smile. His eyes accused her. "You were more than lucky. It's a miracle that child had no damage and those X rays are so clear. How she didn't do anything to her lungs or liver is amazing." His voice was bitter.

"Now, Mark, Mady's had enough for one day," Nate said. Mady extended her hand to thank Dr. Sauer, but he looked at it, turned, and strode down the hall.

"He just lost a boy Foffy's age. Leukemia. He's not back to his office, he did this as a favor, we were in medical school together . . ." Nate hurried away.

"Poor thing, he's still sick with grief, Mady, he didn't mean it," Anne said. "He can't help himself." Mady felt her throat fill. She went in to Foffy.

"Wasn't Dr. Sauer the funniest man, Mommy? He made me do the queerest things, he kept tickling me." She put her arms around her mother's neck. She was so light and this morning she had been so heavy. Dead weight; what an apt phrase. "And now I remember everything," Foffy told her. "I was so scared when I couldn't yell. Did you ever open your mouth and have nothing come out? It's terrible." Mady pulled the child closer.

After they were both dressed she realized she had gotten no instructions. The young nurse was in the hall talking to Anne. Under her arm was a folder marked "Sophia Glazer."

"Nothing special, everything back to normal. Maybe a nap this afternoon and a good supper. Dr. Tolliver will call, and as much television as she wants." She put her hand on Foffy's shoulder. "What's your favorite program?"

" 'Emergency,' " Foffy said, then looked puzzled when everyone, even her mother, laughed so heartily.

In Mady's room her bed was turned down and Foffy's nightgown was folded on the unused pillow. The optimism of children is touching and unsinkable, Mady thought as she watched Anne undress Foffy and tuck her in. She had only enough strength to kick off her shoes and lie down next to Foffy in her clothes. When she had seen Nate's face, she had felt a surge of energy, but it was the same false energy she had had after she gave birth. Now all she wanted was to sleep.

The ringing of the telephone woke her. Foffy gave a little grunt and flung out her arm, then sank back into a deep sleep. Only when she glanced at the clock did she remember Hans. It was four-fifty. Oh, my God, he's still waiting! she thought. She saw him walking up and down those endless stairs in front of the Metropolitan, checking his watch, searching the crowd again, one more time, then, finally, disgustedly, dialing her number.

She hurried into the kitchen. Anne was explaining patiently as she stirred. The kitchen smelled almost obscenely delicious. She was actually hungry.

His voice was ice. Why hadn't she called when she knew she couldn't meet him? He hadn't left his house till after one. "I've been waiting here for almost two hours," he muttered. The operator asked for more money. She pictured him standing in the lobby of the emptying museum with not even a booth around him for protection. She never understood the open phones in that luxurious museum. He was probably standing straighter than ever, his face as controlled as a piece of sculpture. Oh, how had she been so thoughtless! She could hardly believe what she had done. "I'm mortified, Hans. I thought about calling when we got to the hospital, but once I was in the Intensive Care Unit, everything but Foffy flew out of my head."

"How is she?" His voice was less hard.

"Exhausted. The fright tired her and they also put a lot of needles into her. All sorts of tests, X rays. She looked like a pincushion."

"Well, give her my love, I'll talk to you." The phone clicked, he was gone.

Mady was speechless. How could he do that? Her eyes finally filled, tears dribbled down her cheeks. Once she had heard his voice she wanted to see him, talk to him. But he wasn't interested. All he could think of was what she had done to him. And he was right, she was to blame, but still . . .

"He doesn't understand, Mady," Anne said softly, as if afraid someone might hear. "How can he? He's never had a child."

Mady nodded. Her legs had begun to tremble again. She needed a hot shower. Before she went she listened for sounds of the older children. "Where are they?" she asked Anne.

"Nina's in her room reading. Peter left." Anne refused to meet her eyes.

"Left?"

"Yes, he went to Ricky's for dinner. He came in about four and said he guessed he would go to the game as planned. He said to tell you he'd be home about one. He's got his key." Mady stood there, with her hand on her left thigh, trying to quiet its shaking. How could he have gone, didn't he know Foffy had almost died? She searched Anne's face for an answer.

"Don't be too hard on him. After all, he's never had a child either."

Mady finally smiled. "I guess you're right. Still, it's amazing, isn't it?"

Anne chuckled. "It doesn't get any better, but" — she stood with the dish towel suspended from her hand — "that's the way it's supposed to be, I guess. Now you go take a shower. This stew is almost ready, and as soon as you get out I've got to go."

Mady looked at Anne, feeling as selfish as Peter. "Oh, Anne, how can I thank you?"

"You can't. Come on now, get into that shower, you'll feel a hundred times better."

When she got out, she slipped into a nightgown and robe. In the kitchen Anne was pulling on her jacket. Anne looked so tired. Mady was filled with guilt.

"Nate called and spoke to Foffy. He left numbers where he can be reached. We're supposed to go to the Porters' later, if you need me, call." She kissed Madeleine and left.

About halfway through dinner the phone rang. It was Nina's friend Ramona. The girls had been planning to practice a concerto together. When they had heard about Foffy, Ramona's mother suggested they go to her house, and maybe Nina would like to sleep over. Nina was leaving the decision to Mady. If her mother wanted her home she would stay. "But we've got to practice," she warned. *What if your mother wants you home, but not with Ramona and not to practice?* Mady felt like asking; instead she said, "Maybe better there. Then Foffy and I can go to sleep early."

A sigh of relief escaped from Nina. Watching her, Mady realized that both she and Peter needed to get out of here tonight. Foffy's brush with death had frightened them; they were running as fast as they could. Their toughness, their instinct for self-preservation were amazing, marvelous in a gruesome way. Young animals, Mady thought, not without a strange pride as she cleared the table.

After dinner Foffy read more of her book. Except for the bruises on her forearms, which were now covered by her warm pajamas, she looked exactly as she had this morning when she had been reading. Mady shuddered. Another minute and who knew what might have happened, where they would be now? All was well, yet Foffy wasn't the same. No one was the same. She had to let the kids recover as quickly as they could; it wasn't fair to remind them how close Foffy had come, and as she gazed at the child reading so intently, absently scratching her arms where the needles had gone in, Mady knew she would never tell Foffy the whole truth, the might-have-beens about today. Yet she wished she could talk to someone. If only Peter and Nina weren't gone. But that was the point. They didn't want to share this with her. Her parents and Shelley and Mel didn't know what had happened, she realized proudly. Her neighbors knew Foffy was all right and that Anne had been here to help her. She could call Gail, but she was probably out. It was Saturday night in the suburbs.

When "Emergency" began, Mady went into the living room. In the corner stood a large worn music basket. When she got to the tattered French copy of *L'Arlesienne* suite, which she had had since she was a child, she knew that the more difficult music wasn't far away — the Schubert sonatas, then the Mozart, the

Beethoven, the Bach partitas. Soon the room was filled with music. Not the mistakes and stumbles of someone who had not played for years and was practicing, trying to get her fingers to work again, but music made by someone who once knew how to play and needed, badly, to play again. The movements of her fingers warmed her; as the hammers struck the strings she could feel her blood pulsing through her body. How different this was from that night at Shelley's, how different from her earlier attempts to play these last months! Now she felt that she was playing with every cell of her body, and the physical effort combined with the exhilaration she was feeling relieved the loneliness. At least she could do this. Perhaps Sarah was right, perhaps this was the very thing she needed to do again, perhaps this could give her the comfort that not even reading the Russian could give her now. She could think of nothing but the notes in front of her, she had to concentrate wholly on the pattern of sound and rhythm they formed in her head and her hands and feet in order to create the music now filling the room. Her fingers flew across the keys and when, at last, she let her eyes stray from the black notes, she saw Foffy's small face shining. The child stood stock-still in the bell of the piano. For how long Mady had no idea. Time had stopped. Her eyes were bright, amazed. "Oh, Mommy, I didn't know you could play like that!" she cried. Mady held out her arms, then pulled her onto her lap and together they sat, listening to the eerie resonance of music that still lingered in the room.

As she put Foffy into her bed (for the little girl insisted on sleeping there), Mady thought of Mark Sauer — the whiteness rimming his mouth, his hooded eyes, his dry voice.

"Do I have to brush my teeth?" Foffy whispered into her hair.

"No, darling." By the time she tucked her in, Foffy was asleep.

Back at the piano she thought not only of Sarah, but of Larry. He was right, she would survive, but not in the way everyone else had mapped out for her. Like them she had thought her survival depended upon a husband, children to look after, a house, a garden. But that was not the whole story. These last two years had been filled with fright and anger and grief, but also with a strengthening. She could do more than she had ever imagined, more than David, more than her parents or Shelley or even Anne knew. Survival has very little to do with love, she had learned; it has more to do with determination. That black girl Cassandra had that kind of determination. So did Hans. Hans!

She should have known she would end up thinking of him. Where was he? What had he done after he called? Why couldn't he understand what had happened? When your child is in danger, there is nothing else, but how could he understand?

She concentrated on the music. She began with the Bach and played the passages of the fugue over and over, trying to absorb the rhythm, for only when she did that would the voices play against each other as they should. Even this relatively easy fugue was so complex, but that was the fascination. Each time she played it through she saw something else. It would be as challenging in its way as reading Akhmatova or Mandelstam or Tolstoy or Chekhov. Her fingers relaxed as she played and she began to think of how she would prepare to get herself a job at the music school.

At first she didn't hear the doorbell, and by the time she did the ringing was loud, insistent. Probably Nina; she must have forgot something, or maybe she had decided to sleep at home. Mady was surprised to discover she didn't care which.

"Oh!" She nearly jumped back into the shadows. For months she used to dream that David would ring the doorbell and she would open it and they would fall into each other's arms. Time and reality had tarnished those dreams; now they were as remote as her girlhood fantasies.

"Oh, you frightened me!" She stepped forward hesitantly. "Come in, please come in."

Hans stared at her. He made no attempt to take her hands. His eyes were penetrating her skin, her hair, all the outer coverings of her self. He was seeing inside her, she felt; when she opened the door she had been embarrassed to be in her robe, now she knew it didn't matter.

"Why don't you take off your coat?"

He shrugged, then pulled off his raincoat and threw it over a chair. They went into the dining room and he watched her pour some brandy into glasses.

"Skol," he said. Even his anger on the telephone had not prepared her for this dense silence, this stony awkwardness. She pulled out chairs and they sat down. The room was glaringly bright; she rose and dimmed the chandelier, and, at last, he spoke.

"I was so angry, angrier than I can remember, even when I was a boy. After I hung up I had dinner and could barely swallow the food. I finally gave up and walked down to the theater district and got a seat for *Equus* and was sitting there watching all the people come in, and then I asked myself why I was sitting here. Was I going to spend the rest of my life watching other people enjoy themselves? I have spent so much of my life doing it that I don't think much about it. But then I thought of you here, and how stupid I was not to be with you, so I got up and gave my ticket to a priest who kept insisting he wanted to pay me for it, and after I convinced him I didn't want his money, I walked back up to the museum where I had left the car. I could think of nothing but you, my body was leading my mind, I was practically in a trance. Lucky I didn't have an accident, now that I think about it. My mind was in a limbo I have never known. When I saw you on the beach that day, I never dreamed it would be like this. Then, when I pulled up to the house and heard you playing, I thought, 'She's fine, she doesn't need me,' and I knew I should leave and let you be, but I couldn't. I had to see you. I was afraid that if I didn't see you now I would never see you again. Can you understand?" His eyes searched hers, he was seeing her now. She pulled up her robe and smoothed her hair. "I must look like a wild woman," she murmured, and the tension between them was broken — in a second. When they went into the living room, she took up her needlepoint. She couldn't care if it bothered him, she needed its rhythm now, and, besides, she was almost finished.

"I was so disappointed when you didn't come, I was horrible on the phone," he started to say.

"It was my fault," she interrupted. "I should have called. I used to have nightmares like this, especially right after David died, then to have one actually happen — well, I was paralyzed. I was still numb when you called. I thought about calling you when we got to the hospital but when I saw Foffy with all those needles in her I lost all sense of time." She felt foolish and wanted to stop, but something made her say, "Anne was here when you called and when you hung up she said, 'He's never had a child . . .'" The words popped out, but he didn't mind.

"She's right," he said, sighing a little. "There are so many things I don't know, feelings I haven't had. My life has been so solitary. Since we met that day on the beach I scarcely know who I am, and what I feel so much of the time is that I'm not enough, not nearly enough of a person for you. David was so capable, so much in the world, he did everything right. There's so much I don't even know," he said ruefully.

Madeleine shook her head and put down her needlework. All the shyness and embarrassment dropped away as she took his hands into hers. They were cold. She rubbed them. "No, that's wrong, the dead just seem to do everything right. Memory warps. No one does everything right, not even David." She searched Hans's eyes. "Besides, I don't want another David." Her voice was hardly more than a whisper, but she had to say it, once and for all. "I used to, and in the beginning I pretended he wasn't dead. I talked to him, I kept imagining what he would answer, how he would act when I had a problem. Then it occurred to me that if I could find someone like him I might be able to stop pretending. It wasn't conscious, of course, but that's what was happening when I went to all those dinner parties. Then a week or so before we came to Racer's Cove I had a strange dream. I was walking through the house, straightening up before

I went to bed and everything I touched crumbled to dust — the books, the magazines, the kids' shoes in the hall, the piano, even some fruit in the bowl. Then I ran back to our room and David was asleep with the covers up over his head, the way he always slept, and I went to pull the blankets down, but as soon as I touched him his body began to crumble and the blankets sank and instead of David there was a pile of dust. I woke up crying, but after that I think I knew I was on my own. After that I stopped looking for David. And in these last months I've learned to face some of the things I had refused to face when we were married or soon after he died. No, Hans, I don't want another David."

The finality of her words hammered into the silence of the house. She was glad he had let go of her hands because she needed to get up, walk around, make sure she had two firm legs instead of those trembling appendages she had had to cope with so often these last few years. She couldn't believe how good she felt. Her hands grazed the piano, the mantel, the tops of the chairs, a lampshade. They were all there, and so was Hans, watching every gesture she made. She took his outstretched hand and settled against the rough tweed of his jacket. Quietly they talked and soon she could tell him what had happened this morning in a logical sequence. "It feels like a month ago," she said. He nodded. Again his face was filled with that odd light. She wondered if he knew about it and started to ask him when he drew her toward him and gently kissed her. Her body filled with desire, her voice grew thick.

"You'll stay?"

"If you want me to."

He followed her to the linen closet and silently they made up the bed in the den. Then they went into Mady's bedroom. Foffy woke when Mady closed the window. "Who's here?"

"It's me, Foffy, and Hans. He came to see how you are."

Hans bent over the child, kissed her. "Hello, Sophia, I hear you had an adventure."

Foffy laughed. "Will you be here in the morning?"

"Yes, you'll see him at breakfast," Mady said quickly.

"Can we have pancakes?"

The hall clock said eleven-thirty. Peter would be home about one. She wouldn't mention that, and instead thought about her nightgown. It was frayed on the hem and sleeves. Worn nightgown, worn body: stretch marks, darkened veins, she even had a few hairs near the nipple of her right breast. Her child had almost died and here she was — not even twelve hours later — about to make love. She had lost her mind, Shelley was right. Besides, what about precautions? She didn't even know what to do anymore, that part of her life had slipped so far into the past. She belonged back in her bed next to Foffy.

She stopped at the door to the den. Hans was looking at the books. He had taken off his jacket and was undoing his tie. His profile was a shaft of light in the sepia glow of the dim room. She could feel herself pulled to him, attracted by that glimmer that played over his features and might have come from his Nordic ancestors or his African childhood; she found herself wanting to touch the high narrow cheekbones so prominent now that the beard was gone; how she loved the natural reticence of his carriage, even the way his clothes hung on his body. Yes, he was a presence, and she no longer felt she had to deny it.

He turned to look at her and a fierce longing spilled from his eyes. Yet he waited for her to move toward him. He wanted her to be sure, and when her body, which had felt so worn and unused for so long, opened to him, Mady knew there was no turning back. All the details she had worried about didn't matter at all. Yet their lovemaking was awkward, tense. He tried to apologize.

"Shhh." She held her fingers to his lips. "There will be lots more times." Years of love had taught her that awkward sex can be a challenge, but there was no way on earth she could think to phrase it. So she lay back in the crook of his elbow and the space between them filled with the faint hum of their mingled breathing punctuated by a few brief, shorthand-like whispers. They both jumped a little when the phone rang. She reached across him and turned on the light. It was twenty after one.

"Mom, did I wake you?"

"No, no, it's all right. What's wrong, Peter?"

"Ricky's father got a flat on the way home and we're in a gas station. They say they can fix it in about twenty minutes. Can I sleep at their house? I'm sorry, Mom, I couldn't help it." His voice was filled more with guilt for leaving her than for being late.

"It's okay, Peter, don't worry — as long as you're okay. I hope you get home soon, and you can sleep at Ricky's. I'll talk to you in the morning." She wondered if she would ever tell Peter the truth about tonight. No. His life was beginning to be his and hers was hers.

Hans was shaking his head. "I don't know where my head was, I forgot about the older children," he admitted.

"That's because they aren't here. Nina is sleeping at a friend's, and Peter went to a basketball game and Ricky's father got a flat so he's going to sleep there," she explained, then held out her arms. This time their movements were slower, surer, anticipating pleasure, and when she felt her body begin to turn inside out, she also felt tears of relief coursing down her cheeks. Hans gathered her into his arms and soon they fell asleep.

When they woke she could see her watch by the moonlight. Three-fifteen. Foffy! Quickly pulling her nightgown over her head she rushed into the bedroom. But Foffy was breathing evenly on her stomach, her arms curved around her head. Back in the den Hans was sitting up and the light was on. His arms and upper body were thinner than she remembered from the beach. Or was she seeing him differently? They sat quietly for a moment, then he cupped his broad hands around her face and drew her to him for one last kiss. "I'll see you in the morning," she whispered. As she slid into her own bed, careful not to jar her child, she was strangely aware only of the scent of the bath oil that had clung to her body since morning.

CHAPTER 20

Fresh snow was falling as Mady walked out of Grand Central station. She would walk to Dore's, she decided, and stuck out her tongue to catch a wisp of snow. Although it was still that fragile time just before the winter darkness descended, the stores and streets were gaily lit — Christmas was only a few days off — and as people hurried in and out of the shops on Fifth Avenue, an air of excitement flowed onto the streets.

She was meeting Hans for dinner and they were going to the opera. He was supposed to drive in, then he would come home with her for the weekend. Now, with the snow, she wondered what he would do. She had given him Dore's number, perhaps he had called there. She wouldn't concern herself about it. She didn't worry about him the way she used to worry about David, and she knew, with a stab of recognition it was impossible to ignore, that she had worried about too many details and David had tended sometimes to treat her like an anxious child. "He takes up too much of the air," Dore used to say. Well, maybe he did, but maybe it was because she didn't take up enough and concentrated on all the wrong things.

At Forty-first Street she crossed Fifth Avenue to avoid passing right in front of Max's office building. She didn't think she would meet him and felt a little guilty for not stopping in to see him, but she didn't have time. Besides, what was the point? He was so angry at her. Why, she didn't exactly know. Because Hans was so different? A German? A gentile? "Dad would be happier if you were considering marriage," Shelley had told her a few days ago. But that was nonsense. She and Hans had just begun to know each other; no one was getting married these days. "Dad doesn't think it's appropriate for Hans to stay overnight," Shelley had ventured with a question mark in her voice. But they both knew that Max wouldn't care what Mady was doing with a man he approved of.

Below Altman's Fifth Avenue changed quickly — now she was passing the rug dealers, then the office machine shops, then the soft goods. Here it was more working class; she heard Spanish, Italian, finally some loud American obscenities. The snow was falling fast and her boots made prints on the whitened street. With each step her footfalls became softer. She grew aware only of a regular tapping, and at the next corner a young blond man was waiting to be helped across the street. He had the naked handsomeness of the youthful blind. David used to help the blind all the time, but she had never done it before. Tentatively she put her hand under his arm. His coat was pitifully thin. He jumped. "Can I help you?" she said as clearly as she could. Too late she had remembered it was important to be decisive, firm; if you were nervous you made them nervous, she had once read.

"Thank you," he said, then relaxed. After they had crossed he turned to her and said, "It looks like it's going to be a real storm."

"Yes," she answered, "maybe it will be a white Christmas."

At the next intersection he turned to cross Fifth Avenue and she waited until she saw an older man take his arm.

Soon she, too, turned and walked west. Now the wind slapped her face and she could feel that her color was high when she stepped into the lobby of Dore's building, which had, of course, a young woman elevator operator. All the tenants in the building were women; it was an old loft building owned by women, rebuilt by women carpenters, plumbers, electricians, and now was run entirely by women. Dore had moved here a few years ago, after she and Jake were divorced.

"Mady, how fantastic you look!" Dore greeted her at the door and folded her arms around Mady. Then she stood away, holding Mady at arm's length. "You have such good color and you don't look so haggard."

"You look wonderful, too, Dore," Mady replied and slipped out of her coat.

"I put back five pounds but now I'm holding my own. It's terrible, a constant battle. After I lost all that weight I thought my metabolism had changed, but nothing changes as you get older, everything just gets a little worse," Dore said cheerfully. "Oh, your Hans called. He said he was taking the train and would meet you in front of the Metropolitan Opera House at six." Mady waited for some aside from Dore, but Dore had taken her arm and was leading her into the huge room that combined living, dining, and sleeping. Off to the left — to form the top of a T — were the small kitchen and a bathroom and dressing room. Once again, Mady was struck by the starkness of the apartment. Everything was white and angular and obsessively neat. Mady searched for some color, some shape to soften the glaring austerity of the room, and as she sat down her eyes seized upon a huge bunch of strawflowers on the night table next to Dore's low bed.

"How do you keep it so neat?" Mady gestured toward the large uncluttered space and shook her head wonderingly as Dore put a glass of sherry into her hand.

"Oh, I don't keep it. It's a compulsion with me, a disease, really. I think I have to live this way to conceal the disorder in my mind. I once read that — the more chaotic your personality is, the more compulsively neat you are."

"You're making that up, Dore," Mady said with a smile.

"No, I'm not. Erich Fromm, or someone like that."

"Poor Erich Fromm, he gets blamed for everything," Mady murmured. She tried to remember what Dore's house had looked like: the usual suburban house with traditional furniture, children clutter, magazines, newspapers, plants, eucalyptus in the front hall that Mady remembered because of its coppery color, heavy drapes, pillows, shelves and shelves of books.

"What did you do with all the books?" she asked.

"The kids. We gave everything to the kids. Jake didn't want anything and I wanted to start out fresh, too, so the good furniture is in storage and the kids will get it when they want it. They divided the books and records and *chotchkes.* They were thrilled."

"Don't you miss anything?"

"Oh, maybe a few of the art books, but I go to the library, and I have bought new copies of a few of my favorites. I keep them in that cabinet." Dore pointed to a cabinet near the dining room table that was painted a clear pure white like everything else in the apartment.

Mady shrugged. She couldn't imagine giving up everything she lived with so easily. But Dore didn't want to talk about it anymore.

"What are you doing? I saw Mack Solomon a few weeks ago and he is still offended that you didn't take the job translating Chekhov with his publishing house."

"How do you know Mack Solomon?" Mady asked, surprised.

"Through Eli Houseman. I go to Eli's for dinner every six months or so, he's got a charming wife and they're one of the few couples I've kept up with — or rather who have kept up with me — since Jake and I divorced. Anyway, last time they had Mack Solomon and his wife. If you think he's strange you should meet her. She's had her face lifted a few times and looks like she's hiding nuts in her cheeks, and she's got sawdust between her ears. This translation project is her baby, you know."

Mady nodded. "That's what he said."

"They have five people working on the early stories by Chekhov. They sit around a conference table and argue over every word. Mack said sometimes it gets very tense. When they split for lunch, they look like they're about to kill each other."

"Or themselves," Mady said. "That's what I probably would have done. Poor Chekhov! When he wrote those stories I'm sure he didn't envision a team translation. Only in America." She sighed.

"Solomon still thinks you didn't take the job because you sensed he was hot for you," Dore told her. Mady stared.

"He is, you know. He kept asking about you, what you were doing, what kind of marriage you had had, whether you needed the job. I think he had decided you needed the money and he was a little disappointed when I told him you had been left a comfortable widow. He seemed very surprised to hear that most of David's insurance had actually been doubled because he died in a plane crash. He said he thought that was a myth. When I left, he told me two or three times to send you his best."

Mady groaned. "Oh, Dore, he was awful."

Dore nodded and they sat silently for a few moments.

"I've decided to do something with the music. When I'm playing the piano I can't think of anything else, and that's what I seem to need now. I've been taking lessons again, and I'm going to apply for a job at the music school for the spring semester," Mady volunteered. Dore nodded briskly.

"It's a good place." Dore's children had studied there, too.

"Very good. And I think the contact with the other teachers and the students is what I must have now. There are times when I think I'll never be able to do anything with the Russian, I care about it too much, and I'm not willing to make the kinds of compromises you have to make in publishing."

"You'll see. You may feel differently in a year or two. But you certainly don't want to start with Mack Solomon, or his wife. You would have hated her. Her mouth turns down and she's so angry. Perpetually disappointed, her face says."

Dore turned her glass in her hands and when she looked up her eyes were sad. "Anne tells me you've fallen in love. With this Hans."

Mady could feel herself blush. "I don't know about 'in love,' but I do care about him." Dore frowned.

"He's a wonderful man, Dore, a potter. A marvelous potter. He also does some sculpting."

"In stone or wood?" Dore asked.

"Wood." Dore nodded and looked down. "What's the matter?" Mady asked.

"Oh, I don't know. I thought you were going to make it on your own."

"But I have made it on my own — for two years," Mady reminded her.

"I mean completely independent, without a man. After David, I thought you would have had enough to last you for a lifetime, he was such a force."

"Yes, he was. Everyone else admired that in him — except you."

"He was selfish, he never thought about you, only about his needs, his career, and you indulged him. That's why he was able to go so far so young."

"I didn't indulge him, Dore, I loved him. I didn't want anything else then, or if I did, I learned to suppress it."

"But if you didn't know any better, he should have seen it and encouraged you. Not everybody knows Russian as well as you do."

"Oh, Dore, that's crazy. No one, no husband, does that, except maybe in paradise. If you're going to save yourself you have to do it yourself. David and I were your ordinary suburban couple in the late fifties and sixties. He built a career and I took care of the kids."

"You didn't need three."

"No one needs anything, Dore. I wanted three children, so did David. And you and Jake wanted Jane and Andy, you know you did."

Dore shrugged. "Who knows, it all seems so long ago, like someone else's life."

Suddenly Mady felt brave enough to ask Dore what she had never asked but had wanted to know for a long time. "Why are you so down on men, Dore, what happened with you and Jake?" For so many years they had been the model couple, and then — nothing.

Dore narrowed her eyes. "Nothing very dramatic, though everyone thought it was something sordid. We realized after Andy went to college that we couldn't stand each other, that we were doing everything we could to avoid each other. I wanted to go into therapy, and we had begun to talk about it, then one night Jake pulled out these elaborate charts and a huge graph. I couldn't imagine what they were, I thought they were statistics on marriage, on middle-aged couples, or people whose parents were immigrants and who went to college, something like that. And then he announced in what I used to call his 'legal voice' — and you, of all people, know what that is, Mady — that the charts were records of all the times we had had sexual intercourse. I remember he used that archaic term and I thought to myself, 'What a cold hard man he is!' He had kept the charts for twenty-one years and then he had given them to his secretary and she had made a graph and of course what the graph showed was a slowing down of passion and of interest in each other, and here, he said, was the evidence that we should part. Therapy wouldn't help. I was so shocked and repelled that I didn't protest, it was useless to think we could ever stay married. Some things are as definitive as death, Mady. You know, I still dream about those charts," Dore said. Her voice was cold, but her face was beaded with perspiration and she had put down her glass and her knuckles were white as she gripped the arms of her chair.

"I couldn't believe how cruel he was, and that very night I packed up whatever he had given me — the jewelry, the books, all of his gifts — into a suitcase and I handed it to him (he thought I had packed him some clothes) and threw him out of the house. It was true when he told everyone for months afterward that I had thrown him out. He didn't come back for his things until I had found this apartment and the legal proceedings were well on their way. By then he had that young girl who worked in his office and he had decided to go to Chicago."

Finally Dore relaxed a little and sat back in her chair. "I know people think I'm gay now, but I'm not. Sex doesn't seem very important anymore, and there's something pleasant about living such a virginal life. And I'm always a little afraid for other women — like you today — because I wonder if this Hans, or any man, will treat you cruelly. After all, Jake looked like one of the gentlest nicest men on this earth, didn't he, Mady?"

Madeleine nodded. She found it hard to swallow. David had adored Jake when he was young — "such a fine clear mind, such compassion," he used to tell her when he came home from work.

Now Dore was smiling a little, a mocking ironic smile that Mady knew. "Odd, isn't it, Mady? No one knows what goes on in other people's houses, do they? Now do you see why I can't wish you luck, or be happy for you and this Hans? All I feel is plain old gut fear for you."

"But he's a lovely man, really. You'd like him, Dore."

Dore gazed at her; she looked more like her old self. "Does he have a sense of humor in bed?" she asked. Mady looked at her, startled.

"Why, yes, he does. So did David," she answered.

Dore chuckled. "Still the loyal wife," she murmured, then added, "You're lucky, Mady, very lucky. With Jake sex was always a matter of life or death and when I once told him that, he replied, very seriously, 'Of course it is, Dore, the French call orgasm *le petit mort*, you know.' I should have divorced him then, if I had had a brain in my head."

"But don't you miss it? I don't mean the sex," Mady interrupted herself, "but the, the tension."

Dore nodded. "I know what you mean and I did miss it at first. I missed a lot of crazy things — like the excitement you feel now, that glows from you because you're going to meet a man you care about and have dinner and go to the opera. I also missed the pleasure of talking to what we in my generation —remember, I'm almost ten years older than you, Mady — used to call a male intelligence. But I've found friends who are terrifically bright. There is no such thing as a male intelligence anymore, at least the way we meant it, and I like the company of other women. We're more careful with each other, we take care of each other when we're sick, it's very touching."

How different Dore was from the woman she had been in the suburbs, or even the woman who came back to visit her old friends. Here Dore was so much quieter, so much surer of herself, Mady thought, as they walked together upstairs to the studio Dore shared with several artists who lived in the building. A woman was working on a painting — a young woman with prematurely gray hair in a large purple smock dress. She was doing a self-portrait that was harsh and angry-looking, but she seemed completely at ease and content. She glanced up briefly as they entered and smiled. Then Mady looked at the paintings propped in Dore's section of the studio. They were the cycle called *Winter White* that Dore had done last spring — two winter landscapes of a barn and a water wheel and a dammed-up spring, and two abstractions of the same material. The contrast was startling, but even more interesting was the progression. When you looked closely, you could actually see Dore's mind changing and working, and Mady thought, I would love Hans to see these.

"They're wonderful, Dore, absolutely first-rate," she said.

Then Dore led her behind the divider where there were two paintings mostly in shades of green, with some blues and yellows. "These are the beginning of the *Green Spring* cycle that I started last summer," she explained. The colors washed the canvases in such a subtle, suggestive way that Mady felt as if she had wandered into David's garden and all the familiar signs of spring — the newly thawed earth, the early hyacinths, the spots of chionodoxa and crocus color, the drapery of the forsythia and wisteria — were actually surrounding her.

"Like?" Dore said, her eyes proud.

"Not like, love," Mady said, and Dore took her arm and they walked downstairs in silence.

Mady had thought she would stay a little longer, maybe tell Dore more about Hans, but now she knew it would have to wait.

Dore tried to explain. "I'm sorry, Mady, I don't talk very much to people these days and it seems to tire me so quickly.

I've been doing a lot of reading these last few years and one of the phrases I love most is from your Chekhov." Mady smiled at her use of the possessive.

"Remember when Masha says in *The Three Sisters* — 'You must know what you live for or else nothing matters anymore'? Remember that?"

Mady nodded.

"Well, I'm living for those paintings, sometimes I feel as if I'm painting with my blood," Dore said.

Quickly they parted. The snow was coming down in thick large flakes by now and Mady was glad to spot an empty cab cruising.

She settled into the cracked plastic of the shabby cab and her fingers, her back, her whole body welcomed the worn mustiness that seeped into her. When they stopped for a light, the cabby turned slightly toward her.

"Lady, are you all right? You look exhausted."

"No, no, I'm fine. I just went to visit an old friend."

"In the hospital?"

"No, just very different from the way she used to be."

"Well, that's how it goes, lady, that's life — birth, childhood, a little love if you're lucky, a lot of change, growing old, and then death. For some people the biggest event in their life is death," he added.

Mady sighed and leaned farther back into the seat. Behind the scrim of falling snow she watched the West Side slide by. She closed her eyes. Her mind was so cluttered she could feel herself consciously trying to clear it, as you would a messy kitchen. She searched for some rhythm her mind could fix on, but cabs aren't like trains, and all she got was the swish of the cars on the wet streets — like waves slapping in toward shore, if you isolated the sound. Trains had such a soothing rhythm; in a train you could let your mind unravel and think of nothing. Her mind wandered back to a train ride she and David had taken when they were first married. They went to Europe after he got out of the army and they were going from Milan to Florence. It was a scorching day and they found a compartment that wasn't full so she could put her legs up. The only other people in the compartment were an old Italian couple, dressed in black. The woman was very delicate and thin, and she dozed as a falling sun streaked the summer sky and the first signs of twilight appeared. The old man took off his glasses and rubbed them, as if astonished that what he saw was real. She and David exchanged glances and smiled, and then watched, in absolute stillness, as the old man tapped his wife on the shoulder. Patiently he watched her struggle with the light and when she opened her eyes they were filled with anticipation. He gestured out the window. *"Bellissima!"* his wife breathed happily and then all four of them watched until the flaring sun descended below their line of sight.

When the cab pulled into Lincoln Center and she reached into her bag, Mady could feel the cabby's eyes on her. She handed him a bill; while he groped for change he started again. "Don't take it so hard, lady, that's life, that's all there is . . ." he began.

She shook her head. "No, no, that's not all . . ." she started to protest, but what was the use? Quickly she opened the door and left without waiting for her change. When she spotted Hans, she ran to him and hugged him so tightly that even he was surprised.

CHAPTER 21

THE SHARP COLD SENT A RUSH of pain through his sinuses. Max ducked into a candy store and stood in front of the cough drops.

"The Smith Brothers cherry are the best unless it's a dry cough, then the honey drops are good," the woman said.

Max bought both, grateful for her slowness which allowed him to linger. The store was stifling, hadn't she heard of the energy crisis? he wanted to ask, but when she handed him change he saw she was very old. And the cozy warmth she needed was why he was here, and she knew it. The door kept banging to.

"Cold enough for you?" her customers greeted her. The woman's quick smile and patience with the people who came in and even leafed through the magazines, then left without buying a thing, touched Max. Who will run a candy store like this in twenty-five years, or even ten? he wondered as he stepped into the shrieking cold.

He was late. He had to stop and leave the car for service and had missed the 8:56. Now it was almost ten. He could have taken a cab, but he was too stubborn. He always walked from Penn Station to his office on Fifth Avenue and the third day of extreme cold wasn't enough to break a habit of fifty years. He picked his way along the narrow path between two humps of gray snow and breathed in. There, that was better; one had only to get used to it. No trick at all, just stay out in it and breathe.

The tall prism of the Empire State Building glistened in the sun. Still a beautiful city. Before he could think about it, he had pushed himself through the revolving doors and was on his way to the observation deck. He hadn't done this in years, maybe twenty years, and then it had been his twenty-fifth anniversary and the parks and streets were lush with greenery and people.

No one else was in the observation area. From here the snow and ice were white in the glittering sun, and the bare trees, the sharp light veering off steel and chrome, gave the city a bare, otherworldly aspect. Battery Park was almost deserted, Ellis Island forlorn. Large ice floes surrounded the Statue of Liberty. Locked in by the ice, her green even more garish because of the reflected light, the poor girl looked trapped, miserable. Max smiled, remembering when Libby had taken the girls to see her. They must have been about eight and four. How Mady had cried. "She's green!" she accused them both. "No one told me she was going to be green!"

And now, sad lady, choked by the ice, she looked ghastlier than ever.

Still, it was a beautiful city. The iced-over harbor, the mauve tones of winter in the parks, the fumes and smells and complaints and bitter cold so distant, and he so secure and warm, watching. He had never been much of a watcher. When he was young he had liked nothing better than closeness; the comforts of intimacy were among the great goods of life. Yet now he needed distance.

His glance strayed from one bridge to another. The Brooklyn was the prettiest, but the Verrazano gleamed brightest. He had once read that in medieval Europe people killed and buried children in the piers of bridges as a sacrifice to ensure that they would stand. They had lost men while building the Brooklyn

Bridge, but the Verrazano was untainted. Now all the sharp edges of those fabulous engineering minds seemed to shine in these bridges. Yet they depressed Max. Why couldn't we manage our governments, our cities as elegantly as we had learned to build bridges?

It had been such a disappointing fall. He had hoped for a cleansing when Ford came in; instead there was the hedging, the pardon of Nixon, the misery in the cities, among the blacks, more inflation, no leadership, statesmanship, or diplomacy, and everywhere he looked — that wild man Kissinger. While everyone read books about Watergate. It was a phenomenon for anthropologists — all that reading — and throughout the last months Max had become more and more detached. When Libby opened the paper the other night and saw Nixon's photograph and said, "He looks so bad," Max had felt as lonely as he had ever felt in his life.

Then, in addition, Mady and Hans. In these last months — through what had been the hardest part of the last two years: Thanksgiving, Christmas, New Year's — Mady had blossomed in what could have been the most touching way, if only he could get his brain to accept Hans.

The man was intelligent, gracious, and loved not only his daughter but his grandchildren as well. He had not been a Nazi and if his father had, well, the sins of the fathers were not borne by the sons. Max had always believed that. Yet why, when he heard Hans's voice saying the most ordinary things, was he plagued by visions of mass graves, storm troopers banging infants against stone walls, miles of spiky barbed wire, naked emaciated people standing, waiting — always waiting?

Wild flowers grew rampant in the fields that were Oswiecim, known as Auschwitz. Acres and acres covered by a spectacular show of wild flowers that made those fields a lepidopterist's paradise. No wonder. Underneath was ten feet of human loam.

"Let her be," Libby kept saying in a strange reversal of the roles they had had for over forty years. "Let her live her own life, she has to please herself, Max. We are old and she is young. Real love doesn't happen that often, she deserves a little happiness." Libby's imperturbable calm was as irritating now as her irrationality had been before. No pleasing you, Max, he thought as he looked down once more on the winter city.

When he stepped into the street, Max no longer minded the cold. He felt refreshed and even the knowledge that it was almost eleven didn't dampen his spirits. Briskly he walked up Fifth Avenue to his office. A police car was parked in front of the Fifth Avenue entrance; he went to the door on Forty-first Street. Inside was a circle of grim faces. He looked behind him for an ambulance barreling down the street; someone had probably had a heart attack. But when he pushed open the door, he knew it wasn't that; here there was no murmur of expectation, time had ceased to matter. He saw Ed Cary, an architect on his floor. When he touched Ed's sleeve, the younger man jumped. "Oh, Max, it's you!"

"What's wrong, you look like you've seen a ghost."

"That would be a blessing," Ed said, then took in Max's heavy boots, his earmuffs, his scarf and turned-up collar. Max's mind raced along the halls, picking out the ones his age. Who was it?

"What happened?" he asked again.

"No one really knows, but the cops think some thieves surprised Fanny when she was cleaning the penthouse and —" Ed hesitated, his brow rimed with sweat. "And maybe she struggled with them, and maybe she didn't, it's impossible to tell, because" — his voice became a taut thread — "they threw her out the window. A truck driver found her about three-thirty this morning on Forty-first Street. Jesus, Max, it's terrible, Jesus . . ." Ed clasped Max's shoulder and led him toward the edge of the lobby. They stood there a moment, their eyes scalded with disbelief. "After that the bastards went through the building, almost everyone was hit. They took some drafting stools from me and some cash." Ed's shoulders shook as he sobbed.

If only I could sob like Ed, Max thought. His body was

stone, lead-heavy as he shuffled a few steps and leaned into a corner.

"Fanny! Fanny!" he screamed into the phone at Libby after he got himself upstairs. (The murderers had passed him by, his office was intact.) "Fanny, the one who was here as long as I was, the one with five grandchildren," he moaned into the phone and when he hung up, he put his head on his arms. The image of Fanny's thin, honey-colored body falling into the narrow street joined the still-vivid image of David's bloody limbs being scattered as the plane crashed, and Max knew that nothing he did or said or thought or took would erase the mingling of the two, until, perhaps, he died. And he wasn't sure they would be separated, even then.

When Libby called back, he was able to speak sensibly, but he knew she would never understand about Fanny. How could she? He had seen Fanny almost every working day of his life for the last twenty years, he had been charmed by her crooked smile, her beautiful teeth, her thin quickness, as she scooted around the halls and his office, never once feeling sorry for herself. He liked the slant of her handwriting on the thank-you note she sent him every January after he had pressed an envelope into her palm on Christmas Eve. And he could even imagine how light she would be if someone picked her up and walked toward the window carrying her in his arms.

"You'll meet me at the restaurant then, Max," Libby finally said. She was not going to let him brood about Fanny's death, or what it meant, for such a thing never meant anything, Libby believed. It was her way of keeping violence at bay.

"Yes, I'll be there," Max said wearily.

Hans was hardly a ringer for David, yet he and Mady looked well together. They were almost the same height and Hans's solid body complemented her thinness. His brownish-gray hair and hazel eyes and sandy complexion — usually what Max called a "no-color Nordic face" — was not a monotone at all.

Something about the planes of Hans's face made it catch the light, giving it a radiance which matched Mady's amazing blue eyes — which she had inherited from no one he or Libby had ever known.

As they walked from the restaurant up to the Metropolitan Museum for the concert, Hans held Mady's arm and once they stopped while she tied her long scarf more tightly around her head. Hans was hatless, his ears red with cold, and yet they walked more slowly than the rest. When he stepped inside the warm lobby, Max turned to watch them.

"Well, she's certainly happy," Shelley said.

"He's a fine man," Libby answered.

"And she's a big girl," Mel mumbled and took their coats and started for the check line. Only Max pressed his lips together and stared ahead. Never would he be reconciled. His heart felt like a frozen fist in his chest. And the worst part of it was that Mady didn't give a damn what he thought.

"She isn't a child anymore," Libby said quietly.

"If you say that once more to me," Max told her through gritted teeth, "I'm going to slap you." Libby's face blanched and she hurried to the ladies' room.

Oh, God, now what had he done? He was thinking of a dozen apologies, but when she came back he saw she had forgiven him.

"You've had a terrible day, we should have skipped this," she said as they took their seats. Max shrugged. He couldn't go out again, at least he could doze a little when the lights dimmed.

On the other side of him Shelley was talking about the second piece on the program — George Crumb's *Ancient Voices of Children*. "It's very interesting, we first heard it with Bonnie, there's a harp in it. It's based on a cycle of poems from Lorca."

His name was García Lorca, Max wanted to tell her, this first-born child who speaks as though she knows everything. Federico García Lorca, and I heard him read his poems one night at the Low Library in the winter of 1929 — a cold rainy night, not as cold as tonight, but a depressing night filled with a raw cold that went to your bones. A friend of mine had translated some of his poems and he took me and I hadn't yet met your mother and no one even dreamed you or your sister would be born and we were jammed into a small side room and he had the most incredible deep eyes and his face was already rutted with the thinking he did and from a distance he looked a little like Babe Ruth.

The lights dimmed and Max settled into his seat, comforted by the familiar sounds of a Dvořák violin trio, dreaming of Ed Cary and Fanny and his friend Ben who followed García Lorca back to Spain and never came home and taught and translated in Madrid. The applause jolted Max awake and he shuddered slightly as Libby put her hand on his arm. "Darling, shall we go?"

He shook his head, then leaned over, wanting to tell his children about the Spanish poet. He started to clear his throat, which was still thick from dozing, when Mel shushed him. "Later, Dad, it's about to begin."

And then the sounds, the clatter, the shrieks, whispers, the guttural groanings, the screams. Was this music? Could this be what they are now calling music? Occasionally he could discern words. He looked at the program. *"El niño busca su voz./(La tenía el rey de los grillos.) . . . En una gota de agua/buscaba su voz el niño."* What a desecration to those carefully wrought Spanish syllables! Now the singer scampered over to the piano, her voice plunged into short jerky sounds, she leaned over the bell of the piano and pushed her voice so that it vibrated along the strings. Then there was a run on the harp, the plucking of those strange bells — Japanese temple bells, the program said — some tapping on the tom-tom, a sound of mandolin and oboe, and more shouting and then a rasping sound of God knows what. Max looked around. Faces were turned intently toward the stage — interested, some even rapt. Shelley's color was high, she had her head to one side, she loved it. So did Mel. Mady was wary, and Hans — Max wasn't certain, he didn't know him well enough, though from the corner of his eye Max thought he saw Hans wince. Next to Max, Libby's eyes darted from the singer to the instruments, a half-smile about her lips. Only he was unmoved as he sat there.

He thought of Fanny, her body falling, splattering, then he saw her flicking her duster around him again. Only to have her fall once more. Over and over his mind repeated the sequence accompanied by the bizarre sounds that emanated from the stage. Then the troubled yelling that was the climax of the piece. A blessed quiet descended for a moment, then was submerged by a surge of clapping, bravos! "Fascinating!" "I love the quiet parts, especially that line 'each afternoon in Granada, a child dies each afternoon.'" "Such an extraordinary singer! They say Crumb wrote it for her." "Wild, isn't it?"

Sounds, voices, swirled around him and he wanted to grab their arms and shout, "This isn't music, and it isn't García Lorca. His work is coherent and all of a piece, this is disintegration, deterioration!" But he said nothing and watched the people — the men in their well-fitting suits and polished shoes, the women in the expensive warm skirts and sweaters and dresses, their stockings intact, their footwear sleek, their hair smartly cut. Perfect examples of the land of plenty, the leisure class coming to listen to this ridiculous bunch of sounds, taking it seriously because they have forgotten what is important.

But what of the others? What of Fanny?

Then Mady took his arm, as she used to in the old days, and let Hans talk to Mel and Shelley. "Hans didn't like it, he says it has no form, it isn't music. What do you think, Dad?" Her face was so calm, happy; for the first time in years she was out with them as an equal, no longer the odd woman. How could he deny her this happiness? Max's throat filled with remorse, then he swallowed it down, and he was filled with anger toward everyone, even his favorite child.

"What do I think? All of a sudden you're worried about what I think?" he said harshly. Her face clouded and she tried to step away from him, but Max clutched even more firmly at her arm. "As long as you're asking me, I think it stinks!" he said loudly. Then he saw Libby's head snap around quickly, he felt her next to him. Mady's face had closed on him like the steel doors they lowered to protect the stores near his office at night.

"He's very tired, he had a terrible day because of that business about Fanny," Libby explained to Mady as she took his hand. "I think we'd better go home." She spoke as if Max weren't there, and her tone brought him to his senses. He wasn't an invalid, or senile. Yet.

"No we won't. We're staying," he said quietly. "I'm sorry. She asked me what I thought, so I told her. No crime in that, is there? This isn't music, no matter what the rest of them think, no matter what the critics say. It's someone indulging himself and we're fools to pay money to listen to it." Relief virtually exploded on Libby's face.

"Well, at least the last piece is a Mozart quartet, that's safe," she murmured.

For the rest of the concert Max let his mind drift into a peaceful nothingness. At the end, while Mel and Hans went to get the coats, Libby and Mady and Shelley were very quiet, bound by a simple desire not to upset him. He had had enough today. He should feel guilty, but he didn't. He was so tired, weariness filled the very crevices of his bones. He could break the tension by telling them about García Lorca, but he had no strength left to open his mouth. When he sought Mady's eyes, she averted them. She knew the roots of his anger and for a second after his outburst her eyes had said, *Why can't you stop treating me like a child?*

Because you are my child, he would answer, *and you always will be.* But that was foolishness. She was almost forty years old, a widow. In her life she had lived through more than most people twice her years know, more than he knew.

Now Shelley was leafing through the program. "Lorca died such a tragic death," she said in her lecturer's voice. "He was killed by the Fascists in the summer of 1936 when he was fighting for the Republicans." As she spoke Hans approached with some coats. Max saw the skin around Hans's mouth whiten. He waited; suddenly he didn't feel tired, his body was charged with energy.

As Hans helped Mady with her coat he murmured something

in her ear. She whispered something back. Although it looked like an inconsequential exchange, Max knew something important was happening between them. He watched Mady search Hans's eyes, and then he saw Hans shrug a little, almost to himself, and then he heard Hans's still accented voice.

"The program is wrong, Shelley," he said. "Whoever wrote it doesn't have his facts straight, though, admittedly, it's hard to get the truth about García Lorca. They've been trying to make a legend of him since he died. He wasn't a Republican, he wasn't on either side, he was known as an artist — mostly as a playwright because *Yerma* was such a great success. He saw himself as a poet, not as a political person. The day he died he was on his way to visit his family to celebrate his saint's day, and he was taken by the Falangists in a riot with hundreds of others and killed randomly. No one knew who he was, he was thrown into an unmarked grave." Hans's voice had gotten flatter as he spoke, as if he were merely reminding them of facts they knew but had forgotten. So different from Shelley's rambunctious show of knowledge.

Max held his coat in his hand and stared at this stranger, who wasn't a stranger at all, but a man, just like himself. A man all alone in an adopted country where, because of his past, he felt responsible for all sorts of things that had nothing to do with him — like García Lorca's celebrated death. Where he had had to inure himself to misunderstanding and loneliness, where he had chosen a deliberately simple life and, unexpectedly, had fallen in love with a widow who happened to be Max's younger child. How vulnerable Hans was! All that outer facade of control had been stripped away in a matter of seconds as he spoke.

Max felt a surge of that mixture of old-fashioned pity and fear, and as he looked at the younger man he remembered a moving detail he had read, years and years ago when he was young, about Dostoevski. Dostoevski had been blindfolded and forced to go through a mock execution when he was a young man, and he had not been the same thereafter. Mady had told him about Hans's twin brother, and now Max could finally understand Hans's predicament. Max stepped forward and said in a clear firm voice, "You're absolutely right, Hans. I ought to know. I heard García Lorca read once and my old friend Ben knew him well," Max told his surprised children. Libby smiled; she had heard this story long ago when they were courting.

"A lot of nonsense has been written about his life," Max continued, "but after he was killed Ben wrote me a letter and the facts are as Hans said."

They began to walk out of the museum. "I heard García Lorca before you girls were born, before I met Mother," Max began. They passed the empty fountain and their footsteps crunched on the icy streets and as Max spoke he took Libby's arm and he could feel her relax through the thick cloth of their touching coat sleeves. And although he kept up a steady stream of talk — playing the affable knowledgeable aging father (the ornery old man of the intermission had disappeared, to everyone's relief) — Max was thinking of Hans. Finally he knew why Mady was in love with this German. Here was a man who needed her as much as she needed him. As they walked Max wished he could say something to them both, he wished he had the strength and humility to articulate an apology. But he didn't. He couldn't.

And later, while he and Libby were getting ready for bed, he snapped at her as he pulled a button off his pajamas.

"There, there, Max," she said soothingly and got a needle and thread. Before she began to sew she broke off a piece of thread and handed it to him. "Chew on it," she instructed as she began to sew. Max remembered his mother telling him to chew thread too when she had to sew something he was wearing, and the persistence of the mysterious superstition calmed him. When Libby said, "Try not to think about Fanny too much," he kissed her and murmured, "I won't."

CHAPTER 22

IN THE GREENHOUSE crocus, hyacinths, scillas, narcissus, fritillaria, allium bloomed. Outside, masses of snowdrops nodded their wet heads. The sky was gray soup. Let it rain today, Mady thought, and perhaps it would be clear at the end of the week. On Friday she was going to Racer's Cove to spend the day with Hans. He had only a half-day of school; it was the two hundred fiftieth anniversary of the founding of the town. Then over the weekend were the dedication of David Glazer Park and a cousin's wedding.

As soon as she finished watering the plants, she practiced for a while, then left instructions with Clair for the children and drove over to the music school. When she got to the third floor, she paused for a moment before she opened the door. It was just a plain raised paneled door that had been painted a glossy white when the old inn was converted into a music school. Her name was the first on the sheet: Mrs. Glazer — Monday and Wednesday. Whenever she entered the simple room, she felt a sharp sense of pleasure she had not known before she began to teach.

Someone knocked. "Mady?" A secretary stood there with a paper in her hand. "The little Brand girl is sick again, but we've scheduled a make-up for the Mahler boy at four-thirty. And Mary would like to see you before you leave."

The lessons so absorbed her that she didn't have time to think about what Mary, the director of the school, might want. Later, questions assailed her as she walked to Mary's office. Was she doing her job? Had parents complained? The Brand child who was sick so much cried so easily, but the last two weeks had been better. She had been teaching since the middle of January; this was the end of March. She thought things were going well, yet why was she so nervous? Quickly she pushed open the door to Mary's cheerful office.

"Well, Mady, how are you?"

"Fine, Mary, really fine. A little tired," she added and sank into a chair. It was after seven. She had taught for four hours.

"I can imagine. The worst occupational hazard is that we have to teach after school — when everyone is tired," Mary said. Then she pulled out a long paper. She was not a woman who wasted words. "Your students and their parents are so enthusiastic about you we wondered if you would like to teach in our summer program," Mary said casually, but when their eyes met she smiled warmly. The two women had known each other for ten years, but since November, when Mady had started studying with Mary, they had become good friends. "It's only March and with this weather summer seems years away, but it will be upon us before we know it. We need another teacher from nine to three Monday through Thursday. It's a six-week program. Think about it, Mady, and we'll talk some more."

"But they pay next to nothing," Shelley said the next day when Mady called her.

"That's not really so important, is it?" Mady answered.

"Yes, it is. You should get what you're worth."

"Shelley, it's a nonprofit school. They barely make ends meet."

"I know, I know," Shelley grumbled. Then, trying to be cheerful: "And it is nice that they like you." But the job offer was no longer something they could discuss. Mady sighed. She waited. From the silence on the other end of the phone she knew Shelley wanted to talk about something.

"Dad's low again," Shelley finally offered.

"He and Mom need to get away. They haven't been away for months."

"They say they're going to go in a few weeks, they've been waiting for the dedication, but it's not only that they're tired, they're so depressed . . ." Shelly began, but Mady didn't want to talk about it. No matter how these discussions began — and usually with every good intention on Shelley's part — they ended by making Mady the villain because she had only added to Max's weariness by falling in love with Hans. Which really wasn't true. It was the obvious thing to fix on, but since that evening at the concert Mady knew that Max didn't blame her so much; she had seen him come to terms with Hans as best he could, and she knew that his tired eyes and his languid aging gestures were not her fault. Neither was Watergate, nor Ford's insufficiency, nor the economic situation, nor the state of education as a result of open admissions, nor the Moonies who hung around the streets near Max's office, nor the gays marching on Fifth Avenue, nor the thieves who had killed Fanny. Max's world had changed, and she had realized it most poignantly that night he talked about García Lorca. Max couldn't accept those changes, but she refused to take the blame. And neither should Shelley nor Mel nor Libby. There were some things no one could control.

"When they've had a vacation, they'll feel better," Mady said.

Friday morning began with a suffocating fog but by eleven it had begun to clear. As Mady drove, the stolidness of winter gave way to hints of spring quickening along the coast road. When she stopped the car to take off her jacket, she could smell a change in the air that drifted toward her. A light wind ruffled the dunes, and beyond their gentle swaying the sea had a brownish cast, like bronze. Although the air was light and warm, the sea still looked thick with cold. The breakers came in high and wild, probably because of the recent rain.

Hans was waiting on the front steps. He wore an open-necked shirt and a few sprouts of golden-grayish hair on his chest caught the sun. She felt a catch in her throat as they hurried toward each other. They rarely had time alone in Racer's Cove; usually she had Foffy with her, and sometimes Nina and Peter. But today the children were in school and going to Anne's for dinner. She didn't have to be home till evening.

Inside the house the sun lightened corners she had never noticed. "The sun is higher and the leaves aren't in yet," Hans said. They stood at the kitchen window. The needles of the Atlantic white cedar were so blue against the pale nakedness of the copper beech behind it. Once that huge copper beech blossomed everything around it faded, and even now the bare tree was impressive. Its nude immensity reminded Mady of the sensuous sculptures by Elie Nadelman. When she turned from the window, her throat filled with disappointment. Hans was taking plates from the refrigerator. He had made a specially nice lunch, she saw, and it would be so much more civilized to eat. She should be hungry, it was almost one, she had had breakfast at seven. But now all she knew was desire, she had never felt it with such intensity before. Not even for David. Did this kind of need come only after extreme events, or prolonged abstinence, or was it her age? There was a lot of talk about choices when people talked about love, but what she felt for Hans had very little to do with choice. It came from the deepest necessity and reverberated into the farthest corners of her life. As the months passed she was no longer frightened by it, she had learned to accept it. Silently she took the plates from Hans's hands and covered the pleasingly arranged food with Saran and put it back into the refrigerator. Then she led Hans into his spare, austere bedroom where they didn't bother to shut the door or draw the blinds.

Later, when they were leaving the house for a walk on the

beach, they heard strains of "Yankee Doodle" floating from the village. Hans smiled. "You will never believe this," he murmured, "but Hitler's army used to goose-step to something that sounded almost like that."

The sea had calmed. Now it rippled like a huge length of mauve taffeta and had the same comforting constant sound. Hans took her arm and they walked for miles, adding the imprints of their feet to the complicated hieroglyphs the gulls and pipers had left in the damp sand.

When they returned, Mady felt encased in an armor of salt. She was glad she had thought to bring a change of clothes. They were planning to eat out before she started for home. She took a hot shower and put on her skirt and sweater. When she came out, a warm fire was flickering. She pushed her chair back a little; if she got too close to its velvet warmth she would doze. She didn't want to miss a moment now.

She picked up *The French Lieutenant's Woman*. He was almost halfway through. She wished they had more time like this — long leisurely afternoons and evenings to turn the pages of big thick books, reading aloud passages to each other. Sometimes she pictured Hans living in her home, sleeping next to her in her bed, sitting across the table from her night after night. All that seemed possible when she was playing the piano or meandering through the house late at night, but here in his house she couldn't see him anywhere else. Mady flipped the pages. Did he think she would disappear like Sarah Woodruff? When he came in, she was reading it.

"Do you like it?" she asked as he put down two glasses of sherry.

"Now I do. I tried to read it when it first came out, but I couldn't suspend enough disbelief then. Now I'm reading it straight through."

Their eyes met as he sat down. It was so peaceful. Outside the sky was streaked with cloudy yellow light, covering the bare treetops with a soft glow. She looked at her watch. Five-thirty. Peter was picking Foffy up and soon her three children would be sitting around the old table in Anne's kitchen, stirring their hot apple juice (which they wouldn't touch at home) with the long sticks of cinnamon Anne put in the mugs. After Foffy's accident she had thought she would never be able to leave them, but she had. That took more courage than the apparent sacrifice of staying home all the time, hovering over them.

In the village the cobbled streets were stippled with confetti. One of Hans's students waved as he carried a pizza to his car. "Hi, Mr. Panneman, wasn't it a great parade?" Rather than explain, Hans nodded. Then he pressed her arm. "Can we duck into the studio for a minute? I left some mail there that needs to be answered and I'll be looking for busywork to do after you leave." She smiled, delighted with his small confession.

The key jammed in the lock. "That's funny, the handle seems stuck," he said. Then he gave the key a quick sharp turn and the door flew open. Even before he turned on the light Mady knew something was wrong. You could smell it.

The floor of the studio was strewn, almost covered, with shards. When they had discovered no money or supplies or typewriter, the thieves had gone berserk. Every piece of Hans's work that was finished or in progress, every bit of the students' work, even the small children's painstaking efforts, were ground nearly to powder on the old wood floor. Amidst the rubble were broken stools and turned-over work tables, their Formica tops slashed with deep cuts. The only things left intact were the large hunks of raw clay on a metal rack against the far wall and the kiln and the hanging plants at the windows and a large piece of dark wood that stood almost hidden in a corner.

Mady followed Hans's gaze as he searched the floor and walls and high ceilings, as if his eyes could put the pieces together again. His face was pleated with such pain that she had to look away. No one had the right to see this, not even she. All the sorrow of his entire life had surfaced in his suddenly colorless eyes. She turned, pretending to examine the lock for a clue. Only after his single "Why?" had stopped resounding through the bare long room did she dare to step closer to him, to touch his arm.

They stood there together. Nothing was left to sit on; if only they could sit down and face each other, she thought irrationally, then maybe they could gather their senses.

She had no idea how long they stood, propping each other up. Finally Hans moved, but when he went to the phone, which was on the floor, he saw that the wire had been cut. He held the limp wire in his hand and murmured, "Why would they need to do that?" as if it were possible to apply some logic to what had happened.

As they walked silently down the street to the police station, Mady searched for words, but nothing came. She stood near him while he explained to the chief, a Captain Marsden whom he had known for years, and she held his arm when his voice wavered for a few seconds, but there was little else she could do. When the police came back to the studio, even their cynical eyes widened at the extent of the damage.

One thing Mady knew: she didn't want to leave him. He had forgotten she was supposed to go, his entire mind was taken up with the vandalism, she saw the completeness of his grief in the stoic dullness of his eyes and in the trembling of his voice, which annoyed him and which he tried, in vain, to suppress. Only when Mady asked to use the phone did he remember. "You must be starved," he said.

She shook her head. "No. I'm going to call Anne and see if she can keep the children." The clock said seven-fifteen.

She couldn't go home tonight. She could not let Hans go home alone, sleep through the night alone. It was that simple, and as soon as she realized it she was able to explain, reasonably and briefly, to Peter and Nina and finally to Foffy that she was staying with Hans for the night and would arrive tomorrow in time for the dedication. "I can't leave him," she told Anne. "They've destroyed everything, it's unbelievable, it makes you wonder about —" she hesitated — "it makes you wonder about everything, and the only thing I'm sure of is that I've got to stay here tonight. He can't be alone."

When she got back to Hans, he was asking the question no

one else could ask. "Do you think this has to do with my being German?" he said, then wet his lips and seemed to gather courage. "Could they have thought I was a Nazi?" he asked in a firm voice.

Captain Marsden shook his head. His voice was dry, resigned. "That would be easy, too easy. And much easier to deal with. No, this is one of those random things that makes you wonder if we're still human. These animals had no idea who you were or where you were born."

When they left the police station, it was almost nine. "The reporters will descend tomorrow," Captain Marsden said grimly as he shook their hands. "Get some sleep," he said to both of them.

They walked slowly to the car. Hans stopped abruptly. "Let's go back to the studio for a minute, there's something I want to take home."

The studio was eerily still. Their footsteps crunched loudly over the broken pottery. Did the walls and floor feel as bruised, as violated as they did? Mady wondered. Of course; he was heading for the block of wood. In the strange dark Mady could discern a few tentative lines. Hans took off his raincoat and wrapped it around the wood. Then he knelt down and picked it up and when they got back to the house he carried it to a corner of the living room.

She was in the kitchen putting up coffee. She would have liked some brandy, but when he sat down she didn't have the heart to ask him to get up again. Silently he watched her move around the kitchen, he seemed to hear her while she reported her conversation with Anne and the children, but his face registered nothing when she said she was staying. He nodded when she asked, "Scrambled eggs?" and they both ate everything she had prepared.

"Sometimes I think eating is a mechanism for convincing us we're still alive," she said softly as they cleared. He smiled for the first time in hours and she waited for him to say something but he shook his head and fell mute again. His eyes were frosted glass when he handed her some pajamas and after she returned from the bathroom he sat listlessly on the edge of the bed. She held out her arms. He looked away. The room echoed with his silent refusal and she could feel the stifling air of helplessness wash invisibly over them as they lay, entirely separate, next to each other. She wished her presence could comfort him, she had assumed it would, but she also knew that for some things there is, simply, no comfort. He had learned to survive entirely alone and now he had to be alone. She wasn't angry that he couldn't pretend with her and she didn't pity him; rather, in an odd way, she respected him for his weary honesty. And whether he wanted her or not, she wanted to lie here.

She closed her eyes and pretended to sleep. The Mandelstam poem surfaced in her head. She had read it again recently and now she could hear the syllables in her head: *"Can't sleep. Homer. Stretched sails. I've read to the middle of the list of ships: the lengthening flock, the stream of cranes that once flew above Hellas. Cranes in flight crossing strange borders, their leaders soaked with the spray of the gods. Where do you sail? What would Troy be to you, O men of Achaea, without Helen? The sea — Homer — it's all moved by love. But to whom shall I listen? Not a word now from Homer, and the black sea roars like speech and crashes up on the bed."* The sea was bronze and it didn't roar tonight, but otherwise the Russian poet was right about the Greeks, right about love. It had brought her here next to this man whom she had resisted for all kinds of reasons — because he was a German, or a gentile, or, perhaps most important, because he had retreated from the world. Yet there was nowhere else she would have wanted to be tonight, for she had grown to love him as deeply as she could love another person. Whatever happened, she had had that, and more than that she could not ask. Even feeling as helpless as she did at this moment, even feeling so utterly alone. She tried to push her mind to think of tomorrow, but she was too tired. If she had learned nothing else these last few years, she had learned to take each moment at a time, so now she tried to think of nothing and listened to the rhythmic shushing of the waves. A little later she felt him get out of bed, saw him at the window, his profile a lusterless gray-white in the cool filtered moonlight. She yearned to go to him; instead, she turned over on her side and pressed her eyelids together and after a while fell into a shallow sleep.

CHAPTER 23

H E HAD SOMETIMES DREAMED of waking up holding her in his arms, and now, in that moment of half-consciousness before he was fully awake, he wasn't sure she was real. In all the times they had been together they had never awakened in the same bed, for her children were always nearby. Yet here she was, with his pajamas scrunched around her thin shoulders. Then the memory seeped through his skin and into his bones and his brain and he saw the work of almost twenty years lying in the form of coarse sand on the floor. Dust into dust.

He also remembered, in shame, how she had called Anne Levin and made arrangements for the children, how she had prepared their supper and tried to comfort him, and how he had been afraid to touch her. Literally afraid. As he looked down at her sleeping face, which was in itself a miracle to him, he couldn't believe they had slept in the same bed for almost eight hours like strangers.

Now, surely, when she went it would be for the last time. Why should she come back? No woman in her right mind would want to cope with a man as obviously maimed as he was. He had thought he was finished with that crippling fear the night he

came to her house after Foffy's accident, the night they slept together for the first time. He heard Johanna's triumphant voice in
his head: "You will go to Oxford, or Cambridge, or maybe
MIT," she used to tell Karl and him. "You will be somebody, I
promise you, you will be somebody!" Karl was dead, and he
wasn't somebody, or anybody, he wasn't even human. To be so
afraid wasn't human.

Madeleine's sleeping face had the look of an antique statue.
The blunt blueness of her eyes dominated her face when she
was awake, but now one could see the fine bones, the firm chin
and brow, enhanced peculiarly by the frown marks that sat like
a quotation mark above her thin straight nose. She slept with her
narrow wrist curled under her chin and the configuration of her
hand against the tilt of her dark eyebrows sent a quiver through
him. How lovely she was! And she had no notion of it. She saw
herself as middle-aged, too thin and tired. He had never seen her
catch a glimpse of herself in a mirror or a glass door or a car
window. Perhaps it was her not knowing that heightened her
beauty. Who knew? But here it was, before his eyes, and if he
could do nothing right while she was awake, then perhaps he
might preserve a spark of her while she slept. The block of wood
would be a sleeping woman. Quickly, softly, he slid out of bed
and rummaged in his desk for charcoal and some sketching
paper. He had to hurry. Soon he would have to wake her, she
had to go to the dedication of David's park, and who knew if she
would ever return?

How could you explain to someone, he thought as he drew,
what it was like to have a presence constantly near you that you
could almost feel, that would at the most unexpected times place
its hands on your heart and your brain, so that you felt tainted?
When he had come home from his mother's funeral, he had
thought, mistakenly, that Europe was behind him. Yet in these
last months, while he and Madeleine had grown to care for each
other, the presence of his past, his Germanness, his father's Nazism, his alienation even in this country (which for all its flaws,

allowed one to be free) had all merged into a presence that he could consciously feel. At times he could almost give it a body and a head, and when he had switched on the light in his studio last night, he had thought, "It's come at last."

And when she had held out her arms, he had been afraid he would taint her, too.

Yet she had stayed. In spite of him. She knew he was suffering and she didn't want him to be alone. Since his childhood no one had ever done that for him. It wasn't the grand gesture, or even passion, that mattered so much in life, Hans thought, but the simple act of faith, of loyalty. What Sergei Vladimirovitch had called *caritas* when he and Karl were growing up. What he had needed Mady had given: her presence, her self. For that there was no thanks or even speech, and she would probably never know what she had done.

His hand was surer now as he drew. Quickly he ripped page after page from the pad. His heart had expanded in his chest; finally, the fear had flown. As his hand knew better and better what to do, the sound of the charcoal grating on the paper filled the room. That was what woke her up.

For the first time since she had known him, his eyes were not tinged with sorrow. She had thought when he looked at her that he felt sorry for her — because she was a young widow, because she was worn by her responsibilities, or because she was so tied to her children. It was guesswork, and although it had made her uncomfortable at first, she had learned not to see it and had tried to enjoy what they had together. Now those cataracts of sorrow were gone.

As he spoke and as she listened to his halting phrases she realized that the sorrow had nothing to do with her, but with him. Perhaps she had known that when she felt his stare upon her at the beach last summer. Perhaps it wasn't so much the reticence or dignity or that odd ineffable light that radiated from his face, but rather his sorrow that attracted her. Maybe a woman like her needed the challenge of that sorrow, or maybe the need was the legacy of David's death. The distinction didn't matter now, and neither did his effort to explain. Tenderly she folded her arms around him and held him while he wept.

Although she knew it would make her a little late, Mady decided to go with him to the studio before she left. The shafts of north light spreading naked fingers on all that rubble; it would be enough to take the breath away, she thought.

"No, no, you'll be late," he said.

"It'll only take another minute," she said.

A police car was parked outside the studio. Voices bounced off the walls inside. Her stomach tightened. What would the reporters want to know, would anyone ask him why he was in this small town instead of his native Germany? An unreasonable fear for him closed around her.

The studio was swept almost clean and the broken stools were stacked in a corner. The work tables were upright. One of the teenagers was trying to pry the slashed Formica from a table top. There were about twenty of them in the studio, their clothes ghostly gray with dust, their faces smudged and sweaty. She recognized some of the faces from the folk dancing last summer. They were one of the most beautiful sights she had ever seen.

Hans held her hand very hard, tears stood in his eyes. He turned to her. "Well, it's a beginning," he murmured.

Captain Marsden walked toward them, lifting his hat. "They're something, aren't they?" he asked as if he had no idea how they had gotten here.

"They certainly are," Hans replied. "But what about the reporters?"

"They'll be hopping mad we didn't leave everything. You could hear them rubbing their hands as they took down the information on the phone last night. They're due in a few minutes." Then he grinned at them. "Screw the reporters. Racer's Cove doesn't live for reporters. They can't help us find the maniacs who did this. Besides," he added thoughtfully, "they had the parade."

She should have known she couldn't slip in quietly. When she opened the door (of course it squeaked) to the village hall, every eye focused on her. She couldn't have been more conspicuous if she had been nude and covered with incandescent paint. Rather than meet that variegated spotlight of eyes, Mady bent her head and found an empty seat near the back though one was waiting for her next to Foffy. When she looked up, Foffy was staring at her, sucking the inside of her lower lip. She gave her mother a small nod. Mady could see that her blouse was buttoned wrong, pushing the collar up too high on one side of her neck. It gave her a disheveled, waiflike look, and all Mady's guilt surfaced with overwhelming force.

How could she have been late? Everyone was here — everyone they had ever said hello to, even people she didn't know personally, had turned out. The place was packed; a few who had arrived after her stood in the back. Near the children were her parents and Shelley and Mel and Bonnie and Cynthia (who had come home from college for the ceremony), and Woody and Anne and the boys. Then Joe Carpenter and his wife, and Gail and her girls, and all her neighbors and Nate Tolliver and his wife, Joanne, Clair and her husband, and the nurses from the hospital and the children's teachers and principals, and far off to the right was her cousin Natalie, pregnant again, holding onto her small son, David, who had been born the day David's plane crashed. She knew Woody and Anne had made a lot of calls, but she never expected such a crowd on a spring Saturday when everyone should be cleaning their cellars or buying roses.

The door squeaked for yet another time. It was Dore and, a few steps behind her, Fred Howland. Fred wore a tie-dyed jeans suit and an open-necked shirt and a heavy gold chain around his throat. He and Gail were now legally separated and he was living with a much younger woman named Wendy or Robin. Gail could barely look at him. Why should she? Only this week she had called Mady in a fury. When he came to see the girls and she was out, he had taken both Philip Gustons off the wall. "We bought those paintings with money my parents gave us for our birthdays and anniversaries," Gail said.

"What will you do?" Mady said.

"He'll get one and I'll get one, which is absurd, since they were companion pieces."

Divorce is worse than death. So much is unresolved, and so much conflict remains. All Gail wanted was to forget she had ever been married to Fred, yet their daughters could never forget he was their father. What would become of Gail? Would she be like Dore? Now Mady caught Dore's eye and they smiled. Dore looked wonderful; she was still thin and now she was rolling her eyes and looking in Fred's direction. She had never liked him.

The mayor's voice droned on; finally its inflections rose. "And so it is with great pride that the Village Board voted to give this area to the community as a small greenbelt park." Polite applause rippled through the hall. The mayor smiled and gestured to Woody. As she turned to watch Woody, Mady's eyes met her father's. Max's face was filled with disgust. He gestured at the empty seat. Libby's eyes were sad. Why can't you manage your life better? they said.

Woody unfolded his speech and smoothed it on the lectern. His voice carried well. He praised David's accomplishments as a lawyer and teacher and fighter for justice, ending the first part of his speech with a quotation from Felix Frankfurter, who had been an old friend of David's. Then in conclusion he said, "His public contributions were impressive, even startling, for a man who had just celebrated his fortieth birthday, but David Glazer was an extraordinary private man as well. A devoted husband, a loving father, a remarkable friend and a giving member of the community. I don't know how many of you know about his beautiful garden or his knowledge of plants and trees and flowers. He never failed to amaze me when we walked in the woods, he knew the name of everything we passed, of every tree and bush and flower, and some of the birds and butterflies as well. The demands of his work didn't dull the excitement he derived from nature, and it is entirely proper and fitting that this small lush piece of land less than half a mile from his home should be named David Glazer Park."

Even Woody had succumbed to the formality of the occasion. Now he looked embarrassed while the applause reverberated through the old barn. The last time she had been here was the night of the meeting, when the town had been divided, but once the park became a reality even those who had fought it worked to clean it up and were here to applaud. Proof of the flexibility of the human spirit, Mady thought, otherwise how could we survive? Still, when she looked toward her children, her mind filled the empty seat next to Foffy with David. He was smiling, clapping, and then he bent over and said something to Foffy that made the child's face glow with delight. How I still miss him! Mady thought. How they would always miss him! Once she might not have been able to admit that, but her life had changed so much these last months, and she was so grateful for all that she could feel.

Now Woody called Peter's name. As he walked slowly to the lectern Mady sighed. His wrists had pushed themselves out of his jacket.

"On behalf of my mother," he began, then stopped and began again. "On behalf of my mother, Madeleine Hayman Glazer, and my sisters, Nina and Sophia, I thank all of you who have worked so hard to clean up this park, especially my father's best friend, Woody Levin. It was his idea and now it is here and I hope we all enjoy many happy hours in David Glazer Park." Peter looked at her and shrugged. Solemnly he shook Woody's hand and walked back to his seat amidst the applause.

"He looks so much like his father!" "The children are so beautiful!" "The little one doesn't look at all like the other two!" "How proud you must be!" People whispered, jostled her, pressed against her as Mady wormed her way through the crowd. Peter looked confused, unhappy. "When you didn't come, Woody asked me to say something. It was lousy, wasn't it?"

"No, Peter, it was absolutely right. Really," she told him, then looked into her son's eyes. They were more timid than his father's but they were the eyes of an adult. He said quickly, "You know, Mom, at first I thought this ceremony would be bullshit but I think it served a purpose, it completed something . . ." He shrugged again. She understood; the ceremony had given them an opportunity to say good-bye to David, and it was just as well that she was late and Peter had spoken for the family. Even in a jacket he had outgrown.

Then she hugged Nina and Foffy. "Foffy buttoned her blouse wrong, but she was so pleased to have done everything herself I didn't fix it," Nina whispered as they heard Libby say, "Here, Foffy, let's fix your blouse, the collar's up." Mady kissed her mother, then held herself erect for her father's angry kiss.

But Max surprised her. Maybe the sight of Peter standing there in front of this crowd had mellowed him, maybe he had finally understood when she was late what Hans meant to her. Whatever it was, Max had forgiven her, at least for now.

When the family and friends mingled together over Anne's magnificent buffet, their voices were filled with kind nostalgia. Everyone had a reminiscence to share with her and her children — even Dore, and for some reason that touched Mady more than anything else. Yet she could hardly believe she was standing here. If someone had told her after David died that she would be standing here with a glass of soave bolla in her hand, listening so attentively to each story, she would have retorted, "You're out of your mind."

Perhaps time is distance; the better others remembered him, the farther away he became to her. At some times she could see him clearly, like that moment during the ceremony, yet at others, like now, surrounded by loving faces and voices, he was so faint, a mere diaphanous blur.

Only Anne asked about Hans. They were in the kitchen, refilling a tray. "How is he? To have all his work destroyed, it gives me gooseflesh." Her expression was kind, concerned.

"It's terrible, but I think he's going to be all right. His students came and cleaned this morning, it was wonderful to see them," Mady said. Anne's face brightened and she carried the tray out. Mady lingered for a moment. During the drive back she had thought she would someday sit here and tell Anne of her loneliness last night, then her joy on waking this morning to the sight of Hans drawing her, the change she had seen in his eyes. But now she knew she would never tell Anne about last night and this morning. Some things were too precious to be shared.

CHAPTER 24

GINGERLY SHE LIFTED THE BLANKET and eased herself out of the bed. Hans was such a light sleeper that the slightest movement jarred him and once he was up he couldn't go back to sleep and stubbornly refused to nap. She put on her robe and carried her slippers to the living room, then turned up the heat. The temperature had dropped sharply during the night, soon after she and the children had arrived for the weekend. Outside everything was crystal. The blueberry bushes were old-fashioned paperweights of Baccarat or Steuben, etched from beneath with the intricate designs of the slender spreading branches. The birches were weary gardeners, bent almost to the ground. Such a severe ice storm in May was unheard of and before they went to bed the local radio announcer was bemoaning the damage. When she went into the kitchen she saw that the beech had lost a limb; they had heard a crack in the night and Hans had checked the oil burner and walked through the house, but it hadn't occurred to either of them that what they heard could have come from so far away. That huge copper beech looked invulnerable, but there it was — ice encrusting the broken limb that had been pulled from the thick aged trunk. Peter had told her often how heavy water was when it froze, but she never believed him.

She sat down with a cup of coffee at the kitchen table. In the guest room her three children slept. If she held herself very still, she could hear them moving, turning, coughing in their sleep. Although they never slept in one room anywhere else they didn't mind it at Hans's house. This was the first time she hadn't gone through the charade of sleeping in the living room. She had discussed her relationship with Hans openly with Peter and Nina and they had been amused. "What do you think we are, Mom, babies?" Nina had asked.

They had come this weekend for the reopening of Hans's studio. There was going to be a party and both of the older children had changed plans so they could be here. Without her asking them to. Why was it that what wasn't asked for was so much more precious than what was?

She walked with her coffee back to the living room. Out the large window the east light was dipping, swallowlike, into the dark nooks and crannies of the landscape. How comfortable she was in this pleasant room, watching the sun rise over the whirling whitecapped sea. She could feel her own pleasure, as palpable as the warmth that rose through the air.

Last night Hans had mentioned an addition — out this east side, to make the living room bigger and add a hall and another bedroom. She had known, she supposed, since she first saw him that he could never live away from here, and last night he had finally articulated it.

"I need the sound of the sea, Mady. And this house. It may be utterly and absolutely crazy, but at this point I don't think I could live anywhere else." What he couldn't say was that he didn't have the strength to begin again, and that it had nothing to do with his love for her. Once she might not have understood. "If you love me you can do anything," she would have said when she was younger. But she had learned that love is not provable and you can't ask someone you love to do what is impossible for him. To ask Hans to leave Racer's Cove would have been like asking David not to fly.

No, this was his home, he wanted her to use it. That was why he was planning an addition, why he was looking through the piano ads. He would come to her house, but he couldn't move, and, really, neither could she. She had her job, Foffy had school, and even after Peter and Nina went off to college, she wasn't sure she could move. So there was the answer to why they probably would not marry, at least not now. The truth was, it didn't matter. She had never understood people not marrying before. Now she did, and as she watched the sun spread its apricot glow over the iced world outside, she knew that she was happy. And no one came by that knowledge easily.

For breakfast Hans made waffles. He followed the directions to the last letter, wouldn't think of adding an egg whole if it said to separate it and whip the white.

"You're the best waffle-maker," she said as they dawdled over the emptying table. Outside the world was a melting de Chirico or Dali. The temperature was rising several degrees every hour and by this afternoon the weather would be warm, May-like. Pieces of ice fell from the bushes and trees in odd billowy shapes, and Foffy had just announced through the open window that tiny blueberries were forming on the bushes.

"Don't forget to make your bed," Mady reminded Foffy.

"When has she forgotten?" Hans asked. In his eyes Foffy could do no wrong, and sometimes it annoyed her. Today she didn't mind.

"Whenever I've forgotten to remind her," she said cheerfully and together they cleared the table and did the dishes.

His studio was filled with people by the time they arrived and when he entered, flanked by Mady and the three children, Hans felt a pride he had not known he missed before. The pride of fatherhood, he supposed, and wondered if real fathers ever asked themselves, do these lovely-looking people really go with me? Nina and Foffy wore printed cotton skirts and walked with the freedom that comes to all females when the weather turns blessedly warm. Mady was in a loose mauve silk top and white pants.

Even Peter had put on a new yellow shirt, which made his hair look almost blue-black, and his jeans were freshly washed. Hans was touched by their care and consideration for him.

Although the party was to mark the official reopening of The Goldfinch Studio, it was really a celebration for Hans. Like the cleanup that had occurred almost two months before, everything was done by the time he arrived. Newly painted and decorated with white stools and multicolored Formica work tables, the large light room looked like a Mondrian painting. Along the east wall were shelves for display and his students had brought work from home to put there. Some had lent Hans his own pieces back. No one who didn't know about the robbery could have surmised what had happened such a short time ago. In the middle of the room, hanging from the highest beam, was a papier-mâché goldfinch, made as a surprise by Hans's older students. Its bright eye gleamed knowingly over the crowd as people looked up, exclaiming over it.

At the very end of the display area was the wooden sculpture. Nina and Foffy spotted it first and Hans saw Nina touch Peter's arm, beckon him to come with her. Their eyes widened in recognition. Hans tried to see it with their eyes. He had worked almost feverishly on it since he made the first sketches. When Rosa told him about the party, he had decided to try to finish it. Now it stood complete, no longer a part of his daily life. He thought of the Swiss customs official, tried to place him here in this room, but some things were too hard to imagine. Now Foffy said, "It looks exactly like her when she's sleeping."

"Even to the way her wrist curls under her chin," Nina added.

Peter moved closer and fingered the hair. His speechless admiration meant most to Hans.

Then Foffy saw him. "It's beautiful, Hans," she said and put her arms up to hug him. He picked her up, surprised that she wanted to be held so publicly. Again he felt how light she was and remembered the accident. Foffy put her mouth against his ear. "She looks like a great lady, Hans."

"Your mother is a great lady, Sophia," he said and was amused when Nina and Peter stared at him as if he had lost his mind.

The distance between generations is simply too great, Mady thought, as she took a few moments to step back and look around. She must have met fifty people in the last twenty minutes, her head swam as she took a sip of her drink and let it flow through her. Her parents thought they knew what would make her happy, but they were wrong, as she would be wrong about her children.

Foffy tugged on Mady's shirt so hard she almost spilled her drink. "Hey, hold on, Foffy."

"Mommy, did you see the sculpture?" she asked excitedly. "Did you see the wooden bust?" She savored the word and looked at her mother mischievously. "The bust of you?"

Mady knew it was there; she had seen Hans and the children near it, but she was embarrassed by it and afraid to see it. She suspected she wasn't going to like it and was astonished that Hans, who was such a private person, could have done such a public thing.

She let Foffy pull her around the raveled edges of the crowded room. A few people stood in front of it. She looked down, waiting until they moved away.

"Isn't she beautiful, Mommy?"

Mady shivered. Her eyes began to fill. The woman was beautiful, but in such a severe way. He had stripped her of all the outer layers of her life and here, carved in this walnut, was her soul — her struggle to stay alive, her fears, and most of all, her determination and strength. She looked like some biblical figure — a Hagar or a Naomi. A desert wanderer whose skin and eyes and features were bleached by a scorching sun and a rapacious wind. This woman had never been a child and was no one's daughter; there was nothing ladylike or gentle about her. Here was a woman of strong feelings and alliances, here was a woman one had to take seriously, to reckon with in the most primitive way.

"It looks exactly like you when you're sleeping," Foffy said.

"I don't think it looks like me at all, I think it looks like Hans's Aunt Johanna, at least from the photos I've seen," Mady retorted.

"You don't see yourself when you're sleeping."

Later Hans stood next to her as she looked at it again. "I still think it looks like Johanna," she said.

"There's a slight resemblance between you and Johanna around the mouth and chin," Hans conceded, "but that's not Johanna." He cocked his head and looked at it and from his expression she knew he was happy with it. Her approval or disapproval was not what mattered; he had done it — for himself and not for her. And as it sat there, part of his studio, part of his life, she knew, and he knew, that she would get used to it.

Later she heard him tell Rosa, "I've ordered more wood; finally I think I can do what I want in wood."

When they got back to the house, Mady went to the bedroom to lie down. She had a headache. From the sculpture? Hans wondered, then dismissed it. He had about an hour before dinner so he and Peter went into the garden. When Mady got up a little later, they had moved the heavy fallen beech limb and positioned the ladder and Hans was applying the second coat of tree-wound paint. He had changed into an old work shirt and jeans; he looked so different from the way he had looked when she first saw him.

She heard them discussing the tree, as if it were an injured person, and when Hans handed the ladder to Peter, she knew why Peter liked him so much. Hans treated him like an equal, always had, even when Peter hadn't liked him.

"That tree looks like a one-armed woman directing traffic," Nina said and put her arm around her mother.

Mady stared at her. "You see her as a woman, too? I thought I was the only one. It's strange to see such a massive tree as a woman, don't you think?"

"Ever since I first saw it that tree has been a woman," Nina said. They both laughed softly.

Although the day had been long neither of them was tired. Long after Peter and Nina said good-night they sat in the living room reading. It was past twelve when she stood up and stretched. She didn't want the day to end, yet it already had, and tomorrow she had to drive home and go to a concert. Bonnie was playing a solo with her high school orchestra and she and the children were going. The thought of the crowd, Shelley's nervousness, her parents' pride in Bonnie's uniqueness pressed inside her head. She sat down, defeated.

"What's the matter?" Hans looked at her.

"Nothing." She pushed her hair back from her face. "I was thinking of the concert tomorrow, going home, facing my other life." She laughed a little. "Did I tell you that my mother is finishing the needlepoint? She was appalled that I wasn't planning to finish it and frame it, so she took it. She can't understand why I don't want it in the house. I think she's going to give it to Shelley." Hans took off his glasses and smiled at her.

"Unless you want it?" she teased him, then walked to the screen door and out onto the deck. Outside the stars were so close that you felt you could pluck them from the sky if only you had a tweezers long enough. The air was balmy, brushing the skin like soft challis. Tomorrow was predicted to be unseasonably hot. Hans stepped out onto the deck and drew her close to him. Reflected moonlight daubed the sea with smudges of silver.

"Isn't it amazing? This morning everything was covered with ice!" she said. He nodded, then glanced at his watch.

"Want to walk?" he said. "The tide is out now and we can stand in the notch of the Cove, you've never seen that."

She tacked a note on the mantel in case one of the children woke up while they were gone. Then she pulled on a sweater. They walked in comfortable silence. He didn't have much conversation, the party had been as much as he could manage for one day. The rhythm of their steps blended with the constant rippling of the waves. Her mind cleared, the walking was more like floating than walking. She watched the spiraling gulls and thought of nothing. She and Hans might have been walking around the rim of the world, utterly alone, and only once did they hear the faint cough of a car horn and the groan of a motorcycle starting. When they reached the notch, the tide was out, as he had promised. It was a miracle to be standing so safely here on this patch of sand that was usually covered with crashing waves and surrounded by a wall of rocks. He held out his hand and steadied her as they climbed on a ledge. She felt as if she were in the ocean, its pulsing was like a magnet, she could feel herself being submerged by its sounds, its smell, when suddenly Hans cried, "Look!"

Out in front of them, not more than twenty feet from where they sat, was the pointed graceful head of a whale. It held itself for a moment in the air, then dived and its spine skimmed the surface like a piece of tinsel. "It's a baby," he said softly. Then there it was, again, and this time Mady could have sworn it looked at them, saw them. Then it was gone.

"How was the notch made?" she asked after a bit, after it was clear that the whale wasn't going to come back.

"They don't know. Every once in a while geologists come and measure the currents and propose theories based on the ages of the rocks or the metal in them, but no one really knows. According to the local paper, a group of geologists is supposed to come this summer. They claim that the currents have changed since Hurricane Beulah, they say the notch will never be the same." He rose and took her hand. They stood for a moment while the waves curled around the rocks.

Neither will we, she thought proudly, as they walked through the rock tunnel and out onto the moonlit beach.